SURVIVAL
—OF THE—
FITTEST

BOOKS BY JONATHAN KELLERMAN

Fiction

SURVIVAL OF THE FITTEST *(1997)*
THE CLINIC *(1997)*
THE WEB *(1996)*
SELF-DEFENSE *(1995)*
BAD LOVE *(1994)*
DEVIL'S WALTZ *(1993)*
PRIVATE EYES *(1992)*
TIME BOMB *(1990)*
SILENT PARTNER *(1989)*
THE BUTCHER'S THEATER *(1988)*
OVER THE EDGE *(1987)*
BLOOD TEST *(1986)*
WHEN THE BOUGH BREAKS *(1985)*

For children, written and illustrated

JONATHAN KELLERMAN'S ABC OF WEIRD CREATURES *(1995)*
DADDY, DADDY, CAN YOU TOUCH THE SKY? *(1994)*

Nonfiction

HELPING THE FEARFUL CHILD *(1981)*
PSYCHOLOGICAL ASPECTS OF CHILDHOOD CANCER *(1980)*

SURVIVAL

— OF THE —

FITTEST

JONATHAN
KELLERMAN

 Bantam Books

NEW YORK TORONTO LONDON SYDNEY AUCKLAND

SURVIVAL OF THE FITTEST
A Bantam Book / December 1997

BOOK DESIGN BY LAURIE JEWELL

Library of Congress Cataloging-in-Publication Data
Kellerman, Jonathan.
Survival of the fittest : a novel / Jonathan Kellerman.
p.   cm.
ISBN 0-553-08923-4
I. Title.
PS3561.E3865S8   1998
813'.54—dc21   97-3182
CIP

Published simultaneously in the United States and Canada

Bantam Books are published by Bantam Books, a division of Bantam Doubleday Dell
Publishing Group, Inc. Its trademark, consisting of the words "Bantam Books" and the
portrayal of a rooster, is Registered in U.S. Patent and Trademark Office and in other
countries. Marca Registrada. Bantam Books, 1540 Broadway, New York, New York
10036.

PRINTED IN THE UNITED STATES OF AMERICA

BVG 10 9 8 7 6 5 4 3 2 1

To my parents,
David and Sylvia Kellerman

Special thanks to
Detectives Paul Bishop and Vic Pietrantoni,
and to Dr. J. David Smith.

———————

SURVIVAL
—— OF THE ——
FITTEST

1

HOORAY FOR HOLLYWOOD.

Brass stars with celebrities' names were inlaid in the sidewalk but the stars of the night were toxin merchants, strong-arm specialists, and fifteen-year-olds running from family values turned vicious.

Open twenty-four hours a day, Go-Ji's welcomed them all. The coffee shop sat on the north side of Hollywood Boulevard, east of Vine, between a tattoo parlor and a thrash-metal bar.

At 3:00 A.M., a Mexican boy was sweeping the sidewalk when Nolan Dahl pulled his cruiser into the front loading zone. The boy lacked documentation but the sight of the policeman didn't alter his rhythm; cops could care less about *inmigración*. From what the boy had observed after a month, no one in L.A. cared much about anything.

Nolan Dahl locked the black-and-white and entered the restaurant, sauntering the way only 220 pounds of young, muscular cop laden with baton, belt, radio, flashlight, and holstered nine-millimeter could saunter. The place smelled rancid and the aisle of deep red carpet between the duct-taped orange booths was stained beyond redemption. Dahl settled at the rear, allowing himself a view of the Filipino cashier.

The next booth was occupied by a twenty-three-year-old pimp from Compton named Terrell Cochrane and one of his employees, a chubby sixteen-year-old mother of two named Germadine Batts, formerly of Checkpoint, Oklahoma. Fifteen minutes ago, the two had sat around the corner in Terrell's white Lexus, where Germadine had rolled up a blue, spangled legging and shot fifteen dollars' worth of tar heroin into a faltering ankle vein. Now nicely numbed and hypoglycemic, she was on her second diluted jumbo Coke, sucking ice and fooling with the pink plastic stirrer.

Terrell had mixed heroin and cocaine into a speedball and was feeling as perfectly balanced as a tightrope walker. He slouched, forked holes in his cheeseburger, simulated the Olympic logo with five flaccid onion rings while pretending not to watch the big blond cop.

Nolan Dahl couldn't have cared less about either of them, or the five other *things* scattered around the bright room. Elevator rock played softly. A slim, pretty waitress the color of molasses hurried down the aisle and stopped at Nolan's booth, smiling. Nolan smiled back, waved away a menu, and asked for coconut cream pie and coffee, please.

"New on the night shift?" asked the waitress. She'd come from Ethiopia five years ago and spoke beautiful English with a pleasant accent.

Nolan smiled again and shook his head. He'd been working Hollywood night shift for three months but had never patronized Go-Ji's, getting his sugar rush from a Dunkin' on Highland recommended by Wes Baker. Cops and doughnuts. Big joke.

"Never seen you before, Officer—Dahl."

"Well," he said, "life's full of new experiences."

The waitress laughed. "Well, hmm." She left for the pastry counter and Nolan watched her before shifting his blue eyes, making contact with Terrell Cochrane.

Scruffy thing.

Nolan Dahl was twenty-seven and had been formed, to a large extent, by TV. Before joining the force, his notion of pimps had been red velvet suits and big hats with feathers. Soon he'd learned you couldn't prepare for anything.

Anything.

He scanned Terrell and the hooker, who had to be a minor. This month the pimp was into coarse, oversized, insipid plaid shirts over black T-shirts, abbreviated cornrows above shaved temples. Last month had been black leather; before that, African prince.

The cop's stare bothered Terrell. Hoping it was someone else under scrutiny, he looked across the aisle at the three transsexuals giggling and whispering and making a big deal out of eating french fries.

He eased back to the cop.

The cop was smiling at him. A weird smile—almost sad. What did *that* mean?

Terrell returned to his burger, feeling a little *out* of balance.

The Ethiopian waitress brought Nolan's order and watched as he tasted a forkful of pie.

"Good," he said, though the coconut tasted like bad piña-colada mix and the cream was gluey. He was a practiced culinary liar. As a kid, when his mother had served swill he'd said, "Delish," along with Helena and Dad.

"Anything else, Officer Dahl?"

"Not for now, thanks." *Nothing you've got.*

"Okay, just let me know."

Nolan smiled again and she left.

Terrell Cochrane thought, *That smile—one happy fucker. No reason for a cop to be happy 'ceptin' he busted some rodney with no video going.*

Nolan ate more pie and again aimed his smile at Terrell. Then he shrugged.

The pimp looked sideways at Germadine, by now nodding half-comatose into her Coke. *Few minutes more, bitch, then back outside for more gravel-knee.*

The cop ate the rest of the pie, finished his coffee and his water, and the waitress was there right away with refills.

Bitch. After bringing Terrell's and Germadine's food, she'd mostly ignored them.

Terrell lifted his burger and watched her say something to the cop. The cop just kept smiling and shaking his head. The bitch gave the cop his check and the cop gave her money and she turned all grinny.

A twenty, keep it, was the reason.

Fuckers always tipped big, but this? All that smiling, must be celebrating something.

The cop looked into his empty coffee cup.

Then something came out from under the table.

His gun.

He was smiling at Terrell again. Showing him the *gun!*

The cop's arm stretched.

Terrell's bowels gave way as he ducked under the table, not bothering to push down on Germadine's head though he'd had plenty of practice doing *that.*

The other patrons saw Terrell's dive. The transsexuals and the drunken long-haul truck driver behind them and the toothless, senile, ninety-year-old man in the first booth.

Everyone ducked.

Except the Ethiopian waitress, who'd been talking to the Filipino cashier. She stared, too terrified to move.

Nolan Dahl nodded at the waitress. Smiled.

She thought, *A sad smile, what's with this guy?*

Nolan closed his eyes, almost as if he were praying. Opening them, he slid the nine-millimeter between his lips and, sucking like a baby, fixed his gaze on the waitress's pretty face.

She was still unable to move. He saw her terror, softened his eyes, trying to let her know it was okay, the only way.

A beautiful, black, final image. God this place smelled crappy.

He pulled the trigger.

2

HELENA DAHL GAVE ME A MOURNER'S ACCOUNT. THE
rest I got from the papers and from Milo.

The young cop's suicide merited only two inches on page 23
with no follow-up. But the flash-point violence stayed with me and
when Milo called a few weeks later and asked me to see Helena, I
said, "That one. Any idea yet why he did it?"

"Nope. That's probably what she wants to talk about. Rick says
don't feel obligated, Alex. She's a nurse at Cedars, worked with
him in the E.R. and doesn't want to see the in-house shrinks. But
it's not like she's a close friend."

"Has the department done its own investigation?"

"Probably."

"You haven't heard anything?"

"Those kinds of things are kept quiet and I'm not exactly in the
loop. Only thing I've heard is the kid was different. Quiet, stuck to
himself, read books."

"Books," I said. "Well, there's a motive for you."

He laughed. "Guns don't kill, introspection does?"

I laughed back. But I thought about that.

Helena Dahl called me that evening and I arranged to see her in
my home office the following morning. She arrived precisely on
time, a tall, handsome woman of thirty, with very short straight
blond hair and sinewy arms exposed by a navy blue tank top. The
tank was tucked into jeans and she wore tennies without socks.
Her face was a lean oval, well-sunned, her eyes light blue, her
mouth exceptionally wide. No jewelry. No wedding ring. She gave

my hand a firm shake, tried to smile, thanked me for seeing her, then followed me.

The new house is set up for therapy. I take patients in through a side door, crossing the Japanese garden and passing the fish pond. People usually stop to look at the koi or at least comment but she didn't.

Inside she sat very straight with her hands on her knees. Most of my work involves children caught up in the court system and a portion of the office is set aside for play therapy. She didn't look at the toys.

"This is the first time I've done this." Her voice was soft and low but it carried some authority. An E.R. nurse would make good use of that.

"Even after my divorce, I never talked to anyone," she added. "I really don't know what I expect."

"Maybe to make some sense of it?" I said gently.

"You think that's possible?"

"You may be able to learn more, but some questions can never be answered."

"Well, at least you're honest. Shall we get right into it?"

"If you're ready—"

"I don't know what I am but why waste time? It's . . . you know about the basic details?"

I nodded.

"There was really no warning, Dr. Delaware. He was such a . . ."

Then she cried.

Then she spilled it out.

"NOLAN WAS SMART," SHE SAID. "I MEAN SERI-ously smart, brilliant. So the last thing you'd think he'd end up being was a cop—no offense to Rick's friend, but that's not exactly what comes to mind when you think intellectual, right?"

Milo had a master's degree in literature. I said, "So Nolan was an intellectual."

"Definitely."

"How much education did he have?"

"Two years of college. Cal State Northridge. Psychology major, as a matter of fact."

"He didn't finish."

"He had trouble . . . finishing things. Maybe it was rebellion—our parents were heavily into education. Maybe he just got sick of classes, I don't know. I'm three years older, was already working by the time he dropped out. No one expected him to join the police. The only thing I can think of is he'd gotten politically conservative, real law-and-order. But still . . . the other thing is, he always loved . . . sleaze."

"Sleaze?"

"Spooky stuff, the dark side of things. As a kid he was always into horror movies, really gross stuff, the grossest. His senior year in high school, he went through a stage where he grew his hair long and listened to heavy metal and pierced his ears five times. My parents were convinced he was into satanism or something."

"Was he?"

"Who knows? But you know parents."

"Did they hassle him?"

"No, that wasn't their style. They just rode it out."

"Tolerant?"

"Unassertive. Nolan always did what he wanted—"

She cut the sentence short.

"Where'd you grow up?" I said.

"The Valley. Woodland Hills. My father was an engineer, worked at Lockheed, passed away five years ago. My mother was a social worker but never worked. She's gone, too. A stroke, a year after Dad died. She had hypertension, never took care of it. She was only sixty. But maybe she's the lucky one—not having to know what Nolan did."

Her hands balled.

"Any other family?" I said.

"No, just Nolan and me. He never married and I'm divorced. No kids. My ex is a doctor." She smiled. "Big surprise. Gary's a pulmonologist, basically a nice guy. But he decided he wanted to be a farmer so he moved to North Carolina."

"You didn't want to be a farmer?"

"Not really. But even if I did he didn't ask me along." Her eyes shot to the floor.

"So you're bearing all this alone," I said.

"Yup. Where was I—oh, the satanic nonsense. No big deal, it

didn't last long and then Nolan got back to normal teenage stuff. School, sports, girls, his car."

"Did he maintain his taste for the dark side?"

"Probably not—I don't know why I brought that up. What do you think about the way Nolan did it?"

"Using his service gun?"

She winced. "I meant so publically, in front of all those people. Like saying screw you to the world."

"Maybe that was his message."

"I thought it was theatrical," she said, as if she hadn't heard.

"Was he a theatrical person?"

"Hard to say. He was very good-looking, big, made an impression—the kind of guy you noticed when he entered a room. Did he milk that? Maybe a bit when he was a kid. As an adult? The truth is, Dr. Delaware, Nolan and I lost touch. We were never close. And now—"

More tears. "As a little kid he always enjoyed being the center of attention. But other times he didn't want anything to do with anybody, just crawled into his own little space."

"Moody?"

"A family trait." She rubbed her knees and looked past me. "My dad underwent shock therapy for depression when Nolan and I were in grade school. We were never told what was going on, just that he was going into the hospital for a couple of days. But after he died, Mom told us."

"How many treatments did he have?"

"I don't know, three, maybe four. When he'd come home he'd be wiped out, fuzzy about remembering—like what you see in head-injury patients. They say ECT works better now but I'm sure it damaged his brain. He faded in middle age, took early retirement, sat around reading and listening to Mozart."

"He must have been severely depressed to get ECT," I said.

"Must have been but I never really saw it. He was quiet, sweet, shy."

"What was his relationship with Nolan?"

"There wasn't much of one that I could see. Even though Nolan was gifted, he was into typical macho stuff. Sports, surfing, cars. Dad's idea of recreation was . . ."—she smiled—"reading and listening to Mozart."

"Did they have conflict?"

"Dad never had conflict with anyone."

"How did Nolan react to your father's death?"

"He cried at the funeral. Afterward, we both tried to comfort Mom for a while, then he just drifted away again."

She pinched her lower lip. "I didn't want Nolan to have one of those big LAPD funerals, gun salutes, all that crap. No one at the department argued. Like they were happy not to deal with it. I had him cremated. He left a will, all his stuff is mine. Dad's and Mom's stuff, too. I'm the survivor."

Too much pain. I backtracked. "What was your mother like?"

"More outgoing than Dad. Not moody. On the contrary, she was always up, cheerful, optimistic. Probably why she stroked out—holding it all inside." She rubbed her knee again. "I don't want to make our family sound weird. We weren't. Nolan was a regular guy. Partying, chasing girls. Just smarter. He got A's without working."

"What did he do after dropping out of college?"

"Bummed around, worked different jobs. Then all of a sudden he calls me, announces he's graduated from the police academy. I hadn't heard from him since Mom died."

"When was this?"

"About a year and a half ago. He told me the academy was a joke, Mickey Mouse. He'd graduated high in his class. He said he'd called me just to let me know. In case I happened to see him drive by in a car, I shouldn't be freaked out."

"Was he assigned to Hollywood from the beginning?"

"No. West L.A. That's why he thought I might see him, at Cedars. He might come in to the E.R. with a suspect or a victim."

In case I happened to see him. What she'd described was less a family than a series of accidental pairings.

"What kind of jobs did he work before he joined LAPD?"

"Construction, auto repair, crewing on a fishing boat off Santa Barbara. That I remember because Mom showed me some fish he'd brought her. Halibut. She liked smoked fish and he had some halibut smoked."

"What about relationships with women?"

"He had girlfriends in high school, but after that I don't know— can I walk around?"

"Sure."

She got up, covered the room in small, choppy steps. "Everything always came easy to Nolan. Maybe he just wanted to take the easy way out. Maybe that was the problem. He wasn't prepared for when things didn't come easy."

"Do you know of specific problems he was having?"

"No, no, I don't know anything—I was just thinking back to high school. I used to agonize over algebra and Nolan would waltz into my room, look over my shoulder, and tell me the answer to an equation. Three years younger—he must have been eleven, but he could figure it out."

She stopped, faced a bookshelf. "When Rick Silverman gave me your name, he told me about his friend on the force and we got into a discussion of the police. Rick said it was a paramilitary organization. Nolan always wanted to be noticed. Why would he be attracted to something so conformist?"

"Maybe he got tired of being noticed," I said.

She stood there for a while, sat back down.

"Maybe I'm doing this because I feel guilty for not being closer to him. But he never seemed to want to get close."

"Even if you had been close, you couldn't have prevented it."

"You're saying it's a waste of time to try to stop someone from killing themselves?"

"It's always important to try to help, and many people who are stopped never attempt again. But if someone's determined to do it, they'll eventually succeed."

"I don't *know* if Nolan was determined. I don't know *him!*"

She burst into loud, racking sobs. When she quieted I handed her a tissue and she snatched it and slapped it against her eyes. "I *hate* this—I don't know if I can keep doing this."

I said nothing.

Looking to the side, she said, "I'm his executor. After Mom died, the lawyer handling our parents' estate said we should each write a will." She laughed. "Estate. The house and a bunch of junk. We rented out the house, split the money, then after my divorce, I asked Nolan if I could live there, send him half the rent. He wouldn't take it. Said he didn't need it—didn't need anything. Was *that* a warning sign?"

Before I could answer, she stood again. "How much more time do we have?"

"Twenty minutes."

"Would you mind if I left early?"

. · .

SHE'D PARKED A BROWN MUSTANG OFF THE PROPERTY, out on the bridle trial that snakes up from Beverly Glen. The morning air was hot and dusty, the smell of pines from the neighboring ravine piercing and cleansing.

"Thanks," she said, unlocking the car.

"Would you like to make another appointment?"

She got in and lowered the window. The car was spotless, empty except for two white uniforms hanging over a rear door.

"Can I get back to you? I need to check the on-call schedule."

Patient's version of *don't call me, I'll call you.*

"Of course."

"Thanks again, Dr. Delaware. I'll be in touch."

She sped away and I returned to the house, thinking about the meager history she'd given me.

Nolan too smart to be a cop. But plenty of cops were smart. Other characteristics—athletic, macho, dominant, attracted to the dark side—fit the police stereotype. A few years bumming around before seeking the security of a city job and a pension. Right-wing political views; I'd have liked to hear more about that.

She'd also described a partial family history of serious mood disorder. A cop judged "different" by his peers.

That could add to the alienation brought about by the job.

Nolan's life sounded *full* of alienation.

So even though his sister was understandably shocked, no big surprises, so far.

Nothing that came close to explaining why Nolan had sucked his gun at Go-Ji's.

Not that I was likely to get any closer to it, because the way she'd left told me it would probably be a one-shot deal.

In my business you learn to make do with unanswered questions.

3

MILO CALLED TWO DAYS LATER, AT 8:00 A.M.

"They just gave me another cold one, Alex. I'm not sure I can pay you, though we did get brownie points on the last thing, so maybe."

The last thing was the murder of a psychology professor stalked and stabbed a few yards from her home in Westwood. Thinking it unsolvable after months of no leads, Milo's superiors had handed it to him as punishment for being the only openly gay detective in LAPD. We'd learned a few secrets about the victim and he'd managed to close the file.

"Well, I don't know," I said. "Why the hell should I do *you* any favors?"

He laughed. "Because I'm such a pleasant fellow?"

I simulated a game-show buzzer. "Try again."

"Because you're a shrink and committed to unconditional acceptance?"

"Don't go on *Jeopardy!* What's the case?"

I heard him sigh. "A kid, Alex. Fifteen years old."

"Oh."

"I know how you feel about that but this is an important one. If you have any time at all I'd appreciate tossing things around."

"Sure," I said. "Come over right now."

HE SHOWED UP CARRYING A BOX OF FILES, WEARING A turquoise polo shirt that proclaimed his gut, wrinkled brown jeans, scarred beige desert boots. His weight had stabilized at around

240, most of it distributed around the middle of his six-three frame. His hair was freshly cut in his usual style, though to use *style* in conjunction with Milo was a felony: clipped short at the sides and back, shaggy on top, sideburns to the earlobes. Gray was winning the battle with black and the sideburns were nearly white. He's nine months older than I am and sometimes looking at him reminds me time is passing.

He put the box down on the kitchen table. His pocked face was chalky and his green eyes lacked spark. A long night, or several of them. Looking at the refrigerator, he frowned. "Need I spell it out?"

"Solid or liquid?" I said.

"Been working on this since six."

"So both."

"You're the doctor." He stretched and sat heavily and I heard the chair creak.

I fixed him a cold roast beef sandwich and brought it over along with a quart of milk. He ate and drank quickly and exhaled noisily.

The box was filled to the top. "Looks like plenty of data."

"Don't confuse quantity with quality." Pushing his plate away, he began removing bound folders and rubber-banded stacks, arranged them neatly on the table.

"The victim is a girl named Irit Carmeli. Fifteen, slightly retarded. Thirteen weeks ago, someone abducted her and killed her during a school field trip up in the Santa Monica Mountains— some nature conservancy owned by the city. Her school goes there every year, the idea is to get a little beauty into the kids' lives."

"Are all the kids retarded?"

"All with some kind of problem. It's a special school."

He ran a hand over his face, as if washing without water. "Here's how it lays out: The kids were dropped off near the entrance by a chartered bus, and hiked about a half-mile into the park. It gets thickly wooded pretty quickly but there are marked pathways for novice hikers. The kids ran around for an hour or so, had snacks, bathroom breaks, then reboarded. Almost two hours had lapsed by then. They called roll, Irit wasn't there, they went looking for her, couldn't find her, 911'd Westside Division, who sent a couple of units, but they couldn't find her either and called for K-9 backup. It took half an hour for the dogs to get there, another half to sniff her out. The body was about a mile away,

lying in a pine grove. No overt signs of violence, no ligature stria-
tions, no subdermal hemorrhaging, no swelling, no blood. Except
for the positioning they would have assumed she'd had a seizure
or something like that."

"Sexual positioning?"

"No, show you in a second. The coroner found bruising on the
hyoid and the sternohyoid and the pharyngeal muscles. No sexual
assault."

"Strangulation," I said. "Why no external marks?"

"Coroner said you can get that when the choke-force is spread
out over a broad area—using a soft ligature like a rolled-up towel
or a clothed forearm. Gentle strangulation, they call it."

Grimacing, he removed the top file and flipped it open to two
pages of snapshots in plastic strip-fasteners.

Some were of the surrounding forest. The rest were of the girl.
Thin and fair-haired, she wore a white T-shirt with lace trim
around the neck and sleeves, blue jeans, white socks, pink plastic
shoes. Very thin. Pipe-cleaner limbs, the elbows prominent, as if
recently enlarged by a growth spurt. I would have guessed her age
at twelve, not fifteen. Lying on her back, brown earth beneath her,
arms at her sides, feet pressed together. Too symmetrical to have
fallen. *Arranged.*

I studied a facial close-up. Eyes closed, mouth slightly parted.
The dirty-blond hair, long and very curly and spread on the
ground.

More arrangement.

Someone taking the time . . . playing.

Back to the full-body shot. Her hands were next to her thighs,
palms up, curled open, as if asking *Why?*

Insipid olive-gray shadows washed across the pale face like
brushstrokes.

Light filtering through the trees above.

My chest felt clogged and I started to close the file. Then I noticed something small and pink near the girl's right ear. "What's
that?"

"Hearing aid. She was also deaf. Partially in one ear, totally in
the other."

"Jesus." I put the file down. "Irit Carmeli. Is that Italian?"

"Israeli. Her father's a honcho at the Israeli Consulate. Which is why the department's inability to develop a single lead in three months is problematic."

"Three months," I said. "I never read about it in the papers."

"It wasn't in the papers. Diplomatic pull."

"Sounds like a very cold case."

"Any colder and I'd be wearing fur. Any gut impressions?"

"He took his time with her," I said. "Meaning he probably abducted her fairly soon after she arrived. When's the last time anyone saw her?"

"No one's sure. From the moment they let them off the bus it was chaos, kids running all over the place. That was the point of the conservancy. The school had gone there before, thought it was a safe place for the kids to run loose and explore."

"How'd the murderer get in without being noticed?"

"Probably a backroad, the place is full of them on three sides, access from the Valley side, Santa Monica, and from Sunset. There's a thick belt of trees between the hiking area and the nearest road so you'd need to know your way around, meaning the piece of shit was familiar with the area, either hiked or drove. If he drove he parked at a distance because the roads closest to the murder scene were clean, no tracks."

"He parks, walks through the trees, finds a spot where he can see the kids, watches," I said. "Any tracks on more distant roads?"

"Nothing that could be identified because you get heavy enough traffic to blur everything. And I can't tell you they checked every square inch of the park early because in the beginning, it wasn't a crime scene, it was a missing kid. In addition to the K-9s and the teachers and the park rangers, her father came over with a whole posse of consulate people and everything got pretty much trampled."

"What about at the scene itself?"

"Not a trace of anything physical, except for a few pieces of straw that the lab says came from a broom. Looks like the scumbag swept up the area around her."

"A neat one," I said. "Compulsive. That fits the way he arranged the body."

I forced myself to look at the photographs again, picturing a fiendish face bent over the girl. But that's not the way it was. It always came down to people, not monsters.

Arranging. Manipulating.

Sweeping up.

"Strangulation and positioning are usually sexual," I said. "No assault at all?"

"Nothing. She was a virgin. And you know how sex fiends usually position: spreading the legs, displaying the genitals. This was just the opposite, Alex. First time I saw the pictures she looked unreal. Like a doll."

"Playing with dolls." My voice was low and hoarse.

"Sorry for dropping this one on you," he said.

"How retarded was she?"

"The file says 'slightly.' "

"Abducted without a sound and carried a mile from the group. How much did she weigh?"

"Eighty pounds."

"So we're talking someone strong," I said. "Is the theory that she wandered off the path, just happened to be unlucky?"

"That's one of them. The other is that he picked her for some reason. As far as no sound, he could have clamped his hand over her mouth and carried her away. Though if he did clamp, it wasn't hard. No finger marks. Not a bruise anywhere."

"So no evidence of any resistance on her part?"

He shook his head.

"Was she mute as well as deaf?"

"She spoke but not clearly and her main language was Hebrew."

"But she had the capacity to scream?"

"I assume." He finished the milk and crushed the carton.

"Watching til he found a victim," I said. "Stalking the herd and picking off a weak one. How many other kids were in the group?"

"Forty-two. Plus four teachers and two aides. Some of the kids were in wheelchairs and needed close supervision. Another reason the kids who could run around had lots of freedom."

"Still," I said. "All those people and no one saw anything?"

He shook his head, again, and pointed to the files. "Everyone's been talked to twice, three times. Teachers, the bus driver, kids to the extent they could talk."

"How often do they come to the conservancy?"

"Once a year for the past five."

"Was the trip prearranged with the park?"

He nodded. "Lots of schools come up there."

"So someone familiar with the park would know disabled kids were due to visit. Easy victims."

"The first guys on the case—Gorobich and Ramos—interviewed every park and school employee as well as former employees. The only criminal records they found was some old DUI stuff on a couple of the gardeners and their alibis all checked out."

"Sounds like they were thorough."

"Both were competent and a kid victim plus a diplomat father made the case high-priority. But they came up with *nada* and last week they got pulled and transferred to auto theft. Calls from above."

"So now they're trading two detectives for one?" I said. "I know you're good but—"

"Yeah, yeah, I asked the same thing. Lieutenant just shrugged and said, 'What, Sturgis, you mean you're *not* a genius?' Only thing I can think of is the Israelis figure all the teamwork scut's been done, they want to keep it low-key so some Arab terrorist won't get ideas and declare open season on other consulate kids. As to why me?" He shrugged. "Maybe they heard about the Devane solve."

"So you're supposed to clear it quickly but quietly," I said. "Quite a mandate."

"It has that smell of futility, Alex. For all I know someone's setting me up for a fall. Lieutenant was sure smiling a lot." He drummed his fingers on the box.

I picked out the second file. Page after page of transcripted interviews with family members, teachers. Lots of stiff, wordy cop prose. Lots of pain seeping through but no revelations. I put it down.

"So," he said. "Anything else?"

"A planner, a sneak. Maybe an outdoors type. Physically strong, possibly a history of child molestation, voyeurism, exposure. Smart enough to wait and watch and to sweep up. Maybe meticulous in his personal habits. He didn't assault her, so the thrill of the chase probably did it for him. Stalking and capture."

Picking the weak one out of the herd. . . . I said, "If he did choose Irit, why? With all those other kids, what made her the target?"

"Good question."

"You don't think it could be something to do with her father's position?"

"The father claims no and my feeling is if it was political the Israelis would take care of it themselves."

"Being a diplomat's daughter," I said, "did she have any special security training? Did her disabilities cause her to be especially gullible?"

"Gorobich said he asked the father that but the guy brushed him off, kept insisting the murder had nothing to do with Irit personally, that L.A. was a hellhole full of homicidal nuts, no one was safe."

"And because he was a VIP, no one pushed."

"That and basically Gorobich and Ramos agreed with him. It *didn't* look like anything the kid had brought on herself. More like some twisted fuck watched her and snatched her and dispatched her and cleaned up afterward. Like you said, *playing*. Big fucking *game*. God, I *hate* when it's a kid."

He got up and paced, opened the fridge, looked inside, closed it, peered out the kitchen window.

"Have you met the parents yet?" I said.

"I put a call in today, waiting for an appointment."

"Three months with no progress," I said. "The grief may have turned completely to rage. It may be even more difficult to approach them."

"Yeah," he said. "I'll tackle that later. Meanwhile, trees don't have feelings, so how about taking a look at the scene?"

4

IT WAS LESS THAN A HALF-HOUR DRIVE, A RIGHT
turn off Sunset, past the Brentwood intersection with Pacific Palisades. No signs. Sometimes people who love nature don't think
other people should disrupt it.

A suburban street lined with middle-sized ranch homes led to a
brush-shaded single-lane road that kept narrowing. A school bus
would be scraped by branches.

The gate was steel painted ballpark-mustard yellow, latched but
not locked. The first sign, orange city-issue, specified visiting
hours. Opening time was an hour away. I got out, released the
latch, returned to the unmarked, and we drove through more
foliage-banked asphalt. We pressed on, rolling on dirty hardpack,
now, as the brush turned to pines, cedar, cypress, sycamore. Trees
planted so close together they formed deep green walls, nearly
black, just the faintest delineation of branch and leaf. Anyone or
anything could hide back there.

The road ended in a spoon-shaped clearing. Faded white lines
marked off a dozen parking spots and Milo slid into one. Behind
the lot was a ten-foot strip of dry, clipped grass upon which sat
three rickety picnic tables, a U-drive mower, and several fastened
lawn bags, stuffed, shiny-black.

Beyond the grass, more forest.

I followed Milo over the lawn to two signs, one atop the other,
marking the mouth of a dirt path that dipped into the trees. Above:
NATURE HIKE, PLEASE STAY ON TRAIL. An arrow pointed left. Below, a
picture board behind cloudy plastic displayed leaves, berries,
acorns, squirrels, rabbits, blue jays, snakes. A warning under the

western rattler that when the days grew long and hot, the serpents came crawling out for action.

We began descending. The drop was gentle and the trail was terraced in spots. Soon other paths appeared, steeper, skinnier, branching from the side. The trees remained so dense only short portions of walkway resisted the shadows.

We walked quickly, not speaking. I was imagining, theorizing, and the look on Milo's face told me he was doing the same. Ten minutes later, he stepped off the trail and entered the forest. The pine smell was much stronger here—almost artificial, like room freshener—and the ground beneath our feet was littered with needles and cones.

We walked for a long time before he stopped at a small clearing that bore no distinction.

Not even a clearing, just the space between huge old pines with gray, corrugated trunks. Trunks all around, like Greek columns. The space felt enclosed, an outdoor room.

A crypt.

Someone's idea of a death chamber. . . . I said so but Milo didn't reply.

I looked around, listened. Bird calls, distant. Insects scattering. Nothing to see but trees. No backroads. I asked him about that.

He hooked a thumb over his shoulder. "The forest ends about three hundred yards back, though you can't see it from here. There's an open field, then roads, then mountains, and more roads. Some eventually link up with highways but most dead-end. I traipsed around all yesterday, walking and driving, saw nothing but squirrels, couple of big hawks. Circling hawks, so I stopped to check, maybe there was something else dead down below. Nothing. No other predators."

I stared in the direction he'd indicated. No breaking light, not even a suggestion of exit.

"What happened to the body?" I said.

"Buried in Israel. The family flew over, stayed for a week or so, came back."

"Jewish mourning rituals take a week."

He raised his eyebrows.

I said, "I worked the cancer ward."

He paced around the clearing, looking huge in the dark, vault-like space.

"Secluded," I said. "Only a mile from the bus but secluded. It had to be someone who really knew this place well."

"Problem is, that doesn't narrow it down very much. It's public access, there are always hikers."

"Too bad there were none around that day. On the other hand, maybe there were."

He stopped pacing. "What do you mean?"

"The news blackout. How would anyone have known to come forward?"

He thought about that. "Gotta talk to the parents. Though it's probably too late."

"Maybe you can get them to compromise, Milo. Report the murder without identifying Irit by name. Though I agree, it's unlikely to pay off after all this time."

He kicked a tree hard, muttered, walked around some more, looked in all directions, said, "Anything else?"

I shook my head and we retraced our steps to the parking lot. The U-drive mower was in use now, a dark-skinned man in a khaki uniform and pith helmet riding back and forth on the grass strip. He turned briefly and kept riding. The brim of the helmet shaded his face.

"Waste of time?" said Milo, starting up the unmarked and backing out.

"You can never tell."

"Got time to read some of the files?"

Thinking of Irit Carmeli's face, I said, "Plenty of time."

5

THEY HADN'T PAID HIM ANY ATTENTION, HE WAS sure of that.

Waiting until the unmarked car had been gone for twenty minutes, he got off the mower, tied off the last of the leaf bags, got back on, and coasted down toward the park entrance. Stopping a short distance behind the yellow gates, he pushed the machine back to the side of the road. The park service had never missed it. Loose procedures.

Very loose. The girl's misfortune.

Good find, the mower a bonus added to the uniform.

As always, the uniform worked perfectly: Do manual labor in official garb and no one notices you.

His car, a gray Toyota Cressida with false plates and a handicapped placard in the glove compartment, was parked three blocks down. A nine-millimeter semiautomatic was concealed in a box under the driver's seat.

He was lean and light and walked quickly. Ten feet from the vehicle, he disarmed the security system with his remote, looked around without appearing to, got in, and sped off toward Sunset, turning east when he got there.

Same direction they'd gone.

A detective and a psychologist and neither had given him a second's notice.

The detective was bulky, with heavy limbs and sloping shoulders, the lumbering trudge of an overfed bull. The baggy, gnarled face of a bull—no, a rhinoceros.

A depressed rhinoceros. He looked discouraged already.

How did that kind of pessimism square with his reputation?

Maybe it fit. The guy was a pro, he had to know the chance of learning the truth was slim.

Did that make him the sensible one?

The psychologist was a different story. Hyperalert, eyes everywhere.

Focused.

Quicker and smaller than the detective—five ten or so, which still put him three inches above the dark man. Restless, he moved with a certain grace. A cat.

He'd gotten out of the car before the detective turned the engine off.

Eager—achievement-oriented?

Unlike the detective, the psychologist appeared to take care of himself. Solidly built, curly dark hair, a little long but trimmed neatly. Clear, fair skin, square jaw. The eyes very pale, very wide.

Such *active* eyes.

If he was that way with patients how could he calm them down?

Maybe he didn't see many patients.

Fancied himself a *detective.*

With his blue sportcoat, white shirt, and pressed khaki pants, he looked like one of those professors trying to come across casual.

That type often *faked* casual, pretending everyone was equal, but maintaining a clear sense of rank and position.

The dark man wondered if the psychologist was like that.

As he drove toward Brentwood, he thought again of the man's rapid, forward walk.

Lots of energy, that one.

All this time and no one had even gotten close to figuring out what had happened to Irit.

But the psychologist had forged forward—maybe the guy was an optimist.

Or just an amateur, too ignorant to know better.

6

L.A. station. As I headed up the stairs to the front entrance, I heard the whine of Robin's table saw from out back and detoured through the garden to her studio. Spike, our little French bulldog, was basking near the door, a mound of black-brindled muscle melting into the welcome mat. He stopped snoring long enough to raise his head and stare. I rubbed his neck and stepped over him.

Like the house, the outbuilding is white stucco, compact and simple with lots of windows and a tile roof shaded by sycamore boughs. Lateral sunlight flooded the clean, airy space. Guitars in various stages of completion were positioned around the room and the spicy resin smell of crisply cut wood seasoned the air. Robin was guiding a hunk of maple through the saw and I waited to approach until she finished and turned off the machine. Her auburn curls were tied up in a knot and her apron was filmed with sawdust. The T-shirt beneath it was sweaty, as was her heart-shaped face.

She wiped her hands and smiled. I put my arm around her shoulder and kissed her cheek. She turned and gave me her mouth, then pulled away and wiped her brow.

"Learn anything?"

"No." I told her about the park, the leafy vault.

Her brown eyes got huge and she flinched. "Every parent's nightmare. What next?"

"Milo asked me to look over the files."

"It's been a while since you got involved in something like this, Alex."

"True. Better get to work." I kissed her forehead and stepped away.

She watched me go.

BY THE END OF THREE HOURS I LEARNED THE FOL-
lowing:

Mr. and Mrs. Zev Carmeli lived in a leased house on a good street in Beverlywood with their now only child, a seven-year-old boy named Oded. Zev Carmeli was 38, born in Tel Aviv, a career foreign-service officer. His wife, Liora, was four years younger, born in Morocco but raised in Israel, employed as a Hebrew teacher at a Jewish day school on the West Side.

The family had arrived in L.A. a year ago from Copenhagen, where Carmeli had served for three years as an attaché at the Israeli Embassy. Two years before that he'd been assigned to the embassy in London and had obtained a master's degree in international relations at London University. He and his wife and Oded spoke English fluently. Irit, said her father, had spoken "very well, considering."

All the quotes were from the father.

The girl's health problems had followed an influenza-like illness at the age of six months. Carmeli referred to his daughter as "a little immature but always well-behaved." The term *retarded* never came up in the files, but an educational summary report supplied by her school, The Center for Development, indicated "multiple learning problems, bilateral hearing impairment, including total deafness in the right ear, and mild to moderate developmental delay."

As Milo had said, Carmeli was adamant about having no enemies in Los Angeles and brushed off all questions about his work and the political situation in the Middle East.

Detective E. J. Gorobich wrote:

''V.'s father stated that his job is 'coordinating
events' for the consulate. I asked for an example and he
said he'd organized an Israel Independence Day parade

last spring. When I inquired about any other events he'd
coordinated, he stated there were lots of them but that
the parade was a main one. When I inquired about
possible connections between what had happened to his
daughter and his occupational/political position and/
or activities, he became noticeably agitated and
stated: 'This wasn't political, this was a madman! It's
obvious that you have many madmen in America!' ''

The Center for Development was a small private school in Santa Monica specializing in children with mental and physical handicaps. Tuition was high and student-teacher ratio was low.

A school bus had picked Irit up each morning at 8:00 A.M. and dropped her off at 3:00 P.M. Mrs. Carmeli taught mornings only and was always home to receive her daughter. Younger brother Oded was enrolled at the school that employed his mother and attended classes til four. Before the murder, he'd been taken home by car pool or a consulate employee. Since the murder, Mr. or Mrs. Carmeli picked him up.

Irit's academic records were skimpy. No grades, no quantitative testing, an assessment by her teacher, Kathy Brennan, that she was "making excellent strides."

Brennan had been interviewed by Gorobich's partner, Detective Harold Ramos.

''Witness stated she feels 'all torn up' and 'guilty'
about what had happened to V. even though she'd gone
over the events of the day over and over and hadn't found
anything she could have done differently except watch
V. every second of the day, which would have been
impossible because there were forty-two children at the
park including some who needed extra-special care
(wheelchairs pushed on the paths, etc.). Ms. Brennan
also stated that going to the park was a regular thing
for the school, they'd been doing it for years, it was
always considered a safe place where 'kids can just run
around for a while and be kids, without being watched
every second.' As to whether or not she'd seen anything
suspicious, witness stated she hadn't, even though
she'd been 'racking her brain.' Witness then stated

that deceased was a 'really nice kid, so sweet, no
problems ever. Why do the nice ones always have to
suffer!' Immediately following this Ms. Brennan broke
down and was tearful. When asked if she was aware of
other nice ones suffering, she stated, 'No, no. You know
what I mean. All the kids are nice, they all have
problems. It's just not fair that someone would do this
to a child!' '

Next came face-to-face meetings with every teacher and aide present at the field trip, as well as the teachers who'd remained at school; the principal, a Dr. Rothstein; the bus driver, Alonzo Burns; and several of Irit's classmates. No transcripts of the talks with the children were included. Instead, Gorobich and Ramos offered forty-two nearly identical summaries:

''Witness Salazar, Rudy, nine y.o., blind, interviewed
in presence of parents, denies any knowledge.''
* ''Witness Blackwell, Amanda, six y.o., braces on*
feet, not retarded, interviewed in presence of mother,
denies any knowledge.''
* ''Witness Shoup, Todd, eleven y.o., retarded, in*
wheelchair, interviewed in presence of mother, denies
any knowledge . . .''

End of that folder.

A thicker one contained interviews with every employee of the park and the results of a door-to-door canvass of the surrounding neighborhood. Twenty-eight employees, nearly one hundred neighbors. Gorobich and Ramos had "telephonically" recontacted every one of them two weeks later, with the same results: No one had seen or heard anything or anyone unusual in or around the park.

I reread the coroner's files, wincing at the term "gentle strangulation" before moving on to a beefy computer printout, the cover stamped with the seal of the state Department of Justice in Sacramento, Violent Crime Information Network.

Five separate lists of names followed, each tabbed, labeled with an acronym, and subheaded CATCHMENT AREA. For all five sections,

the park's zip code and three adjoining codes were typed on a
dotted line:

1. SAR (Sex Registration)
2. SHOP (Sexual Habitual Offenders)
3. ACAS (Child Abuse Reports)
4. ISU (M.O.'s related to violent crimes)
5. SRF (Persons on probation/parole from CDC/CYA)

Five databases filled with names and information on sex offenders.
I counted 283 names, some overlaps circled in red. Ninety-seven
offenders, including four of the overlaps, had been rearrested and
were in custody. Two turquoise circles identified a pair of child
murderers out on parole, one living three miles from the park, the
other in Bell Gardens.

Gorobich and Ramos had interviewed both killers immediately
and verified strong alibis for the day of the murder. The detectives
then enlisted the help of three other investigators, two civilian
clerks, and three volunteer police scouts to locate the 186 criminals
still out there, though none of the names on the DOJ lists matched
any of the park workers, neighbors, teachers, the principal, or the
bus driver.

Thirty-one men were missing in violation of parole and war-
rants were issued for their rearrest. A handwritten note reported
eleven already apprehended. The others were contacted and presented alibis of varying strength. A note by Ramos indicated no
strong suspects because "No M.O. matches to this homicide were
found among any of these individuals and given the lack of assault
and other sexual patterning, it is still not clear that this was a
sexual homicide."

I read the M.O. file carefully.

With the exception of a few exhibitionists, the child molesters
had all played with, bruised, penetrated, or somehow made physical contact with their victims and the vast majority had been previously acquainted with their victims: daughters, sons, nieces,
nephews, grandkids, stepkids, the children of girlfriends, drinking
buddies, neighbors.

Both of the alibied murderers had killed children known to
them: One had beaten a girlfriend's two-year-old daughter to

death with his fists. The other, a woman, had intentionally scalded her own son in the bathtub.

Nearly two hundred predators, roaming free in this relatively small area . . .

Why only four zip codes?

Because the detectives couldn't be everywhere and you had to draw the line somewhere.

Would doubling, tripling, quadrupling the area have accomplished much?

L.A. was a country-sized sprawl, ruled by the car. Give a stalker some gas money and coffee and he could go anywhere.

Hop on the freeway, weave nightmares, be back in bed in time for the evening news. Munching chips and masturbating, eyes glued to the headlines, hoping for fame.

Aimless driving was one characteristic of sexual sadists.

But Irit hadn't been tortured.

Still, maybe we did have a traveler. Someone who liked the backroads. Maybe this killer was up in Alaska by now, fishing salmon, or strolling the boardwalk in Atlantic City, or in New Orleans, hunkered down in a French Quarter club eating gumbo.

Watching . . .

For all their numerical precision, the printouts seemed primitive. I put them down and picked up the next file, thin and black.

Still thinking of two hundred predators in four zip codes. What kind of society let people who raped and beat children back out on the streets?

It's been a long time, Alex.

Inside the black file were aerial photographs of the murder scene—fluffy, green-black patches of treetop, as distant and artificial as an architect's design sketch.

Tan laces at the upper periphery—the roads. Capillaries feeding mountains, gullies, the city sprawl beyond.

Facing the photos was a crisp white letter on FBI stationery. DEAR DETECTIVE GOROBICH correspondence from FBI Special Agent Gail Gorman of the bureau's Behavioral Sciences Regional Unit in San Diego.

Gorman acknowledged receipt of the aerial shots, the crime-scene data, and the completed questionnaire, but regretted that insufficient information existed for a definitive profile of the killer. However, she was willing to guess that he was most likely male, white, over thirty, of average to above-average intelligence, non-psychotic, probably compulsive and perfectionistic, presenting a neat, clean, unremarkable appearance, probably employed at the present, though possibly with an inconsistent or checkered job history.

With regard to the crime being "sexual in nature," she repeated the disclaimer of insufficient data and went on to say that "despite the obvious organization of the crime, the lack of sadistic or vicious elements mitigate against a sexual homicide, as does the absence of obvious or covert sexual activity at the scene. However, should future homicides bearing precisely these signature elements show themselves, we would be interested in hearing about them."

The letter ended by suggesting that "victim characteristics should be explored further: age, ethnicity, specific disabilities. While this homicide might very well turn out to have been committed by an opportunistic or premeditated stranger, the possibility that the victim knew the perpetrator cannot be ruled out and, in fact, should be looked into, though, once again, this is only a suggestion, not a conclusion. Factors mitigating against victim-perpetrator acquaintance include leaving the body faceup in a location where it would eventually be found. Factors mitigating for acquaintance include the use of diffuse-force ('gentle') strangulation and other evidence of care and time taken to avoid brutalization and degradation of the body."

Average to above-average. Organized, compulsive, perfectionistic.

That meshed with my first impression.

A planner—someone who took pride in setting things up and watching the elements fall into place.

Taking his time—spiriting Irit a mile from the bus so he'd *have* time.

It implied a certain relaxation—self-confidence? Arrogance?

Someone who *believed* he was clever.

Because he'd gotten away with it before?

No M.O. match existed in any of the state files.

Had he evaded detection by concealing other bodies?

Going public, now?

More confident?

I let my mind dance around the data.

Someone who craved control because he'd been controlled as a child, perhaps brutally?

Maybe he was *still* under someone's thumb. A worker bee or submissive spouse?

Faking self-confidence?

Needing release.

Employed, possibly a checkered history . . .

Agent Gorman using sound psychological logic, because psychopaths' achievements nearly always lagged behind their own inflated self-images.

Leading to dissonance. Tension.

The need for release: the ultimate control.

I thought of a killer I'd met in graduate school. A strangler, as it happened, locked in a back ward of County General Hospital, waiting for the court system to evaluate his sanity. A professor who earned extra money as an expert witness had taken us to the killer's cell.

A gaunt, almost skeletal man in his thirties, with sunken cheeks and wispy black hair, the strangler lay on a cot, restrained by wide leather straps.

One of my classmates asked him what it felt like to kill. The gaunt man ignored the question at first, then a slow smile spread across his lips and they darkened, like paper held to a flame. His victim had been a prostitute whom he hadn't wanted to pay. He'd never known her name.

What it feels like? he finally said, in a disturbingly pleasant voice. *It feels like nothing, it's no big fucking deal, you stupid asshole. It's not actually doing it, anyway, it's being* able *to do it, asshole.*

The power . . .

Opportunistic or premeditated.

Had Irit's killer known about the annual field trip in advance or was he just aware that the park was frequented by schoolkids?

Were the Carmelis right about Irit's victimization being one of those wrong-time/wrong-place horrors of chance that give atheists fuel?

Predator leering as the school bus unloads.

Feeling sweet contentment the way a fox might as it views chicklets hatching.

Every parent's nightmare.

Picking a weak one out of the herd—but why Irit?

Special Agent Gorman had suggested the girl's disabilities, but Irit's problems weren't obvious to the casual observer. On the contrary, she'd been an attractive child. No shortage of other kids with more conspicuous handicaps.

Was *that* the cue? The fact that she *looked* normal?

Then I remembered the hearing aid on the ground.

Despite all the care taken to arrange the body.

Not an accident. The more I thought about it, the more certain I became.

Leaving the pink disc behind—a *message*?

Communicating *what*?

I grabbed up the M.O. file again, looked for crimes committed against deaf people. Nothing.

Had the hearing aid told him Irit was the easiest target of all—less likely to be aware as he came up behind her, less likely to scream?

She wasn't mute, but maybe he'd assumed she was.

Gentle strangulation.

The phrase disgusted me. . . .

Care and time taken to avoid degradation of the body . . . No sex at the scene but perhaps he'd gone elsewhere to get off, masturbating to memories, as sex killers usually do.

But sex killers often used trophies to trigger memories: clothing, jewelry. Body parts; the breasts were a favorite.

Irit's body had been left pristine, nothing taken. Posed—almost primly. Expressly *un*sexual.

As if the killer wanted the world to know she hadn't been touched.

That he was *different*?

Or maybe he *had* taken something—something unobtrusive, undetectable—a few strands of hair.

Or had the souvenirs been the images themselves?

Photos, snapped at the scene and pocketed for later.

I pictured him, faceless, standing over her, tumescent with power, arranging—*posing*, snap, snap.

Creating a tableau, a hideous art form.

Polaroids. Or a private darkroom where he could modulate optical nuance.

A self-styled *artiste*?

Taking Irit far enough from the path so no one would hear the click, see the flash.

Cleaning up . . . obsessive but not psychotic.

You have many madmen in America!

I reread S.A. Gorman's letter, everything else in the box.

For all the hundreds of pages, something was missing.

The Carmelis' friends and neighbors hadn't been interviewed. Neither had Mrs. Carmeli, and her husband had been contacted only twice, both times briefly.

Respect for the grieving or soft-glove treatment for a diplomat?

Now, months later, a dead end.

My head hurt and my lungs burned. I'd been at it for nearly three hours.

As I got up to make coffee, the phone rang.

The operator at my service said, "A Ms. Dahl is on the line, Doctor."

"I'll take it, thanks."

"Dr. Delaware? It's Helena. I just got my on-call schedule for the week so I thought I'd try for an appointment. Do you have anything in two days? Maybe around ten in the morning?"

I checked. Several court reports were due. "How about eleven?"

"Eleven would be fine. Thank you."

"How's everything going, Helena?"

"Oh . . . about as well as can be expected . . . I guess I'm going through a point where I really miss him—more than I did . . . right after. Anyway, thanks for seeing me. Bye."

"Bye."

I wrote down the appointment. So much for clinical predictions. What was the chance I could do better for a dead girl?

7

"HOW FAR'D YOU GET?" MILO ASKED THE NEXT morning. It was 9:00 A.M. and we were drinking orange juice in my office.

"All of it." I lifted the offender printout. "New system?"

"Funded by Sacramento in response to the victims' rights movement. Great idea but so far reporting procedures are sloppy and lots of cities—L.A. included—don't have a system in place. Also, most cops are scared of computers so the best way to get info is still the horn and teletypes. What'd you think of the FBI letter?"

"Nothing I disagree with but Agent Gorman's careful not to commit herself."

"So what else is new."

I told him my conception of the murderer. The possibility that photos had been taken.

"Polaroids or a darkroom?" he said. "A professional photographer?"

"Or a serious amateur. Someone with artistic pretensions—there's something pretentious about the *crime*, Milo. Fussy. Arranging the body, sweeping up. A psychopath who wants to believe he's something else. But all that's predicated upon it being a sex crime."

"You don't think it was?"

"Gorman may be right about its having something to do with Irit's background rather than being just a random thing. When Gorobich and Ramos did something, they were thorough. It's what they didn't do that's off. All those interviews with park neighbors but none in Beverlywood. The father talked to twice, the mother not at all."

He wiped his face. "A family thing?"

"Most kids *are* killed by relatives."

"Something about these parents comes across creepy?"

"Just how little attention they've received. And how little information they've offered."

"A parent hiding in that forest—it would have to be the father 'cause the mother wouldn't be strong enough to carry Irit that far. And I know for sure it wasn't the father because when the call came in about Irit's being missing, he was at the consulate in a meeting."

"Okay," I said. "Any other relatives besides the younger brother?"

"Don't know." He put his big hands on the side of the box and rocked it. "It's too weird, anyway, Alex. When relatives kill kids you know it's almost always at home. Or some family outing. I've never heard of them stalking like this. I know Gorobich and Ramos didn't turn over every rock but they claim there was nothing off about the Carmelis. Just parents destroyed by the worst possible scenario. Add VIP to the picture and you could see why they wouldn't want to pry too hard."

"Makes sense," I said. "Get a callback from Mr. Carmeli yet?"

"Nope. And I can't wait to tackle that one. Little old *moi* crashing the halls of diplomacy."

The image made me smile.

"What?" he said. "The tie?"

The tie was a limp, narrow strip of blue-green pseudosilk, too short to stretch the hump of his belly and flipped-up at the tip. Perfect with the beige-and-black-striped shirt and the faded olive sportcoat.

I used to think he didn't know better but a month ago, Robin and I had gone with him to the art museum and he had looked at the pictures the way someone who understands pictures does, talking about how much he liked the Ashcan painters, why Fauvism stank because of the vulgar colors. After all these years I was beginning to suspect the way he dressed was intentional. A distraction, so people would think him inept.

"The tie," I said, "could cause an international incident. Why, are you planning a drop-in?"

"You know me. Mr. Spontaneous."

"When?"

"Soon as possible. Want to come along? No doubt *you've* got a diplomatically correct foulard—in fact, do you have one to lend me? More orange juice, too, long as you're up."

I LENT HIM A CONSERVATIVE PAISLEY AND WE TOOK the unmarked.

The Israeli Consulate was on Wilshire near Crescent Heights, on the top floor of a faceless seventeen-story tower. The first three floors were parking lot and Milo drove in, ignored the WAIT FOR VALET sign, and pulled into a space near the elevator. Pocketing the keys, he shoved a bill at the flustered attendant, flashed his badge, and called out, "Have a nice day."

We rode up. The interior halls were narrow, white, free of decoration, topped by a low, gray, water-spotted acoustical ceiling. The carpeting was mint green with a faint dot pattern. Both needed cleaning and wallpaper seams had come loose in spots. Lots of doors, mostly white and blank.

At the end of the corridor was a TV camera aimed at the last door. A brown plastic sign announced the presence of the consulate and the Israeli tourist office and spelled out hours for visa applications. Just to the right was another plaque—the blue-and-white Israeli flag—and below that a plate-glass window with a steel document tray, a call button, and a speaker.

A young black-haired man in a blue blazer, white shirt, and tie sat behind the glass. His features were sharp and his hair was thick and cropped to the skull. He was reading a magazine and didn't look up until Milo pushed the button.

"Yes?"

"Mr. Carmeli."

"Do you have an appointment?" Middle Eastern accent.

Milo produced the badge again.

"Drop it in, please."

The badge hit the tray and slid into the reception booth. A steel shutter dropped over the slot. The guard inspected the badge, looked at Milo, held up a finger, got up, and disappeared. The magazine was *Sports Illustrated.*

Behind the booth was a nest of white cubicles and I could see two women and one man working at computers. A few travel posters hung on the walls. Everything looked just a bit off— cloudy. Refracted through the inch-thick glass.

The young man came back a moment later. "He's in a meeting—"

"This is about—"

The young man smiled and held up a finger again. *"But,"* he said, "he'll be out soon."

He sat down and returned to the world of soccer.

"Doing us a big favor," mumbled Milo.

A low-pitched whine sounded above. The camera rotated, aiming at us.

Milo pushed the button again and the young man looked up.

"My badge?"

"Mr. Carmeli has it."

We stood in the hall as the guard read. A heavy black woman in blue blazer and gray slacks came from around the corner and walked down the hall, glancing at doors. She saw us and turned around.

Three minutes passed, four, five. The guard picked up a phone, listened, put it back down.

Five more minutes until one of the white doors opened and a tall, pale man came out into the corridor. Stooped, with round shoulders, he wore a gray nailhead double-breasted suit, baby blue shirt, and maroon tie. The shirt's collar was too big and the suit bagged. His cheeks were sunken and the bones of his hawk face were oversized and painfully obvious. Wavy brown hair was neatly trimmed and thinning at the crown. He wore heavy, black-framed eyeglasses.

"Zev Carmeli."

Handshakes were cursory. His fingers were long and very cold. The glasses were bifocals. Thirty-eight but he looked ten years older.

Milo started to speak but Carmeli interrupted him by returning the badge and turning to point down the hall. Leading us to another of the white doors, he unlocked it and motioned us into a windowless room set up with a brown sofa, Danish teak coffee table with brass ashtray, a pair of chrome and brown-tweed armchairs.

Blue carpeting, still nothing on the walls. Behind the couch was another white door, double-bolted.

Milo and I took the chairs as Carmeli relocked the outer door. Reaching in his coat, he placed a hardpack of Dunhills and a matchbook that said LEARN AT HOME TO BE A COURT REPORTER on the table.

He sat down on the couch and lit up, inhaling for a long time while studying the grain of the tabletop. His movements were slow and steady, as if everything required careful planning. He kept smoking, finally looked at us. His eyes were as black as the eyeglass frames, still and flat as a stain. The room fogged with nicotine, then I heard an air conditioner kick in and smoke began rising toward a duct in the ceiling.

Carmeli hiked his trousers up over black socks. His fingertips were stained amber.

"So," he said to Milo, "you are the new detective." Lighter accent than the guard's—Middle East tempered by upper-crust London.

"Milo Sturgis, sir. Pleased to meet you."

Carmeli glanced at me.

"This is Dr. Delaware," said Milo. "Our psychological consultant."

I expected some reaction but Carmeli gave none. Finally he raised the flat, black eyes til they met mine. Another lungful of smoke.

"Good morning, Doctor."

Everything on delay. Everything an effort. I'd met too many families of dead children to be surprised.

"You will be analyzing the murderer, Doctor?"

I nodded.

"And anything else that bears analyzing," said Milo.

Carmeli didn't react.

"We're sorry for your loss, sir."

"Have you learned anything?"

"Not yet, sir, I just got the files. I thought I'd start by touching base and—"

"Touching base," said Carmeli, softly. "We are playing baseball. . . . Your predecessors touched base with me, as well. Unfortunately, they struck out."

Milo didn't answer.

The cigarette was only half-smoked but Carmeli crushed it out. Both of his feet were flat on the ground. He drew them closer to the couch and his knees pointed sharply through his trousers. The shirt collar at least one full size too big, his Adam's apple unusually sharp-edged, like a blade threatening to rip through his neck. A thin man who'd lost lots of weight.

New cigarette. I noticed the dark smudges under his eyes, his fingers squeezing the paper cylinder so tightly it was almost an L. The other hand rested on the couch, curled into a fist.

"A no-hitter," he said. "So . . . we are touching base. What would you like to know, Mr. Sturgis?"

"First of all, is there anything you want to tell me?"

Carmeli stared at him.

"Anything," said Milo, "that's occurred to you since Detectives Gorobich and Ramos spoke to you."

Continuing to stare, Carmeli straightened the bent cigarette, then lit up and shook his head. A very soft "No," emerged from clenched lips. "Nothing."

"Then I'll ask a few questions, sir. Please understand that some of them may be repet—"

Carmeli cut him off with a wave of the cigarette. Smoke ribboned. "Ask, ask, Mr. Sturgis."

"Your work, sir. The Middle East situation. I'm sure you receive threats—"

Carmeli laughed without changing the shape of his mouth. "I'm not James Bond, Detective. My title is deputy consul for community liaison. Did your predecessors tell you what that means?"

"They said something about organizing events. The Israel Independence Day parade."

"Parades, Israel-bond luncheons, meetings at synagogues, talking to Hadassah ladies—do you know what Hadassah is?"

Milo nodded.

"Dear ladies," said Carmeli. "Lovely people who plant trees in Israel. When wealthy donors want to have lunch with the consul general, I arrange it. When the prime minister comes to town to meet with the wealthiest of donors, I organize his itinerary. Double-O-Eight. License to cater."

The free hand shot through his thinning hair.

"So you're saying you never encounter—"

"I'm saying there's nothing controversial or dangerous about my work, Mr. Sturgis. I'm saying what happened to my daughter had nothing to do with my work or my wife's work or our family and I don't understand why the police simply can't accept that."

His voice had risen but remained soft. He leaned his head to the right as if loosening a neck kink. The black eyes were unflinching. He smoked some more, hungrily.

"Then again," he said, "I've dealt with your department in the course of my duties."

"Oh?"

Instead of elaborating, Carmeli smoked aggressively.

"Sometimes," said Milo, "we have to be annoying to do our job properly."

"Do you?"

"Yes, I'm afraid. Asking the same questions over and over."

"Ask whatever you please but if you persist in emphasizing my work the answer will be the same: I'm a bureaucrat. No exploding pens."

"Still, sir. Being Israeli, you have enemies—"

"Two hundred million of them. Though we're now on the road to peace, right?" Now, Carmeli smiled.

"Then how can you be sure this wasn't political? Despite your duties, you're a representative of the Israeli government."

Carmeli didn't answer for several moments. Looking at his shoes, he rubbed the toe of the left one. "Political crimes are based upon hatred and the Arabs hate us. And there are thousands of Arabs in this city, some of them with strong political views. But the goal of even the most violent terrorist is to send a message in a way that will attract attention. Not *one* dead child, Mr. Sturgis. A *busload* of children. Copious amounts of blood, disarticulated limbs, TV cameras recording every agonized cry. Bombs that make noise, Mr. Sturgis. Literally and figuratively. Several years ago when the Palestinians in Gaza and the West Bank discovered that throwing rocks at our soldiers made them international heroes they began phoning the wire services to give journalists advance notice of impending riots. Once the film crews showed up . . ."

He clapped his hands and ash scattered, landing on the table, his trousers, the floor.

"Your predecessors, Detective, informed me that the . . . crime was unusual in its *lack* of violence. Do you agree with that?"

Milo nodded.

Carmeli said, "That alone convinces me there was nothing political about it."

"That alone?" said Milo. "Is there something else that convinces you?"

"Interpreting my phrasing, Mr. Sturgis? I thought *he* was the psychologist—speaking of which, have you developed any theories, yet, Doctor?"

"Not yet," I said.

"Are we dealing with a madman?"

I glanced at Milo. He nodded.

"Outwardly," I said, "the killer probably looks quite sane."

"And internally?"

"He's a mess. But clinically he's not mad, Mr. Carmeli. More likely he's what we call a psychopath—someone with a serious character disorder. Self-centered, lacking normal emotional responses, no empathy, an incomplete conscience."

"Incomplete? He *has* a conscience?"

"He knows right from wrong but chooses to ignore the rules when it suits him."

He rubbed his shoe again and sat up. The black eyes narrowed. "You're describing evil—and you're telling me he could be any man on the street?"

I nodded.

"Why does he kill, Doctor? What's in it for him?"

"Relief of tension," I said.

He flinched. Smoked. "Everyone experiences tension."

"His tension may be especially strong and his wiring's off. But these are just guesses, Mr. Carmeli. No one really understands what leads—"

"What causes this supposed *tension*?"

A sexual warp, but I didn't say that. "Possibly a gap between who he thinks he is and the way he lives. He may pride himself on being brilliant, believe he's entitled to fame and fortune. But he's probably an underachiever."

"You're saying he kills to feel *competent*?"

"It's possible, Mr. Carmeli. But—"

"Killing a child makes him feel *competent*?"

"Killing makes him feel powerful. As does eluding capture."

"But why a *child*?"

"At root, he's a coward, so he preys upon the weak."

His head snapped back, as if struck. The cigarette shook and he jammed it into his mouth. Smoking, he played with a cuff button, stared at me again. "As you said, these are guesses."

"Yes."

"But if there's any truth to them, the killing won't stop, will it? Because his *tension* won't simply disappear."

"It's possible."

"Also," said Carmeli, "he may have murdered before." He turned to Milo. "If that's so, why haven't the police discovered similar crimes?"

His voice had risen and the words tumbled out. Snubbing out the second cigarette, he used his index finger to shape the ashes on the table into a thin gray line.

Milo said, "This may be a beginning, sir. A first crime."

"The killer *began* with my Irit?"

"It's possible."

"Why?" said Carmeli, suddenly plaintive. "Why *Irit*?"

"We don't know yet, sir. That's one of the reasons I'm here to—"

"How extensively have you *looked* for other murders, Mr. Sturgis?"

"Very extensively, but we're still in the process—"

"The process, the process—your predecessors said there's no central crime computer in California. I was incredulous so I checked. And verified it." Carmeli shook his head. "Absurd. Your department claims to be . . . Israel has a population of five million and our crime situation is much less severe than yours and we centralize our files. Excepting political incidents, we experience fewer than a hundred murders per year. That's comparable to a busy weekend in Los Angeles, right?"

Milo smiled. "Not quite."

"A bad month, then. According to the mayor's office, Los Angeles had one thousand and four murders last year. Other American cities are even worse. Thousands and thousands of murders in this vast country. Without centralized files how can you hope to access information?"

"It's tough, sir. We do have some central—"

"I know, I know, the FBI," said Carmeli. "NCIC, various state logs, I know. But reporting procedures are slipshod and inconsistent and there's tremendous variation from city to city."

Milo didn't answer.

"It's chaos, isn't it, Detective? You really *don't* know if similar crimes have occurred and you're unlikely to *ever* know."

"One thing that might help in that regard, sir, would be publicizing the crime. I understand your reluctance but—"

"Again," said Carmeli, clenching his jaws. "Back to me. Us. What could you possibly expect to gain by publicizing the crime other than subjecting my family to more pain and possibly endangering the children of my colleagues?"

"Endangering them how, Mr. Carmeli?"

"Either by inspiring the murderer to kill another Israeli child or giving someone else ideas—go after the Zionists. At that point, we *would* be feeding terrorist fantasies." He shook his head again. "No, there's no point, Mr. Sturgis. Besides, if this killer has struck before, it's been somewhere other than Los Angeles, right?"

"Why do you say that, Mr. Carmeli?"

"Because surely, even with your slipshod procedures, you would have heard about it, no? Surely child murders aren't that routine, even in Los Angeles."

"No murders are routine to me, sir."

"So you'd know if there were others, wouldn't you?"

"Assuming the crime was reported."

Carmeli squinted in confusion. "Why wouldn't it be?"

"Many crimes aren't. Murders that look like accidents often aren't."

"But the death of a child!" said Carmeli. "Are you telling me there are places in this city where parents wouldn't report the death of a child?"

"There are, sir," said Milo, softly. "Because many child homicides are committed by parents."

Carmeli went white.

Milo began to rub his face but stopped himself. "What I'm saying, sir, is that we can't assume anything at this point, and going public could jog someone's memory. A crime that was similar in some crucial way could emerge. Maybe years ago, maybe in another city. Because if we get good media coverage, the exposure would reach other cities. But I can also see your point about the danger. And to be honest, I can't promise it would do any good."

Carmeli breathed rapidly several times and placed his hands on the couch. "Your honesty is . . . laudable. Now I will be frank with you: not a chance. The risk-outcome ratio isn't good, I won't have another child's death on my conscience. So what *other* avenues will you pursue?"

"I'll ask lots of questions. Could I ask you a few more?"

"Yes," said Carmeli, weakly. He reached for a third cigarette, picked up the matchbook but didn't light up immediately. "But if they're about our family life, I'll simply tell you what I told the others: We were happy. A happy family. We never appreciated how happy we were."

The black eyes closed, then opened. Flat no longer. Something burned within.

"Back to the political issue for a second, sir," said Milo. "No doubt the consulate gets threats. Do you save them?"

"I'm sure we do but that's not my area."

"Do you have any objection to turning over copies?"

"I can ask."

"If you tell me whose area it is, I'll be happy to ask, myself."

"No, I'll do it." Carmeli's hand began to shake. "Your comment. About parents killing their own children. If you were implying—"

"I wasn't. Of course not, please forgive me if I offended you. I was just explaining why some crimes don't get reported."

The black eyes were now moist. Carmeli removed his glasses and wiped them with the back of one hand. "My daughter was—a very special girl. Raising her was challenging and I believe we loved her more because of it. We never hurt her. Never lifted a finger against her. If *anything* we spoiled her. Thank *God* we spoiled her!"

He put the glasses back on, slapped his hands back down on the couch. "What other questions do you have?" Hardened voice.

"I'd like to know more about Irit, Mr. Carmeli."

"In what way?"

"The kind of child she was, her personality. The things she liked and disliked."

"She liked everything. A very agreeable child. Kind, happy, always laughing, always wanting to help. I assume you've got Gorobich's files?"

"Yes."

"Then I don't need to go over the details of her . . . medical condition. As a baby she had a fever that did damage."

Slipping his hand under his jacket he drew out a large calfskin billfold. Inside were slots for credit cards. A photo sat in the first one and he slipped it out and showed it to us without relinquishing it.

Wallet-sized headshot of a beautiful, smiling child in a white dress with puff sleeves. Jewish star necklace. The same fair, curly hair and flawless skin, the same face . . . a mature face, no outward sign of retardation. In the death picture she'd looked younger. In this one, sparked by the joy of life, she could have been anywhere from twelve to seventeen.

"*This* was Irit, Detective. Not the images in your files."

"How long ago was this taken?" said Milo.

"This year. At school."

"Could I have a copy?"

"If I can find one." Carmeli pulled the snapshot back, protectively, and returned it to the billfold.

"Did she have friends, sir?"

"Of course. At school. Children her own age were too . . . quick for her."

"What about friends in the neighborhood?"

"Not really."

"Any older kids who'd bothered or bullied her?"

"Why? Because she was different?"

"It happens."

"No," said Carmeli. "Irit was sweet. She got along with everybody. And we sheltered her."

He blinked hard, lit up.

Milo said, "How hard of hearing was she?"

"She had no hearing in the right ear, about thirty-percent function in the left."

"With or without the hearing aid?"

"With. Without the aid she could barely hear at all, but she seldom used it."

"Why not?"

"She didn't like it, complained it was too loud, gave her headaches. We had it adjusted several times but she never liked it. Actually I—"

He buried his face in his hands.

Milo sat back. Now, he rubbed his face.

A moment later, Carmeli sat up. Inhaling the third cigarette, he talked through the smoke.

"She tried to deceive us about it. Wearing it when she left the house, then pulling it out the moment she got on the school bus. Or if not then, in class. Or losing it—we went through several replacements. We had her teachers make sure she wore it. So she began leaving it in her ear but switching it off. Sometimes she remembered to switch it back on when she came home but usually she didn't, so we knew—she was a sweet child, Mr. Sturgis. Innocent, not good at sneaking. But she did have a will. We tried reasoning with her, bribing her. Nothing worked. Finally, we came to the conclusion that she *preferred* not hearing. Being able to shut the world out, create her own world. Does that make sense to you, Doctor?"

"Yes, I've seen that," I said.

"My wife has, too. She's a teacher. In London she worked at a school for special children, said many kids with problems enter their own private worlds. Still, we wanted Irit to know what was going on around her. We never stopped reminding her to use it."

"So that day," said Milo, "even though she was wearing it, you don't know if it was switched on."

"My guess would be that it was off."

Milo thought, rubbed his face again. "Thirty percent in one ear at best. So even with the aid, it's likely she couldn't hear much of what was going on around her."

"No, not much." Carmeli smoked and sat straighter.

"Was Irit very trusting?" I said.

He took a deep breath. "You need to understand, Doctor, that she grew up in Israel and in Europe, where things are much safer and children are much freer."

"Israel's safer?" said Milo.

"Much safer, Mr. Sturgis. Your media play up the occasional incident, but outside of political terrorism, violence is very low. And in Copenhagen and London, where we lived later, she was also relatively free."

"Despite being the child of a diplomat?" I said.

"Yes. We lived in good neighborhoods. Here in Los Angeles, a good neighborhood means nothing. Nothing prepared us for this city—certainly, Irit was trusting. She liked people. We taught her about strangers, the need to be cautious. She said she understood. But she was—in her own way she was very smart. But also young for her age—her brother is only seven but in some ways he was the older child. More . . . sophisticated. He's a very gifted boy. . . . Would Irit have gone with a stranger? I'd like to think no. Am I sure?" He shook his head.

"I'd like to speak to your wife," said Milo. "We'll be talking to your neighbors, as well. To find out if anyone noticed anything unusual on your street."

"No one did," said Carmeli. "I asked them. But go ahead, ask them yourself. In terms of my wife, however, I insist on drawing some ground rules: You may not imply in *any* way that she could be responsible, the way you implied with me."

"Mr. Carmeli—"

"Do I make myself *clear*, Detective?"

His voice was loud, again, and his narrow torso had tensed, the shoulders up, as if he was prepared to strike out.

"Sir," said Milo, "I have no intention of adding to your wife's stress and I'm sorry if I offended you—"

"Not a *hint*," said Carmeli. "I won't permit you to speak to her, otherwise. She has experienced enough pain in her life. Do you understand?"

"Yes, sir."

"I'll be present when you speak to her. And you may not talk to my son. He's too young, has no business with the police."

Milo didn't answer.

"You don't like this," said Carmeli. "You think I'm being . . . obstructionistic. But it's my family, not yours."

He sprang up, stood at attention, eyes fixed on the door. A dignitary at a boring but important function.

We rose, too.

"When can we meet Mrs. Carmeli?" said Milo.

"I'll call you." Carmeli strode to the door and held it open. "Be brutally honest, Mr. Sturgis. Do you have any hope of finding this monster?"

"I'll do my best, Mr. Carmeli, but I deal in details, not hope."

"I see . . . I'm not a religious man, never attend synagogue except for official business. But if there is a life after death I'm fairly certain I'm going to heaven. Do you know why?"

"Why?"

"Because I've already been to hell."

8

DESCENDING IN THE ELEVATOR, MILO SAID, ''THAT room. Wonder if Gorobich and Ramos merited his private office.''

"Putting some distance between the murder and his work?"

"Distance is a big issue for him, isn't it?"

"Can you blame him?" I said. "Losing a child is bad enough without attributing it to your career choice. I'm sure he considered the political angle right from the beginning. The entire consulate probably did, and they decided it wasn't a factor. As you said, if they thought it was, they'd handle it themselves. And what Carmeli said about terrorism as attention-seeking backs that up. The same thing applies to counterterrorism: Send a message. Someone's out for your kids, come down hard and fast and with enough publicity to provide strong deterrence. And something else: Carmeli's demeanor wasn't that of a man who's achieved even the slightest closure. He's hurting, Milo. Starving for answers."

He frowned. "And we haven't given him any. Maybe that's another reason he doesn't like the department."

"What do you mean?"

"That crack about having worked with us before. Someone probably screwed up on his parade or something. Sticking with the baseball analogies, I'm starting out with two strikes against me."

The car was where we'd left it. He gave the parking attendant another tip, backed out, and drove down the exit ramp. Traffic was heavy on Wilshire and he waited to turn left.

"That room," he said, again. "Did you see the way the smoke got sucked up into the ceiling? Maybe he's not James Bond but my

Mossad fantasies are taking over and I keep flashing images of secret tunnels up there, all this cloak-and-dagger crap."

"License to cater," I said.

"And cynical old me thinks: protesting too much . . . any other impressions of him?"

"No, just what I said."

"No special antenna-twang?"

"Why?"

He shrugged. "I can understand his wanting to keep distance between the murder and his job but don't you think he could have been a little more forthcoming? Like volunteering to turn over the consulate's crank mail . . . not that I blame him, I guess. From his perspective we're clowns who haven't done squat."

He made the turn.

"Changing the subject," I said. "The hearing aid. I keep thinking it was left there deliberately. Maybe the killer's telling us that's why he chose her."

"Telling us? A game-player?"

"There's a gamelike quality to it, Milo. Malignant play. And what Carmeli told us about Irit's turning off the hearing aid, retreating to her own private world, would have made her a perfect target. For children, private worlds often mean overt self-stimulation: fantasizing, talking to themselves, strange-looking body movements. The killer could have watched and seen all that: first the hearing aid, then Irit wandering away from the others, acting preoccupied, lost in fantasy. He pulled her out of her script and into his."

"Wandered off," he said. "So maybe we're just talking real bad luck."

"A mixture of bad luck and victim characteristics."

A moment later something else hit me.

"There's a whole other possibility," I said. "It *was* someone who knew her. Knew that even when she wore the aid, she turned it off and was easy to sneak up on."

He drove slowly, jaws knotted, squinting at more than sun-glare. We traveled for three blocks before he spoke.

"So back to the old acquaintance list. Teachers, the bus driver. And neighbors, no matter what Carmeli says. I've seen too many girls brutalized by supposed friends and acquaintances. The wholesome kid down the block who up til then only cut up cats and dogs when no one was looking."

"That why you asked about bullies in the neighborhood?"

"I asked because at this point I don't know what else to ask. But yeah, the thought did occur to me that someone could have had it in for her. She was retarded, deaf, Jewish, Israeli. Choose your criterion."

"Someone had it in for her but took care not to violate the body?"

"He's twisted. You're the shrink." His voice was husky with irritation.

I said, "The M.O. files you gave me didn't classify by victim characteristic other than age and sex. If you can get hold of the information, I'd look into murders of deaf people. Handicapped people, in general."

"Handicapped defined how, Alex? Lots of our bad guys and their victims wouldn't win any IQ contests. Is a dope fiend who OD's and blasts himself into a coma handicapped?"

"How about deaf, blind, crippled. Documented retardation, if that doesn't get too unwieldly. Victims under eighteen and stran-gled."

He put on speed. "That kind of information is obtainable. Theo-retically. Given enough time and shoe leather and cops from other jurisdictions who cooperate and have decent memories and keep decent records. *That's* for L.A. County. If the killer's new to the region, did the same thing two thousand miles away, the chances dwindle. And we already know from Gorman's letter that nothing about the crime tipped off the FBI computers, meaning there's no VICAP match. Even if we do find another case, it'll be unsolved. And if the bastard swept up just as thoroughly, we're not any further along, forensically."

"Pessimism," I said, "is not good for the soul."

"Sold my soul years ago."

"To whom?"

"The bitch goddess Success. Then she cut town before paying off." He shook his head and laughed.

"What?"

"Guy gets his statistics straight from the mayor's office. You see any career boost coming out of this one?"

"Let's put it this way," I said. "No."

He laughed harder.

"Your honesty is laudatory, Doctor."

At Robertson he stopped at a red light and touched his ear.

"Her own little world," he said. "Poor kid."

A few moments later: "Hear no evil."

THAT NIGHT I DIDN'T SLEEP MUCH. ROBIN HEARD ME
tossing and asked what was wrong.

"Too much caffeine."

9

THE NEIGHBORHOOD WAS WORSE THAN HE REMEM-bered.

Nice houses on his friend's street. Big, by his standards, most of them still decently maintained, at least from what he could see in the darkness. But to get there he'd passed through boulevards lined with pawnshops, liquor stores, and bars. Other businesses, to be sure, but at this hour they were all shuttered and the street was given over to girls in minimal clothing and guys drinking out of paper bags.

Night sounds: music, car engines, laughter now and then, rarely happy. People hanging out on corners or half-concealed in the shadows. Dark-skinned people, with nothing to do.

He was glad the Toyota was small and inconspicuous. Even so, occasionally someone stared as he passed.

Watching him, hands in pockets, slouching.

The half-naked girls paraded up and down or just stood at the curb, their pimps out of eyeshot but no doubt waiting.

He knew all about that kind of thing. Knew all the games.

His friend had told him not to be shocked and he'd come equipped, the nine-millimeter out of its box beneath the seat and tucked on the left side of his waistband where he could draw it out quickly with his gun hand.

His gun hand . . . nice way to put it.

So here he was, reasonably ready for surprises, but, of course, the key was not to *be* surprised.

Suddenly his thoughts were drowned out by music from a passing car. Big sedan, chassis so low it nearly scraped the asphalt.

Kids with shaved heads bobbing up and down. Throbbing bass beat. Not music. Words. Chanting—shouting to electric drums.

Ugly, angry rant that passed for poetry.

Someone shouted and he looked around and checked his rearview mirror.

A siren shrieked in the distance. Got louder.

The ultimate danger.

He pulled to the curb and an ambulance passed and Dopplered to silence.

Silence had been Irit's world.

Had she been cued into some internal universe, able to feel the vibrations of her own heartbeat?

He'd been thinking about her all day and into the night, imagining and supposing and replaying the scene. But when he began the drive to his friend's house he forced himself to stop because he needed to concentrate on the present.

Still, so many distractions. This city . . . this neighborhood, all the changes.

Don't be shocked.

He turned off onto a night-black side street, then another, and another, until he found himself in a completely different world: dim, silent, the big houses austere as bureaucrats.

His friend's house looked the same, except for the FOR SALE sign staked in front.

It was good he'd caught him in time.

Surprise!

He pulled into the driveway, behind the dark van.

Touching the gun, he looked around again, got out, alarmed the car, and walked up the flower-lined pathway to the paneled front door.

Ringing the bell, he uttered his name in response to the shouted "Who is it?"

The door opened and he got a face full of smile.

"Hey!"

He stepped in and the two of them embraced briefly. To his friend's left was an old mahogany mail table against the wall. On it, a large manila envelope.

"Yeah, that's it."

"Thank you. I really appreciate it."

"No problem. Got time to come in? Coffee?"

"Sure. Thanks for that, too."

His friend laughed and they went into the kitchen of the big house.

The envelope in his hand, stiff and dry.

The guy had come through. Taking risks.

But when had anything worthwhile ever come easy?

He sat and watched as his friend poured coffee, saying, "Easy drive over?"

"No problem."

"Good. Told you it got bad."

"Things change."

"Yeah, but they rarely improve. So . . . you're back in the game. From the looks of it we've got plenty to talk about."

"That we do."

The hand stilled. "Black, right?"

"Good memory."

"Not as good as it used to be." The hand paused again. "Maybe that's for the better."

10

"IT'S AFFECTING MY WORK," SAID HELENA. "I SEE a suicide attempt wheeled into the E.R. and I want to scream, *Idiot!* I watch the surgeons open a gunshot wound and start thinking about Nolan's autopsy . . . he was so healthy."

"You read the report?"

"I called the coroner until someone spoke to me. I guess I was hoping they'd find something—cancer, some rare disease—anything to justify it. But he was in the pink, Dr. Delaware . . . he could have lived a long time."

She began crying. Pulled a tissue from her purse before I could get to the box. "The damn thing is," she said, catching her breath, "I've thought about him more in the last few weeks than all the years before combined."

She'd come straight from the hospital, still wearing her uniform, the white dress tailored to her trim frame, her nametag still pinned.

"I feel guilty, dammit. Why should I feel guilty? I never failed him because he never needed me. We didn't depend on each other. We both knew how to take care of ourselves. Or at least I thought so."

"Independent."

"Always. Even when we were little kids we went our separate ways. Different interests. We didn't fight, we just ignored each other. Is that abnormal?"

I thought of all the genetically linked strangers who'd passed through my office. "Siblings are thrown together by chance. Anything from love to hate can follow."

"Well, Nolan and I loved each other—at least I know I loved him. But it was more of a—I don't want to say family obligation. More of a . . . general bond. A feeling. And I loved his good qualities."

She crumpled the tissue. The first thing she'd done upon arriving was hand me insurance forms. Then she'd talked about the coverage, the demands of her job—taking time to get around to Nolan.

"Good qualities," I said.

"His energy. He had a real—" She laughed. "I was actually going to say 'love for life.' His energy and his intelligence. When he was young—eight or nine—the school tested him because he was goofing off in class. Turned out he was highly gifted—something like the top half-percent and he'd been tuning out because he was bored. I'm not stupid, but I'm not even remotely in that league . . . maybe I'm the lucky one."

"Being gifted was a burden for him?"

"It's crossed my mind. Because Nolan didn't have much patience and I think that had to do with his intelligence."

"No patience for people?"

"People, things, any process that moved too slowly. Once again, this was back when he was a teenager. He may have mellowed when he was older. I remember him always railing about something. Mom telling him, 'Honey, you can't expect the world to go at your pace,—could that be why he became a cop? To fix things fast?"

"If he did that could have been a problem, Helena. There are very few fast fixes in cop work. Just the opposite: Cops see problems that never get solved. Last time you said something about conservative political views. That could have led him to police work."

"Maybe. Although, once again, that's the last phase I knew about. He could have been into something completely different."

"He changed philosophies often?"

"All the time. There were times he outliberaled Mom and Dad, radical, really. Just about a Communist. Then he swung back the other way."

"Was all this in high school?"

"I think it was after the satanic phase—probably his senior year. Or maybe his freshman year in college. I remember his reading

Mao's Little Red Book, reciting from it at the table, telling Mom and Dad they thought they were progressive but they were really counterrevolutionary. Then for a while he got into Sartre, Camus, all that existential stuff, the meaninglessness of life. One month he tried to prove it by not bathing or changing his clothes." She smiled. "That ended when he decided he still liked girls. The next phase was . . . I think it was Ayn Rand. He read *Atlas Shrugged* and got totally into individualism. Then anarchy, then libertarianism. Last I heard he'd decided Ronald Reagan was a god, but we hadn't talked politics for years so I don't know where he ended up."

"Sounds like adolescent searching."

"I guess it was, but I never went through it. Always middle-of-the-road. The boring child."

"How'd your parents react to Nolan's changes?"

"They were pretty cool about it. Tolerant. I don't think they really ever understood Nolan but I never saw them put him down." She smiled. "Sometimes it was funny—the passion he put into each new phase. But we never made fun."

She crossed her legs.

"Maybe the reason I never went through any of that was I felt Nolan was so unpredictable that I *owed* it to Mom and Dad to be stable. Sometimes it did seem that the family was divided into two segments: the three of us, and Nolan. I always felt close to my parents."

She swiped at her eyes with the tissue. "Even when I was in college I'd go places with them, go out to dinner with them. Even after I was married."

"And Nolan wasn't part of that?"

"Nolan stopped hanging out with us when he was twelve. He always preferred to be by himself, do his own thing. Now that I think about it, he always kept his life private."

"Alienated?"

"I guess so. Or maybe he just preferred his own company because he was so smart. Which is another reason becoming a cop seems so strange. Who's more establishment?"

"Cops can be pretty alienated as a group," I said. "Living with all that violence, the us-them mentality."

"Doctors and nurses develop an us-them, too, but I still feel part of society."

"And you don't think Nolan did?"

"Who knows what he felt? But life must have been pretty damn bleak for him to do what he did."

Her voice was tight, dry as kindling.

"How *could* he, Dr. Delaware? How could he get to the point where he didn't feel tomorrow was worth waiting for?"

I shook my head.

"Dad's depressions," she said. "Maybe it's all genetic. Maybe we're just prisoners of our biology."

"Biology is strong but there are always choices."

"For Nolan to make that choice he must have been profoundly depressed, wouldn't you say?"

"Men sometimes do it when they're angry." Cops sometimes do it when they're angry.

"Angry about what? Work? I've been trying to find out more about his work record, see if he went through any bad work situations. I called the police department to get hold of his file and they referred me to his original training officer, a Sergeant Baker. He's at Parker Center, now. He was nice enough, said Nolan had been one of his best trainees, there'd been nothing out of the ordinary, he couldn't understand it either. I also went after Nolan's medical records, contacted the department insurance office and used some of my nursing skills to pry them loose. Back when I was still hoping for a disease. Nolan hadn't been treated for any medical conditions but he had seen a psychologist for two months before he died. Up til a week before. So something was wrong. A Dr. Lehmann. Do you know him?"

"First name?"

"Roone Lehmann."

I shook my head.

"He's got an office downtown. I left him several messages but he hasn't called back. Would you have any problem calling him?"

"No, but he may not break confidentiality."

"Do dead people have confidentiality?"

"It's an open question but most therapists don't breach even after death."

"I guess I knew that. But I also know that doctors talk to doctors. Maybe Lehmann would be willing to tell you something."

"I'll be happy to try."

"Thank you." She handed me the number.

"One question that I have, Helena, is why Nolan transferred

from West L.A. to Hollywood. Did Sergeant Baker say anything about that?"

"No. I didn't ask him. Why? Is that strange?"

"Most officers consider West L.A. a plum. And Nolan went from the day shift to the night shift. But if he liked excitement, he could have wanted an assignment with more action."

"Could be. He did like action. Roller coasters, surfing, motorcycling. . . . Why why why, all these whys. It's stupid to keep asking questions that can't be answered, isn't it?"

"No, it's normal," I said, thinking of Zev Carmeli.

She laughed, a jarring sound. "I saw this cartoon in the paper, once. That Viking, Hagar the Horrible? He's standing on a mountaintop, with rain and lightning all around, holding his hands up to the heavens, shouting, 'Why me?' And down from the heavens comes the answer: 'Why not?' Maybe that's the ultimate truth, Dr. Delaware. What right do I have to expect a smooth ride?"

"You have a right to ask questions."

"Well, maybe I should do more than ask. There's still Nolan's stuff to go through. I've been putting it off, but I should start."

"When you're ready."

"I'm ready now. After all, it's all mine, now. He left everything to me."

SHE MADE AN APPOINTMENT FOR NEXT WEEK AND left. I called Dr. Roone Lehmann's number and gave my name to his service, asking for the office address.

"Seventh Street," said the operator, reciting a number that put it near Flower, in the heart of the downtown financial district. Unusual location for a therapist but if he got lots of referrals from LAPD and other government agencies, I guess it made sense.

Just as I hung up, Milo called, his voice charged with some kind of energy.

"Got another case. Retarded girl, strangled."

"Pretty quick—"

"Not from the files, Alex. I'm talking brand-new, here and now. Caught the radio call a few minutes ago and I'm headed over to Southwest Division—Western near Twenty-eighth. If you come by now you might get a look at the body before they take it away. It's a school. Booker T. Washington Elementary."

11

verse away from the park where Irit Carmeli had lost her life. I took Sunset to La Cienega, headed south down San Vicente, and picked up the Santa Monica Freeway east at La Brea. Exiting at Western, I covered the next few blocks of inner city with relative speed. Few cars were on the street as I passed shuttered buildings and burned-out lots that hadn't been rebuilt since the riots and maybe never would be. The sky was very pale gray, almost white, looked as if it had given up on blue.

Washington Elementary was old, dun-colored, and cruelly graffitied. Set on acres of potholed playground, the entire property was surrounded by twelve-foot chain-link fencing that hadn't prevented vandals from pretending they were artists.

I parked on Twenty-eighth, near the main gate. Wide open but guarded by a uniform. Squad cars, technical vans, and the coroner's station wagon had converged at the south end of the playground, between the monkey bars and the swings. Yellow tape divided the lot in two. On the northern half children ran and played under the eyes of teachers and aides. Most of the adults watched the activity across the field. Few of the kids did and the yard was filled with laughter and protest, the scrappy doggerel of childhood.

No media cars, yet. Or maybe a murder down here just wasn't good enough copy.

It took a while to get past the uniform but finally I was allowed to make my way to Milo.

He was talking to a gray-haired man in an olive suit and writing in his notepad. A stethoscope hung around the other man's neck and he talked steadily, without visible emotion. Two black men with badges on their sportcoats stood twenty feet away, looking at a figure on the ground. A photographer snapped pictures and techs worked under the swing set with a portable vacuum, brushes, and tweezers. Other uniforms crowded the scene but they didn't seem to have much to do. Among them was a short, bearded Hispanic man around fifty, wearing gray work clothes.

As I came closer, the black detectives stopped chatting and watched me. One was fortyish, five nine and soft-heavy, with a head shaved clean, bulldog jowls, and a dyspeptic expression. His jacket was beige over black trousers and his tie was black printed with crimson orchids. His companion was ten years younger, tall and slim with a bushy mustache and a full head of hair. He wore a navy blazer, cream slacks, blue tie. Both had analytic eyes.

Milo saw me and held up a finger.

The black detectives resumed their conversation.

I took a look at the dead girl on the field.

Not much bigger than Irit. Lying the same way Irit had been positioned, hands to the sides, palms up, feet straight out. But this face was different: swollen and purplish, tongue extending from the lower left corner of the mouth, the neck circled by a red, puckered ring of bruise.

Her age was hard to make out but she looked in her teens. Black, wavy hair, broad features, dark eyes, some acne on the cheeks. Light-skinned black, or Latino. She wore navy sweatpants and white tennis shoes, a short denim jacket over a black top.

Dirty fingernails.

The eyes open, staring sightlessly at the milk-colored sky.

The tongue lavender-gray, huge.

Behind her, a foot of rope hung from the top bar of the swing set, the end cut cleanly. No breeze, no movement.

The coroner left and Milo approached the black detectives while waving me over. He introduced the heavy one as Willis Hooks, his partner as Roy McLaren.

"Pleased to meet you," said Hooks. His hand was baked leather.

McLaren nodded. He had clear, nearly coal-black skin, and clean features. Turning back to look at the dead girl, he set his jaw and chewed air.

"Was she left that way or cut down?" I said.

"Cut down," said Milo. "Why?"

"My first thought was she looks like Irit. The position."

He turned to the body and his eyebrows rose a millimeter.

"Irit's yours?" said Hooks.

Milo nodded. "She was arranged just like that."

"Well, unless the janitor's our killer I don't see any big deal about that."

"The janitor cut her down?" I said.

"Uh-huh." Hooks pulled out his pad. "School custodian, excuse me. Guillermo Montez, that older Mexican guy in the gray uniform. Showed up for work at seven this morning, mopped the main building first then came out here to pick up trash from the yard and found her. Ran back to get a knife and cut her down, but she was dead, had been for several hours. Said the rope was thick, it took work."

"Dr. Cohen said she'd been dead at least three or four hours by then, maybe more," said Milo.

"Cohen's usually pretty close," said McLaren.

"So she was killed sometime during the night," I said, "but the sun's been out since six. No one driving or walking by saw her?"

"Apparently not," said Hooks. "Or maybe someone did." He turned to Milo. "Tell me more about yours."

Milo did.

Hooks listened with his finger to his mouth. "Apart from the retardation, I don't see any big parallels." He looked at his partner.

McLaren said, "No, I wouldn't call this gentle strangulation."

"Ours wasn't raped," said Milo. "Cohen told me there were no obvious signs of rape with yours, either."

"So far," said McLaren. "But who knows. Janitor says her pants were up but maybe the bad guy pulled them up. Coroner'll get in there and let us know for sure."

"The strangulation," said Milo. "From the size of the ligature burn, the rope could have actually killed her, as opposed to his doing it some other way first and then stringing her up."

Hooks said, "Could be. It would be tough stringing up someone who struggled, even a small girl, but if she was flying, maybe. We know she used crack."

"Who was she?" I said.

"Local girl named Latvinia Shaver," said Hooks. "Patrol officer ID'd her before we got here, but I know her myself from working Vice a couple of years ago."

"A pro?" said Milo.

"She's been busted for it, but I wouldn't call her a pro. Just a street girl, nothing cooking up here." He tapped his bald head. "Nothing to do all day, so she gets into trouble, maybe does some guy for a vial or some spare change."

"Big crack habit?"

"Patrol officer said nothing big that she was aware of but hold on, let's ask her."

He went over to the uniforms and pulled a short, slim woman away from the group.

"Officer Rinaldo," he said, "meet Detective Sturgis and Dr. Delaware, who's a psychological consultant. Officer Rinaldo knew Latvinia."

"Just a bit," said Rinaldo, in a subdued voice. "From the neighborhood." She looked to be twenty-five, with hennaed hair pulled into a ponytail and thin, pained features that seemed to be aging quickly.

"What do you know besides her tricking for dope?" said Hooks.

"Not a bad kid," said Rinaldo. "Basically. But she was retarded."

"How retarded?" said Milo.

"I think she was eighteen or nineteen, but she acted more like twelve. Or even younger. The family's pretty messed up. She lives with a grandmother or maybe it's an older aunt, over on Thirty-ninth, people constantly going in and out."

"Crack house?"

"I don't know for sure but it wouldn't surprise me. She has a brother up in San Quentin, used to be big in the Tray-One Crips."

"Name?"

"Don't know that either, sorry. I just remember that 'cause the grandmother told me about him, said she was glad he was gone so Latvinia wouldn't be influenced."

She frowned. "The lady seemed to be trying."

Hooks wrote something down.

"Any gangster boyfriends or known acquaintances?" said McLaren.

Rinaldo shrugged. "As far as I could see she didn't hang with anyone in particular. No gang, I mean. More like whoever was around . . . basically she was pretty promiscuous. She drank, too, 'cause I caught her woozy a few times, with bottles of malt and gin."

"Bust her for it?"

Rinaldo blushed. "No, I just took it away and tossed it. You know how it is out here."

"Sure do," said Hooks. "Anything else in her fun-pack?"

"Probably, but I never saw anything worse—I mean, she didn't shoot heroin, far as I know."

"She have any kids?"

"Not that I heard about. But maybe, she was pretty easygoing, you know? Easy to con. Like a kid with a grown-up body. So who knows."

"Be interesting if she was pregnant," said Hooks. "Can't wait to see the autopsy on this one." He glanced back at the body. "Not that she's showing. Small lady."

"Small," McLaren agreed. "Cohen estimated five one, ninety."

"Yeah, she was small," said Rinaldo. "Anyone could have hurt her."

"Any ideas about who did?"

"Not a one."

"So no known enemies?"

"Not that I heard. Overall, she was a pretty nice kid, but anyone could have conned her. Like I said, she was retarded."

"I'm still trying to get a feel for how retarded," said Hooks.

"I don't know exactly, sir. I mean, she could talk and make sense and at first glance she didn't look weird, but once you talked to her you realized she was immature."

"Like a twelve-year-old."

"Maybe even younger. Ten, eleven. Despite all her fooling around she was kinda . . . innocent." Another blush. "Not a hard kid, you know?"

"Was she in any program?" said McLaren. "Special school, that kind of thing?"

"I don't think she was in school, period. I just used to see her on the streets, walking around, hanging. Sometimes I had to tell her to get moving, go home."

She winced. "The thing is, sometimes she didn't put on enough clothes. No underwear or bra and sometimes she'd wear real filmy see-through clothes. Or leave her shirt unbuttoned. When I'd say what on earth are you doing, girl, she'd giggle and button up."

"Advertising for business?" said McLaren.

"I always thought she was just acting stupid," said Rinaldo.

"Whether or not she was advertising," said Hooks, "going around like that, she probably got business."

"I'm sure," said Rinaldo.

"No boyfriend," said McLaren.

"Not to my knowledge."

"No gangsters in her social life at all?"

"The brother's all I know. You'd have to ask her grandmother."

"We'll do that," said Hooks. "What's the home address?"

"Don't know the exact number but it's on Thirty-ninth a couple of blocks east of here. Green house, old, one of those big wooden ones converted to rooms, chain-link fence in front and cement instead of grass. I know because I took her home one time when she had a short dress and no panties. The wind was blowing the dress up and I just wanted to get her inside." She blinked. "Grandmother's on the second floor."

"When Latvinia was busted," said Hooks, "were you the arresting officer?"

"Me and my partner, Kretzer. We pulled her twice for soliciting. Both times she was out late, over on Hoover near the freeway on-ramp, getting in the way of traffic."

"East ramp or west?"

"West."

"Trying to snag a Beverly Hills guy, maybe," said McLaren.

Rinaldo shrugged.

"When was this?" said Hooks.

"Last year. December, I think. It was cold and she had on a quilted jacket but no top underneath."

Hooks wrote. "So I can get her personal info from the files."

"Probably not, it was a juvey bust, sealed. She was just short of eighteen and I told her she was a lucky girl. If it's just the home address you need, I can take you there."

"The address is a good place to start," said Hooks. He looked at McLaren. "You want?"

The younger man said, "Sure."

He and Rinaldo walked away, got into a black-and-white, and drove toward the south gate.

"See any dramatic parallels, yet?" Hooks asked Milo.

"Not really."

"Yours was a diplomat's kid?"

"Israeli diplomat."

"Nothing in the news on anything like that?"

"They hushed it up." Milo told him Carmeli's rationale.

"Well," said Hooks, "he could be right, but I don't know. Sounds like a fun one."

"Yeah. Where you going with this, Willis?"

"The usual. If we get lucky it'll be some dirt lives next door. If not, who knows? She didn't exactly lead a sheltered life."

Milo glanced across the yard. "Those kids are looking at the body."

"Would have been worse if the janitor didn't get here and they saw it swinging."

"Interesting reaction, his cutting her down."

Four parallel lines in Hooks's forehead deepened. "Civic volunteerism. Maybe he listens to the mayor's speeches. Hold on." He made his way halfway to the crowd in a quick, rolling gait, caught the eye of the man in the gray uniform, and motioned him over.

The janitor came over licking his lips.

"If you got a minute again, sir," said Hooks. "This here is Mr. Montez."

The custodian nodded. Up close, I saw he was closer to sixty with a prizefighter's battered face and a coarse gray beard. Five seven and broad-shouldered, with thick, stubby hands and oversized feet.

"Detective Sturgis," said Milo, holding out his hand. Montez shook it. His eyes were bloodshot.

"I know you told your story, sir," said Milo, "but if you don't mind, I'd like to hear it, again."

Montez looked up at him and put his hands in his pockets. "I come to work at seven o'clock," he said, in clear but accented English. "I clean the main building and bungalow B, like always, then I come out to sweep, like always. I sweep early 'cause sometimes people leave shi—things on the yard. I don't want the kids they should see."

"What kinds of things?"

"Liquor bottles, crack vials. Sometimes condoms, needles. Even used toilet paper. You know."

"So people get into the schoolyard at night."

"All the time." Montez's voice rose. "They get in, do parties, do dope, shootings. Three months ago, three guys got shot dead. Last year, two guys. Terrible for the kids."

"Who got shot?" said Milo.

"Gangsters, I dunno."

Hooks said, "Wallace and SanGiorgio's case. Drive-by, through the fence." Turning back to Montez: "What do they usually do, cut through the lock?"

"The chain. Or they just climb over. All the time."

"Any idea the last time the chain was cut?" said Milo.

"Who knows," said Montez. "We used to change the locks all the time. Now . . . the school they don't have money for books. My grandchildren go here."

"You live around here, sir?"

"No, I live in Willowbrook. My daughter and her husband, they live here, on Thirty-fourth. The husband, he work over at the Sports Arena. They got three kids—the two here and one baby."

Milo nodded. "So you came out and started sweeping and saw her."

"Right away I see her," said Montez. "Hanging there." He shook his head and pain danced across his face. "The tongue . . ." Shaking his head again.

"Did you realize she was dead right away?" said Milo.

"That tongue? Sure, what else?"

"So you cut her down."

"Sure, why not? I figure maybe . . ."

"Maybe what?"

Montez stared at him. Licked his lips, again. "Maybe it's stupid, but I dunno, maybe I figure I help her—I dunno, guess it was . . . the way she was hanging, I didn't want no kids to see it . . . my grandchildren. And she was always a nice kid, I wanted her to look nice."

"You knew her?" said Hooks.

"Latvinia? Sure. Everyone know her, she crazy."

"She came round here a lot?"

"Not inside, on the street." He tapped his temple. "She live on Thirty-ninth, few blocks from my daughter. Everyone see her walking around, no clothes. A little . . . not right."

"No clothes at all?" said Hooks. When Montez looked confused, he added, "She walked around totally naked?"

"No, no," said Montez. "A *little* clothes but not enough, you know?" Another tap. "Not right—you know? But happy all the time."

"Happy?"

"Yeah. Laughing." Montez's eyes hardened. "I do something wrong, cutting her down?"

"No, sir—"

"I go out, I see her up there, think the kids see that. My grandchildren. Go get a knife from the supply closet."

He slashed empty space.

"How long have you been working here, sir?" said Milo.

"Nine years. Before that, I worked over at Dorsey High, twelve years. Used to be a good school, there. Same problems now."

Milo hooked a thumb at the body. "When you saw Latvinia hanging, were her clothes the way they are now?"

"What do you mean?"

"Were her pants up when you saw her hanging?"

"Yeah—what, you think I—"

"No, sir, we're just trying to find out what she looked like when you saw her."

"The same," said Montez, angrily. " 'Zactly the same, pants up, the same. I get a knife, cut her down, and put her on the ground. Maybe a miracle, she not dead. But she dead. I call 911."

"The way you placed her," said Milo.

Montez's eyes were uncomprehending.

"Arms at her side," said Hooks. "Like you wanted her to look nice."

"Sure," said Montez. "Why not? Why shouldn't she look nice?"

HOOKS LET HIM GO AND WE WATCHED AS HE RE-turned to the school's main building.

"What do you think?" he asked Milo.

"Any reason to doubt his story?"

"Not really, but I'm going to do a background on him and if the girl was raped, I'll try to get some body fluids." He smiled. "Some thanks for the good Samaritan, huh? But we've seen plenty of those turn out not so good, right? Thing is, though, if he's the bad guy, why would he do her right here where he works, focus attention on himself.''

"Bloodshot eyes," said Milo. "Maybe he was up late."

"Yeah," said Hooks. "But no booze on his breath and he said he works two jobs. This during the day, part-time at a liquor store on Vermont at night. Says he was at the store last night, that should be checkable. Did he look hinky to you? If he's dirty, he's ready for the Oscar."

He gazed through the fence at Twenty-eighth Street, then took in the traffic on Western. "Somebody driving or walking by could very well have seen her swinging, but you heard what he said about all the crap goes down on the schoolyard. Unlike Mr. Montez, people around here don't volunteer much."

"If it was some dirt next door," said Milo, "wonder why *he'd* take the trouble to hang her here."

"Who knows?" said Hooks. "Maybe they ran into each other around the corner, made a date, headed over here to consummate. Montez said he finds condoms all the time."

"Techs have any idea when the chain was cut?"

"Just that it wasn't fresh, which is also consistent with Montez."

"The school keeps using a broken chain 'cause the minute they put a new one on, someone slices it."

"Yeah," said Hooks. "Nothing like security for our youngsters." He looked at the body again. "Maybe it does mean something, bringing her here, the bad guy making some kind of statement."

"Such as?"

"I hate school." Hooks smiled. "That narrows it down, huh? Pull in all the bad students."

Milo gave a short, hard detective laugh and Hooks laughed, too, fleshy jowls undulating. The four wrinkles smoothed.

"Put your hands up, punk," he said, making a finger-gun. "Lemme see your grade-point average. Two D's and an F? Off to the lineup."

He chuckled some more, exhaled. "Anyway, except for strangulation and both being retarded, I still don't see any parallels with your case."

"Strangulation, retarded, and no rape," said Milo.

"We don't know for sure if there was no rape," said Hooks.

"But if there wasn't any—no assault at all—that's interesting, right, Willis? How many sex fiends don't do anything to the body?"

"Maybe. But who knows what goes on in assholes' heads? Maybe *hanging* her got him off, he watched her dangle, came in his pants, went home, had sweet dreams. I remember one, few years back, guy got off on playing with their feet. Killed 'em first, set 'em up on their beds, played with their feet. That was enough to get him off—what do you think of that, Doctor?"

"Something for everyone," I said.

"This guy, the foot guy, he didn't even have to yank the monkey. Just playing with the toes did it for him."

"I had a foot guy, too," said Milo. "But he didn't kill, just tied 'em up and played."

"Probably woulda killed if he'd kept on."

"Probably."

"You could probably sit down and dig up lots of stories about perverted stuff." Hooks stiffened and shot Milo a quick, embarrassed look. Milo's face remained still. "Anyway, if Mac and I come up with something, we'll let you know."

"Ditto, Willis."

"Yeah."

A young white cop jogged over.

"Excuse me, Detective," he said to Hooks. "Coroner's driver wants to know if we can transport the vic."

"You got anything more you want to do, Milo?"

"Nope."

"Go ahead," Hooks said. The officer hustled back, delivered the word, and two morgue attendants came forward with a gurney and a black body bag.

I noticed movement from the north end of the playground. A few teachers had come closer to the tape and were watching while drinking coffee.

"School days," said Hooks. "I was born on Thirty-second. We moved to Long Beach when I was three, otherwise I woulda gone here."

The attendants got the body into the bag and lifted it on the gurney. As they wheeled her away, the white cop turned his attention to the ground and called over another uniform, a tall black man, even darker than McLaren. Then he jogged back to us.

"It's probably nothing, sir, but you might want to take a look."

"At what?" said Hooks, already moving.

"Something under the body."

We followed him over. The black uniform had his arms folded and his eyes were aimed at a small scrap of white paper, maybe two inches square.

"It's probably nothing," the first cop repeated, "but it was under her and there's something typed on it."

I saw the letters.

Hooks squatted. "D-V-L-L. That mean anything to anybody?"

The cops looked at one another.

"No, sir," said the first.

"Maybe the devil," said the second.

"Any gang using that moniker?"

Shrugs all around.

"And since when do gang bangers type," muttered Hooks. "Okay, you're the eagle eye, Officer . . . Bradbury. Do me a favor and check that graffiti on the school buildings over there, see if the same thing comes up anywhere."

"Yes, sir." As Bradbury approached the yellow-tape border, the teachers backed away. But they watched as he scanned the graffiti.

"DVLL," said Hooks. "Mean anything to you, Milo?"

"Nope."

"Me, neither. And seeing as she was laid down by the janitor, it was probably just something lying there on the cement before she got here. Maybe a piece of school memo or something."

The paper remained motionless in the static, metallic air.

"Should I not bother to tell the techs?" said the black cop.

"No, tell them to bag it, take a picture," said Hooks. "We wouldn't want to be accused of shoddy police work by some scumbag lawyer, would we?"

12

MILO DROVE OUT TO THE STREET AND PARKED BEHIND
my Seville.

"Ah," he said, looking in the rearview mirror. "Finally, the
games begin."

Behind us, a TV van from a local station had just pulled up,
disgorging a gear-toting crew that sprinted for the gate. As the
uniform checked with Hooks, a small gray car pulled away from
the curb and passed us. The driver, Hispanic and wearing the
same institutional-gray Montez had on, glanced at us for an instant
and continued to Western.

"A diplomat's kid on the West Side and a crack-kid down here,"
said Milo. "What do you think?"

"Some physical resemblance between Irit and Latvinia, both of
them retarded, death by strangulation, no sexual assault on Irit, no
evidence so far of an assault on Latvinia. And the position of the
body. But Latvinia wasn't strangled with broad force and the
janitor moved her."

"The janitor."

"You like him?"

"Sure. Because he was there. *And* because he moved her."

"Sparing the grandchildren," I said. "Janitors clean up. Janitors
use brooms."

"Something else, Alex: He cuts her down, arranges her respectfully but doesn't tuck the tongue back in her mouth? Hooks asked
him about that and he said when he realized she was really dead
he didn't want to mess things up. Make sense to you?"

"The average person seeing a hanging body would probably

run for the phone. But if Montez is action-oriented, a family man, with strong attachments to the school, it could fit. But so does another scenario: Montez has a date with Latvinia—he admitted knowing her. They meet on the schoolyard because it's his turf. He kills her, hangs her, then realizes students are going to show up soon, maybe there isn't enough time to get rid of the body. So instead he plays hero."

"Or it was colder: There *was* enough time to get rid of the body but he left her there because he got *off* on thumbing his nose at us. On being a hero—thinks he's smart, a pretender, just like you said. Like those firefighters who torch stuff and show up to hold the hose."

"Another thing," I said. "Montez wears a uniform. His is gray and the park worker I saw mowing at the conservancy was wearing beige, but someone else might not draw the distinction."

His eyes narrowed. "Irit."

"To her it might have connoted someone official. Someone who belonged and could be trusted. Most people relate to uniforms that way."

"Montez," he said. "Well, if there's anything to learn about him, Hooks is as good a detective as any."

"That piece of paper," I said. "DVLL."

"Mean something to you?"

"No. I'm sure it's nothing—what Hooks said, a scrap of school memo."

He turned to me. "What, Alex?"

"It just seemed too cute. Move the body and there it is. Nothing like that was found near Irit. According to the files."

"Meaning?"

"Sometimes," I said, "small things get overlooked."

He frowned. "You think Montez or whoever killed Latvinia left a message?"

"Or it was in her pocket and fell out, either when she was hung or when Montez cut her down."

He rubbed his face. "I'll get to the morgue and look at the evidence bags personally. That is, if the stuff hasn't been returned to the family. Speaking of which, Carmeli called me this morning, said he has copies of the consulate crank mail, I should come by and pick them up. I'll do it around five, after I play phone tag to see if anyone's got deaf or retarded victims that look interesting. If I drop the letters off this evening, could you analyze them?"

"Be happy to, for what it's worth. Quick cooperation on Carmeli's part. Attitude adjustment?"

"Maybe he was impressed 'cause I brought along a psychologist."

"Sure," I said. "That and the tie."

I GOT HOME AT TWO-THIRTY. ROBIN AND SPIKE WERE out and I drank a beer, went through the mail, paid some bills. Helena Dahl had phoned an hour and a half ago—not long after her session—leaving her work number. And Dr. Roone Lehmann had returned my call.

The Cardiac Care Unit clerk told me Helena was in the middle of a procedure and couldn't come to the phone. Leaving my name, I phoned Lehmann.

This time no service; an answering tape with a low, dry-but-mellow male voice picked up, and as I introduced myself, the same voice clicked in.

"This is Dr. Lehmann."

"Thanks for getting back to me, Doctor."

"Certainly. Officer Dahl's sister called, too, but I thought I'd speak with you first. What exactly is she after?"

"Some understanding of why he killed himself."

"I sympathize," he said. "Of course. But can we ever really understand?"

"True," I said. "Did Nolan leave any clues?"

"Was he despondent or profoundly depressed, overtly suicidal or making oblique cries for help? Not when I saw him, Dr. Delaware, but—hold on."

He was off the line for thirty seconds, came back sounding rushed. "I'm sorry. Something came up and I can't talk at length right now. Not that I could, anyway. Even though the patient's dead and even though the courts have been hacking away at confidentiality, I'm one of those old-fashioned fellows who takes our vows seriously."

"Is there anything you can tell me that might help her?" I said.

"Anything," he repeated, drawing out the word. "Hmm . . .

let me think on that—do you ever get downtown? I could give you
a few moments. Because I'd rather not discuss these things on the
phone. A police case and all that, the current climate. One never
knows where the media lurks."

"Do you see lots of police cases?"

"Enough to be cautious. Of course, if it's too much of a problem
to drive all the way—"

"No problem," I said. "When?"

"Let me check my calendar—I do want to emphasize that I can't
promise anything until I go over the file. And I'd prefer not to
speak to the sister directly. Please tell her we talked."

"Sure. Have you had problems with these types of cases?"

"Not . . . as a rule. Ounce of prevention and all that—there's
something you might want to consider, Doctor. As the sister's therapist. The search for understanding is normal, but the value of
digging things up varies from case to case."

"You don't think this case merits it?"

"What I'm . . . let's just say Officer Dahl was . . . an interesting fellow. Anyway, I'll leave it at that, for the moment. I'll be in
touch."

AN INTERESTING FELLOW.

Warning me?

Some dark secret that Helena was better off not knowing?

I thought of what I'd learned about Nolan.

Mood swings, sensation seeking, sudden shifts to political extremes.

Had he stepped over the line—in the course of police work?
Something best left unexplored?

Something political—on the fringe?

A police case and all that. The current climate.

Videotaped beatings of suspects, cops sitting around as rioters
torched the city, bungling of evidence in major cases, case after
case of felonious cops caught in the act. LAPD was as popular as
an abortionist at the Vatican.

The media lurking.

Had Lehmann been involved in other cop cases that had left
him gun-shy?

Whatever the reason, he was definitely trying to steer me away from a psychological autopsy of Nolan.

The department hadn't argued when Helena had chosen to skip the full-dress funeral.

Eager to move things along?

Nolan, bright, different because he read books.

Alienated.

The switch from West L.A. to Hollywood.

Because he liked action?

Illegal action?

Had he gotten himself into something that left suicide the only option?

As I thought about it, Helena phoned, sounding breathless.

"Rushed?" I said.

"Busy. We just had a patient infarct in the middle of an angio. Big artery the cardiologist hadn't known about, he's Roto-Rooter-ing one and the other jams up. But he's okay, the patient, things have quieted down. The reason I called is, right after our session I went over to Nolan's apartment, all motivated to go through his stuff, maybe find something." She paused and I could hear her inhale and blow it out. "I went to the garage first and it was fine but someone broke into the place, Dr. Delaware. It was a wreck. They took his stereo and his TV, his microwave, all his flatware, a couple of lamps, pictures off the walls. Probably some clothes, too. Someone must have come with a truck and loaded up."

"Oh, boy," I said. "I'm sorry."

"Lowlifes." Her voice shook. "Scumbags."

"No one saw anything?"

"They probably did it at night. It's a duplex, just Nolan and the landlord and she's a dentist, out of town at a convention. I called the police and they said it would take at least an hour to get there. I had to be at work by three, so I gave my number and left. What can they do, anyway? Write a report and file it? The damage is already done. Even if the bastards come back, there's nothing to take except . . . Nolan's car—God, why didn't I *think* of that! His Fiero. In the garage. Either they didn't see it or they didn't have time and are coming back—God, I've got to go back there, get someone to take me so I can drive the Fiero over to my place . . . so many things to handle, the lawyer just called me about the final papers . . . robbing a cop. This *damn* city . . . his rent is paid up for the month but eventually I'm going to have to clean everything up and . . . go back there . . ."

"Would you like me to go with you?"

"You'd do that?"

"Sure."

"That's so nice, but no, I couldn't."

"It's okay, Helena. I don't mind."

"I just—you're serious?"

"Where's the apartment?"

"Mid-Wilshire. Sycamore near Beverly. I can't leave right now, too many iffy patients. Maybe midshift, if we're staffed enough. If they take the damn car before then, fine."

"Tonight, then."

"I can't impose on you to come out late, Dr. Delaware—"

"It's no problem, Helena. I'm a night person."

"I'm not sure exactly when I'll be free."

"Call me when you are. If I'm free, I'll meet you there. If not, you're on your own. Okay?"

She laughed softly. "Okay. Thanks so much. I really didn't want to go alone."

"Have a minute?" I said.

"Unless someone else starts dying."

"I spoke with Dr. Lehmann."

"What'd he say?"

"As we expected, nothing, because of confidentiality. But he did agree to reread Nolan's file and if he comes up with something he feels comfortable discussing, he'll meet with me."

Silence.

"That is, if you want me to, Helena."

"Sure," she said. "Sure, that's fine. I started, might as well finish."

13

MILO CHOMPED A DEAD CIGARILLO AND CARRIED THE consulate crank letters in an oversized, unlabeled white envelope.

"A year's worth," he said, remaining out on the terrace.

"What do they do with the old ones?"

"Don't know. This is what Carmeli gave me. Or rather, his secretary. Still haven't gotten past the hall, yet. Thanks, Alex. Back to the phones."

"No luck yet?"

"Lots of callbacks pending. Hooks has started to work on Montez. So far, the guy's clean. Totally. Just to be careful I double-checked the offender files. Nothing. See you."

He patted my shoulder and turned to leave.

"Milo, are you aware of any scandals brewing in the department? West L.A. or Hollywood, specifically?"

He stopped short. "No. Why?"

"Can't say."

"Oh," he said. "The Dahl kid. Someone bad-mouthed him? Do *you* know something?"

I shook my head. "I'm probably overreacting, but his therapist implied I shouldn't ask too many questions."

"No reason?"

"Confidentiality."

"Hmm. Nope, nothing that I've picked up. And even though I'm not Mr. Popular if it was something big-time I think I'd know."

"Okay, thanks."

"Yeah . . . happy analysis."

•   •   •

I EMPTIED THE ENVELOPE ON MY DESK. A SQUARE OF blue paper was stapled to each letter, saying L.A. and listing the date received.

Fifty-four letters, the most recent, three weeks ago, the oldest, eleven months.

Most were short, viciously to the point.

Anonymous. Three main themes.

1. Israelis are Jews and, hence, the enemy because all Jews are part of a capitalist banker/Masonic/Trilateral Commission conspiracy to dominate the world.

2. Israelis are Jews and, hence, the enemy because all Jews are part of a Communist/Bolshevik/cosmopolitan conspiracy to dominate the world.

3. Israelis are the enemy because they're colonial usurpers who stole land from the Arabs and continue to oppress the Palestinians.

Lots of misspellings, more disorganized handwriting than I'd seen in a long time.

The third group—Israel versus the Arabs—contained the most grammatical errors and awkward phrases, and I assumed some of the writers were foreign-born.

Five of the letters in group 3 also carried references to murdered Palestinian children and I set those aside.

But no specific warnings of revenge upon consulate children or other Israelis and no references to DVLL.

I shifted to the envelopes, examining the postmarks. All California. Twenty-nine had been mailed within L.A. County, eighteen from Orange County, six from Ventura, one from Santa Barbara.

Of the five with allusions to children, four were local, one from Orange County.

Another read. Run-of-the-mill racial venom and I couldn't see any way to connect it to Irit.

The office door opened and Robin came in with Spike. As I scratched his neck, her eyes lowered to the letters.

"Fan mail," I said.

She read a sentence, turned away. "Vile. Were these sent to the girl's father?"

"To the consulate." I began scooping up the letters.

"Don't quit on my account," she said.

"No, I'm finished. Dinner?"

"I was going to ask you."

"I could cook."

"You want to?"

"Wouldn't mind feeling useful, if you don't mind quick and simple. How about lamb chops? We've got some frozen. I'll steam some corn. Salad, wine, ice cream—the works, babe."

"Wine *and* the works? My girlish heart swoons."

Concentrating on the grill helped me relax. We ate outside, slowly, quietly, and ended up in bed an hour later. At seven-thirty, Robin was in the tub and I lay atop the sheets.

Ten minutes later, Helena called and said, "I can get away, now, but you really don't have to bother."

I went into the bathroom and told Robin.

"Well," she said, "you've already done your good deeds here, so why not?"

SYCAMORE WAS AN ATTRACTIVE, SHADED STREET JUST west of Hancock Park, full of high-style duplexes dating from the twenties. Nolan Dahl's building was of that vintage, but a plain cousin. White lumpy stucco, no architectural embellishments, narrow windows like wounds, a few yucca plants pushing up against the front window, a fuzzy square of lawn. It gave no hint of falling victim to anything but tight budgeting.

I got there two minutes before Helena drove up.

"Sorry, had some discharge forms to finish. Hope you haven't been waiting long?"

"Just arrived."

Waving a key, she said, "His is the downstairs unit."

We walked to the front door. A business card had been slipped between the door and the jamb and she pulled it out.

"Detective Duchossoir," she read. "Well, thanks for showing up, guy—they never called me for a statement. What a joke."

She unlocked the front door, turned on a light, and we stepped into disarray dimmed by heavy gold velvet curtains that looked as old as the building. The living room was nice-sized with beamed ceilings and off-white walls but it smelled of old dust and sweat and looked like a war zone. The furniture the burglars had left was upended and damaged: broken legs on wooden folding chairs, a brown corduroy sofa with Naugahyde trim turned onto its arms, the bottom slashed open, the wounds exposing coils and stuffing.

A cheap ceramic lamp lay shattered on the green shag carpet, white grit littering the pile. Nothing on the walls but dark rectangles where something had once hung.

In the dining area a card table had been tossed against the wall, cracking the plaster. More folding chairs. In the tiny kitchen, drawers were open, most of them emptied to the yellow paper lining. Nolan's meager collection of crockery was strewn all over the lumpy linoleum floor. As Helena had said, no flatware.

The refrigerator, an old white Admiral too small for the nook provided, could have come from a thrift shop. I opened it. Empty.

Nolan had adopted the Basic Lonely Bachelor lifestyle. I knew it well. Once upon a time.

"They got in here, through the kitchen door," said Helena, pointing to a tiny service porch, past an empty garbage can.

A window was set into the rear door and the glass had been punched out. Crudely—the edges were still ragged. After that, it had been easy to reach in and release the lock.

Simple lock, no dead bolt.

"Not much security," I said.

"Nolan always prided himself on taking care of himself, probably felt he didn't need it."

She picked up a broken bowl. Put it down, looking drained.

Gazing past the mess and seeing how her brother had lived.

We walked down a low, narrow hall past a small, green-tiled bathroom with an empty medicine cabinet. Toothbrush and paste and wadded towels on the floor. The shower was dry.

"Looks like they took the medicine, too," I said.

"If there was any. Nolan was never sick. Didn't even take aspirin. At least when I knew—when he lived at home."

Two bedrooms. The first was totally empty, curtained to gloom. Helena stared in from the doorway before forcing herself to continue. The one where Nolan had slept had a king-sized mattress and box spring that took up most of the floor space. A four-drawer fake-wood dresser—another thrift-shop candidate—had been pushed away from the wall, all the drawers pulled out and tossed on the floor. Underwear, socks, shirts were scattered like buckshot. An aluminum TV stand stood near the foot of the bed, but no set remained. Rabbit-ear antenna in the corner. The black quilted bedspread was drawn back from sweat-stained white sheets and the mattress had been yanked halfway off the box. Two rumpled pillows sat propped against the wall like ghosts pummeled to unconsciousness.

A disc on the wall above the bed said a clock had once hung there.

And that was it.

"The thing I *don't* get," she said, "is where all his books are. 'Cause that's one thing he always had plenty of. He just loved to read. Do you think the burglars could have taken them?"

"Literate criminals," I said. "Were any of them valuable?"

"Collectors' stuff? I wouldn't know. I just remember Nolan's room at home, books all over the place."

"So you were never here?"

"No," she said, as if it were a confession. "He used to have a place out in the Valley and I was there a few times. But after he joined the department, he moved to the other side of the hill . . ."

She shrugged and touched the bedspread.

"It's possible," I said, "that he gave his books away."

"Why would he do that?"

"Sometimes people contemplating suicide give away things that are important to them. It's a way of formalizing the final step."

"Oh." Her eyes misted and she turned away and I knew she was thinking, *He didn't give them to me.*

"There could be another reason, Helena. You said Nolan changed points of view pretty suddenly. If the books were on politics, something he no longer believed in, he could have decided to get rid of them."

"Whatever. Let's get out of here, see if the car's still here."

MORE CARE HAD BEEN TAKEN IN THE REAR GARDEN than in front—well-pruned apricot and peach trees and several flowering citrus that perfumed the air. The garage was a double. Helena pushed up the left-hand door. A pullcord to the right illuminated the narrow, lathe-walled space.

The Fiero was bright red covered with a fine coat of dust, sitting on half-deflated tires. A while since it had been driven.

I went over and looked at the driver's door. Deep gouges near the lock, and the window was cracked but not broken.

"They tried, Helena. Panicked or ran out of time."

She came over and sighed. "I'll have it towed."

The rest of the garage was taken up by a wooden workbench, bracket shelves of paint cans and dry brushes, a bicycle with one wheel, an airless basketball, several cardboard boxes under a crumpled wet suit. The pegboard above the bench was empty.

"His tools are gone," she said. "He had them since high school. He went through an artistic phase—wood carving—convinced Mom and Dad to get him a complete set. Expensive stuff. Soon after, he lost interest. . . . Maybe there are books in those boxes over there."

She went over to check, tossing the black neoprene aside. Five cartons, the top one unsealed.

"Empty," she said. "This is a waste—oh, hold on, look at this."

She lifted a second box. Heavy, from the way her arms tensed.

"Still taped." Using the house key, she tried to slit the binding without success. I took out my pocketknife and cut deeply.

She gasped.

Inside were several large leatherette albums in a variety of colors. The top one was black and said PHOTOGRAPHS in gold script. Helena flipped it open to faded color snapshots under plastic sheets.

She turned pages quickly, almost frantically.

The same image in varying forms: heavyset mother, ectomorph father, two pretty blond children. Trees in the background, or ocean, a Ferris wheel, or just blue sky. Helena no older than twelve in any of them. Had family life stopped, then?

"Our family albums," she said. "I've been looking for these since Mom died, never knew he had them."

She turned another page. "Dad and Mom . . . they looked so young. This is so . . ." She shut the book. "I'll look at them later."

She lifted the box and carried it out to her Mustang. Placing it on the front passenger seat, she slammed the door.

"Well, at least I got something—thank you, Dr. Delaware."

"Sure."

"I'll have the car towed tomorrow." She placed a hand on her chest. The fingers shook.

"Nolan took the albums from Mom's house without saying a thing. Why didn't he tell me? Why didn't he tell me *anything*?"

14

THE NEXT MORNING, AT TEN, DR. ROONE LEHMANN called.

"I've been going through Nolan's file. How's the sister doing?"

"Hanging in," I said. "It's rough."

"Yes. Well . . . he was a complex young man."

"Complex and bright."

"Oh?"

"Helena told me he tested gifted."

"I see . . . interesting. Is she gifted, as well?"

"She's an intelligent woman."

"No doubt—well, if you'd like to come by the office, say around noonish, I can give you twenty minutes. But I can't promise it will be earth-shattering."

"Thanks for your time."

"It's part of the job, isn't it?"

MINUTES LATER, MILO PHONED. ''CORONER SAYS NO sexual assault on Latvinia. Hooks says Montez the janitor is alibied for the time of her murder."

"Good alibi?"

"Not perfect but sometimes it's only criminals who come up with perfect alibis. Working at the liquor store from seven til eleven-thirty. The owner verifies, says Montez has an impeccable work record. Then home to the wife and kids—two older daughters, both of whom were up. All three of them swear he went to bed shortly after midnight, the wife is certain he never left the house. She got up at 3:00 A.M. to go to the bathroom, saw him there. His snoring woke her up again at five."

"The wife," I said.

"Yeah, but Montez is solid as they come: married thirty-five years, Vietnam service record, no criminal activity, not even traffic tickets. The school principal says he gets along great with everyone, always willing to go the extra mile, really does care about the school and the students. Told Hooks cutting the body down was exactly the kind of thing Montez would do. A couple of years ago a kid choked on something and Montez did the Heimlich maneuver and saved him."

"A genuine hero."

"Wait, there's more: Hooks located an old Army buddy of Montez's, a neighbor on the same block. Apparently Montez fended off a horde of Cong, rescued six other soldiers. Lots of medals. Now one thing I remember clearly is Cong stringing up bodies—we cut them down all the time. So that could be another reason. In terms of Latvinia, Hooks and McLaren talked to the grandmother and she said the girl was incorrigible, going out at all hours, wouldn't listen to reason. No steady boyfriends, no gang she hung out with. Just not too bright, easygoing and gullible and sometimes she'd just start acting weird—dancing and singing, pulling up her blouse. Neighbors said Latvinia's rep was a girl you could talk into anything."

"Any drugs in her system?"

"Tox results aren't back yet and the coroner said there were no needle marks on the body. But her nasal passages were significantly eroded and there was some scarring on her heart, so coke for sure. I'm still looking for deaf-girl murders in other divisions and I've also been checking on that DVLL note. Nothing so far. It probably was a random scrap."

"Nothing in Irit's evidence bag?"

"No personal *effects* in Irit's evidence bag. Everything was returned to the parents and the evidence-room log lists no pocket contents of any kind."

"Is returning clothes on an unsolved standard procedure?"

"No, but with no semen or body fluids or any other evidence, and Carmeli being a big shot, I can understand why it happened." Pause. "Yeah, it's a screwup. But at this point I'd settle for a bad guy's lawyer jumping up and down on it."

"Going to ask the Carmelis to look at the clothes?"

"Think it's worth it?"

"Probably not, but why risk another omission?"

"Yeah. I'll bring it up when I speak to the mother. Left a message with Carmeli respectfully requesting blah blah blah, but haven't heard back. For all I know the clothes have already been buried. Do Jews bury the clothing?"

"Don't know."

"Whatever. Okay, I'll call you if anything interesting comes up. Thanks for listening, send me a bill."

I SET OUT FOR DOWNTOWN, AVOIDING THE FREEWAY and taking Sunset. Wanting to *feel* the city from Bel Air to Skid Row. Entering Hospital Row made me think of my days at Western Pediatrics Hospital, my induction into a world of suffering and occasional redemption. Heroics, too. I thought of Guillermo Montez, saving all those lives in Asia, winning all those medals, now a janitor working a second job.

At Echo Park, L.A. became Latin America. Then the downtown skyline came into view behind a cloverleaf of highway, blue steel and white cement and the pure gold of reflective glass towers incising a curdled-milk sky.

Lehmann's Seventh Street office was in a lovely six-story limestone building, one of the older ones, in a circumscribed part of the district where pinstripe and Filofax predominated and the homeless and diseased were invisible.

I parked at a nearby pay-lot and walked over. The entire ground floor of the building was taken up by an insurance company with its own entrance. To the right was a separate foyer for the rest of the structure, generous and chilly, charcoal granite with gold deco trim, two gold-cage elevators, a tobacco-and-aftershave smell, a carved walnut reception desk with no one behind it.

The directory said floors 2 and 3 were occupied by a private bank called American Trust and the fourth by something called the City Club, accessed by private elevator key only. The rest of the tenants were investment firms, lawyers, accountants, and, on the top story, Roone Lehmann, Ph.D., listed as a "consultant."

Unusual setting for therapy and Lehmann wasn't advertising that he was a psychologist.

For the sake of treatment-shy police officers and other reluctant patients?

One of the cages arrived and I rode up six flights. The corridor ceilings were high, white, ringed with garland molding; the hallways, oak-paneled and carpeted in maroon wool printed with tiny white stars. The office doors were oak, too, and identified by small silver plaques that had been buffed recently. Soft, characterless music flowed from invisible speakers. Hunting prints hung on the walls and fresh flowers in glass vases sat on oiled Pembroke tables every twenty feet. Far cry from the plain-wrap ambience of the Israeli consulate.

Lehmann's office was in a corner, neighbored by multiple-partner law firms. His name and degree on silver, again no occupation.

I tried the door. Locked. An illuminated button off to the right glowed ember-orange against the wood.

I pressed it and was buzzed immediately into a very small brown-walled anteroom furnished with two blue wingback chairs and a stiffly upholstered deep green Queen Anne sofa. A glass-topped chinoiserie coffee table bore *The Wall Street Journal,* the *Times,* and *USA Today.* Artless walls. Reluctant light from two overhead recessed spots. Another button on the inner door over a PLEASE RING IN sign.

Before I reached it, the door opened.

"Dr. Delaware? Dr. Lehmann." The dry-mellow voice, more muted than it had been over the phone, almost sad.

I shook a soft hand and we studied each other. He was in his fifties, tall and round-shouldered and soft-looking, with shaggy white hair and thick, flattened features. Bushy eyebrows bore down on fatigued lids. Brown eyes worked their way through a squint.

He wore a double-breasted navy blazer with gold buttons, gray flannel slacks, white shirt, loosely knotted pink tie, white pocket square carelessly stuffed, black wing tips.

Rumpled-looking, though the clothes were perfectly pressed. And expensive. Cashmere blazer. Working buttonholes on the cuffs said hand-tailored. Single-needle stitching on the shirt collar. The tie was silk mesh.

He motioned me in. The rest of the suite consisted of a small walnut-paneled bathroom and a huge butter-yellow office with a high, molded ceiling and distressed herringbone oak flooring that had lifted in places. A frayed blue Persian rug that looked very old spread diagonally over the wood. Two more blue wingbacks and a filigreed silver table formed a conversational area at the rear of the room. Between them and the desk was an empty expanse of rug, then a pair of black tweed armchairs closer to a massive cherrywood desk.

Two Victorian mahogany bookshelves were crowded with volumes but the glass doors to the cases spat back glare from a pair of windows, obscuring the titles. The windows were narrow and high, cut at the outer corners by ruby velvet pull-back drapes, offering rectangles of city view.

Great view. A newer building would have offered a full wall of transparency. When this one was built, the vista had probably been smokestacks and beanfields.

The yellow walls were silk. No credentials, no diplomas. Nothing that identified the purpose of the office.

Lehmann motioned me to take one of the black armchairs and sank behind the cherry desk. The top was green leather with gold-tooled edges and on it were a brown calfskin folding blotter, silver inkwell, letter knife, and pen cup, and a curious-looking silver contraption with a flamboyantly engraved crenellated top. Envelopes extended from compartments. Probably some kind of message rack.

Lehmann ran his finger along the edge.

"Interesting piece," I said.

"Document holder," he said. "Georgian. It sat in British Parliament two hundred years ago. Repository for history. There's a hole at the bottom where it was screwed into the clark's desk so no one could make off with it."

He used both hands to lift it and show me.

I said, "Found its way across the ocean, anyway."

"Family piece," he said, as if that explained it. Spreading his hands flat on the blotter, he looked at a thin gold watch. "Officer Dahl. It would help me to understand what you already know about him."

"I've been told he was bright and mercurial," I said. "Not your typical cop."

"Cops can't be bright?"

"They can be and are. Helena—his sister—described him as someone who'd read Sartre and Camus. I may be stereotyping but that isn't what you generally think of as typical LAPD material. Though if you work extensively with the police, you'd know better."

His hands flew upward and the palms drifted toward each other and touched silently.

"Each year, my practice brings fewer surprises, Dr. Delaware. Don't you find it harder to resist seeing patterns?"

"Sometimes," I said. "Did the department refer Nolan to you?"

Another pause. Nod.

"May I ask why?"

"The usual," he said. "Adjustment problems. The work is extremely stressful."

"What kinds of work problems was Nolan having?"

He licked his lips and white hair tumbled across his forehead. Pushing it away, he began playing with his pink tie, flicking the tip with a thumbnail, over and over.

Finally he said, "Nolan was having both personal problems and difficulties related to work. A troubled young man. I'm sorry, I really can't be more specific."

Why had I driven across town for this?

He looked around the big, ornate room. "*Mercurial.* Is the term Helena's or yours?"

I smiled. "I've got a live patient, Dr. Lehmann. My own confidentiality issues."

He smiled back. "Of course you do, I was simply trying to—let's put it this way, Dr. Delaware: If you're using *mercurial* as a euphemism for affective disorder, I'd understand that very well. *Very well.*"

Letting me know without saying so that Nolan had suffered from mood swings. Depression, only? Or manic-depression?

"I guess it's too much to ask if we're talking unipolar or bipolar."

"Does it really matter? I'm sure she's not seeking a *DSM—IV* diagnosis."

"True," I said. "Do any other euphemisms come to mind?"

He tucked the tie in and sat up straighter. "Dr. Delaware, I sympathize with your situation. With the sister's. It's only natural that she'd seek answers but you and I both know she'll never get what she's really after."

"Which is?"

"What survivors always crave. Absolution. As I said, understandable, but if you've dealt with lots of similar cases, you know that leads them off the track. They haven't sinned, the suicide has. In a manner of speaking. I'm sure Helena is a lovely woman who adored her brother and now she's torturing herself with should-haves and could-haves. Pardon my audacity, but I'd say your time with her would be better spent guiding her toward feeling good about herself rather than fathoming the workings of a very troubled mind."

"Was Nolan too troubled to do police work?"

"Obviously, but that never became clear. Never." His voice had climbed and a flush had spread under his jaw, snaking downward and disappearing under his collar.

Had he missed a danger sign? Covering his own rear?

"It's a tragedy all around. That's really all I have to say." He stood.

"Dr. Lehmann, I wasn't implying—"

"But someone else might and I won't have it. Any therapist worth his salt knows there's absolutely nothing that can be done if an individual's serious about destroying himself. Look at all the suicides that take place on psychiatric wards with full supervision."

He leaned toward me, one hand tugging down at a cashmere lapel. "Tell your patient that her brother loved her but his problems got the best of him. Problems she's better off not knowing. Believe me—*much* better off."

Staring at me.

"Sexual problems?" I said.

He waved me off. "Tell her you spoke to me and I said he was depressed and that police work may have exacerbated the depression but didn't cause it. Tell her his suicide couldn't have been prevented and she had nothing to do with it. Help her plaster her emotional fissures. That's our job. To patch, assuage. *Massage.* Inform our patients they're *okay.* We're couriers of *okay*ness."

Through the anger came something I thought I recognized. The sadness that can result from too many years absorbing the poison of others. Most therapists experience it sooner or later. Sometimes it passes, sometimes it settles in like a chronic infection.

"Guess we are," I said. "Among other things. Sometimes it gets difficult."

"What does?"

"Massaging."

"Oh, I don't know," he said. "One chooses one's job and one does it. That's the key to being a professional. There's no point complaining."

When the going gets tough, the therapist gets tougher. I wondered if he'd used the chin-up approach with Nolan. The department would approve of something like that.

He smiled. "After all these years, I find the work enriching."

"How many years is that?"

"Sixteen. But it's still fresh. Perhaps it's because my first career was in the business world where the philosophy was quite different: It's not enough for me to *succeed. You* must fail."

"Brutal," I said.

"Oh, quite. Policemen are easy, by comparison."

He walked me to the door and as I passed the bulky bookshelves I was able to make out some of the titles. Organizational structure, group behavior, management strategies, psychometric testing.

Out in the waiting room, he said, "I'm sorry I haven't been able to reveal more. The entire situation was . . . bleak. Let the sister maintain her own image of Nolan. Believe me, it's far more compassionate."

"This unspeakable pathology he displayed," I said. "It's directly related to the suicide?"

"Very likely so."

"Was he feeling guilty about something?"

He buttoned his blazer.

"I'm not a priest, Dr. Delaware. And your client wants illusion, not facts. Trust me on that."

AS I GOT BACK ON THE ELEVATOR, I FELT AS IF I'D been rushed through an overpriced, tasteless meal. Now it was starting to repeat.

Why had he wasted my time?

Had he intended to say more but changed his mind?

Knowing he was professionally vulnerable because he'd missed something crucial?

Fear of a lawsuit would make Helena—and me—a major threat.

Not talking to me at all would be seen as unreasonable obstructionism.

But if he was covering, why even hint around at Nolan's serious problems?

Wanting to find out what *I* knew?

The lift opened at 5 to let in three hefty men in gray suits and eyeglasses. Their jovial chatter ceased the moment they saw me and they turned their backs as the taller one slipped a key into the City Club slot. After they exited, the elevator took a while to kick in and I had a view of white-and-black checkerboard marble floor, polished wood walls, softly lit oil landscapes, riotously colored mixed flowers in obsidian urns.

A tuxedoed maitre d' smiled and welcomed them forward. They entered the club talking again. Laughing. Behind them, silverware clattered and red-jacketed black waiters hurried by with covered dishes on trays. As the elevator filled with the smell of roast meat and rich sauce, the gilded door slid shut silently.

I DROVE WEST, TAKING THE FREEWAY THIS TIME, still thinking about Lehmann.

Strange bird. And an old-world quality to his demeanor. British pronunciations. He'd said the right things but was unlike any therapist I'd ever met.

As if reciting for my benefit.

Analyzing me?

Some psychologists and psychiatrists—the bad ones—make a game of it.

Believe me, she's much better off not knowing.

Strange bird, strange location.

Consultant.

All those books on management and psychological testing, nothing on therapy.

Practicing beyond the boundaries of his competence?

Was that why he was edgy?

If so, how had he gotten LAPD's business?

No big mystery, there. Politics as usual. Who you knew.

The custom-made cashmere, the studied carelessness and old-money furnishings.

A consultant with family connections? Downtown connections

could mean big business: a stream of referrals from the police department and other government agencies.

A potential *flood* of referrals because though LAPD maintained a few psychologists on staff, most of their time was spent screening applicants and teaching hostage negotiation and they were chronically overworked.

Something else: Milo had told me, once, that cops considered the in-house shrinks tools of the brass, were cynical about assurances of confidentiality, often reluctant to seek them out for help.

Except when filing for stress disability. Something LAPD officers had engaged in for years at a notorious rate, now even worse in the postriot era.

Meaning *lots* of money could be made contracting to field complaints. The unspoken directive from the department would be *find them healthy.*

Which would explain Lehmann's self-description as a *courier of okayness.*

And why he might have been reluctant to acknowledge warning signs in Nolan.

Had the young cop come to him with a history of mood swings and alienation, complaining of crushing job pressures, only to receive tough love?

One does one's job. That's the key to being professional.

Now Lehmann wanted to quash any budding inquiry.

Let the dead rest. His reputation, too.

WHEN I GOT HOME, I LOOKED HIM UP IN MY AMERI-can Psychological Association directory. No listing. None in any of the local guilds or health-care provider rosters, either, which was odd, if he was a contractor. But maybe LAPD referrals alone gave him enough business and he didn't need to solicit other sources.

Or maybe he really *was* old money, choosing psychology as a second career for personal fulfillment, rather than income. Respite after years in the heartless world of *business.*

The big office and leather desk and books—the trappings of *doctor*hood. Simply props to help him fill the hours before he rode down for a rubdown at the club?

I phoned the state medical board and confirmed that Roone Mackey Lehmann was indeed duly licensed to practice psychology in California and had been for five years. His degree was from a place called New Dominion University and he'd done his clinical training at the Pathfinder Foundation, neither of which I'd heard of.

No complaints had ever been filed against him, nothing irregular about his certification.

I thought about him some more, realized there was nothing I could—or should—do. Bottom line, he was right: If Nolan had been adamant about leaving this world, no one could have stopped him.

Serious problems.

My question about sexuality had evoked a meaningful silence, so maybe that had been it.

A bleak situation.

The sister better off not knowing.

Leading me to the main question: What would I tell Helena?

15

I CALLED HER AT THE HOSPITAL BUT SHE WASN'T IN.
Not at home, either, and I left a message and phoned Milo at the
station.

"New insights?" he said.

"Sorry, no. Actually, I'm calling about Nolan Dahl."

"What about him?"

"If you're busy—"

"Wish I was. Been on the phone all day and the closest case I've
got to Irit is a retarded thirteen-year-old boy abducted a year ago
in Newton Division. Body never found but his sneakers were, full
of dried blood. Left in front of the Newton station. No lightbulb-
over-the-head feeling but I'm driving over later to look at the actual file. What about Dahl?"

"I just met with his therapist, fellow named Roone Lehmann.
Ever hear of him?"

"No. Why?"

"He got the referral through the department and I got the feeling he was on some LAPD list."

"Could be. Is there some other reason you're asking about
him?"

I told him.

"So you think maybe he botched Dahl's treatment and is covering his ass."

"He implied that Nolan had serious problems that Helena
doesn't want to know about."

"Meaning if he missed the boat it was a big one."

"Exactly. And he's an odd one, Milo. Works in a building with bankers and lawyers, labels himself a consultant but doesn't spell out what he does. But he's duly licensed, no checkered history, so maybe I'm being paranoid. I *would* like to know why Nolan went to see him. Would the department keep records?"

"If it was something to do with the job, they sure would, but good luck getting hold of it. Especially now that he killed himself. If he put in for a stress pension or some other compensation, there'd be a record of that, but once again, things get lost when it suits the right people."

"That's another thing," I said. "If he was under stress, why'd he transfer from West L.A. to Hollywood?"

"You got me—maybe he got tired of scumbag celebrities and their battered wives."

"My thought was he craved action. Liked taking risks." I told him about the break-in at Nolan's apartment, the cheap lock on the back door.

"No big surprise," he said. "Cops can be super-security freaks or they become danger freaks and get lax. If the public knew how many times we got victimized, the confidence level would sink even lower. If that's possible."

"But if Nolan craved danger, why would he buckle?"

He grunted. "Your field, not mine. Sounds like we're both running the blind-alley marathon. I'd offer to ask around about his records, but it would be a waste of time. One person who might be able to tell you something would be his training officer."

"Helena already spoke to him and he was baffled by the suicide."

"Name?"

"A Sergeant Baker."

"Wesley Baker?"

"Don't know the first name. Helena said he's at Parker Center, now."

"That's Wes Baker." His voice changed. Softer. Guarded.

"You know him?" I said.

"Oh, yeah . . . interesting."

"What is?"

"Wes Baker training rookies again. I didn't know, but we don't have much contact with the boys in blue. . . . Listen, Alex, this isn't the best time—or place—to have this discussion. Lemme get over to Newton, check out the year-old abduction file, and if nothing else comes up, I can drop by this evening. If you'll be home."

"No plans not to be," I said, realizing I'd been home for nearly an hour and hadn't gone back to see Robin. "If I go out, I'll call you."

"Fine. I'm heading over to the East Side now. *Sayonara.*"

Robin was taking off her goggles when I walked in, and she reached for the vacuum cleaner. At the sight of the hose, Spike began barking furiously. He despises the industrial age. Canine Luddite. When he saw me he stopped, cocked his head, started to trot forward, then changed his mind and returned to attacking the vacuum canister.

Robin laughed and said, "Stop." She tossed a Milk-Bone in a corner and Spike went after it.

We kissed.

"How was your day?" she said.

"Unproductive. Yours?"

"Quite productive, actually." She tossed her curls and smiled. "Don't hate me."

"Because you're beautiful?"

"That, too." She touched my cheek. "What went wrong, Alex?"

"Nothing. Just lots of seek and very little find."

"That little girl's murder?"

"That and another case. A suicide that will probably never be explained."

She put her arm through mine and we left the studio, Spike at our heels, breathing excitedly, Milk-Bone crumbs dotting his pendulous flews.

"I don't envy you," she said.

"Don't envy what?"

"Hunting for explanations."

SHE SHOWERED AND CHANGED INTO A CHARCOAL-gray pantsuit and diamond stud earrings and said how about meat, that Argentinian place we'd tried a few months ago.

"Baked garlic appetizers?" I said. "Not very social."

"It is if we both indulge."

"Sure, I'll eat a whole bowl. Afterward we can tango or lambada, whatever, and fume up each other's faces."

Suddenly she swooned into my arms. "Ah, Alessandro!"

SHE SET SPIKE UP WITH WATER AND SNACKS WHILE I changed and left messages at Milo's West L.A. desk, his home in West Hollywood, and the number he used for his after-hours private-eye business, Blue Investigations.

He'd begun the moonlight gig several years ago after the department took him off duty for punching out a superior who'd endangered his life and banished him to the Parker Center data-processing office in hopes of nudging him off the force. He'd managed to regain his detective position and it had been a while since he'd solicited private work, but he'd held on to the exchange.

Symbol of freedom, I supposed. Or insecurity. For all the talk of diversity and open recruitment, the role of a gay detective was far from comfortable.

Had *that* been Nolan's problem?

Never married. But he was only twenty-seven.

Relationships with women in the past, but, as far as Helena knew, nothing recent.

As far as Helena knew. Which wasn't very far at all.

I thought of Nolan's apartment. Mattress on the floor, no food in the fridge, the dingy furniture. Even accounting for the trashing, not exactly a swinging bachelor lair.

A loner. Flirting with all sorts of philosophies, shifting from one political extreme to the other.

Had self-denial been the latest?

Or had he divested himself of material pleasures because he just didn't *care* anymore?

Or wanted to punish himself.

Lehmann had used the word *sin* but when I'd asked him about guilt he'd said he wasn't a priest.

Somewhere along the line, had he judged Nolan?

Had Nolan judged himself? Passed sentence and carried out the execution?

For what?

I pictured the young cop in Go-Ji's, surrounded by the night denizens he'd been assigned to rein in.

Drawing out his service gun, putting it in his mouth.

Symbolic, as so many suicides are?

Final fellatio?

Stripping himself bare in front of other sinners?

Policemen committed suicide more frequently than civilians, but few did it *publicly*.

"Ready?" Robin called from the door.

"Oh yeah," I said. "Let's tango."

16

THE PSYCHOLOGIST.

His presence complicated matters: attend to him or Sturgis?

Sturgis was the professional, but so far all the big policeman had done was stay in his office all day.

On the phone, probably.

Predictable.

The psychologist was a bit more adventurous. He'd gone on two outings.

Perhaps he could be used to *advantage.*

The first trip had been to that duplex on Sycamore to meet the pleasant-looking but tense-faced blond woman.

Her tension made him think: patient? Some kind of on-the-street therapy?

Of course, there was another possibility: a girlfriend; the guy was stepping out on the woman with the auburn hair who lived with him. A beauty, some kind of sculptress. He'd seen her carrying blocks of wood from her truck to the rear of the house.

He watched the psychologist and the unhappy woman talk, then go inside the duplex. Liaison with one while the other one chipped away?

The blond woman was trim and nice-looking but nothing like the sculptress. And the two times he'd seen the sculptress with the psychologist the affection had seemed genuine. Touching each other a lot, that eagerness.

But logic had little to do with human behavior.

Terrible things had taught him about the self-destructive element that ran through the human soul like a polluted stream.

They stayed inside for twenty minutes, then went out to the garage. The psychologist didn't seem to be relating to her in a romantic way, but maybe they were having a rough time.

No, there was no hostility. She was talking and he was listening as if he cared.

Attentive, but maintaining distance.

Professional distance?

So she probably *was* a patient.

Or a sister. It definitely didn't look romantic.

He copied down the license plate number on the blond woman's Mustang, waited til the two of them had driven off, then sauntered to the rear of the duplex in his electrician's uniform and let himself through the rear door by popping an absurd lock.

Pretty clear why the woman had looked so miserable.

Burglarized.

He poked around in the debris, found utility bills with the name Nolan Dahl on them that matched the address. Later that night, after a cold-sandwich-and-bottled-water dinner and some praying with insufficient conviction, he turned on his computer, hacked into the Department of Motor Vehicles file, and ran the woman's license plates.

Helena Allison Dahl, thirty years old, blond hair, blue eyes, an address in Woodland Hills.

Ex-wife of the burglarized Nolan?

So where was Nolan?

Or maybe the guy was an irate husband who'd ruined his own place to get back at the wife.

She'd call her therapist for something like that.

One thing seemed likely: nothing to do with murder.

Which made sense. Sturgis would be concentrating full-time on Irit, but the psychologist would have a whole other life. To him, Irit would be just another consultation.

Tentative conclusion: Outing number 1 didn't relate to any of *his* concerns.

Neither, as far as he could tell, did the second one.

Downtown, terrible traffic all the way, and following the psychologist's green Cadillac at a discreet distance had been difficult. Another challenge was finding parking for the van near the lot the psychologist chose without losing sight of that curly head for too long.

Getting into the limestone building, though, was easy.

No guard, and the electrician's uniform gave him that air of belonging.

The van, too.

Uniforms and vans. He'd spent so much of his life in them.

His main prop for the building was a nice little toolbox whose contents could serve as more than props. He carried it in his good hand and kept the bad one in his pocket because why attract unnecessary attention.

He made it to the lobby just as the psychologist entered the elevator, watched the lift rise to the top floor.

Moments later, up there himself, he examined the doorplates, trying to figure out where the guy had gone.

Law firms, accountants, investment bankers, and one Ph.D.

Another psychologist? The sign said only CONSULTANT.

Roone M. Lehmann, Ph.D.

One consultant visiting another.

Unless the psychologist was a major investor and had come to check out his holdings.

Unlikely. The guy lived nicely but not extravagantly. Lehmann the consultant was the best bet.

He copied the name down for a DMV run, ducked around a corner that gave him a view of Lehmann's door, pulled out his electric meter, and unscrewed an overhead light fixture. If any of the wood-paneled doors had opened, he was ready to probe and tinker and look official.

Nothing happened until nearly a half hour later when the psychologist stepped into the hall.

Out of Lehmann's office. Lehmann, a big, flabby-looking white-haired guy with bushy eyebrows, watched Delaware depart with no friendliness in his eyes. Stood there looking unhappy til Delaware was on the elevator.

Delaware seemed to surround himself with unhappy people.

Occupational hazard?

Finally, Lehmann went back inside.

The meeting had lasted twenty-eight minutes.

Brief consultation? About something relevant to *him*?

He screwed the fixture back in and put the meter in the box. Under the top tray of tools was a nine-millimeter automatic, not the one from the car, but the identical model, fully loaded, wrapped in black felt. With all the gear he was lugging he was a metal detector's dream.

So few buildings had metal detectors.

Even government buildings.

Last week an employee of the city's electronic-repair plant had come to work with a machine pistol and mowed down six coworkers.

So much madness and violence but people continued to pretend otherwise.

Crime and denial.

He understood that.

BACK HOME, IN THE SILENCE, HE PLAYED.

The DMV listed Roone M. Lehmann, Ph.D., fifty-six, six one, 230, as living in Santa Monica.

The Thomas Guide map placed the address in one of the canyons that led down to Pacific Coast Highway.

Not all that far from Irit.

Another of life's little coincidences.

It was 8:00 P.M. and time to switch gears.

He phoned the West L.A. station and asked for Sturgis. A few moments later the big policeman came on the line. He hung up.

So the guy was still staying put.

Dedicated civil servant.

Back to the psychologist? Probably useless, but since the girl on the playground, nothing interesting had happened and he had to keep busy.

Keeping busy was his nature. It helped fight off the loneliness.

He drove to Beverly Glen and parked a ways down the road from the narrow pathway that curled up to the psychologist's and the sculptress's modern white house.

As luck would have it, eighteen minutes later the green Cadillac nosed out onto the glen and sped by him.

He caught a blur of two good-looking, smiling faces.

Ten minutes later he was at the front door, ringing the bell with a gloved good hand.

From inside, a dog barked. From the sound of it a small dog. Dogs could be dangerous, but he liked them.

He'd once had a dog that he *loved*, a friendly little spaniel with a black spot over one eye. A man had brutalized the animal and he'd killed the man in front of the dog. The dog recovered, though he was never quite as trusting. Three years later a bladder tumor finished him off.

Yet another loss. . . . He examined the door lock. Dead bolt. A good brand, but a common one and he had masters for it.

The eighth key he tried worked and he was inside.

Nice place inside, too. High, airy ceilings, white walls, some art, good furniture, a couple of Persian rugs that looked to be quality.

A high-pitched alarm warning buzzer sounded as the dog raced forward.

Small and cute. Dark brindle, with ridiculous ears and a flat face that couldn't be taken seriously. Some kind of bulldog. A miniature. It charged his pants, snarling and howling and scattering spittle. Deftly, he picked it up—heavier than it looked, he needed two hands to keep it at arm's length as it struggled. Carrying it to a bathroom, he locked it in and it butted the door, over and over.

The alarm buzzer still going.

The keypad by the door flashing red.

Probably less than a minute before the alarm bells kicked in, but no worry, there. Police response in Los Angeles was slow, sometimes nonexistent, and in a remote area like this, with no close neighbors to complain, there was nothing to worry about.

Things had gotten to the point where only blood brought the police out and even then, not with much enthusiasm.

He walked around the house, quickly but calmly, able to block out the noise, smelling lemon wax, looking for a target.

The more he thought about it, the greater was his conviction that choosing the psychologist was the way to go. Whether or not the guy could do any direct good, he had access to Sturgis and was, thus, a conduit.

Two birds with one shot.

Now the bells were clanging. Very loud but it didn't bother him.

The alarm company would be phoning soon. If no one answered, they'd call the police.

In this case, the West L.A. station, but Sturgis, up in the detective office, would be unaware. Some uniformed officer would take the call, jot down the details. Eventually, maybe, someone would drive by.

Crime and denial. . . . What he had to do wouldn't take long, anyway.

He wasn't without some guilt—breaking and entering wasn't part of his self-image. But priorities were priorities.

When he was finished, he let the dog out of the bathroom.

17

WE NEVER GOT TO DANCE.

The call came just as we were thinking about dessert and I took it behind the bar of the restaurant.

"This is Nancy from your service, Dr. Delaware. Sorry to bother you, but your alarm company has been trying to reach you for a while and they finally figured to call us."

"The alarm went off?" I sounded calm but was feeling a needle-stab of panic: not-distant-enough memories of intrusion, the old house reduced to cinders.

"Around an hour ago. The company records it as a circuit break at the front door. They've called the police but it might be a while before anyone gets there."

"An hour and the police haven't gotten there, yet?"

"I'm not sure. Would you like me to phone them?"

"No, that's okay, Nancy. Thanks for letting me know."

"I'm sure it's nothing, Doctor. We get this kind of thing all the time. Mostly they're false alarms."

BEFORE I RETURNED TO THE TABLE, I REACHED MILO, back at West L.A.

"Going to take advantage of our friendship," I said. "How about getting a patrol car to go by my house?"

"Why?" he said sharply.

I told him.

"I'll go myself. Where are you?"

"Melrose near Fairfax. We'll leave in a minute, meet you there."

"Get any dinner down?"

"All of it. We were just about ready to order dessert."

"Order it. I'm sure it's a false call."

"Probably," I said. "But no, even if I could eat, Robin couldn't. Spike's there."

"Yeah," he said. "But who'd steal *him*?"

ROBIN DIDN'T RELAX FULLY UNTIL WE PULLED UP TO the front and she saw Milo standing outside on the landing giving the okay sign. Spike was next to him and Milo looked like a dog-walker. An absurd notion. It made me smile.

The front door was open, the interior lights burning.

We rushed up the steps. Spike tugged, Milo let go of the leash, and the dog met us halfway.

"You're okay," said Robin, sweeping him up and kissing him. He returned the affection and let me know with a look who was top dog.

We entered the house.

"When I got here the front door was locked," said Milo. "Bolted, had to use my key. No windows jammed. Nothing messed and that safe you keep in the bedroom closet hasn't been touched. So it looks like a false. Contact the company tomorrow and have them come out and check the system. Only thing out of sorts is this guy."

I rubbed Spike behind the ears. He harrumphed, turned away, and resumed licking Robin's neck.

"Muscling in on your lady?" said Milo. "You going to stand for that?"

We drifted into the kitchen. Robin's eyes were all over the place. "Seems fine to me," she said. "Let me just check the jewelry I keep loose in my drawer."

She was back in a moment. "Still there. Had to be a false alarm."

"Good thing," I said. "We didn't exactly get quick protection from the department."

"Hey," said Milo, "count yourself lucky you didn't get a false-alarm citation."

"Protect and cite?"

"Anything that brings in revenue."

Robin said, "Let's have dessert here. You up for ice cream, Milo?"

He patted his middle. "Aw shucks, I shouldn't—no more than three scoops and only a quart of chocolate sauce."

She laughed and left, Spike trotting along.

Milo scuffed one shoe with the other. Something in his eyes made me ask if he'd learned anything in East L.A.

"The victim was a kid named Raymond Ortiz. IQ of seventy-five, overweight, some coordination problems, very bad eyesight, Coke-bottle glasses. He was on a school outing in a park at the east end of Newton Division. Tough place, known as a gang hangout, drugs, the usual. The theory is that he wandered away from the group and got grabbed. Never been found but two months later his blood-filled sneakers were left near the front door of the Newton station, resting on top of an old newspaper clipping about the disappearance. Raymond's blood was on record at County Hospital because he'd participated in a retardation study and they got a perfect match."

"Jesus," I said. "Poor, poor kid . . . in some ways it's so much like Irit, but in others—"

"It's nothing like Irit, I know. With Irit—and with Latvinia—we had the body but no blood, with this one, blood and no body. And the blood implies something other than strangulation. At least not gentle strangulation."

"I hate that term, Milo."

"Me, too. Pathologists are such dispassionate bastards, aren't they?"

I thought about what he'd told me. "Even with the differences, we've got two retarded kids, snatched out of a school group in a park."

"What better place to snatch a kid, Alex? Parks and malls are favorite stalking zones. And this park was nothing like the nature conservancy. No trails, no surrounding wilderness. Your basic inner-city place, poorly kept up, bums and junkies on the grass."

"And they took kids there for a field trip?"

"An outing, not a field trip. The school was being painted and they wanted to get the kids away from the fumes. The park's a few blocks away. They were taking them there every day."

"The entire school went?"

"They brought them a few grades at a time. Raymond was with the special-ed kids and they were grouped with the first and second graders."

"So there were lots of smaller children and the killer chose Raymond. Without wilderness, what did he use for cover?"

"There are some big trees behind the public rest rooms. The most logical scenario is Raymond went to the john and got dragged into a stall. Either killed right there or incapacitated. They never found any of his blood in the john, but he could have been killed cleanly, the blood for the shoes taken later. Whatever happened, no one saw it."

"None of *his* blood? Does that mean someone else's?"

"Like I said, it's a drug place, junkies use the stalls to fix. There were blood-specks all over the place. At first they thought it would be a lead, but no match to Raymond. The samples are on file if they ever get a perp but why should the *perp* have bled? They also dusted for prints, found matches to a few local bums with sheets, but all of them had solid alibis and none of them had a history of pedophilia or sex crimes."

Thinking of the boy trapped in a fetid stall, I felt my stomach knot up. "What's the theory about how the killer got him out of the park?"

"The parking lot's about thirty feet behind the bathrooms with the trees in between, a nice green barrier. If the asshole's car was nearby, he could have carried Raymond, tossed him in, driven off."

"What time of day did this take place?"

"Late morning. Between eleven and noon."

"Broad daylight," I said. "Same as Irit—so damned brazen. . . . You said Raymond was chubby. How much did he weigh?"

"Hundred and ten or so. But short. Four seven."

"Heavier than Irit," I said. "Once again, a strong killer. How's the case classified?"

"Open but very cold, not a single lead the entire year. The main

Newton D on the case is an older guy named Alvarado, very good, very methodical. He began the same way we did on Irit: hauled in and interviewed sex offenders. He also grilled all the gang bangers known to hang out at the park. They said they'd never hurt a poor little kid—which is bullshit, they kill poor little kids in drive-bys all the time. But Raymond was actually a popular kid because his older brothers were bangers in Vatos Locos and Dad had been, too. VL rules that area and the family was well-respected."

"But couldn't that be a possible motive?" I said. "Some internecine gang thing and Raymond was used to get a message across to the Vatos? Had the brothers or the father gotten on anyone's bad side? Were they involved in the drug trade?"

"Alvarado looked into that. The father served some time years ago, but he's straight now—works as an upholsterer downtown—and the brothers are low-status punks, not particularly aggressive. Sure they use, like all their buddies, but they're not kingpins and as far as Alvarado could learn, they hadn't pissed anyone off big-time. Plus, if it had been a gang message, some sort of revenge would have been taken. Alvarado's feeling right from the start was a sex crime because of the park setting, the john, the shoes left at the station. To him that was a taunt—a power-trip sicko trying to show how smart he was at the police's expense. Make sense?"

"It makes a lot of sense," I said, remembering the business-world adage Dr. Lehmann had quoted this afternoon:

It's not enough that I succeed. You have to fail.

"Yeah, he was brazen, all right," he said. "Arrogant bastard. To me, sending the clipping also meant he got off on the publicity, was hoping to stir things up."

"How much publicity did the abduction create?"

"Couple of small articles in the *Times*, couple of larger ones in *El Diario*. More than Latvinia Shaver's gotten, by the way. All those media leeches came up with was a thirty-second story on the late news that night, no follow-up."

"Which raises a question," I said. "I can see him killing Irit to get publicity, but then why do Latvinia?"

"Exactly. I don't see enough of a match to consider these anything but three separate cases."

"Did the shoes stir up the case again?"

"Nope. Alvarado never released anything to the press."

"Why not?"

"To hold something back, in case the asshole ever gets caught. I asked about the DVLL thing and Alvarado said it didn't ring any bells. So that scrap of paper probably was just trash."

"Three separate cases," I said.

"You disagree?"

"No," I said. "Not yet. But the similarities do bear consideration: the choice of retarded teenagers, picking them out of a crowd in Raymond's and Irit's cases and in Latvinia's, from plenty of other girls working the street. I keep picturing the same kind of psychopath for each: smug, meticulous, confident enough to spirit a victim away in broad daylight or leave her in a public place like the schoolyard. Leaving the body out in the open in two instances, and a body-surrogate—bloody shoes—in another. Sneaky, but an exhibitionist. A show-off. Taken with himself. Which isn't profound because every psychopath is self-obsessed. They're like cookies out of a cutter: same power lust, same extreme narcissism, same need for excitement and total disregard for others."

"Seen one psychopath, seen 'em all?"

"In terms of their inner motivation that happens to be true," I said. "Psychologically, they're flat, banal, boring. Think of all the creeps you've put away. Any fascinating souls?"

He thought about that. "Not really."

"Emotional black holes," I said. "No *there*, there. Their crime techniques differ because of individual quirks. Not just M.O., because the same killer can change his method if it's not *psychologically* important to him yet still have a *trademark*."

"Yeah, I've seen that. Rapists who'll switch back and forth from a gun or a knife, but always talk to their victims the same way. You see any trademark, here?"

"Just retarded kids with various disabilities," I said. "I suppose that could indicate some twisted notion of eugenics—culling the herd. Though his basic motive would still be psychosexual. Give me a sheet of paper and your pen."

Sitting down at the breakfast table, I drew a grid and filled it in as Milo watched over my shoulder.

	RAYMOND	IRIT	LATVINIA
AGE	13	15	18
SEX	M	F*	F*
ETHNICITY	Hispanic*	Israeli*	Black*
METHOD	? no blood at the scene so possible strang.	manual strang.*	lig. strang.*
JURISDIC.	Newton	West L.A.	Southwest
LOCATION	park*	park*	schoolyard*
TIME OF DAY	morning	afternoon	night
DISABILITIES	retarded* severely myopic clumsy	retarded* deaf	retarded* drug use seizures
BODY POSITION	? (shoe flaunt)	supine, public* (flaunt)	hanging, public* (flaunt)

"The asterisks are matches?" Milo said.

"Yes."

"Where's the ethnicity match?"

"All three were minorities," I said.

"A racist killer?" he said.

"It also fits with the eugenics thing. As does the fact that all three were only mildly retarded, functioning very well. Teenagers. Meaning capable of reproduction. He tells himself he's cleansing the gene pool, he's not just some lust killer. Which is why he doesn't assault the victims."

"Him," he said. "One killer?"

"Hypothetically."

"Usually lust killers prey on their own race."

"The conventional wisdom used to be *always* until cross-racial serial killers started showing up. And murder and rape have been used for years as part of racial and ethnic warfare."

He scanned the chart again. "Park and schoolyard."

"Both are public places where kids congregate. I can't help thinking leaving Latvinia on that yard had some kind of meaning. Maybe to terrify the schoolkids the next morning—expand the violence."

"Culling." He shook his head.

"Just presenting another perspective, for argument's sake."

He picked up the chart and ran his finger down the middle. "Truthfully, Alex, what I see is lots of partials, very little that goes across the board. And one killer operating out of three jurisdictions?"

"What better way to evade notice than by moving around?" I said. "It would lessen the chance of a connection being discovered because how often do detectives from different divisions get together? It could also be part of the thrill: By killing all over the city, he expands his sphere of influence. Rules the city, so to speak."

"The Killer King of L.A." He frowned. "Okay, let's stick with the one-killer hypothesis for argument's sake. Raymond's abduction was a full year before Irit, Latvinia three months after. You say he's compulsive. Not much even spacing there."

"Assuming no murders took place between Raymond and Irit. And even if they didn't, with lust crimes the drive often accelerates as the victims pile up. Or he killed out of town. But let's assume he operates only in L.A. and Raymond was his first. Even with his arrogance he would have been apprehensive, pulling back to see if the investigation turned anything up. When it didn't, he left the shoes. When that didn't get any attention, he struck again. In a safe place, like the conservancy. And *that* success bolstered his confidence so he repeated sooner."

"Meaning the next one could be even sooner." Shoving his hands in his pockets, he began to pace.

"Something else," I said. "If Raymond was his first, maybe he removed the body to *use* it. Kept it for two months until he thought he was finished with it. Or—and this is sickening—until it wasn't usable, anymore. At that point, he disposed of it, keeping the shoes and whatever else as mementos. Maybe he was still at a point where he wanted to quit. But after a while, the shoes no longer worked for him as sexual stimuli so he delivered them to Newton Division, with the clipping, to revive some of the power-thrill. That was temporary, too, and he went stalking. Driving around the city, looking for another outdoor setting. Some place that evoked Raymond's murder but different enough to avoid detection of a pattern."

He stopped pacing. "First a boy, then girls?"

"He's ambisexual. Remember, he doesn't have sex with them. The thrill is the stalking and capture. That's why he took Raymond but not Irit and Latvinia. By then, he was less impulsive, had learned what really turned him on."

"You've got some mind, Doctor."

"That's what you pay me for. When you pay me."

He tapped a foot and studied the rug. "I don't know, Alex. It's a clever construction but there are still too many differences."

"I'm sure you're right," I said. "But here's another thought: All three kids were murdered in public places. Perhaps because the killer—or killers—finds that erotic. Or, he has no access to an indoor killing spot."

"Homeless?"

"No, I doubt it. He's got a car and I still see him as middle-class, neat and clean. I was thinking just the opposite: a family man, living an outwardly wholesome and conventional life. Maybe with a wife, or a live-in girlfriend. Even children of his own. A nice, cozy domestic setup where there'd be no convenient place to play with a dead body."

"What about a van?" he said. "You know how many of these assholes love vans."

"A van might work but sooner or later, he'd have to clean it up. If I'm right about his being a family man, with a job, it would be sooner."

"Not a nine-to-five job, Alex, because he gets away in the middle of the day."

"Probably not," I said. "Someone with flexibility. Self-employed, an independent contractor. Or a work schedule with revolving shifts. Maybe a uniform. Some kind of repairman, or park maintenance worker. A security guard. One thing I'd do is cross-reference the personnel lists for the conservancy and the park where Raymond was killed. If you come across someone who switched jobs from East L.A. to the Palisades, ask him lots of questions."

He pulled out his pad and made a note. "And keep looking for other retarded victims. Other divisions . . ."

Robin came in with three bowls and set them down. Milo folded the chart I'd made and slipped it in the pad.

"Here you go, boys. Chocolate syrup for you, Milo, but the only flavor we had was vanilla."

"No prob," said Milo. "The virtue of simplicity."

18

marked. He lagged behind me on the stairs and his footsteps were halting and deliberate.

"Going home?" I said.

"Nope, back to the office. Gonna call every goddamn night-shift detective in every goddamn division, look for any remotely possible matches. If I don't get any, that'll tell me something, too."

He opened the car door. "Thanks for the input. Now let me tell you about Sergeant Wes Baker. We were classmates in the academy. Two of the oldest guys in the class, he might have been *the* oldest. Maybe that's why he started off thinking we were kindred spirits. Or maybe it was because I had a master's degree and he fancied himself an intellectual."

"And you didn't want to be kindred with him."

"What are you, a shrink? I didn't want to be kindred with anyone at that place, still tucked deeply in the closet, waking up with my jaws clenched so tight I thought my face would break. Every day I memorized another section of the penal code, shot bull's-eyes on the range, did hand-to-hand, the whole macho bit. After Vietnam, no big challenge, but it was like someone else going through it—I felt like an impostor, was sure I'd be found out and lynched. So I kept to myself, avoided after-hours with the other recruits, didn't have to pretend to be a pussy hound and smile through the fag jokes. Why I didn't quit, I still don't know. Maybe after the war I couldn't find any alternatives that seemed better."

A sudden, frightening grin spread across his face. "And that's my confession, Father . . . back to Wes Baker. He was a relative loner, too, because he considered himself above it all, Mr. Experience. He saw me reading Vonnegut and got the idea we could relate because he was into books. Philosophy, Zen, yoga, politics. *Psychology*. Always eager for a meaning-of-life discussion. I pretended to go along, which was easy because he liked to talk and I know how to listen. He told me his life story in weekly installments. He'd knocked around a bit, traveled everywhere, Peace Corps, worked oil rigs and cruise ships, taught school in the inner city, been-there-done-it. He was always complaining he couldn't get a bridge foursome at the academy, that for the other guys poker was an intellectual challenge. He kept trying to buddy up, inviting me over. I kept declining politely. Finally, midway through the course, he asked me to his place to watch a Rams game and I agreed, wondering if he was gay, too. But his girlfriend was there—cute little grad student from the U. And her friend—a budding actress. *My* date."

He smiled again, this time with some pleasure. "Noreen. Great legs, flat voice, maybe the silent era would have treated her better. Wes cooked up this Indian banquet—chutneys and curries, whatever. Okra, which to me is snot from the ground—chicken in a clay pot. He served some esoteric beer from Bombay that tasted like horse piss. The game was on the tube but it never got watched because Wes nudged us into a debate on East versus West, who really enjoyed the greater quality of life. Then he got down on the floor and demonstrated yoga positions, trying to show how they could be used to subdue suspects without undue violence. Gave a whole lecture on the history of martial arts and how it related to Asian religion. His girlfriend thought it was fascinating. Noreen got sleepy."

"Sounds like a fun evening."

"Real chortle fest. After that night, I was friendly to him but really kept my distance. The guy was too intense for me and life was hard enough without having to deal with all his cosmic bullshit. He must have sensed it because he cooled off, too, and eventually we were just nodding hello in the hall, then avoiding each other completely. About a week before graduation, I happened to be having one of my few nights out. Dinner at a place in West Hollywood with a guy I'd met at a bar. Older guy, an accountant, also struggling. He ended up divorcing his wife, had a massive heart attack shortly after and died at forty-two. . . . Anyway, we'd been at this place on Santa Monica and when we came out some cars were stopped at a red light. The guy put his arm around my shoulder. I wasn't comfortable being public, and I moved away. He laughed it off and we walked to the curb to cross the street. Just then I got that back-of-the-neck feeling when someone's watching you, turned and saw Wes Baker in a little red sports car. Looking right *through* me, with this *so-that-explains it* expression. When my eye caught his, he pretended he didn't see me, and jackrabbited the moment the light turned green. A week later someone busted into my locker and filled it with a stack of gay porn. A huge stack, including some really nasty S and M stuff. I could never prove it was Baker, but who else? And a couple of times I caught him staring at me in a weird way. Studying me, like I was some kind of specimen."

"You wondered about his sexuality," I said. "Maybe he was cruising West Hollywood for a reason, was worried that you'd seen *him*."

"And the locker was a best-defense-is-an-offense bit? Could be, but I think it was plain old homophobia."

"Not very tolerant for an intellectual."

"Since when do the two go hand in hand? And to me he's a *pseudo*intellectual, Alex. Surfing the philosophical wave of the week. Maybe he is latent, I don't know. For obvious reasons I couldn't afford to make an issue of it, so I just stayed away. I didn't see him again for a long time. Then around five years ago he made sergeant and got transferred to West L.A. and I thought oh, shit, here come problems. But there weren't any. He made a point of coming up and saying hi, Milo, long time no see, how's everything? Mr. Jovial. I couldn't shake the feeling that he was putting me on. Patronizing me. But D's and uniforms don't have that much contact and his path never crossed mine. A few months ago, he got kicked upstairs to Parker Center. Some sort of administrative job."

"If he fancies himself an intellectual," I said, "how come he stayed in uniform and didn't try for detective?"

"Maybe he likes the streets—putting the cosmic yoga choke hold on bad guys. Maybe it's the image—tailored duds, gun, baton, stripes. Some blues think detectives are paper-pushing wusses. Or could be he likes training rookies, easing little blue-birds out of the nest."

"In some ways he sounds like Nolan. Self-styled scholar, trying on different philosophies. I don't imagine the department operates like a computer dating service, but two guys like that getting to-gether seems awfully coincidental."

"I'm sure it's not. Baker would have been in a position to pick and choose."

"I've been wondering if the suicide had something to do with the job, but Baker told Helena he's baffled."

"The Baker I knew would have had an opinion. The Baker I knew had an opinion about everything."

Thinking about Lehmann's reticence and wondering who else shared it, I said, "Maybe I'll talk to him myself."

"Getting involved in this one, huh? When Rick sent the sister to you, he thought it would be a quickie."

"Why?"

"He said she was a no-nonsense gal. All business. Move 'em up, get 'em out."

I'd had the same feeling about Helena, had been surprised when she'd called for a second appointment. She hadn't returned today's calls, though.

"Suicide changes things," I said.

"True. I called the department's personnel office and Lehmann is on their shrink referral list, along with a bunch of others, but that's all I can get on him."

"Don't spend any more time on it. You've got your hands full."

"*Big* hands," he growled, and held them out, palms up. "For *big* man. With *big* job. Me go back to cave now. Try not to fuck up *big*-time."

I laughed.

He got in the car and started the engine. "Lest I blanket you in total pessimism, Zev Carmeli called me just before I left for New-ton, said I could talk to his wife tomorrow, at the family home. I told him I might be bringing you along, wondered if he'd give me some grief over that—psychoanalyzing the wife. But he didn't. In general, he seemed more cooperative. As if he finally believed I was on his side. Have you the time and inclination?"

"When?"

"Five o'clock."

"Should I meet you there?"

"Probably best 'cause I don't know where I'll be. They live on Bolton Drive." He gave me the address, shifted the unmarked into drive, coasted ten feet, then stopped. "When you talk to Wes Baker, bear in mind that knowing me will not earn you gold stars."

"I can live with that risk."

"What a pal."

THE NEXT MORNING I REVIEWED IRIT'S FILE AGAIN, learning nothing. The theories I'd spun for Milo last night seemed nothing more than random shots.

I wasn't any further along on Nolan's suicide, either. Some elements of the "typical" problem cop were there—alienation, isolation, family history of depression, possible job stress, the dark secrets Lehmann had intimated. But trying to explain self-destruction on the basis of a collection of symptoms is like saying people got poor by losing money.

Lehmann's caginess had accomplished just the opposite of what he'd hoped, piquing my interest.

What Milo'd told me about Baker was intriguing but before I talked with him I wanted Helena's go-ahead and she still hadn't returned my messages. I tried the hospital again and was told she'd called in sick last night. No one answered at her home.

Huddled under the covers, sleeping off a nasty virus?

Should I call Baker anyway? If I asked questions and told him nothing of substance, there'd be no breach of confidentiality.

But grief was a psychic tide, ebbing and flowing in response to the magnet of memory, and Helena's "sickness" could be something of quite a different nature.

Emotional withdrawal? Nothing healed *but* time, and sometimes that didn't work either.

The last time I'd seen her she'd taken home the family snapshot albums.

Memory *overload*?

I decided to try Baker. He'd probably refuse to talk to me, anyway.

. . .

A PARKER CENTER DESK OFFICER TOLD ME SERGEANT
Baker had a day off and I left my name and number, expecting
nothing. But barely an hour later, as I sat typing a child-custody
report, my service called and said he was on the line.

"Dr. Delaware? Wesley Baker, returning your call. What kind of
doctor are you?" Clipped, businesslike. He was older than Milo
but sounded in his thirties, an aggressive young lawyer.

"Thanks for calling back, Sergeant. I'm a psychologist looking
into the death of Nolan Dahl."

"Looking into it at whose request?"

"Officer Dahl's sister."

"A psychological autopsy?"

"Nothing that formal."

"Just trying to get some closure?" he said. "I'm not surprised.
She called me a few weeks ago, trying to get some answers. Poor
woman. I was extremely upset by Nolan's suicide, myself, disappointed that I couldn't tell her much. Because Nolan and I hadn't
worked together for some time and I didn't want to give her information that might be irrelevant. She sounded depressed. It's good
she got professional help."

"Irrelevant in what way?"

Pause. "Not *being* a professional, I wasn't sure what would be
therapeutic and what would be harmful."

"You're saying Nolan had some problems that could upset her."

"Nolan was . . . an interesting kid. Complex."

The same term Lehmann had used.

"In what way?"

"Hmm . . . listen, I don't feel right getting into this without
thinking it through. I'm off today, planned to get a little sailing in,
but if you'll give me a little time to collect my thoughts, you can
come by my boat, we'll see what turns up."

"I appreciate that, Sergeant. When's a good time for you?"

"How say noon? If we're both hungry, we can grab some lunch.
You can even pay."

"Fair enough. Where's your boat?"

"Marina del Rey. She's called *Satori*. I'm docked right near the
Marina Shores Hotel." He gave me the slip number. "If I'm not
there, it means the winds died and I had to tie up and use the
engine. One way or the other, I'll be there."

19

THE BOAT WAS THIRTY FEET OF SLEEK WHITE FIBER-glass with gray trim. Tall masts, the sails tied. *Satori* painted on the hull in black script edged with gold.

The sky over the marina was baby blue rubbed with chalk dust. Not much wind at all. The craft and its neighbors barely bobbed and I wondered if Baker had even gotten out of the harbor. Just a moment's walk away, the rear balcony of the Marina Shores Hotel extended over the footpath that ribboned the edge of the dock. Early lunchers sat nursing iced drinks and forking seafood.

A wall of chain-link sectioned the hotel property from the rental slips but it was unlocked and I walked through.

Satori. I knew it had something to do with Zen and had looked it up before leaving.

A state of intuitive illumination.

Maybe Sergeant Wesley Baker could illuminate Nolan's death.

HE CAME OUT FROM BELOW BEFORE I REACHED THE boat, drying his hands with a white towel. Five nine, stocky, but without visible body fat, he wore a white Lacoste polo shirt, pressed black jeans, and white deck shoes. Looking every year of his age—around fifty, but a well-put-together fifty—he had a dura-ble tan, short dark brown hair silvering at the temples, square, broad shoulders, and well-muscled, hairless arms. His head was slightly small for the blocky torso, the face round, vaguely child-like, despite sun seams and assertive features. Large, gold-framed eyeglasses were turned to ray guns by the midday sun.

A successful businessman on his day off.

He waved, I climbed aboard, and we shook hands.

"Doctor? Wes Baker. Up for lunch? How about the hotel?"

"Sure."

"Let me lock up and I'll be right up."

He was gone for a moment, came back carrying a large black calfskin billfold. More like a purse, really, and he carried it in one hand. We got off the boat and headed for the hotel.

He walked very slowly—as if every movement counted. Like a dancer. Or a mime. Swinging his arms, looking from side to side, a faint smile on thin, wide lips.

Behind the glasses, his eyes were brown and curious. If he was planning to hide facts, it wasn't making him tense.

"Glorious day, isn't it?" he said.

"Beautiful."

"Living up here, you give up space—I make do with four hundred square feet—and the marina's as congested as the city. But at night, when things quiet down and there's a clear view out to the ocean, the illusion of infinity more than makes up for all that."

"Satori?" I said.

He chuckled. "Satori is an ideal, but you've got to keep trying. Do you sail?"

"Infrequently."

"I'm comparatively new to it, myself. Did some work on boats when I was a kid but nothing that taught me how to operate a serious craft. I got into it a few years ago. Trial by ordeal. A few knocks on the noggin and you learn to watch out for the boom."

"Nolan did some work on boats, too."

He nodded. "Santa Barbara fishing boats. He did some abalone diving, too. Didn't care for any of it."

"Oh?"

"He didn't have a taste for manual labor."

We climbed the stairs to the dining patio.

A sign said PLEASE WAIT TO BE SEATED and the host's lectern was empty. Two dozen tables covered in navy blue linen dotted the brick-floored terrace. Three were occupied. Crystal and silver played with the sun. The east wall was glass that looked into an empty dining room.

"Also, he said killing fish turned him off," said Baker, looking around. "Killing, period. He was a nonviolent kid, had become a vegetarian the year before entering the academy. Probably the only vegetarian cop I ever met—hey, Max."

A Chinese maitre d' emerged from inside the hotel. Black suit, black shirt, black tie, and a wide, professional smile full of distress.

"Hello, Mr. Baker. Your table's ready."

We were shown to a waterside table big enough for four but set for two. I could smell brine and boat fuel and someone's sautéed lunch.

"Nonviolent," I said. "Yet he chose police work."

Baker unfolded a navy napkin and placed it on his lap. "Theoretically there shouldn't have been a conflict. The goal of the police officer is to reduce violence. But of course, that's not reality."

Removing his glasses, he looked through them, blew off a speck of something, and put them back on. "The reality is that police work entails being constantly *submerged* in violence. Take a sensitive kid like Nolan and the result can be disillusionment."

"Did he talk about being disillusioned?"

"Not in so many words, but he wasn't happy. Always kind of down."

"Depressed?"

"Looking back, maybe, but he showed no clinical signs." He stopped. "At least that I'd know, being a layman. What I mean is, his appetite seemed fine and he was always on the job, ready to go. He just never laughed or got happy. As if he'd been dipped in some kind of protective coating—emotional lacquer."

"To avoid getting hurt?"

He shrugged. "I'm out of my element here. I'm as puzzled as everyone by what he did."

A young waiter brought French bread and asked for our drink order.

"Vodka and tonic," said Baker. "Doctor?"

"Iced tea."

"I'm ready to order, too. The calamari salad's great if you go for seafood?"

"Sure," I said.

"Two, then, and let's go with a nice white." He looked up at the waiter. The young man's expression said his last audition hadn't gone well. "Do you still have that Bear Cave sauvignon blanc in stock?"

"The eighty-eight? I believe so."

"If you do, bring us a bottle. If not, what's in the same league?"

"There's a good Blackridge sauvignon blanc."

"Whatever's reasonable. The doctor here is paying."

"Yes, sir." The waiter left and Baker sniffed his finger. "Ah, a fine nose. Pretensions of peach and old leaves and the faintest hint of 7Up."

He broke off some bread and chewed slowly. "What Nolan did has been bothering the hell out of me on two levels. Most important, of course, the act itself. The waste. But also narcissistically. Why didn't I see it?"

"How long did you work with him?"

"Three months, day after day. He was the fastest learner I've ever seen. An *interesting* kid. Different from other rookies I'd had but nothing that led me to believe he was high-risk—how much do you know about police suicide?"

"I know it's on the rise."

"Sure is. The rate's probably doubled in the last twenty years. And those are only the acknowledged ones. Throw in guys taking excessive risks, accidents that really aren't, other 'undetermined deaths,' and you probably double the count again."

"Accidents," I said. "Suicide by work?"

"Sure," he said. "Cops like doing it that way because it spares the family the shame. The same thing happens with the people cops deal with: Some profoundly depressed character gets drunk or dusted, stands in the middle of the street waving a gun, and when the patrol car arrives, instead of dropping it he points it at the windshield."

He pulled an imaginary trigger. "We call that suicide by cop. Only difference is, the *character's* family hires a lawyer, sues the city for wrongful death, and collects. Depression and litigation make a great combination, Dr. Delaware."

"Do cops litigate, too?" I said.

He took off his glasses and stared reflectively out at the harbor. "Live ones do, Doctor. Stress pensions, all that good stuff. Lately, the department's been clamping down. Why? Does the sister want to sue?"

Casual tone and he was looking at his bread plate.

"Not that I know," I said. "She's just looking for answers, not blame."

"In the end, it's the suicide who's to blame, isn't it? No one else put that gun in Nolan's mouth. No one else pulled the trigger. Were there signs beyond his not being the life of the party? Not that I saw. He took things seriously, took his work seriously. I saw that as positive. He was no slacker."

Our drinks arrived. As Baker tasted his, I said, "Besides being a fast learner, how was Nolan different from the other rookies?"

"His seriousness. His intelligence. We're talking major bright, Doctor. We'd go on Code 7s—breaks—and he'd whip out a book, start reading."

"What kinds of books?"

"The penal code, politics. Newspapers and magazines, too. He always brought something. Not that I minded. I'd rather read a good book any day than talk about the usual cop stuff."

"What's that?"

"Harleys, Corvettes, guns and ammo."

"He had a sports car. Little red Fiero."

"Did he? Never mentioned it. Exactly the point. When we were out cruising, he concentrated on work. When we broke, he didn't make small talk. Intense. I liked that."

"Did you choose to train Nolan because he was smart?"

"No. He chose me. When he was still at the academy I was over there to give a lecture on rules of arrest. Afterward he came up to me and asked if I'd be his T.O. when he graduated. Said he was a quick learner, we'd get along fine."

Baker smiled, shook his head, and spread thick, bronze hands on the tablecloth. The sun was beating down. I could feel the heat on the back of my neck.

"Pretty damn audacious. I figured what he was really after was a West L.A. placement. But I was intrigued, so I told him to come to the station after shift and we'd talk."

He rubbed the tip of his nose. "The very next day he showed up, on the dot. Not pushy at all. Just the opposite—deferential. I asked him what he'd heard about me, he said I had a reputation."

"For being intellectual?" I said.

"For being a T.O. who'd show him the way things really were."

He shrugged. "He was smart but I didn't know how he'd do on the street. I figured it would be interesting, so I said I'd see what I could work out. In the end, I decided to take him, because he seemed the best of the lot."

"Bad class?"

"The usual," he said. "The academy's not Harvard. Affirmative action has made things more . . . variable. Nolan did well. His size helped—people tended not to mess with him and he never bullied anyone or lorded it over the characters. By the book."

"Did he ever talk politics?"

"No. Why?"

"Just trying to get as full a picture as possible."

"Well," he said, "if I had to guess, I'd say his politics were conservative, simply because you don't find too many flaming liberals in the department. Was he waving any Klan flags? No."

I'd asked about politics, not racism. "So he got along well with the people you policed."

"As well as anyone."

"What about other policemen? Did he socialize much?"

"A couple of times he and I had dinner. Other than that, I don't think so. He stuck to himself."

"Would you say he was alienated from the other rookies?"

"Can't answer that. He seemed comfortable with his own lifestyle."

"Did he ever tell you what led him to become a cop?"

He put the glasses back on. "Before I took him on I asked him that and he said he wouldn't spin me some yarn about helping people or being a New Centurion, he just thought it might be interesting. I liked that, an honest answer, and we never discussed it again. In general, he was a closemouthed kid. All work, eager to learn the ropes. My policing style is to make lots of arrests, so most of the time we were pursuing calls aggressively. But no John Wayne stuff. I stay within bounds and so did Nolan."

He looked away. The fingers remained on the table but their tips had whitened. Sensitive topic?

"So there were no egregious problems on the job."

"None."

"Any alcohol or drug abuse?"

"He was health-oriented. Worked out after-hours at the station gym, jogged before shift."

"But a loner," I said.

He looked up at the sky. "He seemed content."

"Any women in his life?"

"Wouldn't surprise me, he was a good-looking kid."

"But no one he mentioned."

"Nope. That wasn't Nolan's style—look, Doctor, you need to understand that the police world's a subculture that doesn't tolerate weakness. You need real symptoms to justify seeking help. My job was to teach him to be a cop. He learned fine and functioned fine."

The waiter brought our lunch and the wine. Baker went through the tasting ritual, said, "Pour," and our glasses were filled. When we were alone again, he said, "I don't know that we should toast to anything, so how about a generic 'cheers.' "

We both drank and he waited for me to begin eating before approaching the calamari, sawing each squid in half and studying the forked morsel before popping it into his mouth. Wiping his lips with the napkin every third or fourth bite, he sipped his wine very slowly.

"Someone sent him to therapy," I said. "Or maybe he sent himself."

"When was he in therapy?"

"I don't know. The therapist is reluctant to discuss details."

"One of the department psychologists?"

"A private one. Dr. Roone Lehmann."

"Don't know him." He looked away again. Ostensibly at some gulls diving the harbor, but he'd stopped chewing and his big eyes were narrow.

"Therapy. I never knew that." His jaws began working again.

"Any idea why he transferred from West L.A. to Hollywood?"

He put his fork down. "By the time he transferred, I'd moved to headquarters. An administrative carrot they'd been dangling in front of me for a while: revising the training curriculum. I have no great love for paperwork but you can't keep saying no to the brass."

"So you didn't know about his transfer?"

"That's right."

"After the training period you and Nolan lost contact."

He looked at me. "It wasn't a matter of losing contact—breaking off some major father-son relationship. The training period's time-limited. Nolan learned what he needed to learn and went out into the big bad world. I found out about the suicide the day after it happened. Police grapevine. My first reaction was to want to wallop the crap out of the kid—how could someone that smart be so stupid?"

He speared a calamari. "The sister. What does she do?"

"She's a nurse. Did Nolan ever talk about her?"

"Never mentioned her. The only thing he said about his family was that both his parents were dead."

He pushed his plate away. Half the calamari were gone.

"What do you think about the way he did it?" I said. "So publically."

"Pretty bizarre," he said. "What do you think?"

"Could he have been making a statement?"

"Such as?"

I shrugged. "Had Nolan shown any exhibitionistic tendencies?"

"Showing off? Not in the course of duty. Oh, he was into his body—getting buffed, tailoring the uniform, but lots of young cops are that way. I still don't know what you mean by a statement."

"You mentioned before that cops always tried to minimize the shame of suicide. But Nolan did just the opposite. Made a spectacle of himself. Almost a public self-execution."

He said nothing for a long time. Lifted his wineglass, drained it, refilled, and sipped.

"You're suggesting he punished himself for something?"

"Just theorizing," I said. "But you're not aware of anything he might have felt guilty about."

"Not something on the job. Did his sister tell you anything along those lines?"

I shook my head.

"Nope," he said. "That just doesn't make sense."

The waiter approached.

"I'm finished," said Baker.

I seconded the motion, declined dessert, and handed over my credit card. Baker took out a big cigar and wet the tip.

"Mind?"

"No."

"Against restaurant rules," he said. "But they know me here and I sit where the wind carries it away."

He inspected the tight brown cylinder. Hand-rolled. Biting off the tip, he placed it in his napkin and folded the linen over the scrap. Taking out a gold lighter, he ignited the cigar and puffed. Bitter but not unpleasant smoke filled the space between us before dissolving.

Baker eyed the boats in the marina and sat back, catching sun.

Puff, puff. I thought of how he'd likely stuffed Milo's locker full of porn.

"Supreme waste," he said. "It still bothers me."

But sitting there, smoking and drinking wine, cleanly shaved face buttered by sun, he looked the picture of happiness.

20

I LEFT HIM ON THE TERRACE WITH HIS CIGAR AND
the rest of the wine. Just before I stepped onto the pathway that led
back to the hotel parking lot, I stopped and watched him smile as
he said something to the maitre d'.

Man at leisure. No clue he'd been talking about the death of a
colleague.

Would it have bothered me had Milo not warned me about him?

For all his open manner, he'd told me less than Dr. Lehmann:
Nolan had been an isolated, smarter-than-usual cop who played it
by the book.

None of the serious problems Lehmann had alluded to. On the
other hand, Baker had been Nolan's training officer, not his therapist.

Still, it was my second face-to-face meeting for no apparent reason.

People scurrying to protect themselves in the event of a lawsuit?
Over what?

Helena still hadn't called. Maybe she'd decided that only Nolan
would understand what Nolan had done. If she dropped out of
therapy, it was out of my hands, and on some level that didn't
bother me. Because Lehmann was right: Real answers were often
unobtainable.

Once home, I tormented myself with a faster-than-usual run up
the glen, showered and changed, and set out for Beverlywood at
four-fifteen, reaching the Carmeli home with ten minutes to spare
for the five o'clock meeting.

The house was a neatly kept single-story ranch on a block full of them. A negligible lawn sloped up to a used brick driveway. Parked on top were a blue Plymouth minivan and a black Accord, both with consulate plates. The curbs were empty save for two Volvo station wagons and a Suburban parked down the block and an electrical-company van across the street. Other driveways hosted more vans and wagons, lots of infant seats. Utility and fertility.

Tucked east of the Hillcrest Country Club and south of Pico, Beverlywood had been developed in the fifties as a starter community for the families of junior executives on their way to senior partnerships and manses in Brentwood and Hancock Park and Beverly Hills, and some people still called it Baja Beverly Hills. L.A. had essentially abandoned street maintenance, but Beverlywood looked manicured because of a homeowners' society that set standards and kept the trees trimmed. A private security company patrolled nightly. The land boom of the seventies had raised housing prices to the half-million mark and the downslide had kept them at a level where striving families found themselves at the top of their dream, nesting here permanently.

Milo pulled behind me two minutes later. He had on a bottle-green blazer, tan slacks, white shirt, and yellow-and-olive tartan tie. Green giant, but not jolly.

"Finally managed to locate six more creeps from the initial M.O. files, all moved to Riverside and San Berdoo. None check out time-wise, and their P.O.'s and/or therapists vouch for them. Nothing on DVLL, either, so I'm ready to chuck that one into the garbage file."

At the house, Zev Carmeli answered Milo's knock, wearing a dark suit and a grim expression.

"Come in, please."

There was no entry hall and we stepped right into a low, narrow, off-white living room. The deep green carpeting was amazingly similar in hue to Milo's jacket and for a second he looked like a fixture. The tan couches and glass tables could have been rented. The beige drapes drawn over the windows were filmy but most of the light came from two ceramic table lamps.

Sitting on the largest couch was a beautiful brown-skinned woman in her thirties with very long, curly black hair and moist, deep-set black eyes. Her lips were full but parched, her cheekbones molded so severely they seemed artificial. She wore a shapeless brown dress that covered her knees, flat brown shoes, no jewelry. Her eyes were nowhere.

Carmeli moved to her side and hovered and I fought not to stare.

Not because of her beauty; I'd seen Irit's death photos and here was the woman she might have become.

"This is Detective Sturgis and Dr. Delaware. My wife, Liora."

Liora Carmeli began to stand but her husband touched her shoulder and she remained seated.

"Hello," she said very softly, struggling to smile but not getting close.

We both shook her hand. Her fingers were limp and her skin was clammy.

I knew she'd resumed teaching school and couldn't be this depressed with her students. So our visit had raked things up.

"Okay," said Carmeli, sitting next to her and waving at some chairs on the other side of a glass coffee table.

We sat and Milo went through one of those little detective speeches full of sympathy and empathy and possibility that he hates to deliver but delivers so well. Carmeli looked angry but his wife seemed to relate a bit—shoulders straightening, eyes focusing.

I'd seen that before. Some people—usually women—respond to him immediately. He gets no satisfaction from it, always worried that he'll fail to produce. But he keeps delivering the speech, knowing no other way.

Carmeli said, "Fine, fine, we understand all that. Let's get on with it."

His wife looked at him and said something in what I assumed was Hebrew. Carmeli frowned and tugged down at his tie. They were both good-looking people who seemed drained of their life-juices.

Milo said, "Ma'am, if there's anything you can—"

"We know nothing," said Carmeli, touching his wife's elbow.

"My husband is right. There's nothing more we can tell you." Only her mouth moved when she spoke. The brown dress tented and I could see no body contours beneath it.

"I'm sure you're right, ma'am," said Milo. "The reason I have to ask is sometimes things occur to people. Things they think are unimportant so they never bring them up. I'm not saying that's actually the case here—"

"Oh for God's sake," said Carmeli, "don't you think if we knew something we'd *tell* you?"

"I'm sure you would, sir."

"I understand what you mean," said Liora Carmeli. "Since my Iriti is . . . gone, I think all the time. Thoughts . . . attack me. At night, especially. I think all the time, I am always thinking."

"Liora, *maspeek*," Carmeli broke in.

"I think," she repeated, as if amazed. "Stupid things, crazy things, monsters, demons, Nazis, madmen . . . sometimes I'm dreaming, sometimes I'm awake." She closed her eyes. "Sometimes it's hard to tell the difference."

Carmeli's face was white with rage.

His wife said, "The strange thing is, Iriti is never in the dreams, only the monsters . . . I feel that she is there but I can't *see* her and when I try to . . . bring her face into the picture, it . . . flies away from me."

She looked at me. I nodded.

"Iriti was my treasure."

Carmeli whispered urgently to her in Hebrew again. She didn't seem to hear.

"This is ridiculous," he said to Milo. "I request you to leave at once."

Liora touched his arm. "The monster dreams are so . . . childish. Black things . . . with wings. When Iriti was little she was afraid of black, winged monsters—devils. *Shedim*, we call them in Hebrew. *Ba'al zvuv*—that means 'lord of the flies' in Hebrew. Like that book about the schoolboys . . . it was a Philistine god that controlled insects and disease . . . Beelzebub in English. When Iriti was little, she had nightmares about insects and scorpions. She would wake up in the middle of the night and want to come to our bed . . . to help her I told her stories about *shedim*. The Bible— how we—the Philistines were . . . conquered . . . and their stupid gods . . . my culture—my family is from Casablanca—we have wonderful stories and I told them all to her . . . stories with children conquering monsters."

She smiled. "And she stopped being afraid."

Her husband's hands were blanched fists.

She said, "I thought I was successful because Iriti stopped coming to our bed."

She looked at her husband. He stared at his trousers.

"When Irit got older," said Milo, "was she afraid of anything?"

"Nothing. Nothing at all. I thought I'd done a good job with my stories."

She let out a short, barking laugh, so savage it tightened my spine.

Her husband sat there, then shot to his feet and came back with a box of tissues.

Her eyes were dry but he wiped them.

Liora smiled at him and held his hand. "My brave little girl. She knew she was different . . . liked being pretty . . . once, when we lived in Copenhagen, a man grabbed her and tried to kiss her. She was nine, we were shopping for jeans and I was walking in front of her instead of with her because Copenhagen was a safe city. There was a museum, there, on the Stroget—the main shopping street. The Museum of Erotica. We never went in but it was always busy. The Danes are healthy about those things but perhaps the museum attracted sick people because the man—"

"Enough," said Carmeli.

"—grabbed Iriti and tried to kiss her. An old man, pathetic. She didn't hear him—she had her hearing aid off, as usual, probably singing songs."

"Songs?" said Milo.

"She sang to herself. Not real songs, her own songs. I could always tell because her head would move, up and down—"

"She stopped doing that a long time ago," said Carmeli.

"When this man grabbed her," said Milo, "how did she react?"

"She punched him and broke free and then she laughed at him because he looked so frightened. He was a little old man. I didn't even realize anything was wrong until I heard yelling in Danish and turned around and saw two young men holding the old man and Iriti standing there, laughing. They'd seen the whole thing, said the old man was crazy but harmless. Irit kept laughing and laughing. It was the old man who looked miserable."

"That was Denmark," said Carmeli. "This is America."

Liora's smile vanished and she lowered her head, chastened.

"So you feel," said Milo, "that Irit wasn't afraid of strangers."

"She wasn't afraid of anything," said Liora.

"So if a stranger—"

"I don't know," she said, suddenly crying. "I don't know anything."

"Liora—" said Carmeli, taking hold of her wrist.

"I don't know," she repeated. "Maybe. I don't *know!*" She broke free of her husband's grasp and faced the wall, staring at the bare plaster. "Maybe I should have told her *other* stories, where the demons won, so you needed to be careful—"

"Ma'am—"

"Oh, please," said Carmeli, disgusted. "This is idiotic. I *insist* you leave."

He stomped to the door.

Milo and I got up.

"One more thing, Mrs. Carmeli," he said. "Irit's clothes. Were they sent back to Israel?"

"Her clothes?" said Carmeli.

"No," said Liora. "We sent only . . . she—when we—our customs—we use a white robe. Her clothes are here." She faced her husband. "I asked you to call the police and when you didn't, I had your secretary call. They arrived a month ago and I kept them."

Carmeli stared at her, bug-eyed.

She said, "In the Plymouth, Zev. So I can have them with me when I drive."

Milo said, "If you don't mind—"

"Crazy," said Carmeli.

"I am?" said Liora, smiling again.

"No, no, no, Lili, these questions." More Hebrew. She listened to him calmly, then turned to us. "Why do you want the clothes?"

"I'd like to do some analyses," said Milo.

"They've already been analyzed," said Carmeli. "We waited months to get them back."

"I know, sir, but when I take on a case I like to make sure."

"Make sure what?"

"That everything has been done."

"I see," said Carmeli. "You're a careful man."

"I try."

"And your predecessors?"

"I'm sure they tried, too."

"Loyal, too," said Carmeli. "A good soldier. After all this time, the clothes being in my wife's car, what use are analyses?"

"I never touched them," said Liora. "I never opened the bag. I wanted to, but . . ."

Carmeli looked ready to sting, said only, "Ah."

Liora said, "I'll get them for you. May I have them back?"

"Of course, ma'am."

She got up and went outside.

UNLOCKING THE MINIVAN'S REAR HATCH, SHE LIFTED up a section and revealed the spare-tire compartment. Next to the wheel was a plastic bag still bearing an LAPD evidence tag. Inside was something blue—rolled jeans. And a white patch—a single sock.

"My husband already thinks I've gone crazy because I've started talking to myself—like Iriti's singing."

Carmeli stiffened, then his eyes went soft. "Liora." He put his arm around her. She patted his hand and moved away from him.

"Take it," she said, pointing to the bag.

As Milo reached for it, Carmeli returned to the house.

Watching him, Liora said, "Maybe I am sick. Maybe I am primitive. . . . What will you be analyzing? The first police told us there was nothing on it."

"I'll probably repeat what's been done," said Milo. He held the bag in both hands, as if it were something precious.

"Well," she said. "Good-bye. Nice to meet you."

"Thank you, ma'am. I'm sorry we upset your husband."

"My husband is very . . . tender. You will return it?"

"Absolutely, ma'am."

"Can you say when?"

"As soon as possible?"

"Thank you," she said. "As soon as possible. I would like to have it with me again when I drive."

21

SHE TRUDGED BACK INTO HER HOUSE AND CLOSED
the door.

Milo and I returned to our cars. "I love my job," he said. "Those
light and airy moments." The evidence bag was nestled against his
barrel chest.

"Poor woman," I said. "Both of them."

"Looks like things aren't great between them."

"Tragedy will do that."

"Any other insights?"

"About what?" I said.

"Her, them."

"He's protecting her and she doesn't want to be protected.
Pretty standard male-female pattern. Why?"

"I don't know . . . the way she talked about being crazy, primitive. She's . . . something about her made me wonder if she has
a psychiatric history."

I stared at him.

"Like I said, light and airy, Alex."

"Stalking her own child in the park and strangling her?"

"Strangling gently . . . could be a boyfriend, I've seen *that*
plenty of times, guy develops a relationship, sees the kids as impediments—but no, she's not a suspect. I just think ugly by reflex."

His arm dropped and the bag dangled. "I've seen too many kids
killed by mama. Can't be effective if I avoid the shadows."

"True," I said. "My guess is that she might have been wound up
pretty tight—a diplomat's wife—and has unraveled. She probably

used to put on a happy face, suppress things, now she says to hell with it."

He looked down at the bag. "What do you think about her keeping this in her car all this time?"

"A shrine. There are all sorts of them. She knew her husband would be offended so she created a private one but she's willing to risk his disapproval in order to cooperate."

"Offended," he said. "She talked about her culture. As opposed to his? Moroccan as opposed to wherever he comes from?"

"Probably. He looks European. When I was in private practice, I had a few Israeli patients and the East versus West thing came up. When Israel was created it became a melting pot for Jews and sometimes there was conflict. I remember one family with just the opposite situation. The husband was from Iraq and the wife was Polish or Austrian. He thought she was cold, she thought he was superstitious. Maybe Mrs. Carmeli didn't want Mr. to think she was engaging in primitive rituals. Maybe she just knew he'd be grossed out by the clothes. Whatever the reason, she had no hesitation telling you she had the bag."

"One thing for sure, I'm talking to the neighbors. Carmeli will freak but so be it. Worse comes to worst, he gripes and they pull me off the case and someone else gets to feel useless."

I looked up the block. The electrician's van was the only vehicle at the curb.

"Are you really planning to run new lab tests?"

"Maybe. First things first."

I MET HIM AT THE WEST L.A. STATION, UPSTAIRS IN the detective room, relatively quiet now, with one other D, a young black woman, filling out forms. She didn't seem to notice as Milo sat at his metal desk, cleared papers, and placed the bag next to a stack of messages weighed down by a stapler. He scanned the slips, put them down. Then he put on surgical gloves and unsealed the bag.

Removing the jeans first, he turned each pocket inside out. The denim gave off smells of earth, mold, and chemistry lab.

Empty.

Turning the pants over, he pointed out some very faint brown stains that I'd have missed.

"Dirt, from when she lay on the ground."

Refolding the pants neatly, he took out the white sock and its mate, then a pair of white cotton underpants printed with small pink flowers, the crotch cut away cleanly.

"Semen analysis," he said.

Next came tennis shoes. He peeled the insoles free and peered inside, saying, "The Ortiz boy's shoes were obviously bloody but let's check these out anyway—size six and a half, made in Macao, *nada*, no blood, surprise, surprise."

A white cotton training bra caused him to pause for a second before removing the last garment—the lace-trimmed white T-shirt I'd seen in the photos. The front was clean but the back bore brown stains, too. Two breast pockets.

He put a thumb and forefinger inside the first, looked inside, moved on to the second and pulled out a small rectangle of paper, the size of a fortune-cookie slip.

"Aha, Dr. Sherlock, a clue—'Inspected by number 11.' " Then he turned the scrap over and his mouth dropped open.

Typed neatly in the center were four letters.

DVLL

22

THAT NIGHT AT TEN, WE ENTERED THE REAR PARTY-
room of a bar and grill on Santa Monica Boulevard, four blocks
west of the West L.A. station. The plain-faced red-haired hostess
looked happy to see us and a bill slipped into her hand improved
her disposition even further.

The room was big enough for a wedding party, with asparagus-
green wallpaper and brown banquettes that were either real
leather or fake. Dainty Impressionist prints hung on the walls—
street scenes of Paris, the Loire Valley, other places cops were unlikely to go, but the only people in the room were three cops at the
largest booth, up against the back wall.

Southwest Division Detectives Willis Hooks and Roy McLaren
drank iced tea, and a chunky, white-haired man of nearly sixty,
wearing a houndstooth sportcoat and a black polo shirt, nursed a
beer.

As Milo and I slid into the booth, he introduced the older man
as Detective Manuel Alvarado, Newton Division.

"Pleased to meet you, Doctor." His voice was mild, his skin was
dark as a field-worker's, rough as bark.

"Thanks for coming on your night off, Manny."

"A whodunit? Wouldn't miss it. Things are slow in Saugus."

"You live all the way out there?" said Hooks.

"Fifteen years."

"What do you do for fun out there?"

"Grow stuff."

"Like plants?"

"Vegetables."

The hostess reappeared. "Is this the entire party?"

"This is it," said Milo.

"Food, gentlemen?"

"Bring the mixed appetizer thing."

When she was gone, McLaren said, "*Gentlemen.* She obviously doesn't know us."

Obligatory smiles all around.

Hooks said, "Your call was the biggest surprise I've had since my ex-wife told me I wasn't handsome anymore."

"It surprised me, too, Willis," said Milo.

Alvarado took a pack of gum out of his jacket pocket and offered it around. No one accepted and he unwrapped a stick, and chewed. "DVLL. A common thread no one's ever heard of before."

"We checked with every gang-cop and banger and social worker and youth leader in our division," said McLaren.

"Same at West L.A.," said Milo. "FBI has nothing in VICAP or any other files."

"I went back through my copy of the Ortiz file," said Alvarado.

"Your copy?"

"The original was missing, just came back today, some sort of storage screw-up, fortunately I always Xerox. No DVLL message in the bathroom where my victim was probably taken and I copied down every bit of graffiti at the time. I'm still trying to locate the boy's shoes, but from what I remember there was no writing in them at all, just blood. So I can't say mine belongs with yours."

"And yours was a boy," said Hooks.

"And we never recovered the body, which is a big difference from both of yours."

"Not that pattern seems to mean a damn thing here," said Hooks. "West L.A. diplomat's kid and a mid-city strawberry?"

He shook his shaved head. "This is nutty. *Twilight Zone* stuff—right up your alley, huh, Doc? What do you think, does DVLL stand for some devil thing?"

"Could be," I said. "Despite the differences, Latvinia and Irit do have things in common: mildly retarded, non-Anglo teenage girls.

The fact that the killer chose handicapped victims says he despises weakness in others, and maybe himself."

"A handicapped killer?"

"Or someone preoccupied with strength and weakness. Domination. It could mean powerlessness in his life."

"A wimp who kills," said McLaren. His hands were huge and they closed around a spoon handle.

"Raymond Ortiz was retarded, too," said Alvarado. "But being a boy . . . usually when they go for boys, they don't go for girls."

"Usually," said Hooks, "when they go for inner-city street kids they don't go for rich kids on the West Side. Usually when they string one body up, they don't leave the other one stretched out on the ground. So if there is a pattern, it's eluding me."

He looked at me.

"Maybe the pattern here is deliberate *avoidance* of pattern," I said. "To outsmart you guys. Serial killers often read up on police procedure, collect true-crime magazines, for stimulation. This one could have used it for reference material. Learning the rules in order to break them. Varying his M.O., moving from district to district, other surface variables."

"What do you mean by surface?" said Alvarado.

"The core of the crimes will be consistent," I said. "The trademark. Because sex killers are psychologically rigid, crave structure. In this case, it's retarded teens and leaving behind the DVLL message. That could be a private message for him or a taunt, or both. So far, he's not advertising: he left it so subtly he can't have expected anyone to find it. One advantage for the good guys. He doesn't know anyone's made a connection."

"That paper in your victim's pocket, Milo," said McLaren. " 'Inspected by number 11.' Was that preprinted or did he type that, too?"

"That part looks preprinted," said Milo, "but with computers and desktop printers, you can't tell. I sent it over to the lab, maybe they can clarify. Either way, he brought it with him, because the DVLL part was in a different font, the lab says probably a computer, and I don't see anyone with killing on his mind bringing along a PC."

"Hey, you never know," said Hooks, "they make those laptop

suckers pretty small nowadays. And the doctor, here, thinks maybe he took her picture. So if he had a camera, why not a laptop? Maybe he brought along a carful of stuff."

"A vanful," said Alvarado. "Those guys love vans."

"Yeah," said Hooks.

"I always look for vans," said Alvarado. "On Raymond's case, I spent weeks checking out every van in the neighborhood—parking tickets, everything. Never found the killer but I did find quite a few set up as mobile bedrooms and one turkey who actually had handcuffs and burglary tools."

"You bet," said McLaren. "Vans and long-distance truckers, the well-equipped killer. There's probably a mail-order catalog out there somewhere."

"So," said Milo, "DVLL's important to him but he's not ready to advertise."

I said, "Either he's still a beginner and building up his confidence, or he'll never advertise, too cowardly. The fact that he chose especially vulnerable victims points to cowardice."

A knock sounded on the door and Milo said, "Come in, Sally."

The hostess wheeled in a two-tiered cart full of platters. Fried wontons, fried chicken, fried shrimp, fried egg rolls, pigs in blankets, shish kebobs on wooden skewers, each piece of meat capped with fat. Miniature wedges of pepperoni pizza. Bowls of dip in various colors, nachos, pretzels, potato chips.

"Mixed appetizers, gentlemen."

"Sure, why not," said Hooks. "I walked fifteen feet today from the lunch truck to my car, musta burned up two calories."

Sally served us and refilled the drinks.

"Thanks," said Milo. "We're fine, now."

"No more interruptions," she promised. "You want something, stick your head out and holler."

The men helped themselves to food and it didn't take long for half the serving plates to empty.

"I love this," said Hooks, lifting a chicken wing. "Feeling my arteries clog up as we speak."

"Your case," Milo said to Alvarado. "You said the shoes are still missing."

"The log says they're in the evidence room but they're not in the bin in the evidence room where they're supposed to be. Which is no heart-stopper, Milo, it's a year-old case, we've always got storage problems, stuff gets moved. It'll turn up, I'll let you know."

Milo nodded. "Anything else?"

"Latvinia," said McLaren. "We found lots of street creeps who knew her, even a couple who admitted doing her, but no one she hung with habitually. The grandmother says she went out alone at night a lot, the closest we've got to a hangout is that freeway on-ramp she got busted at. She went there from time to time so any-one could have picked her up—a West Side commuter who did her in his car—or van—then brought her back to the school so we wouldn't figure out he was a West Side guy.

"When the ramps are busy," he said, "or when the freeway's metered, you get panhandlers, people selling flowers, bags of oranges. Traffic balls up, Latvinia's out there flashing skin, some joker picks her up. . . . Maybe someone noticed that, some-one stalled in the gridlock. I was gonna see if some TV station would flash her pic, though we couldn't get much exposure, she's just a Southwest hooker got in trouble. Then you told me about the gag order."

"What gag order?" said Alvarado.

"My victim's family," said Milo. "The Israeli Consulate. They insist it stays out of the media for security reasons and they've got major pull with the brass. I checked again today with my loo and he says it's come down from the mayor's office, don't mess with it."

"So we're all gagged," said Hooks.

Alvarado said, "So does that apply to mine, too? I'm still not convinced it's connected."

"Why?" said Milo. "Were you thinking of going to the Spanish papers again?"

"No. I just want to know the rules—what exactly are the secu-rity concerns?"

Milo summed them up. "Now, with the tie-in to Latvinia, it doesn't sound like a terrorist. I explained that to my loo, but . . ." He covered his ears.

"Course it's not a terrorist," said McLaren. "This is a freak."

"Retarded kids," said Hooks, shaking his head.

"So what's the plan?" said Alvarado.

"Keep looking for leads, keep in touch," said Milo.

Alvarado nodded. "The shoes. I'll find them."

"Maybe we'll get lucky and he'll make a mistake," said Hooks.

McLaren said, "Our best friend: good old human error."

"Assuming," said Milo, "that he's human."

23

Milo the bill. Typical cop tip; she looked ready to kiss him.

He pocketed the credit slip but stayed seated and she left. "What do you think?"

"Eight hands are better than two," I said.

He frowned.

"What?"

"I keep flashing to what you first said about Raymond Ortiz. The impulsiveness of a first murder. If that's true, we're right at the beginning of the killing curve . . . DVLL. What the hell does it mean?"

"I'll go to the U tomorrow and play with the computers."

"Sure . . . thanks."

There was iced tea left in his glass and he drained it.

I asked where the men's room was.

He pointed across the room, to a door in the right-hand corner.

I pushed it open and on the other side was a pay phone, the rear door marked EMERGENCY ONLY. The lav was small, white-tiled, spotless, sweet with disinfectant.

Drafty, too. An oft-painted casement window had been left partially open and I heard engine noise from outside.

Then I noticed dry paint flakes on the sill. Recently opened window.

An alley ran behind the restaurant and a car was pulling into it. A van.

Headlights off, but as it backed away it passed under the back-door lamp.

Gray or light blue Ford Econoline. Electrician's logo.

I'd seen it or one just like it this afternoon, parked across the street from the Carmeli house.

The alley was narrow and the van had to manipulate a three-point turn, exposing a side panel.

I tried to force the window wider but it wouldn't budge. Straining, I made out the name of the company.

HERMES ELECTRIC. SPEEDY SERVICE.

Winged-messenger logo. An 818 number I couldn't catch.

A van. These guys love vans.

The Econoline straightened and the tires rotated. Dark windows, no view of the driver.

As it sped away, I tried for the license plate, managed to get all seven digits, kept reciting them out loud as I fumbled for a pen and a paper towel from the dispenser.

MILO GOT UP SO HARD THE TABLE SHOOK. ''STALKING us, the Carmelis? He's that arrogant?''

He hurried back to the bathroom area and shoved the emergency door open.

Outside, the air was warm and the alley smelled of rotted vegetables. I could hear sirens, probably from the station. I handed him the paper towel.

"Hermes Electric," he said.

"An electrician would wear a uniform. One of those anonymous beige or gray things that could resemble a park worker's. Electricians also carry lots of equipment, so who'd notice an extra camera in the back of the van? And I remember something Robin told me when we were rebuilding the house. Of all the tradesmen, electricians tend to be the most precise. Perfectionistic."

"Makes sense," he said. "Slip up and get fried. . . . Was the van at the Carmelis' the whole time?"

"Yes."

We walked through the restaurant, moving quickly past diners. The unmarked was parked in front, in a loading zone.

"Hermes," I said. "The god of—"

"Speed. So we've got a *fast* little motherfucker on our hands?"

. . .

HE USED THE MOBILE DIGITAL TERMINAL TO CONNECT to DMV, then typed in the plate number. The answer came back within minutes.

"Seventy-eight Chevy Nova registered to P. L. Almoni on Fairfax. So the asshole switched plates. This is looking better and better—I'm heading right over to the address . . . looks like between Pico and Olympic."

"The number on the side of the van was an 818."

"So he lives in the city, works in the Valley. Has a personal car and a work van and switches plates around when he wants to play . . . Almoni . . . that could be Israeli, too, right?"

I nodded.

"Juicier and juicier . . . okay, let's see what the state crime files and NCIC have to say about him."

Checking those data banks produced no hits. He started driving.

"Clean record," said Milo. "A goddamn beginner like you said. . . . Let's see how this asshole lives—unless you want to go home."

My heart was pounding and my mouth was dry. "Not a chance."

The east side of Fairfax, a dark, relatively untraveled section of the avenue, was filled with one shabby storefront after another. Every store closed, except for an Ethiopian restaurant with no drapes over the window. Inside, three people sat concentrating on heaping plates.

The sign atop P. L. Almoni's address read NOTARY PUBLIC, PHOTOCOPY SERVICES, MAILBOXES FOR RENT. We got out and looked through the window. Three walls of lockboxes, a service counter in back.

"Goddamn mail drop," said Milo. "Onward to his business."

We got back in the car, where he phoned Valley Information, waited, said, "You're sure?" and wrote something down.

Hanging up, he gave a sour smile. "It's a Valley exchange all right, but the address is in 310 territory. Holloway Drive in West Hollywood. Welcome to the maze, fellow rats."

HOLLOWAY WAS A TEN-MINUTE DRIVE FROM THE MAIL drop, nice and convenient for the convoluted Mr. Almoni. West to La Cienega, then north just past Santa Monica Boulevard, and a left turn onto a quiet street filled with apartment buildings. Well-designed buildings, many of them prewar, some concealed behind tall hedges. I guessed Almoni's would be one of them.

Only a short walk to Sunset Strip but insulated from the din and the lights. I noticed a woman walking a huge dog, its gait and hers long and confident. Tucked among the apartments was an old Mediterranean mansion turned into a private school.

So dark it was hard to read addresses. As Milo searched for the right number, I composed news copy in my head:

Not much is known about Almoni. He was a quiet man, residents in this comfortable neighborhood said.

Suddenly, he pulled to the curb.

Bad guess: Hermes Electric's home base was a newer, well-lit three-story structure with an unshielded brick face and glass doors leading into a bright, mirrored lobby.

A short walk, also, to Milo and Rick's West Hollywood house.

He was thinking the same thing, clenched his jaw and said, "Evening, neighbor."

Out of the car, he studied a collection of parking signs on a lamppost. Bottom line: permit parking only.

Placing an LAPD sticker on the dash, he said, "Not that it'll help. West Hollywood's county territory, the meter-leeches they contract with could give a shit."

We walked up to the glass doors. Ten mailbox slots, each with a call button.

Number 6 said I. BUDZHYSHYN. HERMES LANGUAGE SCHOOL, INC.

"Multitalented," Milo said, squinting at his Timex. "Almost midnight . . . no jurisdiction, no warrant . . . wonder if there's an in-house manager—here we go, Number 2, hope he's not a morning person."

He finger-stabbed Unit 2's button. No answer for several moments, then a thick, male voice said, "Yes?"

"Police, sir. Sorry to bother you but could you come down to the lobby, please."

"What?"

Milo repeated the greeting.

The thick voice said, "How do I know you're the police?"

"If you come down to the lobby, I'll be happy to show you identification, sir."

"If this is some kind of joke—"

"It's not, sir."

"What's this all about?"

"One of your tenants—"

"Trouble?"

"Please come down, sir."

". . . hold on."

FIVE MINUTES LATER A MAN IN HIS LATE TWENTIES came into the lobby rubbing his eyes. Young, but bald, with a light brown mustache and clipped goatee, he had on a baggy gray T-shirt, blue shorts, and house slippers. His legs were pale, coated with blond hair.

Blinking and rubbing his eyes again, he stared out at us through the glass. Milo held out his badge and the goateed man studied it, frowned, mouthed, "Show me something else."

"Great," muttered Milo, "a picky one." Smiling, he produced his LAPD business card. If the goateed man realized the department had no jurisdiction in West Hollywood, he didn't show it. Nodding sleepily, he unlocked the door and let us in.

"I don't understand why you couldn't come at a decent hour."

"Sorry, sir, but this just came up."

"What did? Who's in trouble?"

"No real trouble yet, sir, but we have some questions to ask you about Mr. Budzhyshyn."

"*Mister* Budzhyshyn?"

"Yes—"

The young man smiled. "No such animal, here."

"Unit 6—"

"Is the home of *Ms.* Budzhyshyn. Irina. And she lives alone."

"Is there a boyfriend, Mr.—"

"Laurel. Phil Laurel. Yeah, yeah, as in 'and Hardy.' Never saw a boyfriend, don't know if she dates. She's gone most of the time. Nice, quiet tenant, no problems."

"Where does she go when she's gone, Mr. Laurel?"

"Work, I assume."

"What kind of work does she do?"

"Insurance company, some type of supervisor. She makes a good living and pays her rent on time, that's all I care about. What's this all about?"

"It says language school."

"She does that on the side," said Laurel.

"Budzhyshyn," said Milo. "That Russian?"

"Yeah. She said in Russia she'd been a mathematician, taught college."

"So the school's a moonlighting thing."

Laurel looked uncomfortable. "Strictly speaking we don't allow tenants to conduct business out of their units but hers isn't any big deal, she maybe sees a couple of guys a week and she's very quiet. Very nice. Which is why I'm sure you have the wrong information—"

"Guys? All her students are men?"

Laurel touched his beard. "I guess they have been . . . oh, no." He laughed. His teeth were stained brown from nicotine. "No, not Irina, that's ridiculous."

"What is?"

"You're implying she's some kind of call girl. No, not her. We wouldn't allow that, believe me."

"You've had problems with call girls?"

"Not in this building, but others, farther east, sure . . . anyway, Irina's not like that."

"You own the building?"

"Co-own." Brief glance at the floor. "With my parents. They retired to Palm Springs and I took over to help them out." He yawned. "Can I go back to sleep now?"

"Does she also operate a company called Hermes Electric?" said Milo.

"Not that I know—what's this about?"

"Where's this insurance company she works for?"

"Somewhere on Wilshire. I'd have to go check her file."

"Could you, please?"

Laurel stifled another yawn. "It's really that important? Come on, what is it she supposedly did?"

"Her name came up in an investigation."

"About electricians? Some kind of construction fraud? I could tell you stories about construction. Everyone in construction is a sleaze, the work ethic is totally gone from American civilization."

He stopped. Milo smiled. Laurel rubbed his goatee and exhaled. "All right, hold on, I'll get the file—want to come in?"

"Thanks, sir," said Milo. "Thanks for your time."

Laurel shuffled off, slippers flapping, and came back with a yellow Post-it stuck to his thumb like a tiny flag.

"Here you go. I was wrong, it's an escrow company, Metropolitan Title. On Wilshire, like I said. On her application she put data manager. I'm not comfortable giving information to you without her permission but this you could get anywhere."

Milo took the yellow paper and I read the address. The 5500 block of Wilshire put it somewhere near La Brea.

"Thank you, sir. Now we're going to pay Ms. Budzhyshyn a visit."

"At this hour?"

"We'll be sure to keep things quiet."

Laurel blinked. "No . . . excitement or anything?"

"No, sir. Just talking."

A TINY, MIRRORED ELEVATOR TOOK US CREAKILY UP to the third floor and we stepped into a yellow hallway.

Two units per floor. Number 6 was on the left.

Milo knocked. Nothing happened for several moments and he was about to knock again when the peephole brightened. He showed his badge. "Police, Ms. Budzhyshyn."

"Yes?"

"Police."

"Yes?"

"We'd like to talk to you, ma'am."

"To me?" Husky voice, thick accent.

"Yes, ma'am. Could you please open the door?"

"Police?"

"Yes, ma'am."

"It's very late."

"I'm sorry, ma'am, but this is important."

"Yes?"

"Ma'am—"

"You wish to talk to *me*?"

"About Hermes Electric, ma'am."

The peephole shut.

The door opened.

.   .   .

SHE WAS FORTY OR SO, FIVE THREE AND STOUT AND barefoot, wearing a white Armani X sweatshirt over black sweatpants. Her brown hair was chopped short and her face was pleasant, maybe pretty ten years ago, with a small but bulbous nose shadowing full lips.

Beautiful complexion—rosy cheeks over ivory. Gray eyes, searching and alert under precisely plucked brows.

She'd opened the door just enough to accommodate her hips. Over her head was a darkened front room.

"Ms. Budzhyshyn?" said Milo.

"Yes."

"Hermes Electric?"

One-beat pause. "I am Hermes Language School," she said, pronouncing it *Hoor-meez*. She smiled. "Is there problem?"

"Well, ma'am," said Milo, "we're a little confused. Because your address also matches a company called Hermes Electric out in the Valley."

"Really?"

"Yes, ma'am."

"That is . . . a mistake."

"Is it?"

"Yes, of course."

"What about Mr. Almoni?"

She backed away from the door and narrowed the opening.

"Who?"

"Almoni. P. L. Almoni. He drives a van for Hermes Electric. Has a post-office box not far from here."

Irina Budzhyshyn said nothing. Then she shrugged. "I don't know him."

"Really." Milo leaned forward and his foot slid closer to the door.

She shrugged again.

He said, "You're Hermes and they're Hermes and their number is listed with your address."

No answer.

"Where's Almoni, ma'am?"

Irina Budzhyshyn stepped back farther, as if to close the door, and Milo took hold of it.

"If you're protecting him, you could be in deep trouble—"

"I don't know this person."

"No such guy? It's a fake name? Why does your boyfriend need one?"

Barking out the questions. The stout woman's lips blanched but she didn't answer.

"What else is phony? Your language school? The data-manager job at Metropolitan Title? What do you really do for a living, Ms. Budzhyshyn? Whether or not you tell us, we'll find out, so save yourself some trouble right now."

Irina Budzhyshyn remained impassive.

Milo forced the door wider and she sighed.

"Come in," she said. "We'll talk some more."

SHE TURNED ON A TABLE LAMP SHAPED AND COLORED like a larva. Her living room was like thousands of others: modest proportions, low ceiling, wall-to-wall brown nylon, forgettable furniture. A folding card table and three folding chairs established a dining area. Behind a white Formica counter was a pale oak kitchen.

"Please sit," she said, fluffing her short hair to no visible effect.

"That's okay," said Milo, gazing at a back doorway blocked by strings of wooden beads. Through it I saw an open bathroom door: night-light dimness, underwear over a shower door.

"How many other rooms back there?"

"One bedroom."

"Anyone there?"

Irina Budzhyshyn shook her head. "I am alone. . . . Would you like some tea?"

"No thanks." Milo took out his gun, passed through the beads, and turned left. Irina Budzhyshyn stood there, not moving, not looking at me.

A minute later he returned. "Okay. Tell us about Hermes Electric and Mr. P. L. Almoni."

This time the name made her smile. "I need to make a phone call."

"To who?"

"Someone who can answer your questions."

"Where's the phone?"

"In the kitchen."

"Anything else in there I should know about?"

"I have a gun," she said calmly. "In the drawer next to the refrigerator, but I'm not going to shoot you."

With a few quick strides, he retrieved it. Chrome-plated automatic.

"Loaded and ready."

"I'm a woman living alone."

"Any other arms?"

"No."

"And no P. L. Almoni lurking in some attic?"

She laughed.

"What's funny?"

"There's no such person."

"If you don't know him, how can you be sure?"

"Let me make the call and you'll understand."

"Who're you going to call?"

"I can't tell you until after I make the call. You're not a county sheriff so I don't even have to cooperate with you."

Statement of fact, no defiance.

"But you're cooperating anyway."

"Yes. It's . . . practical. I'm going to call now. You may watch me."

They went into the kitchen and he stayed right next to her, towering over her, as she punched numbers. She said something in a foreign language, listened, said something else, then handed the receiver to him.

As he pressed it to his ear, his jaws bunched.

"What? When?" He was growling now. "I don't . . . okay, all right. Where?"

He hung up.

Irina Budzhyshyn left the kitchen and sat on a couch, looking content.

Milo turned to me. He was flushed and his shirt looked tight. "That was Deputy Consul Carmeli. We're to meet him at his office in fifteen minutes. Sharp. Maybe this time we'll actually get past the goddamn hall."

24

the consulate building. By the time we were out of the car, someone was standing in front of the unlit lobby door.

He studied us, then came forward into the streetlight. Young
man in a sportcoat and slacks. Big shoulders, big hands, one of
them carrying a walkie-talkie. His hair was dark and very short,
just like that of the guard behind the consulate reception window.
It could have even been the same man.

"I'll take you up," he said in a flat voice.

Striding ahead of us, he unlocked the door and walked across
the echoing lobby. The three of us rode up to the seventeenth floor.
He looked bored.

The door opened on Zev Carmeli standing in the corridor. He
said, *"B'seder,"* and the young man remained in the elevator and
rode down.

Carmeli was wearing a dark suit and white shirt, no tie, and he
reeked of tobacco. His hair had been watered and combed but
several cowlicks sprouted.

"This way." He did an abrupt about-face and led us to the white
door of the same conference room. This time we walked through
and out the back into the cubicles of the work area. Office machines, a water cooler, corkboard full of memos, the travel posters
I'd seen through the reception window. The fluorescent panels in
the ceiling were off and light came from a single corner pole lamp.
Nothing to distinguish the place from any other site of repetitive-
motion injury.

Carmeli kept going, hunched, arms swinging loosely, til he

reached a door with his name on it. Twisting the knob, he stood aside and let us enter.

Like Irina Budzhyshyn's apartment, his office was characterless, with blue drapes over what I assumed were windows, a wall of half-empty board-and-bracket shelves, a wooden desk with steel legs, gray sofa and love seat.

A man sat on the love seat and when we came in he stood, keeping his left hand in the pocket of his blue jeans.

Late thirties to forty, five seven, around 140, he wore a black nylon windbreaker, pale blue shirt, black athletic shoes. His tightly kinked hair was black tipped with gray and trimmed to a short Afro. His face was lean, very smooth, café-au-lait skin stretched tightly over finely molded features. A strong nose was anchored by flared nostrils and his lips were wide, full and bowed. Very light brown eyes—golden, really—and shaded by long, curved lashes. Arched eyebrows gave them the look of permanent surprise but the rest of his face contradicted that: static, unreadable.

Probably Middle-Eastern, but he could have been Latin or American Indian or a light-skinned black man.

Familiar for some reason . . . had I seen him before?

He met my stare and volleyed it back. No hostility, just the opposite. Pleasant, almost friendly.

Then I realized his expression hadn't changed. Like a Rorschach card, his neutrality had led me to interpret.

Milo was looking at him, too, but his attention shifted to Carmeli as the consul passed behind the desk and sat down.

His big hands were clenched and I saw him open them. Forcing the appearance of relaxation. During the ride over from Holloway Drive, he'd been silent, driving much too fast.

He sat down on the sofa without being invited and I did the same.

The dark man with the golden eyes was still looking at us. Or past us.

Still pleasantly blank.

Suddenly I knew I *had* seen him. And where.

Driving away from Latvinia Shaver's murder scene. Driving some kind of compact car—a gray Toyota—just as the film crews arrived. Wearing a uniform like that of Montez, the custodian.

Another image clicked in.

A dark-skinned uniformed man had also been at the nature conservancy the day Milo took me to view Irit's murder scene.

Park-worker's uniform. Driving some sort of mowing machine,
leaf bags stacked on the grass.

A pith helmet had hidden his face.

Following us? No, in both cases he'd gotten there before.

Anticipating us?

One step ahead because he had access to police information?

Listening in, somehow.

Milo'd said Carmeli's attitude had seemed to change suddenly.
More cooperative.

Because he'd kept tabs, knew Milo was serious, working hard?

I nodded at the dark man, expecting no response, but he nodded
back. Milo's big face was still full of curiosity and anger.

Zev Carmeli pulled out a cigarette and lit up. Not offering one
to the dark man. Knowing the dark man didn't smoke. Knowing
the dark man's habits.

The dark man remained still, left hand in pocket.

Carmeli puffed several times, cleared his throat, and sat up
straight.

"Gentlemen, this is Superintendent Daniel Sharavi from the Israeli National Police, Southern District."

"Southern District," said Milo, very softly. "What does that
mean?"

"Jerusalem and the surrounding areas," said Carmeli.

"So on your map that includes Southern California, too."

Sharavi leaned back in the love seat. The windbreaker was unzipped and the flaps parted, revealing a thin, flat torso. No shoulder holster, no visible weapon, and the bulge in his pocket was too
small to be anything other than five fingers.

Carmeli said, "Several years ago, Superintendent Sharavi
headed a major investigation into a series of Jerusalem sex killings
called the Butcher murders."

"Several years ago," said Milo. "Must have missed that one."

"Serial murders are almost nonexistent in Israel, Mr. Sturgis.
The Butcher was the first in our history. We're a small country, the
impact was huge. Superintendent Sharavi solved the killings.
There've been none like them since."

"Congratulations," said Milo, turning to Sharavi. "Must be nice
to have spare time."

Sharavi didn't move.

Carmeli said, "Superintendent Sharavi is also familiar with Los Angeles because he was part of the security contingent that accompanied our athletes to the L.A. Olympics. We would like you to work with him on the current murders."

"Murders," said Milo, still facing Sharavi. "Plural, not just your daughter's. Sounds like you've kept abreast."

Carmeli smoked and sanded his desk with the palm of his hand. "We are aware of . . . developments."

"I'll bet you are," said Milo. "So where're the bugs? Dashboard of my car? My office phone? Heel of my shoe? All of the above?"

No reply.

"Probably in my house, too," I said. "The night the burglar alarm went off. By listening in there, they'd have access to lots of information. But the superintendent's been with us well before then."

I faced Sharavi. "I've seen you twice. At Booker T. Washington Elementary School the day Latvinia Shaver's body was found. And at the nature conservancy the day Milo and I looked over the crime scene. You were driving a mower. Both times you wore a uniform."

Sharavi's expression didn't change and he didn't answer.

Milo said, "Isn't that interesting." Striving for calm, too. The air felt ready to implode.

Carmeli smoked hard and fast, stopping only to look at the cigarette, as if the act required concentration.

"Well," said Milo. "It's sure good to meet a genuine expert. A real back-alley sleuth."

Sharavi removed his hand from his pocket and placed it in his lap. The upper surface was glossy with grayish-brown scar tissue and deeply caved, as if a chunk of flesh and bone had been scooped out. The thumb was atrophied and curled unnaturally and I'd overestimated the number of fingers: The thumb was intact but all that remained of the index was a one-knuckle stump and the remaining three were wasted, too, not much more than bare bone with a pallid brown sheath.

He said, "I began looking into the case just before you came on, Detective Sturgis." His voice was youthful, barely accented. "I hope we can put that aside and work together."

"Sure," said Milo. "One big happy family, I trust you, already."

Crossing and uncrossing his long legs, he shook his head. "So, how many felonies have you racked up so far, playing James Bond?"

"Superintendent Sharavi is operating under full diplomatic immunity," said Carmeli. "He's protected from threats and prosecution—"

"Ah," said Milo.

"So it's arranged, Mr. Sturgis?"

"Arranged?"

"A working agreement to share and collaborate."

"Share," said Milo, laughing. "Christ. Show me yours, I show you mine? And if I say no?"

Carmeli didn't answer.

Sharavi pretended to study his ruined hand.

"Let me guess," said Milo. "You put a call in to the mayor's office and I'm off the case, replaced with some lackey willing to *share*."

Carmeli took a deep drag. "My daughter was murdered. I was hoping for a more mature attitude on your part."

Milo stood. "Let me save you the trouble. Get yourself a mature guy and I'll go back to dealing with ordinary homicides with ordinary obstructions. No big loss to you—since you've been following closely, you know we haven't made much progress. Bye—*shalom*."

He started out and I followed.

Carmeli said, "I'd prefer that you remain on the case, Detective Sturgis."

Milo stopped. "I'm sorry, sir. It just won't work out."

We left the office and were back at the door into the conference room when Carmeli caught up with us. Milo turned the knob. It wouldn't budge.

"There's a master lock for the entire suite," said Carmeli.

"Kidnapping, too? I thought you guys *rescued* hostages."

"I'm serious, Detective Sturgis. I want you on my daughter's case. You were assigned to it in the first place because I asked for you, personally."

Milo's hand dropped from the knob.

"I asked for you," Carmeli repeated, "because things had bogged down. Gorobich and Ramos were nice men, they seemed competent enough for routine cases. But I knew this wasn't routine and it soon became clear that they didn't measure up. Nevertheless, I gave them time. Because contrary to what you believe, it was never my intention to obstruct. All I want is to find the garbage who murdered my daughter. Do you understand that? Do you?"

He'd moved closer to Milo, closing the space between them the way—exactly what I'd seen Milo do with suspects.

"That's all I care about, Mr. Sturgis. Results. Do you understand? Nothing else. Gorobich and Ramos produced none so they—"

"What makes you think—"

"—were removed and you were brought in. I conducted some research. The performance of Robbery-Homicide detectives at the West L.A. station. I wanted to know which detectives avoided the quick and easy and had a record of tackling atypical cases. Of those, which detective had the highest solve rate for the past ten years. Things the department doesn't want made public, the data was hard to obtain, but I managed. And guess what, Mr. Sturgis? *Your* name kept coming up. *Your* solve rate is eighteen percent higher than your nearest competitor's, though your popularity rating is considerably lower than his. Which is also fine, I'm not running a social club. In fact—"

"I've never seen statistics like that—"

"I'm sure you haven't." Carmeli pulled out another cigarette and waved it like a conductor's baton. "Officially, they don't exist. So congratulations. You're the winner. Not that it will help your career advancement . . . you were also described as someone lacking in polish and good manners, someone who doesn't give a damn about what people think of him. Someone who can be a bully."

Puff, puff. "There are also people in the department who believe you harbor violent tendencies. I know about the incident in which you broke a superior's jaw. My reading of that was that you were morally justified but that nonetheless it was a stupid, impulsive act. It bothered me, but the fact that you haven't done anything like that in over four years encourages me."

He came even closer, looking Milo straight in the eye. "The fact that you are *gay* encourages me, as well, because it's clear that no matter how liberal a line the police department takes in public, no matter how high the caliber of your work remains, you'll always be an outcast."

Another long drag. "This is as high as you'll go, Mr. Sturgis.

Which, for my needs, is perfect. Someone aiming for the top—someone cautious, a *careerist*—is exactly what I *don't* want. Some ambition-blinded *monkey* scampering up the administrative ladder, looking over his shoulder every other second, keeping his buttocks shielded."

He blinked. "My daughter was *taken* from me. Bureaucracy is the last thing I need. Do you understand? Do you?"

"If you're after results, why make it so difficult for me to get info—"

"No, no, no," said Carmeli, smoking and blinking through the haze. "In terms of reading my motivations, you're not as astute as you think you are. I haven't hidden *anything* important from you. I'd strip naked and parade down Wilshire Boulevard if it would bring the garbage who murdered my Iriti to justice. Do you understand that?"

"I—"

"Life has its ups and downs, no one knows that better than Israelis. But losing a young child is an *unnatural* occurrence and losing one *violently* is an *abomination*. One can never be prepared for it and one finds oneself unable to help those who—" He shook his head violently. "I don't want a *team* player, Milo."

Using the first name as if used to it. "On the contrary. Come to me and inform me that you've found him, that you've shot him or cut his throat, and I'll be a far happier man, Milo. Not *happy,* not jocular or sunny or optimistic. I've never been that sort, even as a child I had a pessimistic worldview. That's why I smoke sixty cigarettes a day. That's why I work for a government. But happi*er*. Partial healing of the wound. Staunching the *pus*."

He touched Milo's lapel and Milo allowed it.

"You saw my wife. Being married to me, holding things in—has always been difficult for her. Now she finds herself unwilling to live a shadow life, to put up with even the most trivial impositions. She works and comes home and won't leave, won't accompany me to functions. Even though I know she can't be blamed, I get angry. We fight. My work helps me escape but hers forces her to look at other people's children, day after day. I've told her to quit but she won't. Won't stop punishing herself."

He rocked on his heels.

"It took thirty-three hours to give birth to Irit. There were complications, she always felt guilty because of Irit's disabilities, even though a fever caused them, months later. Now, her feelings are—when I go home I don't know what to expect. Do you think I want a *team* player, Milo?"

He let go of the lapel. Milo's face was white as moonlight, the skin around his mouth so tight the acne pits had compressed to hash marks.

"The stress," said Carmeli, "has already taken its toll. Some things can't be fixed. But my—I want to *know*. I want resolution—"

"So you want to use me as an executioner—"

"No. God forbid. Stop reading between lines that bear no interpretation. What I want is simple: knowledge. Justice. And now, you'll admit, it's not just for me and my family, is it? That girl on the schoolyard, possibly the poor little boy in East L.A. Why should this . . . monster kill more children?"

"Final justice?" said Milo. "I find him, your boys finish him off?"

Carmeli stepped back, stubbed out the cigarette, and fumbled in his jacket for yet another one. "I'll grant you your moment of outrage. No one likes being watched, least of all a detective. But put your ego aside and stop being obstinate."

He lit up. "We bent some rules to obtain information—fine, now we've confessed. I'm a diplomat, not a terrorist. I've seen what terrorists do and I respect the rule of law. Catch this piece of garbage and bring him to the bar of justice."

"And if I can't?"

"Then your solve rate drops and I seek other solutions."

As Milo regarded him, Carmeli took in lungfuls of smoke and tapped his foot. His eyes had turned wild and, as if realizing it, he closed them.

When they opened, they were dead, and the look on his face chilled me.

"If you refuse me, Milo, I will not make vengeful phone calls to the mayor or anyone else. Because vengeance is personal and you hold no interest for me personally, only as a means to an end. *You* might do well to adopt the same attitude. Think of me as a bureaucratic idiot, curse me every morning for listening in on your conversations. I'll live with your curses. But does your opinion of me mean Irit's murder doesn't deserve your best efforts?"

"That's the point, Mr. Carmeli. You've been *hampering* my best efforts."

"No, I reject that. I reject that absolutely, and if you analyze the situation honestly, you will, too. If the Ortiz boy's shoes were left with the police to get attention, would giving the garbage more attention solve the problem? Be honest."

Looking for an ashtray, he found one in a nearby cubicle, picked it up, flicked.

I thought of the kitchen conversation he'd heard. My theories, Milo's procedures.

Now he was face-to-face with Milo again, inches away, holding his cigarette next to his trouser leg.

Milo said, "Listen, I'm not gonna stand here and make a big deal out of this, because you've been through it, you've got serious rights, here. But I'm also not gonna let you control the investigation because of your outrage or who you happen to be. You're out of your element. You don't know what the hell you're doing."

"Granted."

"The point is, Mr. Carmeli, my job is a lot more perspiration than inspiration and if I do solve a few more cases than someone else it's probably because I try not to get distracted. And you've been distracting me. Right from the beginning, you've been trying to call the shots. And now all this espionage shit. I just spent hours of investigative time chasing down your boy in there, instead of looking for Irit's killer. Now, you order me to adopt him and just—"

"Not an order, a request. And one that could help you. He's a very able detective—"

"I'm sure he is," said Milo. "But one case, in a country where violent crime is rare, has nothing to do with what we're dealing with. And now I've got to take time off from the investigation to figure out where he stuck his goddamn bugs—"

"Not necessary," said a quiet, boyish voice. I hadn't heard Sharavi come out of the office but he was there, hand in pocket again. "I'll tell you exactly where they are."

"Great," said Milo, wheeling on him. "Very comforting." He gave a disgusted look.

Carmeli said, "We meant no harm, Milo. The intention was always to be open, eventually—"

"How eventually?"

"The surveillance was nothing personal. And if you must blame someone, blame me. Superintendent Sharavi happened to be in the

States on other business and I had him brought to L.A. because Gorobich and Ramos were getting nowhere. They talked to me, those two, but they never *told* me anything. I'm sure you know what I mean."

Milo didn't answer.

Carmeli said, "I needed a starting point. Some basic information. In my position, can you honestly say you would have done any differently? The idea, all along, was that if Superintendent Sharavi came up with something, you'd be the first to—"

"Eventually? What if Dr. Delaware hadn't noticed that van in the alley? Would we have ever been told *anything*?" He faced Sharavi. "Screwed up, didn't you, James Bond?"

Sharavi said, "Yes," with an utter lack of defensiveness.

Milo shook his head. "License-plate switches, mail drop, and a phony language teacher to hide your trail? What's Irina, a full-fledged secret agent or just some free-lance? And who the hell is P. L. Almoni?"

Carmeli smiled and hid it behind his smoking hand.

"My mistake," said Sharavi. "I didn't appreciate Dr. Delaware's powers of observation."

"Underestimating Dr. Delaware is no way to win at blackjack," said Milo. "He's a detail guy, attuned to all the nuances."

"Obviously," said Sharavi. "He was the one who urged pursuing the DVLL angle."

"Our first real break," said Carmeli, waving his cigarette. "Finally. We've plugged it into all *our* databases. Here, back in Israel, Asia, Europe. We have resources you don't. If we pool—this is no time to let egos get in—"

"Learn anything from your databases?" Milo asked him.

"Not yet, but the point is, the wider the net—"

"Sometimes the wider the net, the bigger the tangles, Mr. Carmeli." He turned to Sharavi. "So tell me, Superintendent, is *this* conversation being taped, too?"

Sharavi's eyebrows arched higher. He glanced at Carmeli.

Carmeli said, "No, we've disconnected the recorders in the suite. However, you were recorded the first time we met."

Milo allowed himself a tiny smile. Gut instincts confirmed.

"From now on," Carmeli continued, "you have my word that no further surveillance will be conducted without your—"

"Assuming there is a 'from now on,'" said Milo.

"Are you *that* egotistical?" said Carmeli. He turned to me. "When I address Milo, I'm including you, Doctor. In light of the DVLL angle and two other related murders, we're clearly faced with a psychopathologic killer, so psychological input is called for. I'm not trying to get between you and Milo, but whatever he decides, the Israeli consulate is willing to reimburse you for your time at a very generous rate. The consulate is also willing to extend itself to you considerably. Because we know the deck is stacked against success and anything we can do to—"

"Anything?" said Milo. "You're saying the investigation gets the full clout of your office?"

"One hundred percent. It always has."

"Full clout is yours to grant? Being only a social director? License to cater?"

Carmeli was thrown off. "Whatever is in my power I'll—"

Carmeli's eyes shifted over to Sharavi. The dark man said nothing.

"I'm an arranger," Carmeli said. "I arrange all sorts of things."

25

holding on to the stare as if it were precious.

Carmeli moved away first. "I've said what I have to say." He walked quickly back to his office and closed the door.

Milo said, "How do we get out of here?" to Sharavi.

Sharavi reached behind the water cooler and something clicked. As Milo started for the door, Sharavi said, "In line with my promise to tell you everything, here's something important: Someone wrote DVLL in ballpoint pen in Raymond Ortiz's right shoe. Small letters, but discernible under the blood."

Milo's hands clenched again and a dragon grin stretched his mouth unnaturally. "You have them."

"No, they're in the Newton Division evidence room. Some of the blood has flaked away over time and it appears to have been applied thinly—probably with a brush, there seem to be strokes. But once you know what to look for, the letters are clear."

"A brush," said Milo.

"Painting with a child's blood," said Sharavi, looking at me. "Maybe he sees himself as an artist."

Milo cursed silently.

"One thing that interests me," said Sharavi, "is the fact that the writing was done first and then the blood was added. So even back then, when, as Dr. Delaware has pointed out, he was still impulsive, those letters—leaving a message—meant something to him and he planned carefully. He's always had a definite agenda."

"What else interests you?" said Milo.

"Just the elements that you're aware of. The variability in methods and body positioning, the geographic scatter, two girls, one boy. The lack of pattern to throw us off, but despite that, a pattern, as Dr. Delaware has suggested. Retardation's obviously an issue, so maybe DVLL has something to do with that, or handicaps in general—D for defective. Defective devils, something like that."

He took out his bad hand and looked at it. "Until the match between Irit and the Shaver girl came up, I was skeptical about Dr. Delaware's theory of linkage. Even now, there's a disconnected feeling to these killings."

"Disconnected, how?" I said.

"I don't know." The smooth face tightened and lines showed around the eyes. "Not that my opinion means much. I *have* only dealt with one serial killer. In Israel that makes me an expert. Here . . ." He shrugged.

"How'd you get the shoe?" said Milo.

"I didn't get it, I got *to* it. Please don't ask more."

"Why not?"

"Because I can't tell you."

"Open communication, huh?"

"From now on. The shoes are in the past. With three killings on your hands, maybe more, why bother?"

"More?"

"At this level of subtlety," said Sharavi, "there could be DVLL messages never detected. Don't you think?"

Milo didn't answer.

"I understand your not trusting me," said the dark man. "In your position I'd feel the same way—"

"Cool it with the empathy, Superintendent. That's Dr. Delaware's territory."

Sharavi sighed. "All right. Would you like me to remove the bugs tonight or tomorrow?"

"Where are they?"

"All in Dr. Delaware's home."

"Where else?"

"Just there."

"Why should I believe you?"

"No reason," said Sharavi, "except I have no interest in lying to you. Check for yourself. I'll provide debugging equipment."

Milo waved him off. "How many bugs are there in Dr. Delaware's home?"

"Four. In the phone receiver, under the living room couch, under the dining table, and the kitchen table."

"That's it?"

"Hook me up to a polygraph if it'll make you feel better."

"Polygraphs can be fooled."

"Sure," said Sharavi, "by psychopaths with abnormally low levels of arousal. I'm not a psychopath. I sweat."

"Do you?"

"All the time. Now, shall I disconnect the bugs or do you want to do it yourself? Nothing complicated. Four little black discs that pop right off."

"Where's the feed?"

"A phone at my place."

"What else do you have there?"

"A police scanner, various equip—"

"A scanner with tactical lines?"

Sharavi nodded.

"What else?"

"The usual. A fax machine, computers."

"You're hooked into all the police data banks," I said. "DMV, NCIC."

"Yes."

"State offender files, too?"

"Yes." He turned to Milo. "I'm aware of all the work you've done looking into alibis—"

"Who else are you working with besides Ms. English-as-a-Second-Language?"

"I'm working completely alone. Irina is employed by the consulate."

"Big shot's daughter gets killed and they send just one guy?"

"I'm all they have," said Sharavi. "For this kind of thing."

"Just how big is Carmeli?"

"He's considered . . . very talented."

"What kind of case was this Butcher?"

"Sexual psychopath, organized, a careful planner. He murdered Arab women—runaways and prostitutes at first, then he progressed to less-marginal victims—a woman who'd just left her husband and was socially vulnerable. He gained their trust, anesthetized them, then dissected them and dumped their bodies in hilly areas around Jerusalem, sometimes accompanied by pages from the Bible."

"Another case with messages," I said. "What was his?"

"We never had a chance to interview him but we suspect he had some kind of racist agenda, possibly trying to cause a race war between Arabs and Jews. The FBI was informed fully. If you'd like, I'll get you copies of the VICAP case file."

"You never had a chance to interview him," said Milo. "Meaning he's dead."

"Yes."

"How?"

"I killed him." The golden eyes blinked. "Self-defense."

Milo looked down at the damaged hand.

Sharavi raised his arm and the limp flesh bobbed. "He doesn't get all the credit for this. I was partially disabled in the Six-Day War. He destroyed what function was left. I would have preferred capturing him alive in order to learn from him. But . . ." Another blink. "After it was over, I read all I could about people like him. There wasn't much, the FBI was just getting the VICAP program started. Now, they offer profiles but Dr. Delaware's point about profiles relying upon the past is well-taken. What's to stop some clever boy from doing his reading, too, and using it against us?"

"Us?" said Milo.

"Policemen. There is a certain . . . contrived feeling to these killings, don't you think?"

"Self-defense," said Milo. "So now you've been brought over to 'defend' yourself against our guy."

"No," said Sharavi. "I'm not a hired assassin. I'm here to investigate Irit Carmeli's death because Consul Carmeli thought I could be of use."

"And Consul Carmeli gets what he wants."

"Sometimes."

"He said you were in the States. Where?"

"New York."

"Doing what?"

"Security work at the embassy."

"Self-defense work?"

"Security work."

"You speak excellent English," I said.

"My wife is American."

"Is she here with you?" said Milo.

Sharavi gave a low, soft laugh. "No."

"Where's she from?"

"L.A."

"Lots of L.A. connections," said Milo.

"Another point in my favor. Shall I disconnect the bugs?"

"Ever been tapped yourself?"

"Probably."

"You don't mind?"

"No one likes the loss of privacy," said Sharavi.

"You guys are big on that, aren't you? Gadgetry, top security, high tech. But all the Mossad crap didn't help your prime minister, did it?"

"No," said Sharavi. "It didn't."

"That was an interesting one," said Milo. "I'm no conspiracy buff, but it made me wonder: The guy shoots Rabin in the back, from two feet away. Next day there's video footage on TV showing him heckling Rabin at a bunch of rallies, frothing at the mouth, having to be carried away. And within hours of the assassination all his confederates are rounded up. So he was well known to the authorities, but the security guards let him get right next to the target."

"Interesting, isn't it?" said Sharavi. "What's your theory?"

"Someone didn't like the boss."

"There are people who agree with you. Another theory is that even experienced security people couldn't imagine a Jewish assassin. Yet another is that the original plan was to use blanks, make a public statement, and the assassin changed his mind at the last minute. In any case, it's a national disgrace. And it's caused me additional pain because the assassin was of Yemenite descent and so am I—shall I disconnect now or later? Or would you care to do it yourself?"

"Later," said Milo. "I think I'd rather look at your place, first."

Sharavi was surprised. "Why?"

"See how the high-tech half lives."

"Will we be working together?"

"Do I have a choice?"

"There are always choices," said the dark man.

"Then my choice right now is to see your setup. If you can't even give on that, I'll know what I'm dealing with."

Sharavi touched his lip with his good hand and gazed up at Milo. The surprised eyes looked innocent.

"Sure," he said. "Why not?"

HE GAVE US AN ADDRESS ON THE 1500 BLOCK OF LI-vonia Street and told us to see ourselves out and meet him. Then he slipped behind a partition and disappeared.

WE DROVE SOUTH ON LA CIENEGA, PASSING ONE DARK restaurant after another, heading for Olympic. Milo said, "He uses that hand as a prop."

"Handicapped detective on a case full of handicapped victims. It could give the case another dimension for him."

"Despite what he says, think he's really here to clean up the mess?"

"I don't know."

"Just between you and me and the dashboard, Alex, that doesn't sound half-bad. We catch the bastard, the Israelis finish him off, no publicity, no media bullshit, no goddamn lawyers, and the Carmelis and God-knows-how-many other parents get some closure."

He laughed. "Some public servant I am. The rule of law. But someone who'd do that to retarded kids . . ." He cursed. "Painting with blood. DVLL in the shoes. So Raymond's a match, too. What bugs me is that it's only luck that led us to the message. And your hawkeye."

He laughed and it jarred me.

"What?"

"You ever come across this Butcher in your readings?"

"No."

"Bringing in a one-case homeboy." He ran his hand over his face and looked at the dashboard clock. "Jesus, it's after two already. Robin gonna be worried?"

"Hopefully she's sleeping. When I left for the meeting with the other cops I told her I'd be late."

"Why?"

"I was hoping for progress."

"Well, we got some, all right."

"Are you going to stay on the case if it means working with Sharavi?"

"Why should I give it up just because Carmeli's a control freak—oh hell, forget my righteous indignation. The guy lost his daughter, he's flexing whatever muscle he's got. Would I do differently if I had the clout? Not on your life. And it's bigger than just Irit, now."

"Another thing," I said, "by working with Sharavi, you can coopt him. Those resources Carmeli talked about."

"Yeah. All sorts of surveillance toys. But first we need someone to surveil."

We were south on Robertson now. At Cashio, he turned right and laughed again. "Besides, who better than me to work this puzzler, right? I do have the top solve rate in West L.A."

"Eighteen percent higher than the competition," I said. "Hoo-hah."

"My mommy always told me I'd be tops."

"Mom knows best."

"Actually," he said, "what she said was, 'Milo, honey, how come you stay in your room all day and don't go out anymore? And what ever happened to that nice girl you used to date?' "

Livonia was the first block west of Robertson. The 1500 block meant a left turn. He cruised slowly.

"Only a mile or so from the Carmelis' house," I said.

"Maybe the boss drops in for briefings?"

"He probably does. That's why Carmeli's attitude changed. Sharavi told him you knew what you were doing. Or played him the surveillance tapes."

"Endorsement from Big Brother," he said. "Wonder if the neighbors know they're living with James Freaking Bond."

THE NEIGHBORS LIVED IN SMALL, SEVENTY-YEAR-OLD Spanish houses. Nearly obscured by a twisted hedge of Hollywood juniper, Sharavi's pink bungalow sat behind a tiny lawn shaved to the dirt. In the driveway was the gray Toyota I'd seen at the schoolyard.

A porch light yellowed the wooden front door. A small olive-wood mezuzah was nailed to the sidepost. Before we could ring, Sharavi opened the door and let us in.

He'd removed his windbreaker and was wearing the pale blue shirt and jeans. The shirt was short-sleeved and his forearms were hairless, thin but muscled, laced with veins. A wedding band circled the ring finger of the good hand.

There was an alarm panel just inside. The living room and dining room were completely empty: clean, golden hardwood under white ceilings; an unscreened, spotless brick fireplace; pleated blackout drapes over every window.

He waved us through a short, narrow center hall, past a kitchen with gray cabinets, to the rear of the house.

"Something to drink?" he said, passing a small bathroom. The lights were on. Every room was lit—showing us there was nothing to hide?

Milo said, "Let's see your gizmos."

Sharavi surged past a bedroom. Queen-sized bed, topsheet with a military tuck, nightstand with nothing on it but a cheap lamp.

Our destination was the second bedroom at the end of the hall.

Metal-sheet shutters on these windows. A steel-legged desk identical to Zev Carmeli's was against the far wall and a black vinyl chair was wheeled up to it. On the desk were a police scanner, CB and shortwave radios, iron-gray laptop computer, laser printer, battery backup, fax machine, and a paper shredder with an empty catch basket. Empty trash basket on the wooden floor. Stacked neatly between olive-wood bookends was a collection of hardware and software manuals and boxes of backup tapes and CD-ROMs.

Next to the computer were two white phones, three reams of paper, and a pair of maroon velvet bags, each with gold-embroidered Stars of David. On top of the smaller bag was a crocheted skullcap—dark blue with red roses along the border.

Sharavi saw me looking at the bags.

"Prayer equipment," he said. "Shawl and phylacteries and prayer book. I need all the help I can get."

"What do you pray for?" said Milo.

"It depends," said Sharavi.

"Upon what you want?"

"Upon how worthy I feel." Sharavi unzipped the larger bag, drew out a folded square of white woolen cloth with black stripes.

"See, nothing dangerous."

"Having God on your side can be dangerous," said Milo. "Or thinking you do."

Sharavi's arched eyebrows rose higher. "Because I'm religious, I'm a dangerous fanatic?"

"No, I'm just saying—"

"I understand your resentment, we had a bad beginning. But why waste any more time on it? You want to solve these cases and so do I. In addition to the professional incentive, I want to return to Jerusalem, to my wife and children."

Milo didn't answer.

"How many children do you have?" I said.

"Three." Sharavi returned the shawl to the bag. "I surveilled you because it was the only way to get information. Rude? Definitely. Unethical? I could debate that, but I'll say yes. But all in all, no big crime. Because an innocent child was murdered—three children, now. At the least. I'll live with my sins. And I suspect you would, too."

"Know me, do you?"

Sharavi smiled. "Well, I have had a chance to learn about you."

Milo said, "Hah. Do they have stand-up comedy in Jerusalem?"

"In Israel," said Sharavi, "everyone's a prophet. It's the same thing."

He touched the prayer bag. "You're effective, Detective Sturgis, and effective people focus on what's important. That's not an attempt to kiss your rear, just fact. I'm going to get some coffee. Are you sure you don't want any?"

"Positive."

He left us alone in the room.

I looked at the computer manuals and Milo unzipped the second velvet bag. Black leather straps and boxes.

"Phylacteries," I said. "Inside are biblical—"

"I know what they are," he said. "Had a robbery case last year, punks broke into a synagogue not far from here. Vandalized, stole money from charity boxes, ripped Torah scrolls and these things, too. I remember the scene, wondering what all those belts were doing there. The old guy who took care of the place—the sexton—explained it to me. Then he broke down and cried. Said it reminded him of pogroms he'd seen as a kid in Europe."

"Catch them?"

"No. There's also a guy—cop named Decker—in the West Valley who's a religious Jew, actually uses them, himself. I know because someone saw him at a police retreat, getting up early to pray, all wrapped up. His wife got him into religion or something like that. They call him the Rabbi. I helped him on a case couple of years ago—Israeli connections, as a matter of fact. Maybe I should give him a call, see if he knows Carmeli, or this joker."

"Another murder case?" I said.

"Missing family case that turned into murder. I churned some paper for him, no big deal. He was decent, but I don't trust him."

"Why not?"

"He got promoted to lieutenant."

I laughed.

He opened the closet. No clothes on the rod. On the shelf above it were several small, crisp-looking brown cardboard boxes and three oblong black canvas cases.

He hefted the first case, opened it, and slid out something black and metallic.

"Uzi barrel, the rest is in here." Sticking his hand into the case, he drew out submachine-gun components, inspected them, put them back. The other two cases contained a rifle with a telescopic sight and a double-barreled shotgun, both polished to a gleam.

The crisp cardboard boxes—ten of them—held ammunition.

"Ready for the battle," said Milo. "He left us here to show us he's got nothing to hide, but that's bullshit, he's got to have handguns and other stuff he's not showing us."

Sharavi came back with a mug in his good hand.

"Where's the nine-millimeter?" said Milo. "And whatever other small stuff you're hiding."

"I'm not hiding anything," said Sharavi. "Everything in its proper place."

"Where?"

"Where would you keep your small arms? In the kitchen and the bedroom. Go see for yourself."

"That's okay." Milo sauntered to the closet. "Looks like you're ready for the big PLO assault. Sure you're not thinking of doing some hunting?"

"No," said Sharavi. "I don't hunt." He smiled. "Though I've been known to fish."

"What else is in your arsenal?"

"Meaning my grenades, rocket launcher, and nuclear bomb?"

"No, your heavy stuff."

"Sorry to disappoint you," said Sharavi. "This is it." He sipped, lowered the cup. "Except for this."

Removing a black disc the size of an M & M from his pocket, he handed it to Milo, who turned it over.

"This is what I attached to your couch and tables, Dr. Delaware."

"Never seen one this small," said Milo. "Cute. Japanese?"

"Israeli. The ones I installed at Dr. Delaware's are channeled to the phone on the left. The other phone's a conventional line and also connects to the fax. I taped your conversations, transcribed them, destroyed the tapes, gave the transcripts to Carmeli."

"Covering your trail?"

"Obviously not well enough." Sharavi shook his head. "Using the van twice in one day was stupid. Must be jet lag."

"How long have you been here?"

"In L.A., five days. A month in New York."

"Security work."

"They called me over because of the Trade Center bombing verdicts. We knew there'd be a conviction, expected some sort of reprisals. I ended up watching some people in Brooklyn. People I knew from the West Bank."

"They do anything?"

"Not yet. I educated our New York staff, was about to fly home, when Zev's call came."

"Do you know him from Israel?" I said.

"I know his older brother. He's in the police. Deputy commander. The family's prominent."

"Superintendent," said Milo. "What's the equivalent, here?"

"Probably a captain, but there's no real equivalent. It's a small pond, we're all minnows."

"How humble."

"No," said Sharavi. "Religious. It accomplishes the same thing."

"So Carmeli calls you and you can't go back—how old are your kids?"

"My daughter's eighteen, just started the Army. I have two younger sons." The golden eyes squeezed shut for a moment.

"Family man," said Milo.

"Whatever that means."

"Maybe that gives you insights I don't have."

"Because you're gay? You don't believe that and neither do I. Policemen are like anyone else: a few genuine idiots at the bottom, equally few high achievers, the mediocre majority."

"You a high achiever?"

"That's not for me to say."

"Any more ideas about this case?"

"My instincts tell me the defective angle should be looked into, as well as the racial angle because all three victims were non-Anglo. But maybe that's because my case had racial aspects. I need to make sure my limited experience doesn't narrow my perspective."

"Maybe it's your destiny to deal with racist killers," said Milo. "Your karma, or whatever equivalent you've got in your religion."

"*Mazal*," said Sharavi. "Have you heard the expression *mazal tov*?"

"This ain't Kansas, Superintendent."

Sharavi smiled. "How about Daniel?"

"Okay. I know what mazal tov is, Daniel. Good luck."

"Yes, but mazal's not really luck," said Sharavi. "It's fate—like karma. Rooted in astrology. A zodiac sign is a mazal. Yemenite Jews have a strong astrological tradition. Not that I believe in any of that. To me it boils down to hard work and what God wants you to do."

"God wants you on the case?"

Sharavi shrugged. "I'm here."

"Must be nice to have faith," said Milo.

Sharavi wheeled the chair away from the desk, raised his arm, and let the bad hand flop on the headrest. "One way or the other I have to work the Carmeli case, Milo. Will you let me do it with you rather than at cross-purposes?"

"Hey," said Milo, "far be it from me to argue with God."

26

MILO AND I STAYED AT SHARAVI'S HOUSE UNTIL AF-
ter three, wearily establishing a division of labor:

Milo would drive to Newton Division, photograph Raymond
Ortiz's shoes, and record the evidence in the growing case
file. Then, back on the phone, to search for additional DVLL
crimes.

Sharavi would use his computers to scan every available data
bank for the same.

"Something else," he said. "I could contact experts on crime
against the handicapped. All over the world."

"Didn't know there were experts on that," said Milo.

"There may not be, but there are specialists in neo-Nazism, racism, that kind of thing."

"You think this is political?"

"Not per se," said Sharavi, "but the notion of eliminating the
weak comes from somewhere. Maybe DVLL will crop up in racist
literature."

"Makes sense," I said. "Striking at the handicapped could be
the killer's own form of selective breeding—eugenics."

"Since the Berlin Wall came down, racist ideology has been cir-
culating freely in Europe," said Sharavi. "For obvious reasons, we
monitor it, so I have my sources. If similar crimes have been recorded, if suspects have been arrested, it could give us some understanding into our killer's motives—at least the motives he
honors himself with."

"Honors," said Milo. "Yeah, because his main motive is sexual."

He took a sip of the coffee he'd finally accepted from Sharavi and the dark man nodded.

"The asshole prides himself on mopping up the gene pool . . . sure, go ahead, check out all that stuff."

His tone was agreeable but bland. Maybe it was fatigue, maybe he was glad to keep the Israeli busy.

"The gene pool," I said. "Have either of you read *The Brain Drain*?"

They both shook their heads.

"Popular psychology, came out a few years ago. The basic premise was IQ means everything and stupid people—mostly dark-skinned people—are overbreeding, depleting our chromosomal resources. The book's answer was government control of fertility. The smart should be paid to procreate, those with low intelligence should be offered incentives to get sterilized. It was a minor best-seller, generated quite a bit of controversy."

"I remember it," said Milo, "some professor. You ever read it?"

"No," I said. "But someone else might have."

"Our boy uses pop psych for justification?"

"Everybody needs justification. Even sex crimes have a social context."

"That makes sense," said Sharavi. "Sex killers often go for prostitutes because prostitutes are at the bottom of the ladder and easier to dehumanize, right? From what I've seen, *every* killer needs to dehumanize his victim in some way: assassins, soldiers, sadists."

"The social context," said Milo. "He deals with his twisted little brain by convincing himself he's cleansing the world of defectives."

His chin was resting in one hand and he kept it there, looking down at the hardwood floor.

"Death by Darwin," he mumbled.

"It would also fit with the notion of someone who thinks he's superior," I said. "He's operating out of some eugenic fantasy, so he doesn't carry out a sexual assault. And takes care to arrange the body with what he considers respect."

"Only Irit's body," he said. "Raymond was reduced to bloody shoes. I can buy the fact that the killer was just starting out, honing his craft. But what about Latvinia? She came after Irit and he strung her up, treated her rougher."

"I don't know," I said. "Something's off—maybe he's just jumping around to avoid an obvious pattern."

No one talked for a while. Sharavi took a swallow from his third cup of coffee.

"DVLL," he said. "That's the pattern he feels safe sharing."

"Let's get back to the uniform angle," said Milo. "In addition to it helping him snag victims, he could also like it because he's a man on a mission. Maybe someone with a military background or a military wanna-be."

"If he served, he may very well have a dishonorable discharge," I said.

Sharavi smiled weakly. "Uniforms can be valuable."

"Being Israeli," Milo asked him, "would Irit relate in a special way to someone in uniform?"

"Hard to say," said Sharavi. "In Israel, we have a citizens' army, almost everyone goes in for three years and returns for reserve duty. So the country's full of uniforms, Israeli children see that as normal. Irit has actually lived outside of Israel for most of her life, but being around embassies and consulates she was accustomed to guards . . . it's possible. I don't really know much about her psychological makeup."

"The Carmelis didn't fill you in?"

"They told me the usual. She was a wonderful child. Beautiful and innocent and wonderful."

Silence.

Milo said, "We could also be talking cop wanna-bes—like that asshole Bianchi." To Sharavi: "The Hillside Strangler."

"Yes, I know. Bianchi applied to many departments, got turned down and became a security guard."

"Which is a whole other angle," said Milo. "No one screens security guards. You get ex-cons, psychos, all sorts of fools walking around looking official, some with guns."

"You're right about that," I said. "I had a case a few years ago, child-custody dispute. The father was a guard for a big industrial company out in the Valley. Turned out to be flagrantly psychotic—paranoid, hearing voices. The company had issued him pepper spray, handcuffs, a baton, and a semiautomatic."

"Let's hear it for personnel screening. . . . Okay, so what do we have so far: Joe Paramilitary with high-IQ fantasies and weird ideas about survival of the fittest, a sex drive that goes out of whack every so often, maybe photographic equipment. By taking pictures for later usage and arranging the bodies in a way that throws us off, he has his cake and . . ."

He cut himself off, gave a sick look, rubbed his face. Hard. Rosy patches appeared on the pale, scarred skin. His eyelids were heavy and his shoulders sloped.

"Anything else?"

Sharavi shook his head.

"What I can do," I said, "is see if any eugenic-related murders come up in the psychiatric literature. Who knows, maybe DVLL will crop up there."

Sharavi's fax machine began spitting paper. He collected a single sheet and showed it to us.

Paragraphs in Hebrew.

Milo said, "That sure clarifies it."

"Headquarters wants my weekly time-log. Precise accounting of my time."

"Been a bad boy?" said Milo.

"Tardy." Sharavi smiled. "One needs to prioritize. Perhaps I should go to Disneyland, bring the chief superintendent back a Mickey Mouse hat."

Crumpling the paper, he tossed it into the trash basket.

"Two points," said Milo. "You have basketball in Israel?"

Sharavi nodded, managed to smile. He looked exhausted, too, eyes sinking even deeper.

"Basketball but no sex killers, huh? What, you pick and choose what you borrow from us?"

"I wish," said Sharavi. "If only we were that smart."

Milo got up. "I'll take those bugs out myself, if it's only the four you said."

"Only those."

"Then I can handle it." He stared down at the smaller man. "You stay here and talk to Interpol, Nazi hunters, whatever."

27

ONCE THEY WERE GONE, DANIEL LOCKED THE HOUSE, activated the alarm, and went to his bedroom, where he sat on the edge of the mattress.

He indulged himself in a few minutes of loneliness before pushing away thoughts of Laura and the children and assessing how it had gone.

Sturgis didn't trust him one bit, but still the situation was not bad, considering his own stupidity.

The psychologist. Those active eyes . . .

He'd had to notify Zev about being found out, but Zev had been decent about it. Bigger things on his mind. Since Irit's murder everyone said he was a different man.

Daniel understood the difference: craving only one thing.

What was the chance of delivering?

Listening in on Sturgis and Delaware had produced one good outcome: He'd learned that Sturgis was bright and focused, exactly the type of detective he enjoyed working with. He'd known a few guys like that. One with a brilliant future but he'd died horribly for no good reason. . . .

Sturgis's history—his LAPD file full of complaints, striking out at the superior—had prepared Daniel for an outburst. But no fireworks tonight.

Delaware had remained very quiet, the eyes going constantly.

The quintessential psychologist. Though he *had* spoken up from time to time.

Asking about Daniel's accent, wanting to know about Daniel's family.

Like an intake at a therapy session. In the Rehab Center, after his first injuries, he'd spent time with psychologists and hated it less than he'd expected. Years later, on the job, he'd consulted them. On the Butcher case, Dr. Ben David had proved of some usefulness.

It had been a while since he'd been analyzed, though.

Those active, blue eyes, pale, appraising, yet not as cold as they might have been.

Sturgis's were green, almost unhealthily bright. What effect would they have on a suspect, so much intensity?

The two of them, so different, and yet they had a history of working together efficiently.

Friends, too, according to reports.

A homosexual and a heterosexual.

Interesting.

Daniel knew only one gay policeman, and not well. A sergeant major working out of Central Region. Nothing effeminate or overt about the man but he'd never married, never dated women, and people who knew him from the Army said he'd been spotted one night going onto the beach in Herzliyya with another man.

Not a brilliant policeman, that one, but competent. No one bothered him, but the other officers shunned him and Daniel was certain he'd never advance.

Sturgis was shunned, too.

For Daniel, the issue was a religious one, and that made it an abstraction.

For Daniel, religion was personal—his relationship to God. He cared nothing about what others did, if their habits didn't infringe upon his liberties or those of his family.

His family . . . in Jerusalem it was morning, but too early to call Laura. Like many artists, she was a nocturnal creature, stifling her internal clock for years to raise babies and coddle her husband. Now that the kids were older, she'd permitted herself to revert: staying up late sketching and painting and reading, sleeping in until eight or nine.

Feeling guilty about it, too; sometimes Daniel still had to reassure her he was fine making his own coffee.

He drew his knees up, closed his eyes, and thought about her soft blond hair and beautiful face, swaddled in topsheet, puffy with sleep, as he stopped to kiss her before leaving for headquarters.

Oh . . . I feel like such a bum, honey. I should be up cooking your breakfast.

I never eat breakfast.

Still . . . or I should give you other things.

Tugging him down for a kiss, then stopping herself.

My breath stinks.

No, it's sweet.

Pressing his lips upon hers, feeling her mouth parting, the wedding of tongue with tongue.

He opened his eyes, looked around the bare room.

In his Talbieh apartment, the walls were alive with color. Laura's paintings and batiks and the creations of her friends.

Her artsy friends, whom he seldom spoke to.

Painting with blood . . .

What would Laura say about that kind of art?

He never told her anything beyond the most general facts.

For twenty years of marriage, that had worked fine.

Twenty years. By today's standards, longevity.

Not *mazal*. Or the result of some amulet or chant or blessing from a *Hakham*.

God's grace and hard work.

Submerging your ego to be half of a pair.

Doing the right thing.

He wished he knew what that meant in this case.

28

THE FOLLOWING MORNING AS I DROVE TO THE U, I realized Helena still hadn't called.

Put Nolan's suicide to rest. I had plenty to do.

Snagging a Biomed computer terminal, I logged into Medline, Psych Abstracts, the periodicals index, every other database I could find, pulling up references on eugenics but finding none with any relationship to homicide.

Collecting handfuls of bound journals, I went looking for *The Brain Drain*. The book was filed under *Intelligence, Measurement*, three copies, two checked out. The one left was thick, re-bound in crimson, squeezed between manuals on IQ testing. A few books down the shelf I noticed a slim softcover entitled *Twisted Science: The Truth Behind The Brain Drain,* and I took that, too.

Finding a quiet corner desk on the tenth floor, I searched every source for a DVLL citation.

Absolutely nothing. But what I was learning kept me turning pages.

Because the idea that some lives were to be nurtured and others eliminated for the good of society hadn't begun with the Race Hygiene Program of the Third Reich.

Nor had it died there.

SELECTIVE BREEDING HAD APPEALED TO THE ELITE for centuries, but it had earned scientific respectability in the Europe and America of the late nineteenth century after being championed by a very respectable figure: British mathematician Francis Galton.

Unable to produce children himself, Galton had strong beliefs about survival of the ethnically fittest. Qualities such as intellect, zeal, and industriousness, he reasoned, were simple traits, much like height or hair color, and governed by basic rules of inheritance. In order to improve society, the state needed to collect detailed mental, physical, and racial information on every citizen, issue certificates to the superior and pay them for breeding, and encourage inferiors to remain celibate. In 1883, Galton coined the term *eugenics*, from the Greek meaning "well-born," to describe this process.

Galton's simplistic theories of intelligence were undermined by a rebirth of the works of Gregor Mendel, the Austrian monk who bred thousands of plants and found that some traits were dominant, others recessive. Later research showed that most defective genes were carried by outwardly normal parents.

Even vegetables didn't follow Galton's simplistic model.

But Mendel's ability to measure patterns of inheritance spurred on Galton's disciples, and eugenics took hold of the academic mainstream, so that by the twenties and thirties nearly all geneticists assumed mentally retarded people and other "degenerates" should be actively prevented from breeding.

These views made their way into public policy on both sides of the Atlantic, and by 1917, a Harvard geneticist named East was actively promoting the reduction of "defective germ plasm" through segregation and sterilization.

One of East's main influences was someone I'd considered a sage of my chosen field.

I'd been taught that Henry H. Goddard, of the Vineland Training School in New Jersey, had been a pioneer of psychological testing. What I hadn't known was that Goddard claimed "feeblemindedness" was due to a single defective gene and enthusiastically volunteered to administer IQ tests to thousands of immigrants arriving at Ellis Island in order to weed out undesirables.

Goddard's bizarre finding—that over 80 percent of Italians, Hungarians, Russians, and Jews were mentally retarded—was accepted without question by a wide range of intellectuals and legislators, and in 1924 the U.S. Congress approved an immigration act curtailing the entry of Southern and Eastern Europeans. The bill was signed into law by President Calvin Coolidge, who declared, "America must be kept American. Biological laws show that Nordics deteriorate when mixed with other races."

And Goddard wasn't alone. Chasing down footnotes and citations, I came across the writings of another giant of psychology: Lewis Terman of Stanford, developer of the Stanford-Binet IQ test. Though the French Binet test had been developed to help identify children with learning problems so they could be tutored, its American modifier declared his major goal to be "curtailing the reproduction of feeblemindedness" with a subsequent reduction in "industrial inefficiency."

According to Terman, intellectual weakness was "very, very common among Spanish-Indians and Mexican families of the Southwest and also among Negroes. Their dullness seems to be racial . . . children of this group should be segregated in special classes . . . They cannot master abstractions, but they can often be made efficient workers . . . from a eugenic point of view they constitute a grave problem because of their unusually prolific breeding."

But the prime mover of the U.S. eugenics movement was University of Chicago professor Charles Davenport, who believed that prostitutes chose their profession because of a dominant gene for "innate eroticism."

Davenport's method of preserving the future of white America was castration of males of inferior ethnic groups.

Castration, *not* vasectomy, he emphasized, because while the latter prevented breeding, it also encouraged sexual immorality.

Davenport's views influenced the law well beyond immigration statutes, embraced as they were by many social-welfare groups, including some pioneers of the family-planning movement. The term *final solution* was first used by the National Association of Charities and Corrections in the 1920s, and between 1911 and 1937, eugenic sterilization laws were passed in thirty-two American states, and in Germany, Canada, Norway, Sweden, Finland, Iceland, and Denmark.

Most enthusiastic among the self-appointed genetic janitors was the State of California, where in 1909, an order to compulsorily sterilize all inmates of state hospitals judged "sexually or morally perverted, mentally ill or feebleminded" got scalpels clicking. Four years later, the law was broadened to include noninstitutionalized people suffering from "marked departure from normal mentality."

In 1927, forced sterilization reached its highest sanction when a young unwed mother named Carrie Buck was sterilized against her will in Virginia, by virtue of a U.S. Supreme Court decision, written by Oliver Wendell Holmes. Holmes's decision not only allowed the procedure to be carried out, but also praised it "in order to prevent our being swamped with incompetence . . . the principle that sustains compulsory vaccination is broad enough to cover cutting the fallopian tubes . . . Three generations of imbeciles are enough."

Carrie Buck's baby—the "third generation of imbeciles" in question—grew up to be an honor student. Carrie Buck, herself, was eventually paroled from the Virginia Colony for Feebleminded and Epileptics, and lived out her life quietly as the wife of a small-town sheriff. She was later found out not to be retarded.

The Buck decision sped up the pace of forced sterilization and more than sixty thousand people, mostly residents of state hospitals, were operated on all across the U.S., as late as the 1970s.

In 1933, the Carrie Buck opinion was adopted as law in Germany and within one year, fifty-six thousand German "patients" had been sterilized. By 1945, under the aegis of the Nazis, the number had climbed to two million. For as Hitler wrote in *Mein Kampf,* "the right of personal freedom recedes before the duty to preserve the race. The demand that defective people be prevented from propagating equally defective offspring is a demand of the clearest reason and if systematically executed represents the most humane act of mankind."

After World War II, the tide began turning. Revulsion at the Nazi atrocities—but more important, the demands of wartime service upon surgeons—slowed down the rate of eugenic sterilization, and though the practice continued for decades, most eugenics laws were eventually reversed in the face of scientific debunking.

But the cause hadn't been abandoned.

Far from it.

And sterilization seemed tame compared to some of the ideas being tossed about now. I found myself swimming in an ethical cesspool.

Calls for assisted suicide sliding quickly into recommendations that those with nothing to live for be put out of their misery.

A report from Holland, where physician-assisted suicide had been liberalized, that as many as one-third of euthanasias—"mercy killings"—had been carried out without patients' consent.

An Australian "bioethicist" proclaiming religion no longer the basis for making moral judgments and the sanctity of human life no longer a valid concept. His alternative: Fellow ethicists should assign numerical "quality of life" measurements to people and parcel out health care based upon scores.

The retarded, the handicapped, the elderly, the infirm, would find themselves low on the list and be treated accordingly. In the case of deformed and retarded babies, a twenty-eight-day waiting period would be offered so parents could choose infanticide for "a life that has begun very badly."

Anyone who fell short on objective criteria of "personhood: rational thought and self-consciousness," could be killed without fear of penalty. Humanely.

Gentle strangulation, indeed.

Britain's National Health Insurance had recently put forth a policy offering free abortions to mothers of genetically defective babies—rescinding the usual twenty-four-week limit and allowing termination til shortly before birth.

Also in England, the Green party's annual conference proposed a very deliberate 25 percent reduction in the U.K.'s population in the name of saving the planet, leading critics to evoke memories of the Nazi party's infatuation with ecology, natural purity, and anti-urbanism.

The government of China was ahead of all this, having long enforced population control through coerced abortion, sterilization, and starving orphans to death in state-run facilities.

In the U.S., calls for prioritizing health-care services in the age of tight dollars and managed care had led many to question whether the seriously ill and the genetically disadvantaged should be allowed to "dominate" health-care expenditure.

I found a *U.S. News and World Report* article detailing the struggle of a thirty-four-year-old woman with Down's syndrome to receive a life-saving heart-lung operation. Stanford University Medical Center had rejected her because "We do not feel that patients with Down's syndrome are appropriate candidates for heart-lung transplantation," as had the University of California at San Diego because it judged her incapable of cooperating with the medical regimen. Her doctor disagreed and the publicity had forced both hospitals to reconsider. But what of others, languishing outside the media spotlight?

It reminded me of a case I'd seen years ago, while working with child cancer patients at Western Pediatrics Hospital. A fourteen-year-old boy diagnosed with acute leukemia, by then a treatable disease with an excellent prognosis for remission. But this leukemia patient was retarded and several interns and residents began grumbling about wasting their precious time.

I lectured to them, with meager results—because I wasn't an M.D., wouldn't be administering chemotherapy and radiotherapy, simply didn't *understand* what was involved. The attending physician, a passionate and dedicated man, caught wind of the protest and delivered a diatribe about Hippocrates and morality that silenced the grumblers. But it had been a begrudging compliance.

What kind of doctors had those interns become?

Who were they judging, now?

Quality of life.

I'd worked with thousands of children with birth defects, deformities, mental retardation, learning disabilities, chronic and painful and fatal diseases.

Most experienced a full range of emotions, including joy.

I remembered one little girl, eight years old, a thalidomide casualty. No arms, stunted flipper feet, shining eyes, an eagerness to embrace life.

Better quality of life than some face-lifted psychopaths I'd known.

Not that it mattered, for it wasn't my role to judge, either.

The eugenecists argued that society's progress could be measured by the achievement of the gifted, and in part, that was true. But what good was progress if it led to callousness, cruelty, cold judgments about deservedness, a degradation of the godly spark in all of us?

Who'd be the new gods? Geneticists? Ethicists?

Scientists had flocked to Nazism in record numbers.

Politicians?

HMO executives with bottom-line obsessions?

And after we cleansed the world of one group of "degenerates," who'd be next on the chromosomal hit list?

The flabby? The charmless? The boring? The ugly?

Scary stuff, and the fact that psychology had once swallowed it whole disgusted me.

The racist swill propagated by Goddard and Terman still reverberated in my head. Both had been names uttered with reverence in the corridors of the Psych Tower.

Like a child discovering his parents are felons, I felt a cold, dark pit open in my gut.

I'd administered countless IQ tests, had prided myself upon knowing the limitations of the instrument as well as the virtues.

Properly done, testing *was* valuable. Still, the rotten spot I'd just found at the core of my field's golden apple made me wonder what else I'd missed, despite all my education.

It was 1:00 P.M. and I'd been in the library for five hours. Lunchtime, but I had no appetite.

I picked up *The Brain Drain.*

The book's sole premise became obvious within pages:

Material success, morality, happy marriages, superior parenthood—all were caused by high g—a supposed general-intelligence trait whose validity had been debated for years.

This author presented it as a given.

The book had a smarmy, congratulatory tone: addressing itself to "you, the highly intelligent reader."

The ultimate kiss-up, virtue by association.

Maybe that—and a harnessing of upper-middle-class anxiety during hard times—could explain its best-sellerdom.

It sure wasn't the science, because I came across page after page of faulty assumptions, shoddy referencing, articles the author claimed as supportive that turned out to be just the opposite when I looked them up.

Promises to back up assertions with numbers that never appeared. Revival of Galton's one-gene theory of intelligence.

Hundred-year-old nonsense—who'd written this garbage?

The author bio at the back said a "social scholar" named Arthur Haldane, Ph.D.

Resident scholar at the Loomis Institute in New York City.

No further credentials.

No book jacket on the library copy, so no photo.

Ugly stuff.

Ugly times.

So what else was new?

My head hurt and my eyes ached.

What would I report to Milo and Sharavi?

Pseudoscientific crap sold well?

What connection was there to three dead kids?

The killer, watching, stalking, culling the herd . . .

With scholarly justification?

Because some lives just weren't worth living?

So he wasn't really a murderer.

He was a freelance bioethicist.

29

THE ONLY THING I HADN'T GOTTEN TO WAS *Twisted Science*, the critique of *The Brain Drain*, and though I couldn't see what it could add, I checked it out and took it home with me.

One message at my service. Milo's home number but the caller was Dr. Richard Silverman.

Rick and Milo had lived together for years but he and I rarely spoke. He was more prone to listening than talking. Reserved, meticulous, fit, always well-dressed, he was a striking contrast to Milo's aesthetic impairment and some people saw the two of them as an odd couple. I knew they were both thoughtful, driven, highly self-critical, had suffered deeply from being homosexual, had taken a long time to find their niche, both as individuals and members of a couple. Both buried themselves in bloody work—Rick spent over one hundred hours a week as a senior E.R. physician at Cedars-Sinai—and their time together was often silent.

He said, "Thanks, Alex. How's everything?"

"Great. With you?"

"Fine, fine. Listen, I just wanted to ask how Helena Dahl's doing—nothing confidential, just if she's okay."

"I haven't seen her recently, Rick."

"Oh."

"Something wrong?"

"Well," he said, "she quit the hospital yesterday, no explanation. I guess what's happened to her could unnerve anybody."

"It's tough," I said.

"I met the brother once. Not through her. He came in with a gunshot case, never mentioned being her brother, and I wasn't paying attention to nametags. But someone told me later."

"Helena wasn't on duty?"

"No, not that particular night."

"Anything unusual about him?"

"Not really. Big guy, young, very quiet, could have stepped right out of an LAPD recruiting poster. Back when that was the type they recruited. I was struck by the fact that he never bothered to ask for Helena, thought maybe he knew she was off. But when I told her he'd been in, she looked surprised. Anyway, I don't want to pry. Take care. If you do see her, say hi."

"Will do."

He laughed. "Say hi to Milo, too. You're probably seeing him more than I am. This case—the retarded kids—it's really disturbing him. Not that he's been talking about it. But he's been tossing in his sleep."

IT WAS TWO-THIRTY. I HADN'T COME UP WITH A thing on the DVLL killings. Robin was out for the afternoon, the house was too damn big, and the day seemed hollow.

I'd pushed Helena and Nolan to the back of my mind but Rick's call got me ruminating again.

What had caused her to make such a complete break?

Those family photos in Nolan's garage? Primal memories that strong?

She was tough and competent on the job but isolated in her private life.

More like her brother than she'd realized?

Had his self-destruction gotten her wondering about where she'd end up? Paths that hadn't been taken?

Depression ran in families. Had I missed something?

I called her home. The phone kept ringing and worst-case scenarios flashed through my head.

I thought about Nolan's showing up at the E.R., never asking for her.

Even when we were little kids we went our separate ways. Just ignored each other. Is that normal?

That kind of distance could pass for civility when life's rhythms remained shallow. But when things went bad, it could lead to the worst kind of guilt.

Parents dead, abandoned by her husband when he moved to North Carolina.

Going to work each day at the E.R., performing heroics. Coming home to . . . ?

Had the reliable engine finally broken down?

I had nothing to do and decided to take a drive out to her house.

Maybe I'd find her in a bathrobe on the sofa, watching soap operas and stuffing her face with junk food. Maybe she'd get angry at the intrusion and I'd feel like a fool.

I could live with that.

IT TOOK FORTY-FIVE MINUTES TO REACH THE WEST end of the Valley and another ten to find her address in Woodland Hills.

The house was a small yellow structure of no particular style on a hot, wide side street lined with mature bottlebrush trees in full bloom. Red flowers and sticky patches from the trees littered the sidewalks and California jays dove among the branches. The sun bore down through the haze and even though I couldn't hear the freeway, I could smell it.

The front lawn was dry and needed mowing. Big, shapeless margarita daisy bushes pushed up against the front porch. No sign of her Mustang in the driveway and the garage door was shut. The mailbox was empty and my ring and knock went unanswered.

Two cars in the driveway next door, a white minivan and a white Acura.

I went over there. The ceramic plaque beneath the bell said THE MILLERS under a crucifix, and looked homemade. A window air conditioner played a waltz.

I rang and the brass cover on the peephole snicked back.

"Yes?" Male voice.

"My name is Dr. Alex Delaware. I'm a friend of your neighbor, Helena Dahl. She hasn't been around for a while and some of us have been getting a little concerned."

"Um . . . one second."

The door opened and cold air hit my face. A couple in their late twenties looked me over. He was tall, dark, bearded, with a sunburned nose, and wore a pink Hawaiian shirt, denim shorts, no shoes. The can of Sprite in his hand was sweating but he wasn't.

The woman next to him was slim, broad-shouldered, nice-looking, with butter-colored multiflipped hair sporting two curlers on top. An electric blue T-shirt was tucked into black shorts and her nails were long and pearly white.

"Who's concerned about Helena?" he said.

"Her friends, people she works with at Cedars."

No answer.

I said, "She quit her job without explaining why. Has she left town?"

He gave a reluctant nod, but didn't say more. Behind him was a neatly appointed living room, home-shopping show on a big screen hawking a pearl necklace with matching earrings, only 234 left.

"We just wanted to know how she's doing," I said. "Do you know about her brother?"

He nodded. "He never came around. At least not since we've lived here, which is two years."

The woman said, "But they both grew up here. It was their parents' house." Southern accent. "Helena said he was a police officer. How strange, what he did."

"Any idea where she is?" I said.

"She said she was going on vacation," said the man. He took a drink from the can and offered it to his wife but she shook her head.

"Did she mention where?"

"No," he said.

"When did she leave?"

"What'd you say your name was?"

I repeated it and held out my business card and my police-consultant badge.

"You're police, too?"

"I work with them sometimes but that has nothing to do with Officer Dahl."

His posture loosened. "My work's kind of related to police work. I teach traffic school, just opened my own business—you're sure this doesn't have anything to do with him—investigating his death, for insurance or something like that?"

"Absolutely not," I said. "I'm just concerned about Helena."

"Well, she just went away to get some rest. At least that's what she said, and can you blame her?"

I shook my head.

"Poor thing," said the woman.

Her husband stuck out his hand. "Greg Miller, this is Kathy."

"Pleased to meet you."

"She left yesterday," he said. "Pardon the suspicion, but you can't be too careful, all the stuff that goes on, nowadays. We're trying to get a block association together, in order to look out for each other. Helena asked us to watch her house while she was gone."

"Crime problems in the neighborhood?" I said.

"It's not Watts but it's worse than you'd think—mostly stupid kid stuff, now they've got the white kids thinking they're gang bangers, too. There was a party last week, over in Granada Hills. Gang bangers showed up and when they didn't let 'em in, they did a drive-by. Sometimes I work nights so I taught Kathy how to shoot and she's good. Probably gonna get an attack dog, too."

"Sounds like serious problems."

"Serious enough for me," he said. "I believe in prevention. All we had til recently was kids driving by booming their stereos late at night, speeding, screaming, throwing out bottles. But the last few months there've been burglaries, even during the day, while people are at work."

Another glance between them. She nodded and he said, "Last burglary was Helena, as a matter of fact. Just two days ago. With her brother *and* that, you can't really blame her for wanting to take off, right?"

"Two days ago?"

"At night, hers was a nighttime thing. She went out to do some grocery shopping, came back, found the back door jimmied. Kathy and I were out, thankfully they didn't hit us. They took her TV and the stereo and some jewelry, she said. Next day she was packed up and asking us to look after the house. Said she'd had enough of L.A."

"Did she call the police?"

"No, she said she'd had enough of the police, too. I figured she meant her brother, didn't want to push it. Even though I thought we definitely *should* call it in. For block security. But she was so stressed out."

"Of all the people for it to happen to," said Kathy. "She was so down to begin with. And she's such a nice person. Mostly she kept to herself, but she was always real nice."

"Any idea where she went?" I said.

"Nope," said Kathy. "She just said she needed a rest and we didn't want to be nosy. She had a couple suitcases in the back of the car but I don't even know if it was a driving trip or she was heading for the airport. I asked her how long she'd be away but she said she wasn't sure, she'd call to let us know if it was going to be long. If she does call, would you like me to tell her you were by?"

"Please," I said. "And good luck with your block association."

"Luck's what you make it," said Greg. "God helps those who help themselves."

HEAVY TRAFFIC AND BAD TEMPERS ON THE FREEWAY ride back to the city. As I sat in a jam just north of the Sunset exit, I thought of the luck of the Dahl family.

Both Nolan's and Helena's homes defiled.

L.A.'s burglary rate had skyrocketed, but I'd never worshiped at the altar of coincidence and it made me edgy.

Someone out to get them?

Someone looking for something? Information about Nolan's death?

Data Helena had?

The family photo albums were all she'd taken the day I'd gone with her to Nolan's place, but maybe she'd returned, picked through the mess, discovered something that had upset her enough to cancel her therapy, quit her job, and leave town?

Or maybe it *was* just the final straw.

Traffic started again, then stopped.

Honks, lifted middle fingers, shouted expletives.

Civilization.

30

THAT NIGHT, AT EIGHT, ROBIN AND I WERE IN THE bath when the phone rang. She faced me, her hair up, water reaching the bottoms of her breasts.

We played toesies. The damn thing quieted.

Later, drying off, I listened to the taped message.

"It's Milo. Call me on the car phone."

I did and he said, "Found another DVLL case. Hollywood Division, before Raymond Ortiz. Seventeen months ago."

"Another poor kid," I said. "How old—"

"No. Not a kid. And not retarded, either. On the contrary."

I MET HIM AT A TWENTY-FOUR-HOUR COFFEE SHOP ON Highland north of Melrose named Boatwright's. Rocket-to-the-moon architecture, boomerang-shaped counter, three of the stools occupied by pie-eating newspaper-nosers, the Hollywood Strings on scratchy soundtrack.

He was in his usual cop's back booth, sitting opposite a dark-haired woman. He waved and she turned. She looked around twenty-five. Very thin, pretty in a severe way, she had a pointed chin and ski-slope nose, ivory skin, glossy black wedge-cut hair, glossy brown eyes. Her pantsuit was black. In front of her was a big chocolate malt in a real glass. Milo had a napkin tucked under his chin and was eating fried shrimp and onion rings and drinking iced tea.

The woman kept watching me until I got two feet away. Then she smiled, more the right thing to do than amiability. Scanning me from head to shoe, as if measuring for a suit.

"Alex, this is Detective Petra Connor, Hollywood Homicide. Petra, Dr. Alex Delaware."

"Good to meet you," said Connor. A little makeup added depth to eyes that didn't need any more. She had very long, very thin hands with warm, strong fingers that squeezed mine for a second, then flew back to the straw in her malt.

I slid in next to Milo.

"Something to eat?" he said.

"No, I'm fine. What's up?"

"What's up is Detective Connor is an eagle eye."

"Pure luck," she said in a soft voice. "Most of the time I never pay attention to memos."

"Most of the time they're bullshit."

She smiled and twirled the straw.

"Oh yeah," he said. "I forgot. Working with Bishop you probably never hear sullied speech."

"I don't, but Bishop does," said Connor.

"Her partner's a Mormon," Milo told me. "Very smart, very straight, probably be chief one day. Petra and he picked up the case in question a while back. He's currently off with the wife and million kids in Hawaii so she's riding alone."

"The whole thing amazes me," she said. "Being tied into a possible serial. Because ours wasn't even a murder, just an iffy suicide. Not iffy enough to change the coroner's verdict, so we closed it as a suicide. But when I saw your memo . . ."

Shaking her head, she pushed the malt aside and dabbed at her lips. The lipstick she left on the straw had brown overtones. The black in her hair was real. She was probably closer to thirty than twenty-five, but not a line on her face.

"Who was the victim?" I said.

"A twenty-nine-year-old scientist named Malcolm Ponsico. Cellular physiologist, recent Ph.D. from CalTech, supposed to be some kind of genius. He lived in Pasadena, but was working at a research lab on Sunset near Vermont—Hospital Row—and that's where he did it so it was our case."

"I used to work at Western Peds," I said.

"Right there. Two blocks up. Place called PlasmoDerm, they do skin research, developing synthetic grafts for burn victims, that kind of thing. Ponsico's specialty was cell membranes. He killed himself with an injection of potassium chloride—the stuff they use for lethal-injection executions. Did it while working late, the clean-ing lady found him at 4:00 A.M., slumped over his lab table. Big laceration right here, where his head hit the edge.''

She traced a line over well-formed black brows.

''He fell on his head when he died?''

''That's how the coroner saw it.''

''Where's the DVLL tie-in?''

''He left it typed on his computer screen. Four letters, right in the middle of the screen. Stu—Detective Bishop—and I figured it for something technical, a formula. But we asked around, just to be careful, in case it was some kind of coded suicide note. No one at PlasmoDerm knew what it meant and it didn't show up in any of Ponsico's computer files—we had one of our data-processing guys check them out. All numbers, formulas. No one seemed surprised by Ponsico writing something only he understood. He was that kind of guy—major brain in a world of his own.''

''Did he leave a message at his home?''

''No. His apartment was in perfect order. Everyone said he was a nice person, quiet, kept to himself, really into his work. No one had noticed him being depressed and his parents in New Jersey said he'd seemed okay when he called them. But parents often say that. People hide things, right?''

''He *seemed* okay?'' I said. ''That's not a ringing endorsement of his happiness.''

''His parents said he'd always been a serious boy. Their word—*boy.* A genius, they'd always let him do his own thing and he'd always produced. Their word, too. They're both professors. I got the feeling it was a high-pressure household. It played out pure suicide. Ponsico's prints were all over the hypodermic and the potassium vial and the coroner said the position we found him in was consistent with self-infliction. Said also it was a fairly quick death—massive heart attack, though Ponsico could have made things easier on himself if he'd taken a tranquilizer like the ones they give Death Row guys. Then again, no one from the ACLU was looking over Ponsico's shoulder.''

''So what was iffy about it?''

''Ponsico's former girlfriend—another scientist at the lab, named Sally Branch—was convinced there was something wrong and kept calling us up, asking us to keep snooping. She said it didn't make sense, Ponsico had no reason to kill himself, she'd have known if there were something wrong."

"Even though she was a *former* girlfriend."

"My thought exactly, Doctor. And she also tried to cast suspicion on Ponsico's new girlfriend, so we figured it was jealousy. Then I met the new girlfriend and wondered."

She took a sip of water.

"Her name was Zena Lambert and she was weird. She'd worked as a clerk at PlasmoDerm but left a few months before Ponsico's death."

"Weird, how?" I said.

"Kind of . . . nerdy—but in a mean way. Snippy. As in, I'm smarter than you so don't waste my time. Even though she claimed to be grieving over Ponsico."

"An intellectual snob?" I said.

"Exactly. Which was funny because Sally Branch, with her Ph.D., was down-to-earth, and here was this clerk who thought she was the end-all. Still, a bad personality doesn't make someone a suspect and we had absolutely nothing on her."

"Did Sally Branch give some reason for suspecting Zena?"

"She said Ponsico changed noticeably after he started dating her—even quieter, less social, hostile. All of which seemed logical to me. He'd be less social with Sally because he'd broken up with her."

"Did she say why he broke up with her?"

"All Zena. To listen to her, Zena swooped down like some harpy and stole him away. She also said Zena had gotten him into some kind of high-IQ club and he'd become obsessed with his intelligence. Big-time arrogant. But that was it, evidence-wise, and she gave me no motive for Zena wanting to hurt him. Eventually, I just stopped taking her calls. Now, Milo's told me about these DVLL murders, someone getting rid of retarded people, maybe a tie-in with genetic cleansing, so I have to wonder about that high-IQ group."

She shook her head. "Though I still can't see any connection to Ponsico, unless he met your killer at the brainiac club and learned too much for his own good."

"Did Zena get another job after she left PlasmoDerm?" I said.

"Bookstore in Silverlake, it's in the file."

"Did Sally give you a name for the club?" I said, thinking about Nolan Dahl, another high-IQ suicide.

"Meta," she said. "You really think there could be a link?"

I told the two of them what I'd learned in the library.

"Survival of the rotten," she said. "Reminds me of something my father once told me. He was a professor in Arizona, physical anthropologist, did research on wolves, the desert. He said there was a giant study going on—the Human Genome Project—mapping every gene in the human body, trying to figure out which traits are caused by what. The ultimate goal is to collect detailed data on every one of us. My dad said the upside potential for medical research was tremendous but it was also frightening. What if insurance companies got hold of the information and decided to withhold coverage because of some mutation way back in the family tree? Or companies started refusing to hire someone because they were at elevated risk for cancer ten years down the line?"

"Or," said Milo, "Big Bro identifies the mutations and kills off the carriers . . . was PlasmoDerm involved in that kind of research?"

"No, just skin grafts, but even if they were, it doesn't explain why Ponsico would kill *himself*."

"Maybe he found out he had some incurable disease."

"Nope, the coroner said he was perfectly healthy."

Milo pulled out his pad. "Meta. Sounds like Greek."

"It is," said Petra. "I went over the file before I came here and looked it up. Means change, transformation. Something that breaks new ground."

"Brave new goddamn world?" said Milo. "A bunch of arrogant geeks sit around theorizing about improving the species and one of them decides to put it into action?"

Both of them looked at me.

"Sure," I said. "If you thought you were that superior, you might start figuring the rules didn't apply."

OUT IN THE PARKING LOT, CONNOR SAID, "I SPOKE to Stu this morning. He won't be back from Maui for another week, says to give you all our data."

She produced a file from a huge black bag and handed it to Milo.

"Thanks, Petra."

"No problem." She flashed an abrupt white smile. "Just promise that if *I* send around a memo, *you'll* read it."

We watched her drive away in an older black Accord.

"Fairly new on the job," said Milo, "but she'll go far. . . . So I guess the next step is for me to go over this, then give you a look. Then have a talk with Ponsico's two girlfriends."

"It's the best lead we've gotten, so far," I said. Saying nothing about Nolan because I was still bound by confidentiality and there was no reason to violate.

We walked to the Seville. "Thanks for the library work, Alex. Have time to go back there and look up this Meta outfit?"

"First thing in the morning. Sharavi's well-equipped in the computer department. Planning to update him?"

"Haven't decided. Because anything I tell him goes straight to Carmeli and how much do I want a grieving high-powered father to know at this point . . . not that I can put him off too long— hell, if I *don't* cue him in, he'll probably start bugging the phones again."

He laughed, cursed. "Distractions . . . by the way, I think I figured out how Sharavi got Raymond Ortiz's shoes. Same way he got the file—remember how the first time Manny Alvarado looked for it he couldn't find it? Seems a former Newton captain just happened to drop in to visit the station a couple days before. Guy named Eugene Brooker, one of the highest-ranked blacks in the department, they used to think he was on his way to deputy chief. But his wife died last summer and he retired. And guess what—he was a biggie on the same Olympics security Sharavi worked on. So the Israelis are connected to the department, who knows where else. No matter how aboveboard Sharavi acts, I'll always figure he's holding something back. You think his computers can help substantially?"

"I can get academic references from the library, material that's been in the English-language press. But if Meta's an international group, or if it's been implicated in anything criminal overseas, he could be useful."

He thought about that. "All this assumes Meta's some big deal.

For all we know, it's just a group of nerds getting together for chips and dip, patting themselves on the back because God gave them smarts. Even if the killer's one of them, how're we going to pick him out of the group?"

"If there's a membership roster and we get it, we could cross-check with the sex-offender and M.O. files. We can also see if any members present a clear opportunity or motive for the three killings. Like working at the park where Raymond was abducted and/or the conservancy."

"Park worker with a high IQ?"

"Underachiever," I said. "That's the way I've seen it all along."

"Ponsico's second girlfriend—the Lambert woman—sounds like an underachiever, too. Clerking. Not that she's any big suspect, because our boy's definitely male and strong—the way he carried Irit and Raymond, trussed up Latvinia."

I got in the car. He said, "What do you think of that gene project Connor talked about?"

"Just what we need in the age of kindness, Milo. Some map that determines whose life is worth living."

"So you're not willing to depend upon the good graces of intellectuals and insurance companies, huh?"

I laughed. "Gang bangers and dope smugglers and back-alley junkie muggers, maybe. But no, not them."

31

AT 6:00 A.M., AFTER WORKING SINCE MIDNIGHT, DAN-
iel opened the shutters on the computer room's windows and
breathed in light.

Putting on his phylacteries, he prayed without feeling, looking
out at the tiny backyard clad in concrete.

He'd spent most of the night on the phone, accommodating the
European and Asian and Middle Eastern time zones. Making
police-officer small talk in four languages, calling in favors, making his way through the various law-enforcement bureaucracies
that somehow never changed from city to city.

Searching for DVLL references, murders with racial and ethnic
overtones, any hints of serial crimes linked to genetic cleansing,
any major changes in the policies of neo-Nazi and nationalist
groups and others who thought themselves superior.

Quantity wasn't the problem. Plenty of information—as democracy spread over Europe, more and more lunatics crawled out of
their holes and gorged themselves on free speech. But in the end
he was left with no connections to the L.A. murders, nothing even
close to a lead.

He cut his prayers short, apologized to God, wrapped up the
tfillin, and went into the small, dark bathroom where he turned on
the shower, stripped, and stepped in, not waiting for the water to
turn hot.

It took exactly two minutes forty-one seconds for the old pipes
to kick in. He'd timed it yesterday, arranged his morning schedule
accordingly.

But this morning he endured the cold needles.

Flogging himself for the futile night?

He'd begun with Heinz-Dietrich Halzell at the Berlin police, who'd informed him the racist presses continued to churn out the nasty stuff; the moment the *polizei* got an injunction, the slime just moved and started up again. And stupid punks kept beating up Turks and anyone else with a dark skin, starting brawls, desecrating graveyards.

Apology in his voice. *Deeply* sorry, the way only a German could be. Daniel had hosted him at a security conference in Jerusalem, last year. A really decent guy, but weren't they always the ones who let themselves feel?

Murders of retarded kids? No, Heinz-Dietrich hadn't heard of anything like that. DVLL? Not in any of their files, but he'd ask around. What was going on in L.A.?

When Daniel told him, sketchily, he sighed and said he'd ask around seriously.

Uri Drori at the Israeli Embassy in Berlin did some double-checking and verified everything Halzell had said. Daniel called him not because he didn't trust the German, but because sometimes what you learned depended on who you were.

Drori reported a slowly escalating rate of low-level incidents, repeated almost word for word Heinz-Dietrich's lament about the idiots popping up like toadstools.

It will never end, Dani. The more democracy you have, the more you get this shit, but what's the alternative?

Same story with Bernard Lamont in Paris, Joop Van Gelder in Amsterdam, Carlos Velasquez in Spain, all the others.

No murders of defectives, no DVLL.

Which didn't really surprise him. These crimes seemed American. Though he couldn't explain why.

A wonderful country, America. Huge and free and naive; big-hearted people always willing to grant the benefit of the doubt.

Even after the Trade Center bombing, you didn't see large-scale anti-Muslim feelings. The Israeli Embassy in New York tracked that kind of thing.

Free country.

But what was the price?

Last night, taking a coffee break, he'd heard police sirens, loud, close, looked out the same rear window and saw a helicopter circling low, beaming down on backyards, like some giant mantis scouting for prey.

His police scanner told him they were searching for an armed-robbery suspect—holdup at Beverly Drive and Pico.

A mile away, right near Zev Carmeli's place.

Not far from the house on Monte Mar where Laura had grown up. Her parents had sold it and bought two tiny condos. Beverly Hills, and Jerusalem, where they were now.

Before he'd left for the States, his father-in-law had warned him: Be careful, things have changed.

Gene said, *Total breakdown, Danny Boy. Going to school can be hazardous to a kid's health.*

Which was one reason Gene had sold his big house in Lafayette Park. Heading for Arizona . . . no real reason for Arizona, except that it was warm and "I'm not exactly worried about melanoma, right?"

Gene looked old. Since Luanne's death, his hair and mustache had turned snow-white and his skin bagged.

An untimely death, the poor woman had been only sixty when the massive stroke had knocked her to the floor of her kitchen. Gene discovering her, another reason to sell the house.

High blood pressure. A doctor friend of Daniel's told him blacks had more of it. Some said it was their diet, others genetics. His friend thought racism had a lot to do with it.

Daniel understood that. He couldn't count the times he'd been called a dirty Jew by Arabs and, because of his skin, a nigger by all sorts of people.

When it happened, he didn't react visibly but his heart pounded in his ears . . . he wondered if Gene was taking care of his diabetes. Cookies on the counter when he'd gone there to pick up the Ortiz file and the boy's shoes said otherwise.

His friend had come through for him and Daniel liked to think the favor had been good for Gene, too.

Nothing but time on his hands, poor guy. He'd called three times since returning the stuff, offering to do whatever Daniel needed.

But Daniel wouldn't go to Gene for any more favors. The man was ill, no reason to draw him in deeper.

If Sturgis cooperated.

He'd said he would, but hard to tell.

Sturgis would never score high on the Trust Index.

He stepped out of the shower just as the water warmed up, dried off, goose-bumped, amazed he hadn't felt any discomfort.

America.

Democracy had begun in Greece but its real home was here. Birthplace of official compassion, too—no country had been as kind as America. Now Americans were paying for their compassion in drive-by shootings, the breakdown of rules and values, child-murderers let out on parole.

Same thing back home. For all his country's image as a tough little fighter state, Daniel knew Israel as one big, soft heart populated by survivors and rooters for the underdog with a reluctance to punish.

That's why victory doesn't sit well with us, he thought. Why we end up the first country in history to voluntarily give back land won in battle in exchange for an ill-defined peace with people who hate our guts.

He'd watched, during the intifada, as the Palestinian Arabs made the most of Israeli democracy: staging rehearsed events masquerading as spontaneous shows of protest, exaggerating the very real brutality of the occupation with hyperbole, kids with rocks playing for the camera. The press, of course, gobbled it up like a rich dessert. Day after day of photo-op baton-to-skull and rubber-bullet hailstorm broadcast worldwide, while Assad executed tens of thousands of potential enemies in Syria and got maybe two lines of newsprint.

Still, who ever said life was fair. He'd rather live in a free society . . . though sometimes . . .

And now he was thinking of Elias Daoud again, resolutions tossed to the wind.

The ginger-haired Christian Arab from Bethlehem had been his best homicide detective, playing a major role in the Butcher investigation, never letting the divided-loyalties thing get in the way though it hadn't been easy—no one but Daniel had trusted *him*.

The closing of the Butcher file got everyone on the team promotions, but Daoud's had taken a bit more prodding of the pencil pushers.

Daniel had been obdurate and finally Daoud ended up a

mefakeah, Southern Division's first Arab inspector. The raise in pay for a guy with seven kids had made it more than just another ribbon.

Daoud was kept on Daniel's squad and Daniel assigned him to the few nonpolitical homicide cases that came up: Old City gang stuff, the drug and watermelon rackets, nothing with any security overtones. For Daoud's protection as well as for the brass. Daniel didn't want him branded a collaborator.

Then the intifada heated up. More rhetoric, more audacity, more violence—the wall of fear broken down, vermin scurrying through the rubble.

Religious militancy found new life, too, and Christians in Bethlehem, and Nazareth, and everywhere else Christian, remembered Beirut and grew less vocal, many of them bribing their way across the border to Jordan and onward to families in Europe and the States.

One morning, in the midst of a serious investigation into the Ramai gang's role in the hashish trade, with Daoud scheduled to give a progress report, everyone waiting in a restaurant on King George Street, the guy didn't show.

Right away Daniel knew something was wrong. The man was a walking wristwatch.

He dismissed the griping detectives, called Daoud's house, got a disconnected line.

The usual twenty-minute drive to Bethlehem took him less than fifteen. Before he got to the city outskirts he saw the military jeeps and the police Ford Escorts, blue lights flashing, people milling around, the simmering feel of an impending riot.

He showed his badge and made his way past grim faces to Daoud's house. Police tape had been wrapped around the little limestone cube and chickens circled the muddy ditch that passed for a yard. No more olive-wood crucifix in Daoud's window— when had that changed?

It had been a long time since Daniel had been there. Now, he realized what a sorry place it was, objectively. Not much better than the hovel in Yemen where Daniel's father had been born. But the promotion had allowed Daoud to finish payments on it, the guy had been so proud.

The uniform at the door warned him not to go in for his own

sake, but he did anyway, thinking of Daoud, the young, fat wife Daoud loved madly and plied with chocolates, seven little kids . . .

The kids gone, no one knew where. Months later, Daniel found out they'd somehow showed up with relatives in Amman, but that was as far as the information went.

Daoud and the fat wife, still here.

Slaughtered like sheep for the market.

Sliced, trussed, dismembered, tongues severed. The wife a leaking bag of yellow adipose, eyes rolled back. Daoud castrated, his penis hacked off, the organ stuffed in his mouth.

Hatchets, the medical examiner said. And long knives, probably six or seven attackers, a midnight blitz.

Flies, so many flies.

Arabic scrawl on the wall in blood:

GOD IS GREAT! DEATH TO COLLABORATORS!

He drove back to French Hill, kept his feelings to himself.

Always, constantly, completely.

Like the Dead Sea, flat and bitter, yielding nothing organic.

Wanting to be dispassionate when he asked to run the investigation into the slaughter, so his superiors would consider it.

Of course, they refused, saying it was an Arab issue, he could never get close enough, no one would talk to him.

He kept asking, demanding, got the same answer, over and over. Refusing to give up, knowing he was being an idiot, he drove home each day with an inflamed belly and a raging headache, the strain of smiling at Laura and the kids just short of unbearable.

A case number was assigned to the Daoud murders but no one seemed to be actually investigating.

He lost interest in his gang cases; the Ramais could sell dope for another few months, big deal. And if they shot each other, no great loss.

He wrote memo after memo, received no answer.

Finally, in Laufer's office, after yet another dismissal, he exploded at the commander.

Is this what it's come to? He was an Arab so it's not worth the time and effort? Different values for different lives? What are we, Nazi Germany?

Laufer had looked him up and down, chain-smoking, sleepy eyes full of contempt, but he hadn't said a word. Daniel's solving the Butcher had gotten *him* kicked up from deputy commander. Who knew what other value the Yemenite might have for him?

After that, a few suspects were hauled in for questioning, but it led nowhere, the file was never closed, never would be.

Daniel thought from time to time of the savages who'd done it. Dispatched from Syria or Lebanon? Or locals, still living in Bethlehem, passing that house, now demolished, and really believing they'd shown God to be great?

And what of the seven kids? Who was raising them? What had they been told?

That the Jews had done it?

Daddy and Mommy, martyrs to Palestine?

The Arabs loved martyrs. After the intifada ended, there'd been a martyr shortage, young guys with scraped feet or the flu claiming they'd gotten hurt fighting the Zionists.

The virtue of suffering.

We, their Jewish cousins, aren't much different, are we? he thought. Though we're a little more subtle about it.

Democracy . . .

And now these *American* killings.

Three homicides of children in three separate police districts— Delaware had a point about that. Spread out over a vast, shapeless thing that calls itself a city.

Retarded kids, how could you get any crueler?

Gene said they called them something else nowadays . . . developmentally challenged.

"Nowadays, everyone's challenged, Danny Boy. Short people are vertically challenged, drunks are sobriety-challenged, criminal scumbags are socially challenged."

"Socially challenged sounds more like someone shy, Gene."

"That's the point, my friend. It's not supposed to make sense. A con game, like that book, 1984. Change the names to confuse the good guys."

Socially challenged.

So what does that make me on *this* case? And Sturgis and Delaware.

Solution-challenged?

No, just stuck.

32

SEVEN-THIRTY A.M. I WAS AT THE DOORS TO THE BIO-
med library when they opened, barely awake, showered but unshaven, still tasting gulped coffee.

I worked for two hours, finding only one reference to the group
called Meta. But it was enough.

Wire-service piece, three years old, carried locally by the *Daily
News.*

GENIUS GROUP EDITORIAL
CAUSES CONTROVERSY

NEW YORK—Opinions supporting selective breeding to
improve genetic stock as well as mercy killing of the
retarded, published by an organization of self-
described geniuses, have raised controversy among
members of social-advocacy organizations and put the
group under an unaccustomed spotlight.

Meta, a little-known Manhattan-based club founded
ten years ago to provide information about creativity
and giftedness, now finds itself accused of fascism.

The article under fire was written by Meta director and
attorney Farley Sanger in *The Pathfinder,* the group's
quarterly newsletter. In it, Sanger calls for a ''new
utopia'' based upon ''objectively measured
intellectual ability'' and questions the value of
providing special education and other services,
including medical care, to the developmentally

disabled, whom he labels meat without mentation.

Sanger also suggests that those lacking the ability to reason and care for themselves are not fully human and, thus, do not merit constitutional protection under the law. ''An effective social-policy analogue,'' he argues, would be ''animal-protection statutes. Just as sterilization and euthanasia are widely held to be humane policies for cats and dogs, so should they be considered for those 'quasi-human' organisms whose genetic makeup causes them to fall well short of the intellectual goalpost.''

The article, published several months ago without fanfare until it was brought to the attention of the press, has generated a predictably hostile reaction from advocates for the mentally retarded.

''This is fascism, pure and simple,'' said Barry Hannigan, chairman of the Child Welfare Society. ''Ugly stuff reminiscent of Nazi Germany.''

Margaret Esposito, director of the Special Children Foundation, an advocacy group for the retarded, said, ''We've worked so hard to erase the stigma associated with developmental delay only to see something like this come along. I can only hope we're talking about a fringe group and that reasonable people will see it for what it is.''

Similar sentiments were echoed by clergy, social scientists, and jurists.

''Reprehensible,'' said Monsignor William Binchy of the Manhattan archdiocese. ''The Church believes only God should play God.''

The editor responsible for publishing the article in *The Pathfinder*, Wall Street securities analyst Helga Cranepool, was unfazed by these comments. Admitting that Sanger's essay contained ''some push-the-envelope phraseology and adventurous notions,'' Cranepool defended them on free-speech grounds and ''the right of our members to be exposed to a wide spectrum of opinions. Two characteristics of very bright people are a willingness to take reasonable risks and an unquenchable curiosity. We're not for everyone, nor do

we claim to be. We'll continue to do everything in our
power to stimulate and challenge ourselves through an
unfettered exchange of ideas.''

Author Sanger, reached at his Midtown law office,
refused to comment beyond saying, ''The writing speaks
for itself.'' Both he and Cranepool declined to offer
the names of other Meta members, with Cranepool
describing the group as ''small and selective. We don't
seek publicity.''

The chairman of the Manhattan chapter of the better-
known high-IQ group Mensa, Laurence Lanin, described
Meta as ''one of our wackier imitators. There are lots
of them, but they rarely endure.'' He estimated Meta
membership at no more than a few dozen.

As with Mensa, sources say admittance to the group is
based upon scores on a self-designed IQ test. Mensa
membership is based upon an upper 2 percent score and
Meta is believed to be more selective. When asked if
Mensa members shared Sanger's views, Lanin said, ''I
can only speak for myself but I find them repellent.''

I photocopied the article and searched local phone books for Meta
listings. None. Big surprise.

How did they recruit members?

Mensa imitator . . . the better-known group *was* listed. West
L.A. number, no address.

A recording listed the time and address for the next meeting and
said messages could be left after the beep.

I said, "My name is Al and I'm an East Coast transplant looking
for info on Meta. Are they out here?" and left my number.

Next, I reached Milo at his desk.

"Just the one article?" he said.

"That's it."

"So maybe that was Ponsico's club, too. Maybe Sharavi *can* find
something on his computers."

"You're going to call him?"

"He called me. Seven A.M., gotta give him points for industriousness. He said he'd been working all night with the foreign police
and Israeli contacts—zippo. I think he was telling the truth, I know
that pissed-off tone of voice. Now that we have a name, maybe he

can pull something up. I'll arrange a meet at his place this afternoon but first I've got a lunch appointment with Malcolm Ponsico's first girlfriend. Sally the scientist, more than eager to talk about Zena the clerk. She's working out in Sherman Oaks now, near the burn center, and I'm supposed to meet her at an Italian place on Ventura and Woodman. In the mood for pasta?"

"The stuff I've been reading lately has killed my appetite," I said. "But the company sounds fine."

33

SALLY BRANCH SPEARED A PIECE OF MUSSEL FROM A nest of linguini and stared at it clinically.

She was thirty-one but had a teenager's eager, nasal voice— Valley Girl inflections overlaid on long, articulate phrases—thick, wavy chestnut hair, a broad, plain, freckled face, brown eyes, and a knockout figure enhanced by a black knit dress. A white lab coat was draped over her chair.

She said, "Malcolm was never a very communicative person but he got worse after he met her."

"How long before his death did you have contact with him?" said Milo.

"A few days before, we had lunch in the PlasmoDerm cafeteria." She colored. "I saw him and sat down. He seemed preoccupied but not depressed."

"Preoccupied by what?"

"His work, I assume."

"He was having work problems?"

She smiled. "No, on the contrary. He was brilliant. But every day something new comes up—specific experiments."

Milo smiled, too. "You'd have to be a scientist to understand?"

"Well, I don't know about that."

She ate the mussel.

I said, "So he never actually talked about something bothering him."

"No, but I could tell."

"The breakup," said Milo. "Was it friendly?"

She swallowed and forced another smile. "Is it ever really

friendly? He stopped calling, I wanted to know why, he wouldn't say, then I saw him with her. But I got over it—I guess I kept thinking Malcolm would come to his senses. Listen, I know I sound like just another jealous woman but you need to understand that suicide would have been a totally illogical choice for Malcolm. His life was going great, he never lost interest in his work. And he liked himself. Malcolm was someone who truly liked himself."

"Good self-esteem?" said Milo.

"Nothing obnoxious but he was brilliant and knew it. He used to make wisecracks about winning the Nobel prize but I knew it wasn't a total joke."

"What was he researching?" I said.

"Cell permeability—moving ions and chemical compounds of increasing complexity through cell walls without causing structural damage. It was still at a theoretical level—mouse cells. But the practical potential was enormous."

"Getting drugs into cells without damage," I said.

"Exactly. Drugs are basically cellular-repair agents. Malcolm was studying drugs that enhance tissue growth in burn patients. He described it as playing with toy trains on a cellular level."

"Cellular repair—like patching up defective chromosomes?"

"Yes! I suggested that to Malcolm but he said he'd stick to medications. That it was possible inborn defects shouldn't be tinkered with."

"Why's that?"

She looked at her plate. "Malcolm was a bit . . . stodgy. A determinist—he believed some things should be left alone."

"Healing burns was okay but genetic problems shouldn't be fixed."

"Something like that—I don't want to make him sound unsympathetic. He wasn't. He was kind. But extremely brilliant people are sometimes like that."

"Like what?" said Milo.

"Snobs."

Milo picked up a piece of garlic bread and ate it. "If he didn't commit suicide, what do you think happened, Dr. Branch?"

"He was murdered. Detective Connor said he had a wound on his forehead from falling but couldn't it also mean someone came from behind and slammed him down on the table, then injected him with the potassium chloride?"

"Any suspects in mind?"

"Absolutely," she said. "Zena. The only thing I can't figure out is why."

"Is she a large woman?" said Milo.

"No, on the contrary. She's tiny—a real shrimp. But coming from behind, she could have compensated for that."

She coiled linguini around her fork. "She took Malcolm from me but that's not why I suspect her. She's a nasty little witch. Very taken with her image: bad little girl. When she worked at Plas-moDerm she'd walk around with weird reading material—maga-zines on body-piercing, serial killers, those violent, X-rated alternative comics. One time I saw her handing something to Mal-colm in the hall and went up to him later. He showed it to me. A photo of a man with a wire connecting his tongue to his penis. Piercing both. It nauseated me."

"What was Malcolm's reaction?" I said.

"He said, 'Isn't that strange, Sally?' As in, why would anyone do anything so foolish."

"Was he repulsed by it?" I said.

"He'd have had to be. Did he *show* his repulsion? No, Malcolm rarely showed feelings."

She put the fork down. "This conversation is frustrating me. He's coming across as an oddball and he wasn't. He was just dif-ferent because his IQ was up in the ionosphere. Even at Plas-moDerm he stood apart."

"Zena Lambert was a clerk at PlasmoDerm," I said. "Who'd she work for?"

"The maintenance office—keeping track of the janitors. See what I mean?"

"Not exactly intellectual stuff," said Milo.

Her shoulders sagged. "I'll never understand it. What could Malcolm have *seen* in her? The only thing I can come up with is she was a good listener. Maybe I challenged him too much. We used to have little debates. About technical things. Social issues—I'm an unapologetic liberal and as I said, Malcolm didn't have much pa-tience for . . . problems. We debated all the time, I thought he enjoyed it."

"You think Zena may have been submissive to him?" I said.

"That's what doesn't make sense! Submissive's the last thing you'd call her. At PlasmoDerm she had a reputation for being cheeky. Relating to the professional staff as if she were one of them."

She pushed away her plate.

"Now I sound like a snob, too. But the fact is, Zena was a file clerk who acted as if she had a doctorate. Insinuating herself into conversations she couldn't have really understood—pretentious. That sums her up better than anything: intellectually pretentious. Yet, Malcolm became infatuated with her." Her eyelids quivered.

"Was there anything appealing about her?" I said.

"I suppose you could think she was attractive. In a contrived way. She has a decent figure—meet her, judge for yourself."

"Where can we find her?"

"Malcolm said she was working at a bookstore named Spasm. An amusing place, he called it."

"More body-piercing?" said Milo.

"Probably. Spasm. Does *that* tell you something?"

"Was she fired from PlasmoDerm?"

"Malcolm said she left."

"When?"

"Two weeks before Malcolm's death."

"Any idea why?"

"No. Her occupational history wasn't of very much interest to me. I was glad she was gone. . . ." She looked down at the table. "I guess I was hoping with her out of the immediate environment, Malcolm and I might reconnect."

"Was she at his funeral?"

"There was no funeral," she said, still studying the white linen. "Malcolm's parents had him shipped back home and they cremated him. Look, I know you think the fact that she took him from me is coloring my opinion, but the facts are clear: She got her hooks into him, and not long after, he was dead. For no good reason."

I said, "Detective Connor told us she got Malcolm into some kind of high-IQ group—"

"Meta. People who thought Mensa was for dummies. Malcolm went to a meeting with Zena and joined up. He said it was great even though the food was lousy and the wine was cheap. To me it sounded like losers with nothing to do but talk about how smart they were."

"What did Malcolm like about it?"

"He said it was a pleasure to meet like-minded individuals—but how selective could they have been? Zena was a member!"

She smoothed her hair back and let it fall and the thick waves reverted to their original shape.

"I'm glad someone's finally looking into it. Maybe if Malcolm's parents had insisted, it would have happened sooner, but they didn't want to rake things up."

"That's unusual," said Milo. "Parents generally deny suicide."

"You'd have to know *Malcolm's* parents. Both are professors of physics at Princeton—Dudley and Annabelle Ponsico. He's mechanical, she's particle, they're both geniuses. Malcolm's sister is a physical chemist at MIT and his brother's a mathematician at Michigan. We're talking major gray matter in the lineage but none of them talk. They just calculate."

"You met them?"

"Once, last Christmas, they all visited and we had dinner at their hotel. Silent. The person I spoke to after Malcolm's death was the father and he just said let it rest, young lady, Malcolm has always been a moody boy."

"A moody boy," I said.

"Quaint," she said. "But he's English. Maybe it was too soon after and they didn't want to hear about foul play. I guess I was insensitive."

I'd read Ponsico's file this morning. Both parents had been interviewed over the phone by Petra Connor. Both had been grief-stricken, saying only that Malcolm had never done anything "unexpected" before but that he had been subject to mood swings since adolescence and, at age fifteen, had been treated for a year by a psychiatrist for sleep disturbance and depression.

Things he'd never told Sally.

"Did anyone else from PlasmoDerm belong to Meta?" said Milo.

"No one I know about. Why?"

"You suspect Zena. We're trying to learn more about her."

"Well, that's all I know—would you like to see a picture of Malcolm?"

Before we could answer she produced a color snapshot from her handbag.

She and a tall young red-haired man in a rose garden. She wore a sundress, a big straw hat, and sunglasses and stood with her arm around Malcolm Ponsico's waist. He was well over six feet, narrow-shouldered, slightly overweight. The red hair was curly and thinning and he wore a ginger Abe Lincoln beard with no mustache. He had on a red polo shirt and brown slacks and had the loose-muscled stance of someone with no use for mirrors. She was grinning. His expression was noncommittal.

"We took this at the Huntington Library. An exhibit on Thomas Jefferson's scientific letters."

Milo gave her back the picture. "Those letters on Malcolm's computer screen—DVLL. Mean anything to you?"

"Probably some devil reference that *she* put there. That's exactly the kind of thing she would have gone for."

"She was into satanism, too?"

"It wouldn't surprise me—the salient point here is she stole him and got him involved in who-knows-what and soon after he was dead. I'm not a paranoid person, gentlemen, but the facts speak for themselves. Ask anyone who knows me, my reputation is for being dependable, level-headed, rational."

Her fingers twisted around one another. "Perhaps that's the problem—I was *too* rational. Perhaps, if I'd yelled and kicked and put up a fuss when she went for him instead of standing back and assuming Malcolm would come to his senses, he would have understood how I really felt about him. Perhaps if I'd *emoted*, he'd still be alive."

34

SHE THANKED US FOR LISTENING, PUT HER LAB COAT on, and left the restaurant.

"Woman scorned," said Milo. "And Ponsico had mood problems, even his parents didn't doubt the suicide. Without DVLL and that Meta article you found, I wouldn't spend another second on it."

"Some pattern we've got," I said. "Retarded kids and a genius with no sympathy for the genetically impaired. The only link I can see to our murders is Ponsico learned something at Meta that made him a threat. The killer chitchatting too explicitly about his plans, and Ponsico's contempt for the unfortunate didn't extend to homicide."

"Dr. Sally's convinced this Zena was the killer but Zena's tiny and that part about her surprising Ponsico from behind is nonsense. The wound would have hurt but a big guy like that could have fought her off easily. So if he was murdered it was by someone strong. Just like our kids."

"What about Zena and someone else?"

"A killing team . . . why not, we're entertaining all kinds of fantasies, but the only strike against this girl is the other girl hates her guts. Somewhere down the line, though, she may turn out useful."

"As an entrée to Meta."

He nodded. "Meantime, let's see what our Israeli friend has to offer."

. . .

IN THE DAYLIGHT, SHARAVI'S HOUSE WAS SHABBY. When he came to the door he was close-shaved and neatly dressed. Cup of tea in his hand. Mint sprig floating on top. I became aware of my own stubbled face.

He looked out at the street and let us in. The tea gave off steam. "May I offer you some?"

Milo said, "No, thanks. Hope your computer's working."

We walked to the back room. The PC was on, a screen-saving pink hexagon dancing on the black screen. Sharavi had arranged two folding chairs in the middle of the carpet. The velvet bag for his prayer equipment was gone.

Milo showed him the article about Farley Sanger's Meta editorial and told him about Malcolm Ponsico.

He pulled up to the workstation and began punching keys, using a one-handed hunt-and-peck that was faster than I would have believed.

The bad hand rested on his lap, an inert hunk of flesh.

I watched data bank after data bank flash and disappear.

After a while, he said, "If this group has done something criminal, none of the major agencies knows about it. I'll check academic bases."

The keyword *Meta* brought up hundreds of irrelevant topics from university data stations: meta-analysis in philosophy, scores of chemical compounds, references to metabolism, metallurgy, metamorphosis.

When we'd waded through all of it, he said, "Let's try the Internet. It's become an international trash can, but who knows."

"Let's try the phone first," said Milo. "New York Information for Meta."

Sharavi smiled. "Good point." He dialed 212 Information, waited, hung up. "No listing."

"Maybe," I said, "the publicity about Sanger's article drove them out of business."

"Could be," said Sharavi. "Though hate's a hot commodity. It could also drum up more business. Shall I try the Internet, now?"

Using a coded password, he hooked into an on-line network I'd never heard of. No cute graphics or chat lines, just stark black letters on white screen.

Several seconds passed and he sat there without moving or blinking.

WELCOME R. VAN RIJN flashed.

Rembrandt's surname. Had the Israeli police assigned him the moniker or did he fancy himself an artist?

A brown hand flew nimbly over the keyboard and within seconds he was web-crawling.

Another flood of unrelated topics: an entomologist in Paris doing research on a larva called metacercaria, a holistic healer in Oakland promising to cure aches of the metacarpal bones.

Twenty minutes later, he stopped.

"Suggestions?"

"Try Mensa," said Milo. "Meta's an imitator, meaning there's probably some hostility between the groups. Maybe some Mensa faithful wants to express feelings."

Sharavi swiveled around, attacking the keyboard.

"Plenty on Mensa," he said.

We watched him scroll slowly through page after page. Times and places for Mensa meetings around the world, Mensa-related topics.

A similar organization in London calling itself Limey Scumdogs discussing its favorite things. Members with nicknames—the Sharp Kidd, Sugar Baby, Buffalo Bob—listing "bad puns," "strong coffee and dialectics," "debates from hell," "cuddles and house-broken Afghan hounds." And so on.

Some of the notations were in foreign languages and Sharavi seemed to be reading them.

"What was that?" said Milo, pointing, as Sharavi skipped one.

"Dublin Mensa. Probably Gaelic."

More scrolling.

A real-estate broker in Fond du Lac, Wisconsin, advertising his services and listing Mensa membership as a job qualification.

Same for a personnel manager in Chicago, a dental hygienist in Orlando, Florida, an engineer in Tokyo, dozens more.

Unemployment hadn't spared the top of the bell curve.

Next came an IQ MEASUREMENT section. Several writers, all men, displaying questions from intelligence scales—quickie tests, the type featured in know-your-IQ-paperbacks. Most selections were followed by variations of the assertion that "this is an extremely rigorous set of questions constructed to show a stratospherically high level of intelligence."

```
The Punchline:
ROBERT'S IQ.
HORACE'S IQ.
KEITH'S IQ.
CHARLES'S IQ . . .
```

Some pages had accompanying artwork—Einstein's face was a favorite.

All with CLICK HERE TO SEE MY SCORE boxes.

Sharavi's clicks brought up graphs with little stars for Robert and Horace and Keith and Charles and . . .

All in the 170-plus range.

"Such smart people," said Sharavi. "So much free time."

"Weenie-land," said Milo. "Send 'em applications to the Get a Life Club."

Sharavi moved through several more pages with no success.

"The information age," said Milo. "You spend lots of time doing this?"

"Less and less," said Sharavi, hand continuing to move. "When the Internet began it was more valuable as an investigative tool. Professors talking to professors, scientific data, agencies communicating. Now, there's too much to wade through for the little you get. It seems to have become one big chat-room for lonely people."

He turned and looked at me. "I suppose that serves a purpose, Doctor."

"Keep going," said Milo.

After two more hours of viewing, we had nothing.

"I assume you've already looked up DVLL," I told Sharavi.

"That and all the hate groups who run bulletin boards. No progress, I'm afraid."

"What about a different keyword," I said. "Galton, sterilization, eugenics, euthanasia."

He typed.

STERILIZATION BROUGHT UP MORE REFERENCES TO food-safety than castration and most of the discussions of eugenics were glorified personal ads: "I hereby splay my DNA out on the platter of public scrutiny. Women desiring choice nucleic protein are cordially invited to apply."

Sharavi printed it all out, anyway, page after page landing in the bin silently. From time to time Milo got up, removed sheets, scanned them, put them back.

At five-thirty, he said, "Enough. They obviously keep a low profile."

"We could act rather than just react," said Sharavi. "E-mailing something about Meta into some of the data banks and see what turns up."

"Can you be sure your identity's totally protected?" said Milo.

"No. I change passwords and addresses regularly but you can never be sure."

"Then, no, not yet. I don't want to alert anyone."

"I already did that with my call to Mensa," I said, describing the message I'd left.

Milo said, "No big deal," but I could tell he was bothered and I felt like an amateur.

He turned to Sharavi. "Any other insights?"

"Ponsico's suicide. Despite the lack of evidence, it does sound irregular. Using poison, for starters. Poisoners tend to be women, right?"

"Ponsico was a scientist."

"True," said Sharavi. "Which leads me to another issue: As a scientist he'd know what to expect. Potassium chloride causes a quick death, but it's far from painless—sudden cardiac arrhythmia, a severe heart attack. When you execute criminals with it, you add sodium pentothal for pre-sedation and pancurium bromide to stop breathing. Couldn't Ponsico have chosen an easier death for himself?"

"Maybe he was punishing himself," said Milo. "Thought he *deserved* cruel and unusual."

"Guilt?" I said, thinking again of Nolan. "Over what?"

"Maybe he'd played a part in something really nasty. Our killings or something else. Or maybe he was just a guy with mood swings who ended up profoundly depressed in the lab and just happened to have access to poison. And even if he did make things rougher on himself than he had to, it was still relatively fast and clean. Helluva lot better than some of the stuff I've seen people do to themselves. Right, Superintendent?"

"Daniel," said Sharavi. "Yes, that's true. Self-hatred can be an amazing thing. But . . . I guess I'd like to learn more about this young man."

"I'll call his parents," said Milo. "The professors in Princeton. Maybe some of his other coworkers at PlasmoDerm."

"It's a biomedical company?"

"Skin research. Ponsico was working on improving the success of skin grafts. Why, you see some sort of work connection?"

"No," said Sharavi. "Though I suppose if there was a dissatisfied customer—someone whose graft didn't take . . . but no, they would have poisoned the surgeon, not the researcher . . . no, I have no ideas."

He drank tea and put the cup down. "I have good sources in New York. If Meta does exist, they'll be able to find out. We could also tap Zena Lambert's line—"

"Forget it. We've got no grounds for any kind of warrant, let alone a tap. On the off chance she's connected to anything, I don't want to screw up the evidentiary chain."

"Good point."

"Don't even think about it," said Milo.

"Of course," said Sharavi.

"I mean it."

"I realize that."

"The bookstore Zena works in," I said. "Spasm. An offbeat name so maybe it's a meeting place for people with offbeat ideas. There could be a bulletin board, maybe with a posting by Meta."

"No phone listing but they announce meetings at a store?" said Milo.

"An out-of-the-way store that attracts the target audience. Want me to drop in and look around?"

He rubbed his face. "Let me think about it—I want to get the most out of anything we do."

Sharavi got up and stretched, raising both arms above his head, the bad hand dangling. "I'm getting more tea—are you sure you wouldn't like some? The mint's fresh. I found a big patch growing out in back."

"Sure," I said. "Thanks."

When he was gone, Milo scowled at the computer. "Garbage in, garbage out. . . . So what's with the Arafat look, Alex—scratch that in view of present company—the porcupine look?"

"I rushed over to the library, didn't take the time to shave."

"That's half a day's worth?"

I nodded.

"Taking those testosterone pills, again?"

I flexed a bicep and grunted and he gave a tired smile.

Sharavi came back with the tea. Scalding, slightly sweet, the mint flavor gliding above the heat.

As I sipped, I used one of the phones to call my service.

"Hi, Doctor, there's just one. A Loren Bukovsky, from . . . looks like Mensa. Though it says here he asked for Al. The girl—a new one—tried to tell him different but he insisted you were Al. You do get some strange ones, Dr. Delaware, but that's your business, right?"

"Right. What did Mr. Bukovsky have to say?"

"Let's see—sorry, this new one has terrible penmanship . . . it looks like he *was* . . . no, he *has* nothing to do with Mela, or Meta . . . something like that . . . anyway, he wants nothing to do with Mela or whatever . . . um, but if you have the . . . sorry, Doctor, this isn't very polite."

"What does it say, Joyce?"

"If you have the poor taste to want to . . . looks like *fraternatize* with . . . idiots . . . go to a place called . . . looks like Spastic . . . but he doesn't leave an address . . . very strange, even for you, Dr. Delaware."

"That's all of it?"

"He also said don't call back, he's not interested in you. How rude, huh?"

"Very," I said. "But maybe he's got his reasons."

"STRONG OPINIONS," SAID MILO, WRITING DOWN Bukovsky's name.

"And now it's out that we're looking into Meta. Sorry."

"But at least we know the bookstore's worth looking into." He turned to Sharavi. "How about using some of that illegal DMV access on Mr. Bukovsky and Ms. Lambert?"

Sharavi put his mug down and faced the computer.

Moments later:

"Loren A. Bukovsky, an address on Corinth Avenue, Los Angeles, 90064."

"West Los Angeles," said Milo. "Minutes from the station. Might as well pay him a visit."

"When should I visit Spasm?" I said.

"Let me check out Bukovsky first."

Sharavi said, "If Bukovsky has something interesting to say, perhaps Dr. Delaware can do more than just drop in at Spasm."

"Such as?"

"If Meta still holds meetings, he could try to attend. Who better than a Ph.D.? He could pose as someone interested in—"

"Forget it," said Milo.

Sharavi blinked but didn't move, otherwise. "All right."

"And don't think about going yourself, Superintendent."

Sharavi smiled. "Me? I lack the qualifications."

"The same goes for any of your people."

"My people?"

"Put it out of your mind. No undercover operations that I don't know about."

"All right."

"All right? Just like that, huh?"

"Just like that."

Saying it in a near-whisper but for the first time, the Israeli was showing emotion. The faintest tightening around the golden eyes, a twitch along the jawline.

"I'm doing my best to cooperate," he said softly.

"I'm a skeptic and a pessimist," said Milo. "When things go too smoothly it worries me."

Sharavi's jaw relaxed and he brought up a smile—mechanically, as if evoking data from the computer.

"Shall I make your life difficult, then, Milo?"

"Why break a trend?"

Sharavi shook his head. "I'm going to eat."

He left the room again and Milo thumbed absently through the printout in the bin. "I'll try to interview Bukovsky today. And call Ponsico's parents. I just hope this whole Ponsico thing hasn't gotten us too far afield."

He got up and paced. The house was small and I could hear Sharavi working in the kitchen.

"If I visit the bookstore," I said, "I could sound out the Lambert woman, see if I can get her to talk about Meta."

"Alex—"

"In an unobtrusive way. Even if the killer's a Meta member, that doesn't make the whole group a homicidal cabal. And if I did get into a meeting and was able to look them all over—"

"Delete the thought, Alex."

"Why?"

"Why do you think?"

"Because Sharavi suggested it?"

He whipped around, glaring. "Ten points off for a very bad guess."

"Hey," I said, "I'm brutally frank 'cause I care."

He started to retort, dropped his shoulders, laughed. "Look at this. I'm trying to protect you and you're dissing me. You think it's a smart idea hobnobbing with a group of genetic snobs, one of whom could be a goddamn serial killer?"

"I don't think attending one meeting is going to put me in danger."

He didn't answer.

"Also," I said, "I think Sharavi's involvement still bothers you to the point where you run the risk of throwing the baby out."

He rubbed his face hard and fast. "This is great. Him on one side and you on the other . . . for all I know he's got this goddamn room bugged."

"Okay, I'll shut up. Sorry."

He grimaced. Laughed again. Circled the room.

"What the hell am I doing here—yeah, yeah, you're right, having to deal with him *does* piss me off. I don't like . . . too many layers." He shoved his arms in front of him, breaststroking air. "Like suffocating under a dozen blankets."

"Sure," I said. "But unless some progress is made on the killings, you run the risk of a dozen more blankets. As in task force."

"What is this, tough *love*?"

"It's for your own good, sonny boy."

"Dr. Castor Oil—you really want to play secret agent, don't you? Couple of days with Mr. Mossad and you're itching for code names and fountain-pen cameras."

"That's me," I said. "Agent Double-O-Shrink. License to interpret."

Sharavi returned with a sandwich on a cheap plastic plate. Tuna and lettuce on egg bread. Very little tuna.

He put the plate down next to the phones. His face said he had no appetite.

"I have two police scanners. The one in the kitchen was on. A call just went out on one of your tactical bands. Central Division Homicide detectives calling in a dead body in an alley. A 187 cutting. It's probably unrelated, but next to the body was a white cane. I thought you should know."

Picking up the sandwich, he took a small, decisive bite.

35

DANIEL WATCHED THE TWO OF THEM DRIVE AWAY through a slit in the living-room drapes.

He'd kept up a bland front during the meeting. Taken things in, given very little out.

Could Delaware see through it?

The psychologist seemed more agreeable, but with psychologists you never knew.

Another meeting. How many had he attended over the years, leaving with those same feelings of frustration?

Like Sturgis, he preferred working alone.

Like Sturgis, he was seldom able to.

Coating himself with the veneer of reason, when he itched to be as negative as Sturgis.

Dead children . . .

He seldom showed his feelings to anyone, even Laura.

Sobbing about Daoud and his fat wife, twice, both times alone in the cool, dark privacy of a tiny, cavelike Yemenite synagogue near the Mahane Yehudah market. An empty synagogue, because he'd chosen the dead time between the morning *shaharit* service and the afternoon *minhah*.

Reciting a few psalms, returning home that evening presentable for Laura and the children.

Why expose them to even a hint of the pain?

The Bethlehem hatchet wielders would never be punished.

Not in this world, anyway.

Now, this. Irit, the other kids. Maybe a blind man. What could be more hideous?

Would this Meta thing lead anywhere? Probably not.

One walked the desert sands, sank shafts, hoped for oil . . .

So he and Sturgis were probably feeling similar emotions—hey, let's have a discussion group, like the ones the department organized when a sapper got blown up or one of the undercover guys took a knife in a back alley of the Old City.

Daniel could just see it. Sturgis and him, sitting in a circle, each daring the other to be human. Delaware in the middle, the . . . what was the word—the *facilitator*.

Sturgis grumbling. An ill-mannered bear, that one. But smart.

Zev Carmeli was feeling better about the guy.

Like most diplomats, Zev didn't forgive. Forced to put on a polite front all day, he was judgmental, essentially a misanthrope.

Daniel remembered the call.

"Guess who they've given me now, Sharavi. A homosexual."

Daniel had sat in a rear room of the New York embassy, listening as Carmeli complained. Carmeli reiterating his opinions of the "moronic L.A. police."

"A homosexual," he repeated. "Who he screws is his own damn business but it makes him an outcast, so how can he possibly be effective? I ask for the one with the highest solve rate and this is who they give me."

"You think they're playing with you?"

"What do *you* think? This is some city, Sharavi. Every group hates the other. Like Beirut."

Or Jerusalem, thought Daniel.

"Maybe he is the best, Zev. Why dismiss him before you know?"

Silence.

"You?" said Carmeli. "A guy with a yarmulke and you approve of that kind of thing?"

"If he's the one with the highest solve rate and the right kind of experience, then you're doing well."

"I'm surprised, Sharavi."

"About what?"

"Such tolerance. The orthodox aren't known for their tolerance."

Daniel didn't respond.

"Well," said Carmeli, "that's why I'm calling you. You come out here and check things out, whatever it takes. If you say keep him on, I will. But ultimately, it's your responsibility."

Then he'd hung up.

Poor Zev.

Years ago, they'd both been students at Hebrew U. Daniel a twenty-five-year-old senior with three years of Army experience, Zev, younger, one of the few whizzes exempted out because of high test scores and family connections. Even then Zev had been serious for his age and openly ambitious. But you could talk to him, have a discussion. Not anymore.

The man had lost a daughter.

Daniel knew about fathers and daughters.

Zev could be forgiven just about anything.

ALONE IN THE HOUSE, HE FINISHED HIS SANDWICH, though it might as well have been dust on plywood, then phoned an attorney in New York who received half of his income from the embassy, and asked him to quietly investigate Meta and fellow lawyer Farley Sanger, the one who'd written that retarded people weren't human.

Two more hours at the computer earned him nothing but a sore hand.

Carpal tunnel, the police doctor at French Hill had announced. If you don't watch out you'll have no hands. Ice it and don't use it so much.

Expert advice; Daniel had suppressed laughter and left the examining room wondering what it would be like to have no hands.

At 8:00 P.M., he drove to a kosher market on Pico and stocked up on groceries, putting on his yarmulke in order to blend in. The woman at the register said, "Shalom," and he felt more at home than he had since arriving.

At ten he called Laura in Jerusalem.

She said, "Darling, I couldn't wait to hear from you. The children want to speak to you, too."

His heart soared.

36

"BODY'S ZIPPED, ALMOST READY TO GO," SAID THE
Central Homicide detective. "Your basic frenzied cutting."

His name was Bob Pierce and he was in his fifties, thick in the
middle with wavy gray hair, a big jaw, and a Chicago accent. On
the way over Milo told me he'd once been a top solver, was two
months from retirement now, thinking only about Idaho.

This evening, he seemed resigned and stoic, but his fingers gathered and released the bottom hem of his suit jacket, pinching, letting go, pinching.

He stood with us on Fourth Street, at the mouth of the alley
between Main and Wall, as the crime-scene crew worked under
portable floodlights. The lights were selective and the filthy strip
lined with dumpsters sported strange, blotchy shadows. A rotten-
produce smell poured out to the street.

"Working alone today, Bob?" said Milo.

"Bruce has the flu. So what's your interest in our alleged felony?"

"Cold case of mine, a retarded kid, so I'm looking into any 187s
with handicapped vics."

"Well, this one was handicapped. Coroner said his eyes were
clearly nonfunctional. Atrophied sclera or something like that.
Probably born blind. Yours black?"

"No."

"This one is."

"Any ID?" said Milo.

"Lots." Pierce pulled out his notepad. "Medi-Cal card, a few other things next to the body, along with his wallet, all the money gone."

He put on half-glasses, and flipped pages. "Melvin Myers, black male, twenty-five, home address on Stocker Avenue."

He closed the pad and turned to watch the techs.

"Stocker's the Crenshaw district," said Milo.

"Don't know what he was doing here but one of the uniforms said there's a school for the disabled not far from here—off L.A. Street, near the garment outlets. I'll find out tomorrow if Myers was a student."

"What happened to him?"

"Walking through the alley, got stabbed from behind about ten times with a big knife, then ten more times in the front."

"Overkill," said Milo.

"I'll say." Pierce's hands worked faster at his hem. "Can you imagine, unable to see it, just *feeling* it—this is some so-called alleged civilization we're allegedly living in."

He directed the last words at me, staring, as he'd done off and on since being introduced. Was it my unshaven face or the fact that Milo had introduced me as a consultant?

Milo said, "Any estimates when it happened, Bob?"

"Sometime late in the afternoon. M.E. said the body was pretty fresh."

"Who discovered him?"

"One of our patrol cars—how's that for something new? They were rolling up the alley, saw a leg sticking out from behind one of the dumpsters. At first they figured him for a crackhead who fell asleep and got out to roust him."

"Late afternoon," said Milo. "Working hours. Pretty risky."

"Not if you're a no-brain sociopath. And he got away with it, didn't he?"

Pierce gave a sour look. "The thing is, even though it's working hours, this particular alley's been pretty quiet, lots of the buildings on Wall are vacant. And for the most part the people who work either on Main or Wall stay out of it because it used to be a crack market. The only citizens who do go in there are the janitors who take the garbage to the dumpsters."

Milo peered down the alley. "The dumpsters give good cover."

"You bet. One after the other, like rows of shacks. Reminds me of those little green houses in Monopoly."

"So it's not a crack market anymore?"

"Not this week. Policy order from headquarters: Mayor says get a handle on quality-of-life offenses, let's make our downtown a real downtown so we can pretend we're living in a real city. HQ says knock the dope rate down pronto but without any additional personnel or patrol cars. Which is about as likely as O.J. feeling remorse. The way it plays out is we up patrol for one alley, the crackheads move to another. Like Parcheesi—bumping and moving, everyone goes in circles."

"How often are the patrols?"

"A few times a day." Pierce pulled out a pack of mints. "Obviously not at the right time for poor Mr. Myers. Helluva place for a blind guy to get lost in."

"Lost?" said Milo.

"What else? Unless he was a crackhead himself, looking for something recreational, didn't know the action's three alleys over. But I'm choosing innocent til proven guilty unless I learn different. At this point, he got lost."

"I thought blind guys had a good sense of direction," said Milo. "And if he went to school around here, you'd think he'd know about the neighborhood, be extra careful."

"What can I tell you?" said Pierce. Another glance back. "Well, there it goes."

Coroner's attendants lifted a black body bag onto a gurney. As the wheels moved over the ravaged asphalt, the car rattled.

Milo said, "One second, Bob," strode over, said something to the attendants, and waited as they unzipped the bag.

"So you're consulting," Pierce said to me. "I've got a daughter at Cal State, wants to be a psychologist, maybe work with kids—"

Milo's voice made us both turn.

He'd walked past the coroner's station wagon, was standing near the east wall of the alley, half-concealed by a dumpster, the visible slice of his bulk whitened by a floodlight.

Pierce said, "What, now?" He and I went over.

The chalk outline of Melvin Myers's body had been drawn unevenly on the pitted tar. Right-angled. Folded. I could see where his foot had stuck out.

The oily rust of bloodstains all around.

A pothole in the center of the outline created a symbolic wound.

Milo pointed at the wall. His eyes were bright, cold, satisfied but enraged.

The red brick was blackened by decades of smog and grease and garbage distillate, a mad jumble of obscene graffiti.

I saw nothing but defacement. Same with Pierce. He said, "What?"

Milo walked to the wall, stooped, put his finger near something just inches from where the brick met the floor of the alley.

Behind the spot where Melvin Myers's head would have rested in death.

Pierce and I got closer. The garbage stench was overpowering.

Milo's fingertip pointed at four white letters, maybe half a hand-breadth tall.

White chalk, just like the body outline, but fainter.

Block letters, printed neatly.

DVLL.

"That mean something?" said Pierce.

"It means I've complicated your life, Bob."

Pierce put on his reading glasses and pushed his big jaw up to the letters.

"Not exactly permanent. Usually the idiots use spray paint."

"It didn't need to be permanent," I said. "The main thing was to deliver the message."

37

to Fourth Street.

"Different M.O.s, different divisions for each one," said the Central detective. "Some piece of crap playing games?"

"That's what it looks like."

"Who're the other Ds?"

"Hooks and McLaren in Southwest, Manny Alvarado in Newton, and we just picked one up that doesn't fit except for a DVLL link that's Hollywood's. D-I named Petra Connor, works with Stu Bishop."

"Don't know her," said Pierce. "One day Bishop's gonna be chief. Why isn't *he* in on it?"

"On vacation."

"So what're we talking about, some coordinated effort?"

"Nothing to coordinate so far," said Milo. "We've just been trading info and not much of it. Gorobich and Ramos did the whole crime-scene thing with the FBI and didn't get much either."

Leaving out one particular detective.

Pierce clicked his upper teeth against his lowers. Perfect teeth. Dentures. "What do you want me to do, here?"

"Hey, Bob, far be it from me to tell you what to do."

"Why not? My wife does. And her mother. And my daughters. And everyone else with a mouth. . . . Okay, what I'm gonna do tonight is write this up as a 187 committed during a robbery. Then I'll try to see if Mr. Myers has a family. And a drug record. If there's a family, I make *that* call. If not, I visit the trade school tomorrow, see if he was a student, take it from there."

Pierce smiled. "If I'm feeling really nasty, I call Bruce at midnight and tell him hey, guess what you'll probably still be working on when I'm fishing at Hayden Lake, trying to figure out which of my neighbors is an Aryan Nations nutcase and which one just hates people on general principle."

"Would it traumatize you," said Milo, "if I try to find out about Myers tonight? Run him through the files, maybe check out the school."

"The school's closed."

"Maybe they've got an off-hours number, someone who can confirm he was a student, tell us something about him."

Pierce's eyes seemed to twinkle but the rest of his face expressed nothing. "Insomniac?"

"I've been living with this one for a while, Bob."

"Yeah, go ahead, why not? You can call the family, too. And while you're at it, take my dog to the vet to get his anal glands squeezed."

"Forget it. Don't mean to muscle in."

"Hey, I'm kidding—go ahead, do what you want. I've got forty-eight days left before I trade smog for Nazis and no way am I gonna finish this one by then. Just keep me cued in from time to time, I need straight paper."

He faced me. "This is police work in action. Enjoying the consulting, so far?"

DRIVING AWAY, I SAID, ''THERE'S NO WAY ANYONE else would have noticed those letters. A message but a private one."

He twisted the wheel, drove to Sixth Street, hung a sharp left, and headed west, racing through the dark downtown streets. The only people visible were living out of shopping carts.

"Mug a blind guy, fake a robbery," he said. "Telling us: Look how goddamn clever I am—press here for *my* score."

He rolled up onto the freeway.

"Learn anything from the body?" I said.

"Not really. The poor guy was hashed."

"So much for neat and clean," I said. "So much for mercy kill-ing. He's picked up the pace and increased the violence level. And the risk level: broad daylight. He may think he's got a serious philosophy but he's just another psychopath."

"What's really picked up is his confidence level, Alex. He has no idea we even know what's going on, and with Carmeli's gag order we can't flush him out. Though what kind of warning could we issue? Anyone with a dark skin and a disability is a potential vic-tim? Just what this city needs."

"Anyone with dark skin and a disability plus Malcolm Ponsico. Who joined a group that just might believe handicapped people aren't human. Myers's death says we need to get closer to Meta, Milo. And why not use the fact that the killer doesn't know we're on to him as an advantage? I'll go to the bookstore, see if they've got a bulletin board, check out Zena Lambert. Maybe I *can* get invited to the next Meta party."

We were going eighty-five on the 10, now. He passed under the bridge at the Crenshaw exit. "If Lambert turns out to be a literal femme fatale, chatting her up could be more than just a social thing."

"Femme fatale," I said. "So now you like the idea of a boy-girl killer team?"

"At this point, I'm not dismissing anything."

"A collaboration could explain some of the diversity in M.O. Two self-rated geniuses getting together to play human chess. She serves as a lure, he steps in and does the heavy lifting. So when do I go to Spasm?"

"Thought you hated parties."

"Sometimes I'm more social than others."

WE STOPPED FOR COFFEE AT A FAST-FOOD STAND ON La Cienega, where I called Robin and told her there'd been another murder and I'd be late.

"My God—another retarded child?"

"A blind man."

"Oh, Alex . . ."

"I'm sorry. It might be a while."

"Yes . . . of course. How did it happen?"

"Fake mugging," I said. "Downtown."

I heard her inhale sharply. "Do what you have to do. But wake me when you get in. If I'm asleep."

IT WAS AFTER ELEVEN BY THE TIME WE RETURNED TO Sharavi's house. He took a while to answer the door, had clearly been sleeping but he did his best to hide it.

The gold eyes were red-rimmed. He wore a plain white T-shirt and green cotton athletic shorts. As he ushered us in, he revealed his good hand and the black-matte pistol dangling from it.

"Plastic," said Milo. "Glock."

"No, a smaller manufacturer." Sharavi slipped the weapon into a pocket of the shorts. "So the blind man *was* part of it."

Milo told him what we'd learned and we returned to the computer room. Moments later we learned that Melvin A. Myers had no criminal record and had received various forms of public assistance for most of his life. No family.

"Let's try the school," said Milo. "Central City Skills Center."

Unsurprisingly, no one answered and Sharavi played with data banks for a while, finally locating a two-year-old article on the school in the *Los Angeles Times.* The director at that time had been a woman named Darlene Grosperrin.

"At least it's not Smith," said Milo. "Look her up."

He was sitting on the edge of his folding chair, moving in rhythm with Sharavi's one-handed stabs at the keyboard. Unaware of the harmony.

Sharavi complied. "Yes, here it is, DMV: Darlene Grosperrin, Amherst Street, Brentwood."

Milo's long arm shot forward as he grabbed the phone and dialed 411. He barked, listened, wrote down the number. "Grosperrin, D., no first name, no address, but how many of those can there be. . . . Here's what you get for your trusting nature, Ms. G. A midnight call."

He punched numbers again.

"Darlene Grosperrin? This is Detective Milo Sturgis of the Los Angeles Police Department, sorry to call this late—pardon, ma'am? No, no, not your daughter, sorry to scare you, ma'am . . . it's about one of the students at the skills center, a gentleman named Melvin A. Myers—no, ma'am, unfortunately, he's *not* okay . . ."

He put the phone down ten minutes later.

"Top student, she says. And not retarded, smart, one of their best trainees, could type over one hundred fifty words a minute on the computer. He was due to graduate in a few months, she was sure he'd get a job."

He rubbed his face.

"She was pretty broken up, couldn't tell me what he'd been doing in the alley. Sometimes he ate dinner downtown before heading back to Crenshaw but there'd be no reason for him to wander in there. And he was pretty good with that cane, knew the street layout."

"So he *was* lured," I said. "What about family?"

"None—lucky for Bob Pierce. Myers has been living alone for the last five years, since his mother died. Apparently she sheltered him and after she was gone he decided to pull himself together. First he took some training at the braille center, then he enrolled at the school. They've got an eighteen-month computer program and he was acing it. The address on Stocker is a state-financed group home."

Sharavi removed the black-matte pistol and placed it next to the computer. "A blind man . . . my contact back east called me while you were gone. He's found nothing on Meta in New York, but the lawyer who wrote that article in *The Pathfinder*—Farley Sanger—is still practicing at the same Wall Street firm. The editor—that woman stock analyst, Helga Cranepool—is still working at her job, too. Neither of them comes up in Lexis, so Sanger doesn't go to court on important cases. My source says the firm does estate planning for rich people."

"What kind of car does he drive?" said Milo. "What kind of shampoo does he use?"

"Mercedes station wagon, one year old. I'll try to find out about the shampoo. And if he uses cream rinse."

Milo laughed.

Sharavi said, "The Mercedes is registered in Connecticut. Sanger's got a home in Darien and an apartment on East Sixty-ninth Street. He's forty-one years old, married, has two children, a boy and a girl, no record of criminal activity."

"So Sanger's being watched."

"For a while. I also looked up Zena Lambert, the bookstore clerk. No criminal record for her, either. She's twenty-eight years old, lives on Rondo Vista Street in Silverlake. The bookstore's nearby. She has a MasterCard but rarely uses it. Last year, she earned eighteen thousand dollars."

He smiled. "I'll check into her hair-care, as well."

"You surveilling her, too?" said Milo.

"Not without your agreement."

"How long are you planning to surveil Sanger?"

"Long as necessary. In view of his belief that retarded people are—what was the phrase, Dr. Delaware—"

"Meat without mention," I said.

"—meat without mention, it seems a good idea, maybe he'll do something that tells us more about the group. On both coasts."

"Speaking of coasts, any chance of accessing his travel records?" said Milo. "Corporate lawyers fly back and forth all the time, nice cover."

"Good idea," said Sharavi. "I'll do it tomorrow, when offices open in New York. In view of Myers's murder, I did call all the major hotels here in L.A., just to check if Sanger's registered and he's not. But he could be traveling under a different name."

"Thanks for all the work."

Sharavi shrugged. "What next?"

"I've got an appointment to meet with Mrs. Grosperrin tomorrow morning, see if I can learn more about Myers, why he was lured, as opposed to some other student."

"For one, he was black," I said. "Every single victim—except Ponsico—was non-Anglo."

"A racist eugenicist," said Sharavi.

"The two have generally gone together. A look at the books Spasm sells might give us some information. Something tells me the place doesn't specialize in children's literature. When do I go?"

Sharavi's eyebrows rose.

Milo told him, "He wants to play Superspy. I blame *you*."

"Are you thinking of going as yourself, Doctor?"

"I wasn't planning to show ID."

"Then maybe you should take alternative ID." Sharavi turned to Milo. "It's the kind of thing I could be helpful with."

"Undercover hoo-hah?" said Milo.

"For his protection. If he's up for a bit of role-playing."

Talking about me in the third person.

Sharavi gave me an appraising look. "You've already made progress on a beard."

38

AT THAT POINT, SOMETHING IN THE ROOM CHANGED.

Milo and Sharavi found several points of agreement:

Undercover work was serious business—temporary dissociation, Sharavi called it.

"We're talking a visit to a bookstore," I said.

"A visit that could lead to something, Doctor. You need to be extremely careful from the start."

"Meaning?"

"Go as someone else, get comfortable being someone else."

"Fine."

"And," said Milo, "you need Robin's okay on this."

"Don't you think this is a little—"

"No, Alex, I don't. What will probably happen is you'll go there, look at some weird books, come home. Even if you do hook up with Meta, it could dead-end, maybe they're just weenies. But Daniel and I both know police work's ninety-nine percent boredom, one percent panic at the unexpected. We are dealing with a person who stabbed a blind man in the back."

He asked Sharavi, "How long would it take you to get him false papers?"

"Half a day," said the Israeli, "for driver's license, credit cards, social security. I can also get him clothes, if that's necessary, and a car."

"The address on the ID," said Milo. "Bogus or real?"

"Real is better—I know of a place in the Valley that's available right now, but I may also be able to find one in the city."

"Just cover or actual use?"

"In the event of a prolonged role-play, he could use it."

Milo turned to me. "What if you need to move for a while, Alex? Are you ready for that?"

Hard voice. I knew what he was thinking. The last time I'd relocated, the move had been coerced. Running from the psychopath who'd burned my house down.

"I assume we're not talking long-term."

"Probably days, not weeks," said Milo. "But what about patients?"

"No active ones," I said. Since Helena Dahl had dropped out. I thought of her brother, another high-IQ suicide . . .

"What about old patients in crisis?"

"I can always check in with my service. Most of what I've got is paperwork—reports due."

"Good," said Sharavi. "So far, your lifestyle seems to fit this nicely."

Milo frowned.

They both gave me more rules:

In order to avoid accidental slipups, I needed to use a false name similar to my real one and a personal history that grew out of my own.

"A psychologist, but not one in active practice," said Milo. "Nothing traceable."

"How about someone who attended psychology graduate school but dropped out before finishing?" I said. "ABD. All but dissertation."

"Dropped out for what reason?"

"Personality conflicts," I said. "He was too smart for them, so they messed him up during his dissertation. My instinct is that's a Meta-compatible profile."

"Why?"

"Because people who spend lots of time talking and thinking about how smart they are generally don't accomplish much."

Milo considered that and nodded.

"So far so good?" he asked Sharavi.

"Yes, but you should start thinking in terms of *you*, Doctor, not *he*."

"Okay," I said. "They messed *me* up because I threatened them. My research threatened them. The genetics of IQ, politically incorrect—"

"No," said Milo. "Too close—too cute."

"I agree," said Sharavi. "These people may not be as smart as they think they are but they aren't stupid. You can't come in there agreeing with them too strongly."

"Exactly," said Milo. "Way I see it, you need to show casual curiosity but not jump on their bandwagon. If it goes that far."

"Okay," I said, feeling vaguely foolish. "I'm essentially an anti-social guy, don't trust groups, so I'm not itching to join any new ones. . . . My research was on—how about sex-role stereotypes and child-rearing patterns? I did some work on that in grad school, then I switched to hospital work and never published, so there's no connection in writing."

Sharavi wrote something down.

"Fine," said Milo. "Go on."

"I ran out of money, the department wouldn't support me because I refused to play the game and—"

"What game?" said Sharavi.

"Interdepartmental politics. That's also something I can talk about with authority."

"When did all this happen?" said Milo.

"Ten years ago?"

"What school?"

"How about an unaccredited program—one that's gone out of business? During the eighties there were plenty of them."

"I like that," said Sharavi. He glanced at Milo, who grunted assent. "I'll find one and create some paper for you."

"Seeing as your print shop's that good," said Milo, "how about some twenty-dollar bills?"

Sharavi waved at the dismal little room. "How do you think I finance such luxury."

Milo chuckled, turned serious. "Speaking of financing, how've *you* supported yourself since dropping out, Mr. All But Dissertation?"

"Family money?" I said. "A small inheritance? Just enough to get by, but no luxuries. Yet another reason for my frustration. I'm brilliant, too good for my station in life."

"Do you work?"

"Nope. Still searching for something fulfilling. Your basic L.A. slacker."

They both nodded.

"So what's my name?" I said. "How close should I get?"

"Close enough to make it easy to remember," said Milo, "but not so close that you use the real one by mistake."

"Allan?" I said. "Allan Del something—Delvecchio? I could pass for Italian."

"No," said Milo. "Let's keep ethnicity out of this. They may not like ethnics of any kind and I don't want you to have to fake some conversation about Mama's gnocchi recipe."

"How about Delbert? Delham—or just plain Dell."

"Allan Dell?" he said. "Sounds phony. And too close."

"Arthur Dell? Albert, Andrew?" I said. "Andy?"

"What about Desmond?" said Milo. "Like the old biddy in *Sunset Boulevard*. Andy Desmond—can you live with it?"

I repeated it to myself several times. "Sure, but now I expect a big house, Daniel."

"Sorry," said Sharavi. "There are limits."

"Andrew Desmond," said Milo. "Would-be psychologist—Mr. Would Be. So can we get papers tomorrow?"

"We could but I suggest we hold off for a few days."

"Why?"

"To give Alex a chance to get comfortable with the role. And to let that beard grow—do you wear contact lenses?"

"No."

"Good. I can supply glasses with clear lenses, it's surprising how effective they can be. And you might consider a haircut. A short one. Those curls are a little . . . conspicuous."

"A buzz. Robin's gonna love that," said Milo.

"If it's a problem—"

"It's no problem," I said.

Silence.

"Fine, then," said Sharavi. "Let's hear more about you, Andrew—tell me about your childhood."

A glance at Milo. "I always wanted to say that to a psychologist."

39

THE NEXT MORNING I TOLD ROBIN.

She said nothing. Then: "And it has to be you."

"If you really don't—"

"No," she said. "If I stopped you it would be . . . if something else happened that could have been prevented I'd never forget that—you're sure they can keep you safe?"

"It's just a visit to a bookstore."

"Just a visit. Browsing the shelves, huh?"

"Robin—"

She gripped my arm. "Be careful—I guess I'm saying it more for myself than for you."

Her fingers loosened. She kissed me and went to the studio.

I called my service, told them I'd be out of town for a week on vacation, would call in regularly.

"Somewhere nice, I hope, Dr. Delaware?" said the operator.

"Somewhere very private."

THAT EVENING, DANIEL SHARAVI CALLED AND ASKED if he could bring over some of my new ID at ten.

"Does Milo know?"

"I just spoke to him. He's briefing the other detectives on Melvin Myers. He'll come by while I'm there."

"Fine."

When he showed up carrying a black vinyl satchel, Robin and I were in the living room playing hearts and she got up to get the door. We rarely played cards; her idea.

I made the introductions. Robin knew about the break-in and the bugging, but she smiled evenly and shook Sharavi's hand.

I heard the dog door slam shut, then Spike's mini-gallop across the kitchen floor. He raced into the living room, snorting and panting. Stopping several feet from Sharavi, he tightened his neck muscles and growled.

Robin stooped and tried to calm him. Spike barked and wouldn't stop. "What's the matter, handsome?"

"He doesn't like me," said Sharavi. "I don't blame him. When I was here, I had to put him in the bathroom for a few minutes."

Robin's smile withered.

"I'm sorry, Ms. Castagna. I used to have a dog of my own."

"C'mon, handsome, we'll let them do business." Spike followed her back into the kitchen.

"You're still willing to do this?" he said.

"Any reason I shouldn't be?"

"Sometimes people get enthusiastic, then they reconsider. And Ms. Castagna—"

"She's fine with it."

We sat down and he placed the satchel on the table. "I've learned more about the New York lawyer, Farley Sanger. His last trip to Los Angeles was two weeks before Irit's murder. He stayed at the Beverly Hills Hotel and as far as we can tell, conducted business for his firm. So far, we've got no records of his being back since, but those kinds of things can be hidden."

He removed papers. "Still no trace of Meta. After the publicity from Sanger's article, the group either dissolved or went underground. When it was active, the meetings were held in a building on Fifth Avenue. A very exclusive building and this particular suite houses the Loomis Foundation—a charitable group started by a wealthy Louisiana farming family over one hundred years ago. A relatively small foundation, from what we can tell. Last year they gave out less than three hundred thousand dollars. One-third went to a psychological study of twins in Illinois, another third to agricultural research, and the rest to various scientists conducting genetic studies."

"Did the twin research have a genetic bent, also?"

"The researcher's a professor of comparative biology at a small college. These are the data." He handed me a stapled reprint.

The journal was *Proceedings of the Loomis Foundation*, the title: *Homogeneity of Traits and Longitudinal Patterns of Encoded Behavior in Monozygotic Twins Separated at Birth.*

"Loomis . . . sounds familiar. What do they farm?"

"Tobacco, alfalfa, cotton. The Loomis family prided itself on its geneology—links to European nobility, that kind of thing."

"Prided?" I said. "They're no longer around?"

"The family name died out but a few cousins remain and they run the business and the foundation. No new cash has been added to the principal for years."

"Is there any record of their funding Meta?"

"Not so far, but the fact that Meta used their office says something."

"And controversy from Sanger's article could attract unwanted attention."

"Exactly. So maybe that's why the group was disbanded."

"Or moved to L.A.," I said. "Loomis—one sec." I went into my office and pulled *The Brain Drain* from a shelf.

The author bio on the back flap.

Arthur Haldane, Ph.D., resident scholar, the Loomis Institute, New York City.

I brought it back to Sharavi.

"Oh," he said. "I bought the book yesterday, haven't gotten around to reading it. . . . So there's an institute in addition to the foundation."

"Maybe other money you didn't trace."

He turned the book over, opened it, and inspected the table of contents. "May I use your phone?"

He made a calling-card connection, spoke briefly in Hebrew, hung up, returned to the table.

"A best-seller," I said. "If any of the royalties were returned to Loomis, that kills their tax-free status. With their cash depletion, they might have been willing to take the risk."

"Both Sanger and that securities analyst, Helga Cranepool, work in financial fields. Her specialty's farm commodities."

"Loomis's product," I said. "Assuming they still farm."

"Oh, they do," he said. "Not in America, overseas. Cotton, hemp, jute, alfalfa and other feeds, various packing materials. They own plantations in Asia and Africa. I'd assume because of the lower wages."

"Oh, for them mint-julep days," I said. "Does the foundation keep offices out here?"

"Not under the Loomis name. I'm looking into it."

"Fifth Avenue suite in New York and all we know about them here is a possible link to a bookstore in Silverlake. Bit of a contrast."

"We know they're snobs," he said. "Maybe it extends to their view of California."

I made coffee while he sat, motionless, almost entranced. When I brought back two mugs, he thanked me and gave me a white envelope. In it were a social-security card, Visa, MasterCard, Fedco membership, Blue Shield enrollment, all made out to Andrew Desmond.

"Health insurance," I said. "What's the deductible?"

He smiled. "Ample."

"In case I get hurt?"

"I'll do my best to take care of you."

"What about a driver's license?"

"We'll need a photo for that and I want to wait til Thursday or Friday when your beard's thicker. I'll have some educational credentials for you at that time, also. We've come up with an L.A.-based, unaccredited psychology program that closed down ten years ago. Even if by some strange coincidence you happened to meet another alumnus, it was home-study, no contact between the students."

"Sounds perfect."

He squared the stack of papers. "Few civilians would disrupt their life to this extent, Alex."

"I'm a masochist. And frankly, I think we're overdoing the espionage bit."

"Better that than the opposite. Should you need a home away from home, you've got one. I was able to get a place in the city. Genesee Avenue. The Fairfax district."

He waved his good hand around the room. "I'm afraid it's nothing like this, but the neighbors don't pry."

From his pocket came a ring bearing several keys. He spread them on the table, touched each in turn.

"Front and back doors, garage, your car. It's a Karmann Ghia, ten years old, but customized with a new engine, and runs better than it looks. It's in the garage."

He slid the keys across the table.

"Sounds like you've thought of everything," I said.

"If only that were possible."

MILO RANG THE BELL JUST AFTER TEN-THIRTY AND Petra Connor was with him. She was dressed in a pantsuit again, this one chocolate brown, wore less makeup, and looked younger.

Milo said, "Superintendent Sharavi, Detective Petra Connor, Hollywood Division."

They shook hands. Connor's dark eyes shifted to me, then to the false ID.

"Something to drink?" I said.

"No, thanks," she said.

Milo said, "If you've got coffee left, I'll have some. Where's Robin?"

"Out in back."

I filled a mug and Milo studied my social-security card. "Just finished interdivisional show-and-tell. Pierce couldn't make it, McLaren and Hooks were out on other cases, so it was Alvarado, Detective Connor, and me."

Connor twisted a cameo ring. "Thanks for letting me in on this. I recontacted Malcolm Ponsico's parents in New Jersey but once again, they were no help. And I couldn't tell them it might not be suicide, my line was I was just touching base. I also looked into Zena Lambert's background and it's spotless. She left PlasmoDerm voluntarily, wasn't fired, nothing iffy in her personnel file, and she's the registered owner of the bookstore, so it looks like an attempt at self-employment."

She looked at Milo.

He said, "The only morsel that came up at the meeting was that Alvarado dug through Recreation Department files and found a guy named Wilson Tenney who'd worked at the park where Raymond Ortiz was abducted and was fired a few weeks later because of personality problems. Wouldn't take orders, showed up when he wanted to, sat on a bench and read instead of raking. They warned him several times, finally gave him the boot. Tenney contested the firing, made noises about a lawsuit, reverse discrimination because he was a white male, but then he just went away."

He handed me a sheet printed with a photocopied driver's license. Tenney was thirty-five, five ten, one fifty. Green eyes, shoulder-length hair, light brown, unless the black and white copy was inaccurate. Hard eyes, tight mouth. If you were looking for something. Nothing else remarkable about the face.

"Angry man," I said. "Resentment of minorities. Reading on the job because he's a self-styled intellectual? Interesting."

"We ran him through, and he's as clean as Lambert and didn't go crosstown for a job at the conservancy. He did split from his last known address—apartment in Mar Vista. And guess what he drives?"

"A van."

"Seventy-nine Chevy, lapsed registration, so that raises the hunch quotient a bit. If he's living on the street, he's not on the dole, no welfare applications."

"He might have a history of psychiatric treatment," I said. "Could be hospitalized."

"Alvarado's already starting to check public hospitals; at this point, private places would be impossible to crack. I also dropped by that Mensa president's place—Bukovsky. It's his business, an auto-parts yard, and he wasn't in. I decided not to leave a card. Suggestions, so far?"

"No," said Sharavi, "just information." He repeated what he'd told me about Sanger and the Loomis Foundation.

"Fifth Avenue," said Milo. "And maybe they're silent partners with the creep who wrote that book . . . maybe partners with Zena Lambert, bankrolling Spasm. One way for a clerk to go self-employed overnight."

"Venture capital for a new utopia," I said.

"And if the store brings in money," said Sharavi, "maybe it goes back to the Loomis Foundation. Interesting way to launder."

"So you'll keep checking Sanger's travel records?" said Milo. Sharavi nodded.

"What about the editor, Cranepool?"

"She lives alone in an apartment on East Seventy-eighth Street, works long hours at the brokerage house, comes home and rarely goes out except to shop and run errands."

Three photos came out of his pocket. The first landed upside down and he left it that way. The second was a snapshot of a tall, beefy man around forty with sloping shoulders that good tailoring couldn't conceal. His hair was dark and combed straight back and his features were thick, slightly flattened. Dark eyes, droopy lids. He wore a gray suit, white shirt, navy tie, and carried a soft leather attaché. The camera had caught him walking down a crowded street looking preoccupied.

The third featured a tight-lipped, harried-looking woman ten years older, wearing a bulky beige sweater and dark green plaid slacks. Light brown hair was pulled back from a broad face. Large gold earrings, gold-rimmed glasses. More flattened features and I asked if she and Sanger could be related.

"Good question," said Sharavi. "I'll try to find out."

I examined the shot of Helga Cranepool some more. She was in motion but a fast lens had captured her without blur—stepping out of a door holding two white shopping bags. The window behind her displayed apples and oranges. The lettering on one of the bags said D'AGOSTINO.

"He was on his way to a business lunch," said Sharavi. "We found her grocery shopping on Lexington Avenue on Saturday."

"Both of them are pretty grim-looking," said Petra Connor.

"Maybe being brilliant's not what it's cracked up to be," said Milo.

Sharavi flipped the first photo over. Farley Sanger in a red polo shirt and canvas hat, a pretty blond woman, and two blond children sitting in a motorboat still moored to a dock. Flat, green water, hints of marsh grass at the periphery.

Sanger still looked unhappy and the woman seemed cowed. The children had turned away from the camera, showing thin necks and yellow hair.

"Not exactly Norman Rockwell," said Connor.

Milo asked if he could have the pictures and Sharavi said sure, they were copies for him.

I thought about the fact that he'd waited til Milo arrived to display them. Waited to let loose with details.

Cop-to-cop. I was a very small part of this.

"Onward," said Milo. "The Melvin Myers stabbing. I met with Mrs. Grosperrin, the director at Myers's trade school. At first she kept describing Myers as the perfect student. Too perfect, so I pressed her and she finally admitted he could also be a giant pain: quick temper, chip on his shoulder, always looking for signs of discrimination against the handicapped, complaining the school patronized the students instead of treating them like adults, the facilities sucked, the course offerings sucked. Grosperrin figured it was because Melvin's mother had cooped him up for so long, now he was feeling his oats. She said Myers saw himself as a crusader, tried to turn the student council into some big deal—greater voice for the students, more respect from the administration."

"A leader but abrasive," I said. "Someone who could have made enemies."

"Grosperrin denied he'd had any conflict with anyone, claimed the faculty understood where he was coming from and admired him. For his spunk, quote unquote."

"What about the people at Myers's group home?"

"Four residents, I talked to three and the landlady, over the phone. They said basically the same thing. Melvin was bright, but he could piss you off with his smart mouth."

"Still," said Connor, "none of the other victims was abrasive. It sounds like who they *were* made them victims, not what they *did*."

"Did Mrs. Grosperrin have any idea what could have lured Myers into that alley?" said Sharavi.

"None," said Milo. "But one thing's for sure: He didn't get lost. She said he knew the area like the palm of his hand, had trained himself to memorize the entire downtown grid. So someone offered him motivation to walk through that alley. And that's where we stand. You schedule a time for visiting the bookstore yet, Alex?"

"Daniel suggested Thursday or Friday. To give the beard some time."

"Good idea," he said, "Andrew."

40

THE THREE OF THEM LEFT, TALKING PROCEDURE, COP-
to-cop, as I thought about Nolan Dahl.

The parallels to Ponsico; another bright boy destroying himself.

Not very profound. IQ was no defense against pain. Sometimes
it hurt to perceive too clearly.

But the next morning it stayed with me.

Dr. Lehmann's *bleak situation*. The things Helena was better off
not knowing.

Things that left Nolan drowning in guilt?

I'd assumed a sexual secret, but maybe not. Helena had talked
about Nolan's embracing extremes.

How far had he taken it?

Had he transferred out of West L.A. because of something he'd
done in West L.A.?

Irit had been murdered in West L.A. When I'd visited the killing
site after Latvinia's murder, I'd thought about a monster in a uniform.

A cop?

A big, strong, smiling, handsome young cop?

Disgusting . . . but a West L.A. cop would know the park's
backroads, be able to lose himself.

A cop could always offer a reason for being somewhere.

West L.A. didn't patrol the park, the rangers did . . . a cop on
lunch break?

Code 7 for doughnuts and homicide?

But no, that made no sense. Nolan had been dead several weeks
by the time of Latvinia's and Melvin Myers's murders. And there

wasn't a shred of evidence that Nolan had ever hurt anyone but himself.

Malignant imagination, Delaware. The time line, all wrong.

Unless there was more than one killer.

Not just a boy-girl thing, a killing *club*. That would explain the varying M.O.s.

A group game: dividing the city up, one police district per player. Nolan telling them how to do it because he was an expert on procedure . . .

Enough. I was defaming a dead man because he'd been smart. No doubt Nolan *had* revealed secrets Lehmann thought best left buried.

Still, Helena *had* run away.

Why?

HER HOME PHONE WAS DISCONNECTED NOW. LONG-term move.

With both parents gone, no close family, who would she turn to in times of stress?

Distant relatives? Friends? I didn't know any of them.

Didn't know much about her at all.

She had mentioned one former relative: the ex-husband.

Gary's a pulmonologist, basically a nice guy. But he decided he wanted to be a farmer so he moved to North Carolina.

I called Rick at Cedars and he came on the line sounding impatient but softening when he learned it was me.

"Sure," he said. "Gary Blank. He used to work here, too. Good lung man, Southerner. Kind of a country boy at heart. Why?"

"I'm wondering if Helena would have turned to him for support."

"Hmm . . . the divorce was friendly. As divorces go. And Gary's an easygoing type. If she asked him to put her up, my guess is sure, he'd hold the door wide open."

"Thanks."

"So . . . you're still trying to reach her."

"You know me, Rick. Never developed a taste for unfinished business."

"Yup," he said. "Used to be that way, myself."

"Used to be?"

He laughed. "Yesterday."

NORTH CAROLINA HAD THREE AREA CODES—704, 910, 919—and I tried Information for all of them before cashing in with 919.

Gary S. Blank, no degree. A rural route near Durham.

Dinnertime in North Carolina.

Helena answered after two rings.

She recognized my voice right away and hers got strained. "How'd you find me?"

"Lucky guess. I don't mean to be intrusive, but I just wanted to see how you're doing. If this makes things worse for you, just say so."

She didn't answer. I could hear music in the background. Something baroque.

"Helena—"

"It's okay. You just caught me off-guard."

"I'm sorry—"

"No, it's okay. I'm—I guess I'm touched that you cared. I'm sorry for skipping out without an explanation but . . . this is very hard, Dr. Delaware. I—it's just hard. You *really* caught me off-guard."

"No need to—"

"No, it's okay. It's just—I got stressed out, decided to make a clean sweep."

"Was it something you learned about Nolan?"

Her voice got higher. "What do you mean?"

"You never made another appointment after finding that family photo album in Nolan's garage. I was just wondering if there was something in there that upset you."

Another long silence.

"Jesus," she finally said. "Shit."

"Helena—"

"Jesus Christ—I really *don't* want to talk about this."

"No problem."

"But I—Dr. Delaware, what I'm saying is, it's water under the bridge. Nothing I can change. None of my business, really. I've got to concentrate on what *I* can do. Get past this, move on."

I said nothing.

"You're good," she said. "Brilliant—uncanny—I'm sorry, I'm not making sense, am I?"

"Yes, you are. You learned something upsetting and don't want to rake it up."

"Exactly. Exactly."

I let a few more moments pass. "One thing though, Helena. If Nolan was involved in something that's still continuing and you have the ability to—"

"Of course, it's continuing! The world stinks, it's full of . . . that kind of thing. But I can't bear the responsibility for every bit of—what? Hold on."

Muffled voices. Her hand over the phone.

She came back on. "My ex heard me shouting and came in to check." Deep breath. "Listen, I'm sorry. Nolan's death was bad enough, but then to learn he was . . . I'm sorry, I just can't deal with this. Thanks for calling, but no. I'm fine. I'll cope . . . it's really beautiful here, maybe I'll give country life a try. . . . Sorry for being so edgy, Dr. Delaware, but . . . please understand."

Three apologies in not many more seconds.

I said, "Of course. You have nothing to be sorry for. Even if Nolan was part of something extreme—"

"I wouldn't call it extreme," she said, suddenly angry. "Sick, but not extreme. Guys do it all the time, right?"

"Do they?"

"I'd say so. It's the oldest profession, right?"

"Prostitution?"

Silence. "What?" she said. "What did *you* mean?"

"I was just wondering if Nolan got into some sort of extreme political activity."

"I wish. *That* I was used to." She laughed. "So you're *not* a mind reader . . . politics. If only. No, Dr. Delaware, I'm just talking about good old whoring around. My noble police-officer brother's apparent obsession."

I said nothing.

She laughed again. Kept laughing, louder, faster, until her voice took on a glassy edge of hysteria. "I couldn't care *less* about No-lan's politics. He *was* always jumping from one crazy thing to an-other, big deal. The truth is, at this point, I couldn't care less about *anything* he did." Her voice cracked. "Oh, Dr. Delaware, I'm so *angry* at him! So goddamn, goddamn *angry* at him!"

She rescued herself from tears by laughing some more.

"You're right, it was the photo album," she said. "Filthy Polaroids, Nolan's private little stash. He kept it right in the middle of one of the books. Mixed in with pictures of Mom and Dad, our old family stuff. First he takes the album from Mom's effects and never tells me, then *uses* it for his goddamn sicko *porno* stash!"

"Porno," I said.

"*Personal* porno. Pictures of *him*. And *hookers*. Young girls—not little kids, thank God it wasn't *that* sick. But most of them looked young enough to be illegal—fifteen, sixteen, skinny little black girls and Hispanics. Obviously hookers from the way they were dressed—spiked heels, garter belts. They all looked stoned—with a couple you could actually see the needle tracks on their arms. In some of them, he left his uniform on, so he probably was doing it on the job—that's most likely why he transferred to Hollywood. To be closer to the hookers. He probably picked them up when he was supposed to be out fighting crime, took them God-knows-where, took *pictures*!"

I heard her snort.

"Garbage," she said. "I turned them into confetti and threw them out. After I closed the garbage-can lid, I thought, what are you doing here? This city, everything's nuts. Then the next night, someone broke in and that was it."

"What an ordeal," I said.

"Dr. Delaware, I never really knew Nolan but nothing could have prepared me for those pictures. It's just so hard to reconcile, someone you grew up with. . . . Anyway, here I *do* feel safe. Gary's got forty-five acres with horses, all I see when I look out the window is grass and trees. I know I can't stay here forever, but right now, it's working. No offense, but, at this point, a change of scenery seems a lot more valuable than therapy. Anyway, thanks for calling. I haven't told anyone. Actually, it wasn't bad being able to unload. Knowing it won't go any further."

"If there's anything else—"

"No." She laughed. "No, I think this has been quite enough, Dr. Delaware . . . dear little brother. First he goes and kills himself on me, then he leaves me souvenirs."

·   ·   ·

CODE 7 FOR HOOKERS.

A sleaze, but not a killer.

Plenty of reason for guilt.

A bleak situation.

Perhaps Nolan had been found out, referred to Lehmann. Talked it out, got no easy answers. Lehmann letting him know he'd have to leave the force. Nolan opting for final exit.

Now I could understand Lehmann's nervousness.

Confidentiality issues and beyond. He made a living as an LAPD contractor. The last thing he needed was to expose yet another LAPD scandal.

Feeling sad but relieved, I went into my office and thought about being Andrew Desmond.

PLACE OF BIRTH: ST. LOUIS. SUBURBIA: CREVE COEUR.

Self-made father, bourgeois, conservative, looks down on psychology, Andrew's intellectual pretensions.

Mother: Donna Reed with an edge. Civic volunteer, sharp-tongued. Convinced Andrew was precocious, had his IQ tested as a child. Frustrated at the boy's chronic underachievement but explains it away as the school's failure: not stimulating poor Andrew.

For simplicity's sake, no sibs.

Poor Andrew . . .

ROBIN CAME IN AT SIX. "WHAT'S THE MATTER?"

"Nothing, why?"

"You look . . . different."

"Different how?"

"I don't know." She put her hand on my shoulder, touched my stubbled cheek. "A little down?"

"No, I'm fine."

The hand moved back to my shoulder. "Alex, you're so *tight.* How long have you been sitting hunched like that?"

"Couple of hours."

Spike waddled in. Usually he licks me.

"Hi," I said.

He cocked his head, stared, left the room.

41

ON TUESDAY NIGHT, AT 11:03, DANIEL WAS WAITING for retired Captain Eugene Brooker in the parking lot of a bowling alley on Venice Boulevard in Mar Vista. He'd noticed the lot that afternoon, when he'd driven by Wilson Tenney's former apartment—a dismal, earthquake-cracked, ten-unit box bordering an alley.

Wearing a suit and tie, he'd represented himself as an insurance claims adjustor to the old Mexican woman who lived in the manager's unit.

The former park worker, he'd told her, had filed an earthquake claim for damaged personal effects and he wanted to verify Tenney's residence at the address during the Northridge quake.

"Yeah," she said, and nothing else.

"How long did he live here?"

Shrug. "Couple years."

"Was he a good tenant?"

"Quiet, paid his rent."

"So nothing we should worry about?"

"Nope. Tell the truth, I hardly remember him." The door shut.

His look into Tenney's background had been more of the same. No Medi-Cal records or state hospitalizations, no citations on the Chevrolet van, not a single entry or cross-reference to any crime files.

Tenney hadn't applied for welfare or for a job at any other city, county, or state park within a hundred-mile radius—Daniel had lied creatively for half a day to find out.

So either Tenney had moved, or just disappeared.

Still, Daniel felt something about the guy—an intuition, what else could you call it? So fuzzy he'd never mention it to another detective, but he'd be foolish to ignore it.

The first thing was what he knew about Tenney's personality—a loner who flaunted the rules, reading on the job instead of working, that remark about being a white male. Put it all together and it resonated.

Second: a van. He could not erase the image of Raymond Ortiz being spirited away in a van.

A vehicle that hadn't been seen since Tenney's firing from the park. Shortly after Raymond's abduction.

Bloody shoes . . .

He'd said nothing about Tenney to Zev Carmeli.

The deputy consul had taken to calling him every day, between 5:00 and 8:00 P.M., getting irritated when Daniel was out, even though he knew Daniel was working on Irit and nothing else.

Tonight, Zev had caught him just as he sat down to a tuna sandwich, the police scanner going in the kitchen. "Are they giving you what you need, Sharavi?"

"They're being cooperative."

"Well, that's a switch. So . . . nothing, yet?"

"I'm sorry, no, Zev."

Silence on the line. Then the same question: "Sturgis. You're sure he knows what he's doing?"

"He seems very good."

"You don't sound enthusiastic."

"He's good, Zev. As good as anyone I've ever worked with. He takes the job seriously."

"Is he taking *you* seriously?"

About as seriously as could be expected. "Yes. No complaints."

"And the psychologist?"

"He's doing his best, as well."

"But no brilliant new psychological analysis."

"Not yet."

He didn't mention Petra Connor or Alvarado or any of the other detectives. Why complicate things?

"All right," Carmeli finally said. "Just keep me fully informed."

"Of course."

After Zev hung up, Daniel bolted down the sandwich, said grace after the meal, then the *ma'ariv* prayers, and resumed reading

The Brain Drain. Some of the details flew over his head—graphs, statistics; a very dry book, but maybe that was the point.

Dr. Arthur Haldane trying to obscure facts with verbiage and numbers. But the message came through:

Smart people were superior in every way and should be encouraged to breed. Stupid people were . . . during good times, a nuisance. During bad times, an unnecessary obstruction.

Dry, but a best-seller. Some people needed others to lose in order to feel like winners.

He'd looked into Haldane's background.

Yet another New Yorker.

The book listed him as a scholar at the Loomis Institute, but Sharavi's Manhattan operative hadn't traced any calls from Haldane to Loomis's office. Haldane's apartment was in Riverdale, in the Bronx.

"Decent place," the operative had said. "Healthy rent, but nothing that special."

"Family?"

"He's got a wife and a fourteen-year-old daughter and a dog. A mini Schnauzer. They go out to dinner twice a week, usually Italian. One time they had Chinese. He stays in a lot, doesn't go to church on Sunday."

"Stays inside," said Daniel.

"Sometimes for days at a time. Maybe he's working on another book. He doesn't own a car, either. The one phone we know about, we've secured, but he could be using E-mail and we haven't found any password yet. That's it, so far. Nothing more on Sanger and that sour-faced woman, either. Helga Cranepool. They both go to work, they go home. A boring bunch."

"Boring and smart."

"So you say."

"So they say."

The operative laughed. She was a twenty-eight-year-old Dutch-born woman whose cover job was photographer for *The New York Times.* No connection to the Israeli government except for the cash that was deposited for her each month in a Cayman Islands bank.

"Any pictures?" said Daniel.

"What do you think? Coming right through. Bye."

The snapshot that slid through the fax machine was of a slight, bearded, gray-haired man in his late forties or early fifties. Curly hair, bushy at the sides, eyeglasses, pinched face. He wore a tweed overcoat, dark slacks, and open-necked shirt, and was walking the little Schnauzer.

Wholly unremarkable.

What did he expect, monsters?

Hannah Arendt had called evil banal and the intellectuals had all jumped on that because it fit in with their disparage-the-bourgeoisie philosophy.

But Arendt had maintained a long-term, pathetic, masochistic relationship with the anti-Semite philosopher Martin Heidegger, so her judgment, in Daniel's opinion, was questionable.

From what he'd seen, *crime* was often banal.

Most of it was downright stupid.

But evil?

Not the evil he'd experienced in the Butcher's dungeon of horrors.

Not this, either.

This was not humanity-as-usual.

He refused to believe that.

GENE TAPPED ON THE PASSENGER WINDOW AND DAN-iel unlocked the Toyota. The older man slipped in. In the darkness, his ebony face was nearly invisible, and his dark sportcoat, shirt, slacks, and shoes contributed to the phantom image.

Only the white hair bounced back some light.

"Hey," he said, shifting around in the small car, trying to get comfortable.

The bowling alley would close soon but there were still enough cars in the lot for cover and Daniel had chosen a poorly lit corner. And a neighborhood where a black man and a brown man could talk in a car without the police swooping down.

Gene's big Buick was parked across the asphalt.

"Seems you're right, Danny Boy," he said. "Sturgis has sleuthed me out. Asking about me a few days ago at Newton. But what can he do? I'm out of there."

"He probably won't do anything, Gene, because he's busy and knows how to prioritize. But if the case goes completely sour, who knows? I'm sorry if this ends up complicating your life."

"It won't. What's the felony, pulling a file?"

"And the shoes."

Gene grinned. "What shoes—hey, I was Newton captain for seven years, always took an interest in unsolved cases, everyone knows that. Anyway, in answer to your question, Manny Alvarado is a very good detective. No fireworks, a plodder, but thorough."

"Thanks."

"You like this Tenney as a suspect?"

"Don't know yet," said Daniel. "He's all we've got so far."

"I like him," said Gene. "At least from what you've told me—the timing, the whole disturbed loner thing. Anything at the conservancy, yet?"

"Tenney definitely never worked there or applied for a job under any name. No other parks, either."

"Ah . . . too bad. Still, he could have held on to his old city uniforms and used them to lure the kid. Believe me, the city's sloppy when it comes to that kind of thing, and a naive kid like Irit, what would she know about the different uniforms?"

"True," said Daniel. "We'll keep looking."

Not mentioning the other depressing fact: Tenney was nondescript; medium-sized, fair-haired, forgettable. Literally. The gang members from the park where Raymond Ortiz had been abducted hadn't recognized Tenney's snapshot. None of the park-goers had, and Tenney had worked there for two years.

Just another bland white face in a uniform.

Even reading on the job, he hadn't drawn anyone's attention.

"So," said Gene, "you're okay working with Sturgis, so far?"

Daniel said, "I'm fine with it, Gene. I think he's good."

"So they say." Gene stretched his feet. He'd put on weight and his belly extended past the lapels of his sportcoat.

"You have doubts?" said Daniel.

"No," Gene said quickly. "Not in terms of doing the job. They all say he's good . . . excellent, actually. Want me to be honest? The gay thing. I'm from a different generation, it puts me off. When I was a rookie, we used to bust gay bars. Which was wrong, no question about it, but the things I saw—I was just wondering about you, being religious."

Same thing Zev had said. Belief in God made you an ayatollah.

"What I mean," said Gene, "was with this kind of thing, you need a cohesive team. Top of everything else, Sturgis is a cowboy."

"I'm fine," said Daniel. "He's professional. He concentrates on what's important."

"Good. Now for the Myers boy. I know you're not going to like this but the reason I wanted to meet you was I went by that group home in Baldwin Hills, made like a cop, talked to the landlady and the other residents."

Daniel kept his voice even. "That puts you at risk, Gene." *Me, too, my friend.*

"I was convincing, Danny, believe me. Sturgis already did telephonic interviews, so why not be more thorough? I told the landlady—a Mrs. Bradley—that I was following up on Sturgis's interviews. She's black, they all are, it didn't hurt, believe me. And guess what? I talked to a fellow Sturgis hadn't spoken to because he was out that day. Lived right next door to Myers. Closest thing Myers had to a friend."

"Closest thing?" said Daniel. "Myers didn't have real friends?"

"The picture I got was that Myers was hard to like, full of attitude. Didn't hang out with the others, mostly stayed in his room reading braille and listening to jazz. This particular fellow likes jazz, too, so he and Myers had that in common. He's a paraplegic in a wheelchair, says Myers was always after him to look into different exercises, vitamins, alternative remedies, try to rehab himself. The guy had been shot in the spine, said, 'What the hell did he expect me to do, grow a new backbone?' But he tolerated Myers because even though Myers could be a pain he really seemed to care. He also said Myers had been talking about going to school to become a psychologist. Anyway, the main thing I got out of this guy was that Myers didn't like the trade school one bit. On the contrary: He hated it, was planning to write some article about it as soon as he graduated."

"An exposé?"

"That's what it sounded like, Myers never gave him specifics. It's probably nothing but it does give us a victim with higher-than-average enemy potential. I figure the next step is, find out if there was anyone at the school who had an especially hostile relationship with Myers. Which makes sense on another level, because whoever got him into that alley probably also knew the neighborhood."

"The director said there was no one Myers had problems with."

"Maybe she didn't know or maybe she's lying to keep the school out of the spotlight. Heck, for all we know this Wilson *Tenney* got a job at the school and ran into Myers. As a custodian. Let's say he stole stuff and Myers found out. Here's Tenney, already killed three people—nonwhite people—and Myers was an abrasive black guy mouths off to him one time too many, threatens to blow the whistle."

Daniel said nothing.

"It's wild but it's plausible," said Gene. "You agree it should be looked into?"

"I'll look into it."

Gene shifted around again. "I've got time, just sitting around. I could go over to the school as one of those kindly retired gents looking to volunteer—"

"Thanks, but I'll do it, Gene."

"You're sure?"

"I'm sure. I've got the perfect equipment." Daniel lifted his bad hand.

Gene's mouth closed. Then he said, "How're you going to pull it off without putting Sturgis's nose out of joint?"

"I'll find a way."

Gene sighed. "Okay, just call me if you change your mind."

"Believe me, I will. And Gene—"

"I know, keep my nose out of it."

"I really appreciate everything—"

"But keep my nose out of it." Gene laughed.

"How's the packing going?" said Daniel.

Gene laughed some more. "Changing the subject? The packing's finished. My illustrious life in boxes. I finally heard from the leasing agent. She's got a couple who'll take the house til the market gets better. Physical therapists, they work full-time at Luther King, so they should be able to keep up with the rent. I'm in good shape, ready to live the good life in the land of sun and sand."

"Great," said Daniel, pleased that Gene could think in positive terms without Luanne. Or at least fake it. "So the new house will be ready soon?"

"Five more days, they claim." Gene slumped. "Guess I better get used to feeling useless."

"You've been very useful, Gene."

"Not really. A file, shoes, big deal . . . to be truthful, it's more than that, Danny. It's the case itself. Ugly. Even for guys like us, it's ugly. And pardon me for saying so, but it doesn't sound as if you're getting much movement."

42

ON WEDNESDAY MORNING, MILO CALLED TO TELL ME he'd caught up with Loren Bukovsky, the local Mensa chapter chairman.

"Not a bad fellow, understandably curious about why I was looking into Meta. I told him it was a financial thing, large-scale covert investigation, hinted around that it had something to do with stolen computers, and asked him to keep it to himself. He promised to and my sense is he might keep his word, because he doesn't like Meta, thinks they're 'insufferables' who look down on Mensa."

"Because Mensa folk aren't smart enough for them?"

"Bukovsky denies that. Emphatically."

"What if Bukovsky doesn't keep it to himself and it gets back to someone in Meta?"

"Then we deal with it. It could even work out to our advantage: One or more of their members turn out to be bad guys and show their hands and give us moving targets. Which is better than none."

"That," I said, "sounds like rationalization."

"No, Alex, it's the truth, you didn't screw things up. As it stands, we're nowhere with this group. Even Bukovsky, for all his hostility, didn't know much about them, just that they'd started back east, cropped up in L.A. two or three years ago, then took a low profile."

"Two years ago," I said. "Right around the time of Sanger's article. And publication of *The Brain Drain*."

"Next item: got hold of Zena Lambert's tax returns for the last three years. Her sole income was the salary from PlasmoDerm.

Before that she made no money at all. So how she started the store is still an open question."

"Maybe a trust fund," I said. "Like Andrew Desmond."

He looked at me. "Andrew's got rich parents?"

"Comfortable." I gave him the profile.

"Sounds like a charming fellow," he said. "The only other thing to report is Melvin Myers's body was clean of drugs and Bob Pierce says none of the local crackheads knew him, so it wasn't dope that got him in that alley. . . . You're really up for this secret-agent stuff, aren't you?"

"Got my shoe-phone in gear."

AT 4:00 P.M., DANIEL PHONED.

"I'd like to show you the cover apartment on Genesee. You may never actually have to use it, but this way you'll be accustomed to it."

"I'll meet you there. What's the address?"

"I'm near your house," he said. "If you don't mind, I'll come by and take you."

He was there ten minutes later and he gave me a brown paper Ralph's Market bag. Inside was a change of clothes: lightweight black cotton pants, black cotton mock turtleneck washed nearly gray, baggy gray herringbone sportcoat with the label of Dillard's department store in St. Louis on the inside breast pocket, rubber-soled black shoes from Bullock's, L.A.

"Costume rehearsal?" I said.

"Something like that."

"No underwear?"

"Underwear is underwear."

"True. I don't see Andrew going for flaming red silk."

I inspected the jacket. The wool emitted a weak scent of insipid cologne.

"The St. Louis touch is nice," I said, "but Andrew's lived in L.A. for several years."

"I don't see him as someone who likes to shop," he said. "His mother sent it to him."

"Good old Mom." I put the clothes on. The sportcoat was a little baggy but not a bad fit.

The mirror showed me a nicely shabby getup that would play

well in lots of L.A. settings. The beard helped, too. It had grown into the itch stage, thick and coarse and straight with more gray hairs than I'd expected. From my cheekbones to my Adam's apple I was covered, the lower half of my face effectively obscured.

We drove down the glen in the gray Toyota. Just past the Beverly Hills line, he said, "Try these," and gave me a pair of eyeglasses. Tiny, round lenses, gray-tinted, in bronze frames.

I slipped them on. No prescription.

"I like the effect," he said, "but I'd remove them from time to time. Your eyes are good for the part—nice and red. Have you been sleeping well?"

"Yes," I lied.

"Well," he said, "you look world-weary, anyway."

"Method acting."

"Andrew's an insomniac?"

"Andrew's not a happy man."

THE GENESEE BUILDING WAS A TWO-STORY STUCCO quadriplex nearly the exact gray of the Toyota, between Beverly and Rosewood. Flat roof, barred windows, all the charm of a storage depot. The front door was locked.

"The small round key," he said.

I turned the latch and we entered a central corridor carpeted in cheap maroon felt. Boiled-onion smell. Stairs at the back, four-slot brass mailbox just inside the door.

The paper DESMOND label was on Unit 2. Brown paper, water-stained. My neighbors were Weinstein and Paglia and Levine.

Two was the ground floor, right-hand unit. A pair of nail-holes pierced the doorpost like the fang-holes of a big-jawed snake. Between them was a three-inch column one shade paler than the surrounding woodwork.

"Andrew removed the mezuzah?" I said.

"He's not Jewish."

"Still, to go to the trouble—"

"Apparently, he's not a man of much faith, Alex. The square key opens both locks."

Two good dead bolts, each shiny, with the crisp feel of new fixtures.

The apartment was dim and stuffy, more of that same weak cologne overlaid with must and mothballs.

Bare wood floors in need of varnish, some of the boards bowing. Off-white walls, off-white polyester drapes over the small protected windows, each with borders of little turquoise yarn-balls. Thrift-shop furniture in hues of ash and earth and not much of it.

A living room with one wall of plywood shelving crowded with books and a Taiwanese stereo system. The kitchen looked greasy but felt clean. Down a skinny dark hall were a cracked-tile bathroom, mattress-on-the-floor bedroom, and a rear door out to the tiny yard with a sagging clothesline and three-car garage.

It reminded me of something. Nolan Dahl's place.

Lonely bachelor living. The places it could lead . . .

"What do you think?" said Daniel.

I looked around. Everything was worn and stained and nicked in all the right places. No one would suspect it was a set.

Who lived here the rest of the year?

"Perfect," I said, and he led me back to the back door and out into the yard. Half dry grass, half bird-specked cement.

"An alley runs behind the property," he said. "The garage can be entered from both sides." From his pocket he removed a remote control and pushed the button. The central garage door opened. Inside was a Karmann Ghia painted legal-paper yellow.

Back in the house, he gave me the remote and we returned to the living room, where he stood back, inviting me to inspect. I checked out the stereo and the books. The music was a mixture of LPs, tapes, and CDs. Small collection, maybe fifty selections in all: Beethoven, Wagner, Bruckner, Mahler, Bach, Cat Stevens, the Lovin' Spoonful, Hendrix, the Doors, the Beatles' *Abbey Road*, nothing recent. Some of the covers bore resale labels from Aaron's on Melrose. The store had moved to Highland years ago.

The books were on psychology, sociology, anthropology, history, a smattering of other subjects, some with USED stickers, many bearing the conspicuous irrelevance of assigned texts. At the bottom was fiction: Hemingway, Faulkner, Kerouac, Burroughs, Camus, Sartre, Beckett. Piles of old psych journals and magazines—*Evergreen Review, Eros, Harper's, The Atlantic Monthly. The Nation* resting comfortably atop the *National Review*. Like Nolan, Andrew Desmond had covered a wide swath of political territory.

Except for that, it could have been my library from college, though my apartment on Overland had been half the size of this place, a stuffy cell neighboring an auto-repair shop. I'd struggled each month to make the ninety-dollar rent; no trust fund . . .

I pulled out an abnormal-psych text. Foxed pages gave off the vomitous odor old books sometimes acquire. Inside was the inked stamp of the student bookstore at the University of Missouri, Columbus. Sold and resold twice. Pages full of yellow underlining.

A newer-looking tome that I recognized as the major grad-school work on the same topic came from the Technical Bookstore on Westwood Boulevard in L.A. Purchase date ten years ago.

Meticulous.

"I guess you have the original receipts, too."

"I didn't see Andrew as someone who'd save receipts."

"Unsentimental?"

He sat down on a sagging couch and dust puffed.

"Lucky I'm not allergic," I said.

"Yes. I should have asked."

"Can't think of everything."

"Is there anything you'd change, Alex?"

"Not so far. Where are the bugs?"

He crossed his legs and managed to get his bad hand on his knee, where it rested like a lumpy gray toad.

"In the phone," he said, "in a bedroom lamp, and here." He hooked a thumb toward the front windowsill. I saw nothing out of the ordinary.

"How many phones?" I said.

"Two, here and in the bedroom."

"Both tapped?"

"Neither's been tampered with, actually. The entire line is monitored."

"What cologne is that?" I said.

"Pardon?"

"There's a scent in the apartment. On this jacket, too."

His nostrils widened. "I'll find out."

Neither of us spoke and I found myself focusing on sounds. Someone's air conditioner rattling upstairs, the occasional car from the street, the chitter of passing conversation.

"Anything else?" I said.

"Not unless you've got suggestions."

"You seem to have covered everything."

He stood and so did I. But as we headed for the door, he stopped, reached behind his waistband, and took out a pager and looked at it.

"Silent," he said. "Excuse me, I just got a call."

He walked to the living-room phone and punched numbers, greeted someone with "*Alo?*" and listened, eyebrows arching. Wedging the receiver under his chin, he reached in his jacket and extricated a small notepad. A miniature pencil was Velcroed to the back and he peeled it off.

"Okay," he said, placing the pad on a fake-wood end table and leaning over, pencil poised. "American—*eyzeh mispar?*"

He copied, said, "*Todah. L-hitra'ot,*" hung up.

As he tucked the book back in his windbreaker, I saw the black plastic gun nesting in a black mesh nylon holster under his right armpit.

"That," he said, "was a source in New York. Our lawyer friend Farley Sanger has booked a flight to Los Angeles this Friday. American Airlines, Flight 005, scheduled to arrive at seven P.M. We almost missed it, the arrangements weren't made through his firm's travel agent. One of our people followed him to a meeting with Helga Cranepool. Sanger had dinner with her at the Carlyle Hotel and then the two of them took a cab downtown to lower Manhattan. To a travel agent we hadn't known about. Which means there may have been other trips we never found. She paid for the ticket but it's his. He's not traveling under his own name. He's calling himself Galton."

"Francis Galton?" I said.

"Close," he said. "Frank."

43

"FRIDAY," SAID MILO. "BUT HELGA STAYS IN NEW York."

"Helga's back to her routine," said Daniel. "She works and goes home. The TV can be heard through the door of her apartment. CNN, situation comedies. She goes to bed at ten, precisely."

It was Wednesday night and the three of us were back at my house, seated around the kitchen table. Robin was across the room, on a stool at the counter, reading *Art and Auction* with more intensity than usual.

"Frank Galton," said Milo. "So the asshole fancies himself the boss eugenicist. Helga goes with him to pay for the ticket, meaning it's Meta business or Loomis business—maybe it *is* a killing trip and they plan 'em in New York and do 'em here. This speeds things up. If Alex is gonna visit the bookstore it's got to be tomorrow."

"I agree," said Daniel.

"And the next day we get on Sanger and stay with him. Who picks up his trail at the airport?"

"That's up to you," said Daniel. "As far as we know, he didn't book a limousine, leaving three possibilities: a rental car, a cab, or a friend's meeting him. If I pose as a cab driver and it's a friend or a rental car, I lose him."

"So you're saying a two-man thing. One at the gate, one at the curb."

"It would help."

"Using your people?"

"If that's not a problem for you."

"Whatever I want, huh?" said Milo. "Too much more of this and I'll start to think I've got free will—tell you what, I'll give you Petra Connor for the airport, she's itching to get involved. Divide it any way you want. My priority is going to be keeping my eye on Alex from the time he starts out on this Spasm/Zena thing. Maybe it'll end tomorrow, but maybe it won't. We're talking a no-wire deal, right? Too much potential for screwup with a wire."

"I agree."

"Is there a tracer on the Karmann Ghia?"

"There will be," said Daniel.

"Soon as possible."

Robin looked up briefly and returned to her magazine.

Daniel put his good hand against one cheek. He looked uncomfortable and Milo picked up on it.

"What?"

"Some information came my way regarding Melvin Myers. A cotenant at his group home said Myers hated the trade school, was going to write an article about it when he graduated."

"Came your *way*," said Milo. "A pigeon dropped a note through the window?"

"Human pigeon," said Daniel. "I'm sorry—"

"A large *black* pigeon?"

"From now on, he's back in the coop, Milo. Once again, I'm sor—"

"What kind of article was Myers planning to write?"

"From the sound of it, an exposé. It may mean nothing, but I thought you should know."

"When exactly did you find this out?"

"Last night."

"Ah . . . I was planning to visit the home. Myers's school, too, but now with you watching Sanger and me watching Alex and trying to track down Wilson Tenney, we're spread a little thin."

"If you think it's worth following up," said Daniel, "I can visit the school before Sanger arrives." He lifted the arm with the bad hand. "I'll tell them a sad story, injury, depression, disability. Claim I want to make a new start."

Milo looked at the ravaged limb. "Putting you out there asking questions is more of an active role than we discussed."

"I know," said Daniel.

"We're talking a brief drop-in, you ask for vocational training, check the place out, that's all?"

Daniel nodded. "Myers was learning computers. I'll ask for computer training. I've already been through it. At a rehab center in Israel."

I thought of his one-hand lightning peck.

"I'll be subtle," he said. His mouth was taut as he slipped the crippled hand under the table and out of view.

"Okay," said Milo. "Make it a really sad story. Tug at their heartstrings. But watch your back. I don't need any goddamn international incident."

44

I'd slept fitfully but was awake at six, ahead of Robin for a change. Lying flat on my back, I watched her doze and thought about being Andrew Desmond.

At six-thirty she awoke and looked at me.

Her eyes were puffy. I kissed them. She lay there.

"Today," she said.

"Just a bookstore visit," I said. "Shouldn't take long."

"Hopefully not. When's he getting here?"

"Nine."

She touched my hair, rolled away from me.

We both got out of bed. She put on a robe, tugged the sash tight, and stood there for a moment.

I stood behind her and held her shoulders. "I'll be fine."

"I know you will." She turned sharply, kissed me hard on the cheek, almost an assault. Then she went into the bathroom and locked the door.

Yesterday, we'd made love twice. The second time, she said, "I feel like an adulterer."

Daniel arrived at nine and sat me down in the kitchen. Covering me with a black barber's sheet, he snipped my hair with scissors, then used electric clippers to reduce it to a Marine-recruit buzz.

"You're a barber, too?"

"The Army," he said. "You learn all kinds of things. Not that I'm ready to open a salon."

He gave me a hand mirror.

Silver glints peppered my scalp; gray hair unearthed.

Bumps on my cranium that I'd never known about.

I looked ten years older, ten pounds thinner.

The haircut and the beard gave me the appearance of an Islamic radical.

I put on the tinted glasses. Scowled.

"Smile," said a voice from the door.

Robin stood there.

I grinned at her.

"Okay, it's still you," she said. But she didn't smile back.

DANIEL SET UP A PROFESSIONAL POLAROID CAMERA on a tripod, took three dozen shots, left, and returned an hour later with Andrew Desmond's California driver's license. To my eyes, indistinguishable from the real thing.

I added it to the rest of the fake ID now occupying my wallet. "Hopefully I won't get stopped by a cop."

"If you do, it's okay," he said. "We've managed to enter the serial number into the system. Your graduate school's the Pacific Insight Institute. Have you heard of it?"

"No."

"It closed down years ago. Master's degrees and Ph.Ds in education and psychology. Headquarters was a one-room office in Westwood Village. Fifty-three graduates. To our knowledge, none passed the state licensing exams."

"So they went to work as psychic friends and made twice the money," I said.

"Could be. Access to the spirits often pays off. So do diploma mills, apparently. Tuition was nineteen thousand dollars per year."

"Couldn't buy licensure. Is that why it closed down?"

He shrugged. "Enrollment dropped each year. The former dean sells insurance in Oregon. His degree was self-granted. For the first year, Pacific was actually able to obtain partial federal loans, but that ended when the government clamped down on diploma mills."

"You've done quite a bit of research."

"More than we intended," he said. "Because while finding a place for you, I learned that the Loomis Institute was involved in funding similar schools. Two in Florida and one in the Virgin Islands. Another possible profit-making scheme while claiming tax-free status, though all we know so far is Loomis awarded grants to these places."

"Where'd you find this out?"

"A book written in response to *The Brain Drain*. One good thing that did come my way through the Internet. A collection of essays. The one that caught my eye was by a professor at Cole University in Mississippi whose field of study was diploma mills. He found out the school in the Virgin Islands had links to Loomis and may have really been a way to fund eugenics research."

"A book," I said. *"Twisted Science?"*

"That's the one. You've read it?"

"I checked it out but never got around to reading it, figured why waste time on something I agree with. What's this professor's name?"

"Bernard Eustace."

"I assume you've contacted him."

His gold eyes were steady. "We tried. He died fourteen months ago."

"How?"

"Auto accident. He was visiting his parents in Mississippi, drove off the road late at night."

"Jesus," I said.

"It's recorded as an accident, Alex. Maybe it was. Milo and I agree that digging further right now is too risky because the crash site is rural, any questions from out-of-town police will be conspicuous."

The fingers of his good hand had bowed, tips pressing into the tabletop.

"Mississippi," I said. "Was Eustace black?"

"White. A historian, not a psychologist. We may eventually talk to his wife, but right now, following Farley Sanger and your meeting Zena Lambert seem more useful. Are you ready?"

"Yes. Where's Milo?"

"He'll be following you but we thought it better that you didn't know where he was. That way you'd be less likely to look his way accidentally. I'm sure you don't doubt his protectiveness."

"Not a shred of doubt," I said.

. . .

BEFORE I LEFT, I STOPPED IN TO SEE ROBIN AGAIN. The shop was quiet, all machines switched off, her apron still folded on a workbench, as she talked on the phone, her back to me.

Spike barked and trotted forward and Robin turned. "I'll call you when it's done. Bye."

She put the phone down. "You look—like a French cinematographer."

"Is that good or bad?"

"Depends if you like French cinema—it does have a certain . . . hungry elegance. C'mere."

We embraced.

"What's that cologne?" she said.

"Andrew's scent. Do you find it alluring?"

"Oh, yeah. Baguettes and pessimism." She pulled away, held me at arm's length. "You're certainly giving them their money's worth. When will you be back?"

"Depends on how it goes," I said. "Probably sometime this afternoon."

"Give me a call as soon as you can. I'll get us something for dinner."

I held her tighter. Her hand reached up and touched my bristly head. Paused. Stroked.

"Fuzzy Wuzzy was a bear," I said.

"If I run out of .000 sandpaper, I'll draft you into service."

She pulled away again. Studied me. "Definitely different."

"Overkill," I said. "It's a bookstore visit in Hollywood, not sneaking into Iran, but they're the professionals."

"Have you seen Hollywood recently?"

I chuckled. Thought about Nolan's Hollywood.

She stroked my head some more. "Three kids, that blind man. Some things grow back."

45

DOWN IN FRONT, PARKED NEXT TO DANIEL'S TOYOTA, was the Karmann Ghia from the Genesee garage, cream-colored, not yellow, in the sunlight, with a scarred hood and a dented door.

He handed me a small color photo.

Headshot of a young woman with a narrow face, white-blond hair cut almost as short as mine.

Her features were good but her skin was beyond pale—Kabuki white. Black liner enlarged her blue eyes and emphasized a hypermetabolic glow. Despite that, she looked bored. Resentful. I resisted the urge to interpret; standing in line at the DMV could make anyone feel that way.

"Driver's license?" I said.

He nodded, took the picture from me, and put it in his pocket. "The store is at 2028 Apollo Avenue. Good luck."

We shook hands and he drove off.

THE KARMANN GHIA'S SEAT WAS ADJUSTED TO MY height and the car started up easily. Plenty of power, as Daniel had promised. The interior was trashed—torn upholstery and headliner, crumpled paper cups and fast-food boxes tossed behind the seat.

The AM-FM radio was old enough to be original. I turned it on. KPFK. The guest was a black "sociopolitical theoretician and author" who believed Jewish doctors had created AIDS in order to kill off inner-city babies. The host let him preach for paragraphs at a time, then threw him grounders that evoked more hatred.

Daniel was a planner and I wondered if he'd preset the dial.
Getting me in the mood.

I switched to jazz and drove.

Spasm's address put the store just past the border between Hollywood and Silverlake. I passed Sunset's Hospital Row and the
Hillhurst intersection, where the boulevard veers southeast toward
downtown—today just a smog-shrouded theory. Then a quick left
on Fountain, which I followed until it became a side street, yielding to two lanes of dips and curves—Apollo.

The street was planted with huge, untrimmed trees. Old trees;
this was the kind of one-story, mixed-use neighborhood you see
only in older parts of L.A.

Mostly it was auto-body shops and printing plants and used-tire
yards, but interspersed among the dreary lots were liquor stores
and other small businesses, and small houses—some converted to
commercial use, some still sporting gardens and laundry lines, one
a Pentecostal church.

A nail parlor, a tattoo parlor, a *botánica* advertising crystals and
herbs. Unmarked buildings, many with FOR LEASE signs. Looking
down on all of it were the steep embankments of Silverlake, weedy
and tree-shrouded where they weren't toasted golden. Dry spots;
primed for the arsonist's match.

The hillside was planted with uneven rows of residences, like
shrubs sprouting from a careless garden. Some of the houses
flamingoed on stilts, others rested at skeptical angles on tremor-
throttled foundations. I saw cracks snaking down stucco, parted
seams, roofs missing entire sections of shingle, porch beams bent
like reeds. The whole neighborhood looked off-kilter. A mile away,
the city was excavating a subway.

The 2000 block appeared and I spotted Spasm right away.

The black window was the tipoff. Small black plastic letters
were placed near the top of a gray door, illegible from the street.

Empty curb; no problem parking. As I got out I made out *spasm
books*.

On both sides of the store were body shops, then an acre of
asphalt bearing the badge of an official police tow yard. Across the
street was a mom-and-pop taco joint, its doors shut, a CLOSED sign
hanging on the knob.

It was impossible to tell if Spasm was open for business but
when I pushed the gray door, it yielded and I stepped into a long,

skinny, tunnel-like charcoal-colored room vibrating with loud calypso music. Skimpy lighting was turned even murkier by the tinted lenses of my glasses but I kept them on and tried to affect an air of mild curiosity.

To the left, a bald, wildly tattooed man sat at a checkout booth and smoked energetically. Leather vest over blue-and-crimson flesh. He was swaying to the music, didn't look up.

The booth was three panels of plywood pushed up against the wall. On the floor were loose piles of throwaway papers—*The Reader, The Weekly, The Maoist Exile Wanderer*—flyers for *Divas in Drag: Where You Can Be What You Want To Be; MaidenHead in Concert; Tertiara Malladonna: A One-Wimin Show About Tampon-Sucking and Rice Confiscation; Uncle Suppurato's Body-Piercing Studio*, schedules of night readings in Barnhard Park of poetry concerned with "quantum physics and gum disease."

Leather Vest continued to ignore me as I passed him. Both side walls were lined with slanting shelves of books displayed face-out. Accent lights brightened the covers. Toward the back was a cable-and-plank staircase leading to an upper loft. On the back wall, another gray door.

Three customers on the ground floor: a wan-looking, clean-cut man in his twenties with bad posture and a fearful frown. He wore a madras button-down shirt, khakis, and sneakers, and glanced over his shoulder nervously as I approached. I could imagine him masturbating in his car, dreading discovery, yet hoping for it. The paperback in his hand said *Cannibal Killers*.

The other two browsers were a man and woman in their late forties, both with pemmican faces shellacked with a sun-and-booze luster. Long hair, missing teeth, lots of beads, a shopping bag full of scraps. Had their tie-dyes and serapes been clean, they could have been traded on Melrose as antiques.

They were sharing a white-covered paperback and cackling. I heard the woman say, "Cool," in a grandmother's voice, then the man returned the book to the rack and they left looking jolly.

HeilRock: Marching Songs of the Waffen SS.

Peace, love, Woodstock had come to this.

The man with the cannibal book brought it up to Leather Vest and paid. Now I was the sole patron. The calypso soundtrack shifted to Stravinsky. The illustrated clerk lit up another cigarette and began tapping his knee to no discernible rhythm.

Time to browse.

Maybe I'd be lucky and find a DVLL reference.

I decided to start with the second floor, out of view of the clerk.

The staircase took me up to half a loft—just one long wall, with the same face-out display and spotlighting.

One copy of each book. Nothing labeled by subject matter or author, no alphabetization, though I did find clumps of volumes that seemed related.

Collections on sadomasochism, lavishly illustrated, some taken to the blood-wound-pus level.

Prison diaries, crudely printed. A glossy thing called *Penitentiary Magazine*, with stories on "Lifer in the Top Bunk: My Favorite Celly," "Stand Up for Your Rights and Don't Let the System Buttfuck You," "Why Writers Don't Know Shit about Crime," and "The Best Jack-Off Videos of the Year."

Another cluster on human oddities, most written with cold, leering tones.

Racist comics.

Alternative comix that glorified incest.

The Turner Diaries and other white-supremacist tomes.

Lots of that: *The Biological Jew; The Secret History of Zionism; Bloodface; Pickaninny Palace; The Mud People: Why Africa Has No Culture.*

The savant on the radio would have liked at least some of it.

No DVLL.

I came upon a shelf of academic texts, mostly philosophy and history. Toynbee, Bertrand Russell, a Frenchman named Bataille.

Shelves of practical paranoia: how-to primers on bomb-making, wiretapping, exacting revenge, getting away with slander and libel, dirty tricks.

Knife Fighters of the Philippines.

The Bizarre Magazine Compendium.

Fetishism, bondage, coprophagy. Step-by-step photo-essays cobbled from operating-room videos: sex-changes, face-peels, brain-tumor removals, liposuction, autopsies.

The Firearms Bible. The Freemen's Manifesto; The Anarchist's Cookbook; Trotsky's Roach Motel: Exterminating Capitalists.

A big black-covered thing called *The Demon's Workshop*, offering exquisitely detailed instructions on building silencers, converting conventional weapons to automatic, imbedding poison in bullets.

A pictorial history of the Chinese Revolution, devoted to carnage. Its centerfold was a double-width sepia print from the twenties showing a royalist scholar being torn to pieces by a mob, chunks of his flesh gone, ribs and viscera exposed. Fully conscious. Screaming.

The Pinhead Review: one hundred pages of empty-faced, clown-suited microcephalics in sideshow booths. Accompanying cartoons and jokes about sex among the retarded.

Einstein's theories alongside astrology.

Slavic dictionaries neighboring *The Art of Harassment*. How to disappear, how to find anyone.

Computer science. The I ching, hypnosis, *Raising Swine for Slaughter*.

The collected works of George Lincoln Rockwell; erotic aromatherapy; *A History of Natural Disasters; The Thinking Man's Guide to Idol Worship*.

The organizing criterion seemed to be Stuff Other Stores Won't Carry.

Nothing on DVLL.

On the last rack was a collection of solemn-looking hardcovers from a well-respected scientific publishing house: forensic pathology, homicide and rape investigation, gunshot wounds, crime-scene techniques, toxicology.

Densely worded manuals for police detectives, eighty bucks each.

Had someone considered them primers, as well?

I pictured Wilson Tenney or some other cruel loner up here, browsing, maybe even buying.

I opened the book on homicide procedure.

The usual cop mix of detached writing and close-up views of the destruction visited upon human flesh by shotgun, blade, blunt instrument, strangulation. Toxicology and lividity charts. Rates of putrefaction. Victims, sexually posed, mutilated; the blank, helpless face of death.

The *modus operandi* section said that while some serial killers traveled the highways, most tended to work within circumscribed areas.

Patterns to be broken?

Replacing the book, I returned downstairs. The clerk had switched to a cigar and was trying to create his own toxic cloud.

He stared at me for a second, leaned forward, twisted something, and Stravinsky blared well above the ear-bleed range.

Not into user-friendly.

I used, anyway.

The first floor started off as more of the same brutal eclecticism and I skimmed, trying to look casual.

Then I found the eugenics books and slowed down.

The Collected Essays of Galton. Desktop publishing by New Dominion Press—why did that sound familiar?

The publisher's address, St. Croix. The Virgin Islands.

Another Loomis venture?

The book was nothing more than what it claimed to be.

Next came Dr. Charles Davenport's 1919 report to the Cold Springs Eugenics Society. Hereditary charts of patients whose "degenerative spawn" had been curtailed by sterilization.

Annotations at the bottom by Dr. Arthur Haldane, resident scholar at the Loomis Institute.

I checked this one out carefully.

Published five years before *The Brain Drain.* Haldane's pre-bestseller days.

In it, Haldane remarked upon the relative unsophistication of turn-of-the-century science but reaffirmed Davenport's thesis: society was doomed unless "genetic restructuring utilizing advanced technology" became public policy.

I flipped to the index.

Still no DVLL.

Nothing on Meta, either.

I found six more books on selective breeding and quality-of-life issues, one by the Australian ethnicist who'd recommended killing retarded babies. Same old crap, nothing new.

The stench of the clerk's cigar had enveloped me and I looked up and realized I was fifteen feet from the register. No insights, no Zena Lambert. Mr. Tattoo was reading something called *Wet Bandage.*

Then, just as I was about to give up, I found one more nugget: a fifty-page pamphlet, that same laser-printer look under brown paper covers.

Humanness: New Perspectives
by Farley Sanger, attorney-at-law

An expanded version of the article from *The Pathfinder*, supplemented by charts and graphs, government statistics on crime, race, unemployment, out-of-wedlock births, DNA testing, the Human Genome Project and how it could be used to "cleanse the dross."

Dry as a legal brief.

Lawsuit against the disadvantaged . . .

Sanger ended with a call for "the brutally efficient elimination of mind-set censorship of indisputably valid areas of research simply because certain elements with vested interests are offended or justifiably frightened of what can only be regarded as the logical conclusions of carefully tested hypotheses."

Golden prose. Pity the poor judges who had to read his work-product.

Twenty-two-dollar price tag. I tucked the book under my arm, returned to the Galton book, and took that, too.

The door at the back of the store opened and Zena Lambert came out.

46

SHE'D DYED HER HAIR BLACK AND GROWN IT TO shoulder length, with thick bangs that covered her brow and a Doris Day flip. But the face was the same, narrow and pale. The same black eyeliner. In real life, less Kabuki than bone china. Clean, balanced features, the nose small and straight, the lips narrow but full, glossed pink. Prettier than in the photo.

The kind of guileless, all-American face favored by casting directors for detergent commercials.

Sally Branch had said she was small but that was an understatement. Maybe five feet, no more than ninety pounds, she was a child-woman with small, sharp breasts and thin but supple-looking arms exposed by a sleeveless pink polyester top.

Tight black jeans covered trim hips. Tiny waist. Proportionately long legs for someone so small.

She wore black plastic earrings and pink high-heeled sandals with clear plastic bows on the instep.

Even with the lift, she was tiny. Twenty-eight years old but she could have passed for a college sophomore.

Hips-swiveling walk. Black, pink, black, pink.

Both of us in costume?

Hers appeared to be fifties retro. Nostalgia for the good old days when men were men and women were women and defectives knew their place?

She'd assembled herself to attract attention, might very well be looking for stares. I hid my face behind a book on dwarfs, trying to observe inconspicuously.

She noticed.

"Hi," she said in a high, bright voice. "Is there anything I can help you with?"

I gave her Andrew's best surly headshake, put the book back, and returned my attention to the rack.

"Happy browsing." She swayed up to the register. Before she got there, Mr. Cigar left the booth without comment and exited the store.

"Stinky!" she called after him as the door closed. Climbing atop the stool, she lowered Stravinsky to a tolerable level, made her own twisting motion, and switched to a harpsichord fugue.

"Thanks," I said.

"Welcome," she chirped. "Being a reader means never having to herniate your tympanic membranes."

I turned back to the book I'd selected randomly—a quarterly called *Earthquake Sex,* and stole glances at her. She picked up the copy of *Wet Bandage* left on the counter, put it aside, and took out what looked like an accounting ledger. Holding it on her lap, she began writing.

I brought Sanger's pamphlet and the Galton book up to the booth.

Columns of figures; definitely a ledger. She slid it out of sight and smiled. "Cash or charge?"

"Charge."

Before I got my hand on my wallet, she said, "Thirty-two sixty-four."

My surprised look was genuine.

She laughed. White teeth, one frontal incisor chipped. A speck of lipstick on another. "Don't trust my addition?"

I shrugged. "I'm sure you're right but that was rather quick."

"Mental arithmetic," she said. "Intellectual calisthenics. Use it or lose it. But if you're skeptical . . ."

Laughing again, she snatched both books off the counter and punched the register.

Ding. Thirty-two sixty-four.

She licked her lips with a tiny pink tongue.

"A-plus," I said. I gave her Andrew's new MasterCard.

She glanced at it and said, "Are you a teacher?"

"No. Why?"

"Teachers love to grade."

"I seldom grade."

She put the books in an unmarked paper bag and handed them to me. "The nonjudgmental type?"

I shrugged.

"Well, enjoy the books, A. Desmond."

I started for the door.

"Not looking forward to it?" she said.

I stopped. "To what?"

"Reading what you just bought. You look positively sullen. It's not for pleasure?"

I stopped and gave her my best downbeat smile. "Until I read, I won't know that, will I?"

Her smile freeze-framed, then widened. She tugged a wave of black hair and let it bounce back. Elastic; I'd seen hair like that as a child. Black-and-white TV commercials for Tonette do-it-yourself permanents.

"On top of being a skeptic, he's an empiricist," she said.

"Is there an alternative?"

"There are alternatives to everything," she said. Then she waved a small, delicate hand. The nails were long, tapered, and— what else—bright pink. "Ta-ta, go on your way, A. Desmond. Didn't mean to intrude but the topic caught my eye."

"Oh?" I looked into the bag. "You've read them? Have I made good choices?"

She lowered her eyes from my face to my chest to my belt. Lingering. Continuing to my shoes then swooping upward for an eye-lock. "Quite good ones. Galton was the progenitor of it all. And yes, I have read them. It happens to be something I'm interested in."

"Eugenics?"

"Societal improvements of all kinds."

I conceded a miserly smile. "Well, we've got common ground, there."

"Do we?"

"I think society sorely needs fixing."

"A misanthrope."

"That depends on what day you catch me."

She leaned on the counter, small breasts spreading on the wood. "A Swift or a Pope?"

"Pardon?"

"The Swift-Pope dichotomy on the Great Yardstick of Misanthropy. Not familiar, A.?"

I shook my head. "Must have missed that one."

She examined a pink thumbnail. "It's really quite simple: Jonathan Swift hated humanity as a structural unit but managed to muster affection for individuals. Alexander Pope professed a love for humanity but couldn't countenance interpersonal relationships."

"Is that so."

"Quite so."

I put a finger to my mouth. "Then I suppose I'm both a Swift and a Pope—again, depending upon which day you catch me. There are also times I'm an equal-opportunity despiser. Such as when I read the paper too early in the day."

She laughed. "A sourpuss."

"So I've been told." I slouched forward, put my hand out. "Andrew Desmond."

She stared at the hand, finally touched my fingertips very lightly. "How sociable of you to actually grant me a greeting, Andrew Desmond. I'm Zena."

"A to Z," I said.

She turned off the music. "How cute. We traverse the alphabet in one fell swoop."

I stepped closer and she moved back, sitting higher on the stool. She took another look at her nails.

"Interesting location you've got," I said. "Have you been here long?"

"A few months."

"I only noticed it because I was picking my car up from the tow yard and saw the sign."

"Our customers know us."

I looked around the empty room. She watched me but didn't react.

"Anywhere to get lunch around here?" I said.

"Not really. The Mexican place across the street is closed because the owner's son got shot last week—gang morons, the usual ethnic entropy."

Waiting for my reaction.

"That's the only place?" I said.

"There are a few others just like it farther down Apollo. If you like that kind of thing."

"I like good."

"Then, no. We're talking roacharama." Another pull of her hair. "Lard-encrusted pinto beans and shredded pork elevated to palatability only by abject starvation. Are you starving, Andrew?"

"Never," I said. "Nothing's worth that kind of self-debasement."

"*Precisement.*" A corner of the ledger was visible on the shelf beneath the register and she pushed it in.

"I'd rather dine than eat," I said. "Where do you go?"

She bunched her lips, creating a mocking rosebud. "Is that a come-on?"

I removed the tinted glasses. Rubbed my beard.

"If you accept, it was an invitation. If you don't, it was a factual inquiry."

"Guarding the old self-esteem, eh?"

"Honor bound to," I said. "I'm a psychologist."

"Are you?" She looked away, as if trying not to show interest. "Clinical or experimental?"

"Clinical."

"Do you practice around here?"

"I don't practice anywhere at the moment. Actually, I'm ABD. All but degree."

"All but degradation," she said. "A quitter?"

"You bet."

"Proud of it, are you?"

"Neither proud nor ashamed," I said. "As you said, nonjudgmental. I served my sentence in grad school, learned primarily that psychology is crumbs of science mixed in with dollops of nonsense. Expositions of the obvious passed off as profundity. Before I took it further, I decided to spend some time figuring out if I can live with that." I raised the bag with the books. "Ergo this."

"Ergo what?"

"Unassigned reading, not the PC swill they shove at you. I want to decide for myself whether or not any of it's relevant. In terms of the aforementioned improvement. Putting a brake on the slippery slope toward mediocrity. When I came in here, I had no idea what you were about. When I saw these"—rattling the bag—"they said 'buy me.'"

She leaned forward, elbows on the counter. "The slide toward mediocrity. I'd say we're well past that."

"I was trying to be charitable."

"Don't be. Charity leads to delusion. Then again, you *are* an almost-psychologist. Making you an almost-keeper of the sacred chalice of self-esteem."

"Or selfish steam," I said. "Depending upon your point of view."

She laughed. Too much more of this and I'd be ready to puke.

"Well, A., in answer to your question, I tend to *dine* at a French joint in Echo Park. La Petite. Provençal and all that good stuff."

"Cassoulet?"

"It's been known to appear on the menu."

"Maybe I'll be lucky. Thanks."

"Maybe you will, at that." She half-closed her eyes, displaying blue lids.

"So," I said, "what's it to be, invitation or factual inquiry?"

"The latter, I'm afraid. I'm working."

"Chained to the rock? Some boss looking over your shoulder?"

"Hardly," she said, suddenly peeved. "It's my store."

"Then why not fly?" I said. "As you said, your customers know you. I'm sure they'll forgive a brief absence."

Her grin was wide but close-mouthed, almost regretful. "How do I know you're not some dangerous psychopath."

"You don't." I bared my teeth in a wolfish grimace.

"A carnivore?"

"All animals weren't created equal on the food chain." Another shake of the bag. "That's the point of all this, isn't it?"

"Is it?" she said.

"For me it is, Z. However, if your sensibilities are bruised, apologies."

She gave me a long, hard look, then pulled a key out of her jeans and locked the register. "I'll fetch my purse and lock up. Meet you out front."

FIVE MINUTES LATER, SHE EMERGED RUBBING HER hands together and got in the Karmann Ghia.

"All but drivability," she said, wrinkling her nose at the mess in back.

"Had I known, I'd have brought the Rolls."

The news was on the radio. She said, "Go," fiddled with the dial until she found elevator music, stretched her legs, wiggled her toes in the open pink sandals, looked behind. "No cops, Andrew. Make a U and get back to Sunset, then go east."

Orders. She stared out the open passenger window. Said nothing as I drove.

A block later, she reached over and grabbed my crotch.

47

TWO SQUEEZES AND THE HAND WAS BACK AT HER hair, stroking slowly. She aimed the rearview mirror at herself and checked her lipstick. Was Milo back there?

As she fooled with the radio dial again, I prepared for anything. But she placed her hands in her lap and turned to me, looking smug. "Honk, honk. Guess that's why they call it goosing."

"Sauce for the gander."

"Ha! Don't go getting ideas, A. Desmond. I'm empowered to shop without buying."

"I'm sure you shop and return."

"What's that supposed to mean?"

"That you're a selective woman," I said. "At least that would be my assumption."

"Why's that?"

"Just a guess."

She wiggled her toes some more. "This could get interesting—turn here."

NO FURTHER CONVERSATION. SHE KEPT STARING OUT the passenger window, sticking her head out from time to time to breathe in smoggy wind. The rearview mirror remained askew. I straightened it and took the opportunity to glance back.

Lots of cars behind me but no way to know if Milo was in any of them.

"Right here," said Zena. She arched her back and I saw the outline of her nipples, sharp and defined against pink polyester.

I hadn't noticed that in the store. Had she removed her bra?

I had a pretty good idea how she'd captured Malcolm Ponsico from Sally Branch.

"Here," she said.

La Petite was misnamed—a big mock chateau on a generous property—more old L.A.—the only business in sight without a Spanish sign. The parking lot was nearly empty but the cars I saw were expensive. Red-vested valets lounged near the porte cochere. One of them held Zena's door open and eyed the Karmann Ghia as if it were contagious.

The restaurant's interior was a couple of lumens above pitch-dark. Oak tables and ceiling beams, leather booths, Impressionist copies, dessert carts heaped with sculptural pastries on doilies. Suddenly I remembered the place. I'd eaten there once, fifteen years ago. A hospital administrator with an expense account explaining why surgery was heroic and psychology wasn't but that I was expected to speak to the volunteer luncheon anyway because genteel women didn't want to know about scalpels and retractors.

Up front was a trio of worried-looking Frenchmen in tuxedos. They aimed cold looks of recognition at Zena. She walked ahead of me and announced, "Two."

The baldest and oldest of the three stiffened, said, "Mademoiselle," and snatched up a pair of huge tasseled menus before hurrying after Zena as she headed for a remote corner booth.

Her usual trysting place?

The maitre d's chilly expression congealed as he watched her snap her napkin open. When I caught his attention, he gave me the same appraisal. *"Bon apetit."*

"Do you have cassoulet today?" she said.

"No, mademoiselle, I'm afrai—"

"What's decent?"

His smile was so pained it could have used anesthesia. "What did you have last time, mademoiselle?"

"Sole Véronique but it was mushy."

"Mushy?"

"Mushy, soft, flabby, pulpous. In need of another minute in the skillet. Which I saw to."

He grabbed his bow tie and entertained homicide. "Very well. I will inform the chef."

She smiled. "Two ice waters with lemon while we decide, and bring a bottle of a decent white wine."

"Decent," he muttered.

"A California wine," she added. "Chardonnay, whatever year was decent."

When he was gone, she said, "The French are such *pompous* fucks. Pomposity in the face of substance is one thing, but they're so fucking socially and intellectually *bankrupt,* that it's reduced to pathetic posturing. Obsessed with their moribund *culture,* their snot-nosed *language,* in pathological denial of the fact that no one speaks it anymore because it's linguistically *anorexic.*"

"How do you really feel about it?"

She giggled.

"By anorexic," I said, "you mean not enough words?"

"Oh, there're enough words to order pressed duck," she said, "but insufficient for anything serious. As in technology. When's the last time computer software originated in *French?*"

"It's a beautiful language," I said.

She laughed. A Mexican busboy brought water.

"The *chef,*" she said. "More like a short-order cook with no green card—probably *that* one's uncle."

We were two feet apart in the booth and I could smell her perfume—light, floral, old-fashioned. Probably French. I smiled at her and she began to scoot farther away, changed her mind and stayed put. Licking a finger, she traced a vertical path down the frost on her water glass. Then another. Two lines. She crossed them twice, made a tic-tac-toe board, erased it.

"As you can see," she said, "I have my Swift-plus-Pope days, as well."

"Common ground."

"If you're lucky."

I laughed.

"What?" she said.

"You don't lack confidence."

She arched her back again. "Should I?"

Before I could answer, a tiny hand clamped around my wrist. Small fingers, all bones, but soft at the tips. Hot, like those of a child with a fever or too much enthusiasm.

"Should I lack confidence, Andrew?"

"I'd say no," I said. "You're obviously endowed on many levels."

The hand tightened and I felt her nails digging into my arm.

"Am I?"

"Intellectually and physically," I said. The hand loosened and her index finger began massaging the space between my thumb and forefinger. Small, circular motions. Annoying, but I didn't resist.

Abruptly, she pulled away.

"Maybe it's psychological," she said, grinning. "My confidence, that is. All through my childhood, my parents told me how wonderful I was."

"Good child-rearing," I said.

"I didn't say they were good. Just free with the praise."

Her voice had hardened. I looked into her eyes. In the weak light, the blue irises were deep gray.

"Actually," she said, "they were excellent. Brilliant, educated people who taught me standards. What about yours?"

I shook my head. "Wish I could say the same."

"Abused child, tsk-tsk?"

"No," I said. "But far short of excellent."

"Poor snookums," she said. "His mummy didn't nurture him— is that why you chose psychology?"

"Probably."

"Probably? You don't know?"

"I'm not much for self-analysis."

"I thought that was the point."

"The point," I said, "is to try to understand as much as you can of this psychotic world so you can do what you feel like. I get into other people's heads but stay away from my own crap. If that's inconsistent, so be it."

"Grumpy, grumpy, *cher* A. I'm getting the feeling that you get off on conflict. When things get too easy you lose interest, correct?"

I didn't answer.

"*True?*" she said, elbowing my arm hard.

"As I said, self-analysis chafes, Z." I picked up a menu. "What do you suggest?"

Refusing to play. Her lean face was rigid with anger. Then she smiled.

"Well," she said merrily, "I'd go for the sole Véronique."

I turned and stared at her. "Not mushy today?"

"If it is, we throw it in their fucking faces."

IT WAS FIRM.

Presented by the maitre d' with a hateful flourish. He studied me as I tasted, then Zena. I nodded, she kept eating. He turned on his heel.

I watched her dissect the fish, examining every forkful, chewing slowly but steadily, never pausing. She finished and moved through the side dishes with silent drive, and by the time I'd had enough, she'd cleaned her plate. Even the parsley.

"Another talent," I said.

"Are you one of those men who thinks women shouldn't eat?"

"Heaven forfend."

"Good. I *like* to eat." She sat back and wiped her lips. "And not an ounce ends up here." Patting a flat tummy. "I just *burn* calories. A surfeit of energy."

"You would have made a good cheerleader."

A flash of dentition spread across her face. "I was a *great* cheerleader." Snapping her fingers, she began moving her head from side to side, threw her arms up, shaking imaginary pom-poms. A few more people had come into the restaurant but all had been seated in the adjoining room. Zena earning her privacy with past displays?

" 'Rah, rah, rah! Sis-boom-boom! The other side stinks! So clear the room! You think you're *cool*, you think you're *hot*! We're here to say you're definitely *not!* ' "

Her arms floated down slowly.

"Bracing," I said. "High school?"

"Where else? The great crucible of cruelty. Pretty lame material but those were the days before you could get away with, 'Block that kick, block that pass, if that doesn't work, just fuck 'em in the ass!' "

"Didn't know things had gotten that loose."

"Oh, they have, they have. A complete lack of standards. Ergo the slippery slope. We're talking a return of the medieval age, Andrew, the only difference being the new nobility's that which earns it."

"How?"

"Intellectually."

I pretended to think about that.

She snapped her fingers at a busboy and demanded a mai tai. I watched her suck it slowly through a straw. "One thing will never change: The vast majority are relegated to serfdom. Serfs think they want freedom, Andrew, but they're incapable of dealing with it. Serfs need structure, predictability, someone to show them how to wipe their glutei."

"How vast is the vast majority?"

"At least ninety-nine percent."

"And they get regulated by the remaining one percent."

"You don't agree?"

"I guess that would depend upon which group I ended up in."

She laughed. "Do you doubt your own abilities?"

More feigned deliberation. "No," I said. "And I agree with your assessment. In principle. Things have deteriorated beyond belief. I just hadn't come up with a number."

"I thought that's what you psychologists were all about."

"ABD," I said. "All but dogmatism."

She touched my hand briefly, pulled away, played with a black curl. "One percent is *generous*. Probably less than one-half percent are qualified to make choices."

The maitre d' came over and asked if everything was acceptable.

She waved him off and said, "Maybe a third. And even in that range some individuals wouldn't qualify. Because they lack conviction. I've known people perceived to be geniuses who turned out to have all the backbone of an oyster."

"Is that so."

"Oh, quite. The requisite gray matter but no spine."

A tightening of her lips and I knew she meant Malcolm Ponsico. Keeping my voice even, I said, "Ideologically weak?"

"Ideologically *mushy*." She put her hand on my sleeve. "*Cher* Andrew, a brain without a spine is only half a central nervous system—but no matter, we're not here to fix society's problems."

"True. We'd need lunch and dinner for that."

The faintest smile. The mai tai was nearly gone and she sucked foam noisily, then leaned over suddenly, placed a frigid tongue tip on my cheek, and traced a wet trail to my earlobe.

"What *are* we here for, Andrew?" she whispered.

"You tell me."

Another cold tongue-dart, then a small, painful bite of the lobe. She snuggled closer, nibbled. I could hear her breathing, rapid and shallow, smell the alcohol on her breath. She put her hand on my chin, swiveled my face, bit my lower lip, pulled away, pinched my thigh, touched my knee. She was arrogant, disturbed, pathetic, quite possibly evil, but dammit, all of it had its effect and when she reached under the table and groped me again, she found exactly what she wanted and it brought a triumphant grin to the plump, pink lips.

Then she pulled away, took a gold lipstick tube and matching compact out of her purse, made them pinker.

"Well, *you're* an eager boy. Which creates a moral dilemma for me."

"Oh?"

She smiled for the mirror. "The issue at hand is: Do I fuck the hell out of you today and risk having you think me a slattern, or shall I let you simmer until your balls turn turquoise and then— just maybe, *if* you behave—fuck the hell out of you and leave you begging for more?"

Her hand returned to my groin. "Hello, Mr. *Gander*."

"Such problems," I said. "Call in the ethicists." Gently, I removed her fingers and placed them on the seat. "Take some time to figure it out, then call me."

She stared at me, outraged, grabbed her glass, nearly threw herself halfway down the booth and showed me her back.

I saw her neck muscles tighten and loosen.

I was dealing with something fragile, easily bruised, maybe more dangerous because of it.

"Take me back, asshole."

"Zena—"

"Fuck *off!*"

"Suit yourself." I stood, hot-faced, teeth clenched, not having to fake it. She started to slide out of the booth but I blocked her exit, leaning over the table, glaring down at her.

"Get the hell out of my—"

"Ms. Third-of-a-Percent," I whisper-growled. "Because I don't feel like creaming my slacks right here, I've *failed* you? Shouldn't the elite be a little more *secure*?"

My tone made her flinch. She was trying to outstare me but little things gave her away—nostrils flexing, spots of color sprouting on her face.

Pink spots, like a mild case of eczema. Her mouth trembled. Her nipples were bigger than ever, poking at the pink fabric.

I threw cash on the table. "It's been an experience. Let's go."

"I'll leave when I'm ready."

"Suit yourself." I began walking out.

"Where the *fuck* do you think *you're* going?"

"Somewhere without pressure, Z."

"Can't handle pressure?"

"Can but prefer not to." I kept going. Suddenly, she was at my side, grabbing my bicep with both hands, clawing through tweed.

"Hold *on,* dammit, or I'll rip your shirt off right here!"

I stopped.

She moved around and faced me, reached up and cupped my chin in one hand. When Robin stands on tiptoe she barely brings herself to eye level with me. Zena missed by several inches and her breasts were up against my abdomen, our faces nearly touching. Someone watching might have thought it affectionate but she was squeezing my face too hard for affection and as I felt her nails graze my jawline, I prepared to bleed.

"Such a tough boy," she said. "Such a tough, tough boy—when's the last time you were laid?"

"I don't keep records."

She laughed. "Exactly as I thought. Okay, I'll attribute your lack of manners to drive level. You deserve release. My place. I'll show you how to get there."

I DROVE BACK TO APOLLO WITH HER SITTING AS close as the gearshift would allow, one hand around my neck, caressing idly as she hummed along with the Bartok she'd found on the radio. Her singing voice was coarse, off-key. I wanted to tell her to shut up.

"Tough boy," she said. "Obviously, I need to be *tender* with you."

I smiled. Thinking, what the hell am I going to do?

For all Milo's and Daniel's cautiousness, nothing had prepared me for this.

I thought of Robin's good-bye, two hours ago.

How far was I willing to go?

I tried to put it in perspective by picturing Irit's body among the trees, Latvinia hanging in the schoolyard, Raymond's bloody shoes, the pain Melvin Myers had felt. But what if this creature *hadn't* been part of that—nutty but not dangerous—

"Lyric's the next corner," she said. "Make a left."

As I turned, I allowed myself another look-around for Milo. Once again, moderate traffic, but no one followed me up the steep, shady road.

Lyric offered barely enough room for one car and I drove slowly, trying to sort out my thoughts. Zena began to drum her fingers on my thigh.

"Keep going to the top."

I checked out the neighborhood. Houses to the right, dry embankment to the left. Draped with cactus, of all things. Between the homes was an eastern view that would have been stunning but for a saucer-shaped suspension of airborne filth hovering over the skyline.

"All the way up," she repeated, sounding impatient. "Right here—okay, now turn left over there—that's Rondo Vista. I'm a block up—pull in right here."

The Karmann Ghia came to rest on a cracked cement pad. It could have been any L.A. hilltop neighborhood, silent, hot, precarious, houses of all sizes and designs, unevenly tended.

Facing the pad was a closed double garage, next to that, a flat-roofed white box with blue wood trim in need of touch-up. Leading to the blue door was a short walkway topped with corrugated fiberglass panels and lined with hanging spider plants, most of them dead. Pink geraniums in a window box set on the ground weren't doing well, either. A rusting hibachi sat near the front steps, leaking orange onto the cement.

"*Ma maison*," she said. "French *is* the language of physicality."

She kissed my cheek, waited for me to open the passenger door, then jumped out and marched ahead, as she had in the restaurant, bare arms swinging, narrow hips swaying, pink heels clacking.

She got to the door when I was ten feet behind and opened it. Then she stopped, stared inside, gave a small wave—greeting someone—and closed it.

"*Merde*, Andrew. We are stymied."

"What's going on?"

She touched my face gently. "Tsk-tsk, the poor lad is suffused with lust and nowhere to spend. . . . Guests, Andrew. Friends staying over. They were supposed to be gone all day, they've changed their plans. *Le grand dragorama*, but such is our reality."

I frowned. "So much for spontaneity."

"So soddy, my dear."

I kept the frown going. She put a finger to her lip and looked at her watch.

"I suppose," she said, glancing at the garage, "I could take you in there and give you a nice quick suck . . . but, such a shame to reduce our first collision to that—where's your place?"

"The Fairfax district."

She studied me. "A taste for bagels?"

"A taste for cheap."

"Do you live alone—of *course* you do—but, no, it would take too long to get all the way to Semite-town and back, and I really must return to the shop."

The shop. As if she were selling dainty things.

I said, "Great."

She stood higher and pulled me down at the same time. Kissed my nose.

"Oh, Andrew, I've done you *wrong*. Obviously, it just wasn't meant to be. Thanks for lunch."

"My pleasure."

"Was it?"

Another kiss, softer, on my chin.

"Yes," I said. "Very much so."

"That's *nice*, Andrew. You're being so *gallant* about this—look at us, standing here being so civil. Aren't we both being wonderfully *decent*?"

I laughed and she joined in.

"I tell you, dear," she said, placing a hand on my chest. "If the erotic moment hadn't passed, I *would* have dragged you into the garage, laid you across my friends' car, and sucked you to the root. Alas."

I DROVE HER BACK TO THE STORE AND THIS TIME SHE opened the door herself and jumped out.

"Bye, Andrew," she said, through the open window.

"Shall we meet again?"

"Shall we, shan't we . . . that depends upon whether or not you'll settle for less than all of me."

"Meaning?"

"Meaning, in the very immediate future all I can offer you is social contact, dear. Meaning, the closest you'll get to my precious parts might be a surreptitious grab punctuating the chitchat."

"Chitchat with your houseguests?"

"And others." She gave a happy-kid grin. "I've scheduled a soiree, Andrew. Tomorrow night. Cocktails at nine o'clock, casual dress. And you are now invited."

"What's the occasion?"

"No occasion, Andrew. A carpe-diem kind of thing—good fellowship and social intercourse. Fun. Surely you remember *fun*?"

"With the top one-third of a percent? Are you sure I qualify?"

"Oh, Andrew, is this all too diffuse for you?"

"Diffuse?"

"Sharing me, after we've worked ourselves up."

She squeezed her small torso farther into the car window and put my hand on her left breast. Pressing down so I squeezed. The mound was unfettered, small, very soft, the nipple a weapon piercing my palm.

"I suppose I'll have to take what I can get, Z."

She took the hand, flung it off. "Why doesn't that surprise me? Nine tomorrow. Bye-bye, A."

48

"THE OLD CHARM WORKS ITS WONDERS," SAID MILO, stretching in the car. Not the unmarked. A brown Honda I'd never seen before.

Pine boughs darkened the car's interior. He'd pulled up next to me at Sunset and San Vicente and told me to follow him.

The place he chose was in Beverly Hills, the alley behind Roxbury Park's western border. Lots of toddlers and mothers and nannies, the ice-cream man playing his jingle while dispensing popsicles and drumsticks, plenty of parked cars, no reason to notice ours.

"If I needed an ego boost, this wouldn't be it," I said. "She's beyond aggressive."

"Aw, don't sell yourself short . . . Little Miss Sex Pistol, huh?"

"Both guns blazing. Ponsico must have been a trout in a bathtub. It's a good bet it was him she meant when she talked about brains without spine. The DVLL murders probably originated at a Meta meeting—maybe not the whole group, just a splinter. The scenario I like is that Ponsico was enthusiastic in theory but when it came to action, he got cold feet and disappointed her and her friends. Some of whom are staying over, will probably be at the party tomorrow night. Add Sanger's trip tomorrow and it smells like a big night for Meta. And Andrew's invited."

He frowned.

"What's wrong?"

"I worry when things go too well."

"Don't you think we're finally due for some good luck on this one?"

"I suppose."

"There's no way she'd suspect anything, Milo. The time we spent together was divided between intellectual pretentiousness and sex talk. The sex came from her. I played Morose Andrew as hard as I could without turning her off. At one point, I thought I'd gone too far."

I described Zena's rage at perceived rejection. "Lots of talk about how wonderful she is, but at the core she's fragile."

"Fragile?" he said. "Or just a rotten temper?"

"The two often go together. The point is, for all her posturing about being brilliant and sexy and slender and peppy, she lives in a shabby house and runs a bookstore with very few customers. The whole femme-fatale bit had a pathetic edge to it, Milo. It didn't take much to touch a nerve. She also called high school a 'crucible of cruelty,' meaning she probably *hadn't* been Miss Popular Cheerleader. She was so upset when I moved her hand away, it actually blemished her face. That kind of volatility could have spelled bad news for Ponsico. Other people, too."

"Now you're saying Ponsico was killed because he offended her personally? I thought it was because he betrayed Meta."

"Maybe it was both," I said. "Someone like Zena might not separate the two. One thing's for certain: She's a eugenics fan. My buying the books is what caught her attention and it didn't take long before she offered her views on the elite and the masses."

My two purchases were on the dashboard. He'd thumbed through them.

"Mr. Galton and Mr. Neo-Galton," he said. "Nasty stuff."

"Nasty store."

"Speaking of which, we can't find any business partners. Sharavi managed to trace her parents. Lancaster. Mother's dead and her father's a groundskeeper at Santa Anita racetrack, has a drinking problem. No trust fund."

"She said her folks were educated, brilliant. More posturing."

"She may be smart but she's not too educated, herself. Lancaster High, less than a year of junior college, then she worked at Kmart before getting the job at PlasmoDerm. And listen to this: When she was in JC, she signed up as a police scout with the Lancaster sheriffs. She wanted to join the force but was too small."

"Anything weird on her academic record?"

"No. She spent half a year, dropped out."

"Underachiever. It fits our profile," I said. "So does her being a police wanna-be. I'd never have thought of a woman in those terms."

"A woman with pals, Alex. No way would she have been physically able to pull off any of the murders by herself."

"Maybe the pals who're staying at her house."

"Yeah . . . and maybe pals who fund the store."

"The Loomis Foundation?"

"Wouldn't that be nice."

"What if, after the flap about Sanger's article, Meta shifted its emphasis to L.A.?" I said. "Sanger could be the group's bagman and he's flying out tomorrow to deliver cash."

"Mr. Mossad's working on untangling their accounting, we'll see what he comes up with."

"Heard from him on the trade school, yet?"

"Nope." He blew smoke rings out the window. The ice-cream man drove away; lots of pint-sized satisfied customers. So cute . . . everybody starts off cute . . .

I said, "I skimmed as many books as I could but found nothing on DVLL. But some of them had no index and I couldn't cover everything in detail. If I stay friendly with Zena after the party, I'll have an excuse to get back to the store."

He flicked ashes and rubbed his face. "You've done good work, Alex, but there's a bad smell to this. You're sure you want to stick with it?"

"If it means getting a closer look at Meta, I do. My main concern is how to avoid Zena when she decides she does want to take me into the garage and yank down my pants."

"Tell her you've got herpes."

"It's a little late for that and besides, this woman would check. I'll figure out something."

"Well, don't do anything you'll regret. Even LAPD has its standards."

I thought of Nolan Dahl's time-outs with teenage hookers. "How close were you following me?"

"I was at the store before you got there, parked two blocks up Apollo, used some Zeiss binocs Sharavi gave me and had a clear view of you going in and coming out with her. She looks a lot different than the picture Sharavi gave me—the hair—but her size was the tip-off. Her body language was affectionate, so I figured it was going well. When you left for the restaurant, I was four cars behind you. While you ate French food, I had a bad burrito in the car."

"Such sacrifice."

"Yeah, workmen's comp time. When you left the restaurant, I followed you but when you turned up Lyric, I held back because it's a quiet road and I didn't want to be conspicuous."

"Daniel supply the car?"

He nodded. "One of the things that smells bad, Alex, is the layout. In terms of maintaining a close watch. Too damn isolated, too damn quiet, and her house is at the top, no way to get above it."

"So you did drive up there."

"I waited a few minutes, drove to where Rondo Vista splits off from Lyric and stayed on Lyric, where I parked about a hundred feet down. Then I went on foot. I had on a uniform—gas company—and a stick-on gas-company sign for the car door. I was carrying one of those little meter gizmos, no reason for anyone to give me a second look. But there's a limit to that kind of thing, Alex. Gas guys don't show up often. I ambled from house to house, managed to catch you getting back in the Karmann Ghia."

"Never spotted you."

"I was two houses down, peeking around some plants. Zena's body language was even better—big-time hots, so I figured you weren't in any immediate danger, but I don't like it."

"It's just a party," I said. "The elite and me. The biggest threat will be her hormones."

49

Back in Israel, before joining the police force, he'd consulted his father, a learned man, about the issue. Abba Yehesqel had sought the counsel of Rav Yitzhak, a ninety-year-old Yemenite *hakham*, and received a quick answer.

The law was clear: Saving a life took precedence over *shabbat*. As with military duty, when police work involved a life-or-death situation, not only was Daniel permitted to work, he was obligated.

Over the years, he'd used the ruling sparingly, working extra hours on weekdays in order to free up Friday night and Saturday. Not hesitating, of course, to go full-force on things like the Butcher, rapists, suicide bombers. As he climbed the ranks and was given more administrative duties in lieu of streetwork, it became easier. The only advantage of becoming a pencil pusher.

Now, here he was, at the airport, sitting at the wheel of a yellow cab at the pickup-zone of the American Airlines terminal.

Back in Jerusalem, he'd be praying in the tiny, ancient Yemenite synagogue near the Old City. Even if he hadn't been on the job, he'd have avoided group worship here, needing to maintain the lowest of profiles, not wanting to have to reject some well-meaning shul-goer who, learning he was an Israeli "software technician" consulting to some anonymous company out in the Valley, just *had* to have him over for shabbat.

Early this morning, he'd called Laura and the kids, telling them he'd be back as soon as possible but not knowing what that really meant.

His eldest, eighteen-year-old Shoshana, was home for the weekend, furloughed from national-service assignment up in Kiryat Shemona. Assigned to a mental-health clinic where she tried to comfort small children terrorized by Hezbollah bombs from Lebanon.

"I've been thinking, Abba. Maybe I'll study psychology in university."

"You're well-suited for it, *motek*."

"The kids are so cute, Abba. I'm finding out that I like helping people."

"You always had a talent for it."

They talked a bit more, then she told him she loved him and missed him and went to get the boys. As he waited, he fantasized introducing her to Delaware someday, getting her some career guidance from the psychologist. Daddy arranging things for her, with his contacts. Delaware would be happy to help. . . . The more he worked with the guy, the more he liked him, that intense drive and focus—

"Abba!" Mikey's twelve-and-a-half-year-old voice, still unchanged, burst from the receiver. Six months away from bar mitzvah, a big party to be arranged, Laura's parents wanted the Laromme Hotel. Then Benny's bar mitzvah, a year after that. A busy period coming up for the Sharavis, something to look forward to.

"Hey, Mike. How's the studying going?"

"It's okay." Suddenly downcast. Not the student his sister was, the boy would have preferred to be playing soccer all day, and Daniel felt bad for bringing it up. But the bar mitzvah meant memorizing a Torah portion to be read in synagogue. Too bad *his* father wouldn't be there to see it. . . .

"I'm sure you're doing great, Mike."

"I don't know, Abba, just my luck to get the longest portion in the entire *chumash*."

"Not the longest, he-man, but definitely long. Maybe God gave you that birthdate because he knew you could handle it."

"I doubt it. I've got a brain made out of marble."

"Your brain is fantastic, Mikey. So's your heart—and your muscles. How's soccer?"

"Great! We won!" The boy's tone lifted and they stayed on sports til it was Benny's turn. The little one, once wild as an Old

City cat, was now studious like Shoshi. Math was his thing. A gentle voice.

Talking to his family gentled Daniel's soul.

THE ARRANGEMENT WITH PETRA CONNOR WAS CLEAR: The female detective, dressed in an Alaskan Airlines flight-attendant's uniform and equipped with a carry-on suitcase with push-me handle, was to hang around the terminal, read a paperback, and keep her eyes out for the New York lawyer.

In the suitcase, among other things, was a cellular phone preset to the one in Daniel's taxi.

Once Sanger/Galton deplaned, she was to stick with him. Once she became aware of his luggage status—carry-on versus checked-through—she was to phone Daniel.

If Sanger/Galton picked up a rental car, she'd notify Daniel of the company, make, model, and license number, and try to reach her borrowed car—a dark green Ford Escort—in time to join in and create a two-person tail.

Likewise if some friend was there to greet the attorney.

If Sanger/Galton needed a taxi and Daniel ended up being his driver, Daniel would call Petra and report his destination, pretending to be contacting the dispatcher. If some other driver snagged the fare, Daniel's tail would be hampered and Petra would have to take the lead and wait til Daniel avoided another fare and made it out of the airport.

One way or another, the would-be eugenicist was covered.

Nothing from Petra, yet.

She seemed good. Quiet, serious, all business. So far all the L.A. people he'd met were good, Zev's experience notwithstanding.

Shabbat . . . still, he was happy to be doing something. Especially after the wasted afternoon at Melvin Myers's trade school.

Nothing strange about the place, they truly did seem to be training handicapped people to get jobs. He hadn't been able to get to Darlene Grosperrin, settling for a brief interview with a young social-work assistant named Veronica Yee.

Each of them thinking the other was the subject.

Smiling, courteous, Ms. Yee had taken a brief history and told him the school was well-established, twenty years old, funded mostly by government money, offering a full range of educational services, including job and psychological counseling. And yes, they would probably have something for him but not until the new term began in two months. He was welcome to fill out the application and get back to them.

Handing him a sheaf of papers—the application, government pamphlets on rights of the handicapped, availability of educational grants, public-relations stuff on the school.

He'd looked for some sign that Melvin Myers's death had caused an impact—a funeral notice, memorial service, anything, and had found only an announcement on the bulletin board. "We regret to announce . . ." Letters and braille.

It had given him the opportunity to work Myers into the conversation with Ms. Yee.

She'd said, "Yes, he was murdered downtown. Terrible. I have to be honest with you, it is a tough neighborhood, Mr. Cohen."

Honest, open.

Nothing to report.

The taxi in front of him edged up the line and he rolled forward.

He'd waited until the queue stretched beyond the pickup area before taking a position at the back. Hoping things stayed slow and he wouldn't reach the front before Sanger arrived, then be forced to zoom past a fare, attracting attention.

The phone rang.

"He's here, the plane arrived early," said Petra. "No one met him at the gate. A briefcase, a carry-on, and a wardrobe, so he probably didn't check anything through—I'll make sure. . . . He's getting on the moving sidewalk, I'm thirty feet in back of him. He's big, about Milo's size, wearing a blue blazer with gold buttons, khaki slacks, dark blue polo shirt. Dark hair slicked back, tortoiseshell glasses, heavy face. The carry-on and briefcase are olive green and the wardrobe's black. . . . Okay, we're at the end now—he's definitely bypassing the carousel . . . heading for . . . Avis. Looks like he's got paperwork already prepared."

Something else Daniel's sources hadn't come up with. Maybe Sanger had used one of those Airfones, set up the car rental while in flight.

"He's filling out an express form," said Petra. "I'm pretending to be using a pay phone across the hall, will let you know when he heads for the Avis lot."

.   .   .

SANGER'S CAR WAS A BROWN OLDSMOBILE CUTLASS
and as it headed east on Century Boulevard, Daniel's taxi was just
ahead.

Both vehicles eased into the traffic and Daniel switched to the
left lane and slowed, allowing Sanger to get ahead, managing to
get a look at the lawyer through the driver's window.

Sanger *looked* big, sitting high in the seat. Serious expression;
smooth, ruddy cheeks well into the jowl stage. Soft around the
jowls. A thick, rosy nose. A cigarette dangled from his lips, already
half-smoked. He drove quickly, inattentively, flicking ashes out the
window.

Daniel followed him toward the airport's outer reaches, passing
freight depots, commercial hangars, commuter hotels, import-
export sheds, nudie bars.

"I'm on Century approaching Aviation," said Petra. "How far
ahead are you?"

"Approaching the 5 Freeway," Daniel told her. "We're making
good time. He's getting on the freeway, headed for—looks like
North—yes, North. We're on the freeway now, merging."

Sanger stayed in the slow lane for a couple of minutes, then
shifted one lane over and maintained a steady speed of sixty.

From Daniel's perspective, traffic was ideal: light enough for
movement, no jam-ups with the unpredictability that could bring,
yet sufficiently dense to give him three car-lengths' cover. Who'd
notice a taxi?

Sanger went past the Santa Monica Freeway interchange and
exited shortly after on Santa Monica Boulevard, east. He took the
lightly traveled street past Century City into Beverly Hills, turned
left on Beverly Drive, and drove north through the wide, residen-
tial street lined with mansions.

Trailing him here was a little trickier and Daniel had to work a
bit to keep a Jaguar and a Mercedes between the taxi and the
brown Cutlass. Petra had just called in; she was a half-mile back,
stopped at the Beverly–Santa Monica light.

Sanger crossed Sunset and drove straight into the entrance of
the Beverly Hills Hotel, refurbished recently by some oil sultan,
reputed to be the richest man in the world. Years ago, during his
Olympic assignment, Daniel had done some security work at the
hotel, guarding a cabinet minister's wife in a bungalow, finding
the place amazingly pink, somewhat decrepit.

Still pink, even brighter. The Israeli Consulate threw no parties here because the sultan was anti-Israel. Plenty of bar and bat mitzvahs, though.

Pink and shiny. Sanger had stayed here last time, but he'd have thought an East Coast corporate lawyer would have chosen something quieter.

Maybe when he came here, he went Hollywood.

The no-tie look for Sanger supported that theory. Preparing for Zena Lambert's casual-dress party?

Without telling Milo, Daniel had driven up Zena's street this morning, early, before the trade school opened. Hoping for a look at this strange-sounding woman as she left the small white house with the blue trim, maybe with one of her guests. Maybe the garage door would be open and he could copy down a license-plate number.

No such luck. But it was good that he'd seen the site firsthand, verifying what Milo had said about a tough surveillance situation.

He'd been driving a pickup truck at the time, a lawn mower and other gardening equipment in the bed. With his dark skin he'd be pegged as a Mexican gardener and rendered, for all intents, invisible.

Not a long-term solution because there wasn't much gardening to do up there, mostly concrete pads like Zena's instead of lawns, and the sloping hillside lots in back were untendable.

He sped away, mentally rationing his time, thinking about when and how to return to Rondo Vista. Wondering about the boundaries of loyalty.

PARKING THE CAB AT THE MOUTH OF THE SLOPING hotel driveway, he climbed toward the entrance just in time to see a bellman hold the brown Cutlass's door open for Sanger, then open the trunk and take out the two pieces of luggage.

Sanger breezed through the main entrance, seemingly unaware as the doorman held the door open for him.

Accustomed to being served.

The luggage followed moments later.

Daniel retreated down the drive, walked to Sunset and, when the light turned green, crossed the boulevard by foot. On the south side, Beverly and Crescent and Canon met in a confusing intersection. The hub was a park where Daniel had once taken his children to see the Florentine fountain spouting into a pond full of Japanese carp—fish like Delaware's. Now, however, the fountain was dry and most of the flowers he remembered were gone. He waited at the south edge until Petra arrived.

PETRA ENTERED THE HOTEL.

Her flight-attendant's uniform minus wings and insignia was just another tailored suit, and with her short dark hair, fine-featured face, and discreet makeup, she looked like just another Beverly Hills working woman.

The black crocodile valise said a very well-employed working woman. She strode confidently to the front desk. The lobby was crowded—lots of check-ins, mostly Japanese tourists. Several harried-looking clerks, male and female pretty-faces, were on duty, typing, dispensing keys. Petra waited in one of the lines, allowed an old Japanese man to go past her, so she could get a male clerk.

Nice-looking guy, blond, struggling actor, yawn, yawn. The poor dear was clicking away, miserable through his smile.

She looked at her watch. "I'm from DeYoung and Rubin with the delivery for Mr. Galton. Has he checked in yet?"

Blondie gave her a half-second lookover, then a real smile, as he tapped computer keys.

"Frank Galton," she added, a little more impatient. "He phoned from the plane, said he'd be in by now."

"Yes, he is—just arrived. Shall I call him for you?"

Chest tightening, Petra checked her watch again. "No need, he's expecting this, said to have you bring it right up."

Blondie looked past her at the undiminished line.

Petra tapped her nails on the granite counter. "Okay, I'll do it—what room?"

"Three fourteen," said the clerk, refusing eye contact. "Thanks."

DANIEL LIT UP THE OFF-DUTY SIGN AND MOVED HIS taxi to Hartford Way on the west side of the hotel, where he exchanged it for the gray Toyota and changed into an olive-green uniform with the name Ahmed embroidered over the pocket.

Petra had a Coke in the hotel bar, avoiding the stares of men, making several trips to the third floor.

The third time, Daniel was up there, too, holding a broom, and she returned to the lobby and read a newspaper, looking all-business.

At 9:00 P.M., Daniel saw a room-service waiter bring Farley Sanger a club sandwich, a Heineken, and coffee.

No food at the party? Going late to the party?

He phoned Petra and told her he was returning to the Toyota, to let him know if Sanger came downstairs.

Circling the hotel property, slowly.

At 10:00, just as he pulled up to the mouth of the drive for the fifth time, Petra called. "Still no sign of him. Maybe he's not going to the party, after all."

Maybe, indeed, thought Daniel. Was this whole evening, like so much police work, a wrong guess based on fine logic?

By 10:15, Daniel was ready to believe the lawyer had turned in—for Sanger, still on East Coast time, it was 1:00 in the morning.

Give it another hour to be safe.

Five minutes later, Petra said, "Here we go. He's wearing a light gray sportcoat, black shirt, black slacks."

Daniel thanked her and started his taxi, told her to have a nice night.

"Sure you don't need me?" she said.

"I'm fine. Thanks. Stay on call."

She didn't argue, understood that one strange car near the house on Rondo Vista was enough.

At 10:20, the lawyer pulled out onto Sunset, going east, and Daniel was ready for him.

SANGER STAYED ON THE BOULEVARD, LEAVING BEV-erly Hills, and cruising the Strip, the Sunset Plaza boutique district, continuing into Hollywood, where marble and granite and sultans' fortunes were the last things on anyone's mind.

Daniel could see him well enough to know the lawyer was smoking steadily, progressing from one cigarette to another, flicking still-lit butts out the window, where they sparked on the asphalt.

The scenery was ancillary film businesses—photo-processing places, color labs, sound studios—plus convenience and liquor stores, cheap motels with the requisite prostitutes out front.

Cruising for something the wife back in Manhattan would never know about? A little fun *before* the party?

Wouldn't that be interesting?

But, no. Sanger kept looking but never stopped.

Smoking his third cigarette since leaving the hotel.

And that briefcase said business . . .

They stopped at a red light at the Fountain intersection and Daniel prepared himself for a right turn toward Apollo, but when the light changed, Sanger stayed on *Sunset.*

Speeding up.

Continuing east, toward a sparkle of lights in the distance.

Downtown.

DANIEL STAYED WITH HIM UNDER THE PASADENA Freeway overpass to Figueroa. Figueroa south to Seventh Street, Seventh to the corner of Flower, where Sanger parked in a pay-lot, got out, looked around for several seconds, and began walking down the street.

Financial buildings, now dark and deserted.

Sanger looked a bit nervous, checking over his shoulder, glancing from side to side.

Holding the green briefcase close to his body.

That much cash in a tough neighborhood?

Daniel parked across the street, in another lot, watched Sanger stop at a six-story limestone building. The lobby was lit, faintly, but enough for Daniel to see charcoal granite with discreet gold trim.

The shock of recognition.

This time, a uniformed security guard sat behind the small desk.

Sanger stood at the locked double doors, tapped a foot, until the security guard saw him, opened the doors, and escorted him in.

Surprise, surprise.

Daniel sat in his car, trying to make sense of it.

50

I left the house at seven, spending some time at the Genesee apartment, wanting to get used to the place in case Zena had the impulse to come here. To *Semite-town*.

Robin had asked me what Zena was like and I'd said only, "Weird, just what you'd expect."

Robin and I had made love at six. Because she wanted to and I wanted to. And I had another reason: Anything that weakened the reflexive response to Zena was welcome.

It made me feel dishonest.

Four murders—maybe five—helped me live with it.

I sat on Andrew's dusty couch, listening to Andrew's music, thumbing through Andrew's books. Then *Twisted Science*, the first few pages of the late Professor Eustace's essay on the Loomis Foundation.

Eustace's tone went well beyond academic criticism, as he accused the group of racist underpinnings, exploiting slave labor in Asia. Funding diploma mills in order to churn out "eugenic foot soldiers." Apex University, Keystone Graduate Center, New Dominion University—I'd set my watch for 9:30 P.M. and it chimed. Placing the book under the mattress, I went out to the garage and pulled out the Karmann Ghia. Children's voices filled the block and the smells of supper drifted from nearby buildings. Edging into the alley, I drove up Fairfax to Sunset and traveled east, very slowly. Twenty-five minutes later I was at Apollo and Lyric.

Well past the cocktail hour. Late enough, I hoped, for me to be lost in the activity and able to observe.

Enough activity to occupy the hostess.

The souped-up Karmann Ghia chewed its way up the nearly black road. Treacherous if someone came barreling down from the summit. The parked cars began well before the corner of Rondo Vista and I had to pull over and continue on foot.

I tried on the tinted glasses. The night rendered them hazardous and I returned them to my pocket and continued on, inspecting the cars. Average cars. No vans. A few lights shone from neighbors' windows but most were dark. Night wind had blown away some of the smog, and blades of view between the properties sparkled. As I got closer to Zena's house, I heard music.

Calypso, just like in the bookstore.

Bongos and happy vocals. Just another hillside party.

Who were these people? How many of them, if any, were killers?

Murdering out of some warped notion of genetic cleansing? Or just for *fun*?

Or both.

There was precedent for that kind of thing. Seventy years ago, two young men with stratospheric IQ scores had stabbed to death an innocent fourteen-year-old boy in Chicago. Motivated, they claimed, by the challenge of pulling off the perfect "motiveless" crime.

Leopold and Loeb had been sexually twisted psychopaths and I was willing to bet the DVLL crimes had roots in something beyond intellectual exercise.

I'd reached the white-and-blue house. Lights poked through drawn drapes, but barely. Turning, I sighted down the road, at the line of parked cars.

Had Milo already arrived? Copied down license numbers, sent them along to Daniel for a quick screen?

Calypso shifted to Stravinsky.

The exact same tape from the bookstore.

Frugal? Probably cheap booze, too.

No matter; I wouldn't be drinking.

THE DOOR WAS LOCKED AND I HAD TO RING SEVERAL times before it opened. The man in the doorway was in his middle thirties with a bushy, wheat-colored beard and a crew cut. He wore a gray sweatshirt and brown pants, was holding a glass of something yellow and filmy.

Small, alert eyes. Small, unsmiling mouth.

He held the door open just wide enough to accommodate his wiry frame. Rough hands, dirty nails. Behind him, the room was dotted with a few colored lights but otherwise dark. I caught a glimpse of faces, moving mouths, but the music pounded, blotting out conversation.

"Yes?" I saw the word, couldn't hear it.

"Andrew Desmond. Zena invited me."

He held up a finger and closed the door. I stood there for several minutes before Zena came out. She wore a full-length dress, royal blue silk crepe, printed with tangerine-colored orchids. Long-sleeved, low neckline, no waistline, generously cut. I supposed it was a muumuu, probably vintage. On a large woman it might have looked tentlike. But the filmy fabric flowed over her tiny body, heightening a sharp pelvis and somehow lengthening her, making her appear taller.

Loose and flowing . . . easier access to the precious parts?

"I was starting to wonder about you," she said. "Fashionably late?"

I shrugged, looked down at her feet, again in high-heeled sandals. Pink toenails. Three-inch heels. She was able to kiss me without straining.

Just a peck. Her lips were supple. Then she took my chin as she had in the restaurant and her tongue impelled itself between my lips. I offered some tooth resistance, then let her in. Her hand dropped, cupped my butt and squeezed. She moved back, taking my hand, twisting the doorknob. "All those who enter, abandon all hope."

"Of what?"

"Boredom."

She took my hand. The house was packed, the music well past loud and into painful. As she led me through the crowd, I tried to look the place over without being obvious. Just past the entry were two doors—a bathroom designated LE PISSOIR by a computer-printed sign, and an unmarked one that was probably a closet. An unrailed staircase led downstairs. Like many hillside homes, bedrooms on the lower floor.

A gray-haired woman in a black dress with a white Peter Pan

collar waited edgily near the lav, not looking up as we passed. The jam of bodies was bathed in Stravinsky and barely illuminated. Some people danced, others stood and talked, managing to communicate despite the din. The colored lights were Christmas bulbs strung from the low-beamed ceiling and they did little but blink in opposition to *The Rite of Spring*. I saw shadows rather than people.

No other signs or banners, nothing identifying it as a Meta bash. What did I expect?

Zena dragged me forward. The other partygoers moved aside with varying degrees of cooperation but no one seemed to notice us. The house was smaller than I would have guessed, the entire second floor just one main room, a waist-high counter sectioning off a two-step kitchen to the right. Every inch of counter was filled with plastic soda bottles, bags of ice, beer cans, packages of paper plates, plastic utensils.

What I could see of the walls was hung with prints in metal frames. Florals, nothing telling. It didn't seem like Zena's style, but who knew how often she reinvented herself?

One thing was certain, she wasn't into decorating. The few pieces of furniture I saw weren't much better than Andrew's, and the books that filled two walls sat in flimsy-looking shelves nearly identical to his.

Spooky prescience on Daniel's part. If he ever tired of police work, a career as a matchmaker awaited.

Zena's hand burned my fingers as she continued to guide me past a long folding table covered with white paper. Behind it were yet more people, eating and drinking.

Then, the only feature elevating the house above low-rent crackerbox: glass doors onto a balcony, beyond them a symphony of stars.

Man-made constellations twinkling from houses half a mile across a darkened ravine and the real stuff set into a melanin sky.

Drop-dead view, a real-estate agent would claim, working mightily to show the place at night.

As we neared the food, I played passive and managed a rough body count. Sixty, seventy people, enough to congest the modest room.

I looked for Farley Sanger. Even if he'd been there, I'd have been unlikely to spot him in the darkened crush.

Sixty, seventy strangers, as average-looking as their cars.

Men seemed to outnumber women. The age range, thirty to mid-fifties.

No one particularly ugly, no raving beauties.

It might have been a casting call for Nondescript.

But an *active* bunch. Fast-moving mouths, a mass lip-synch. Lots of gesturing, posturing, shrugs, grins, and grimaces, finger-stabs of emphasis.

I spotted the thickly bearded man who'd answered the door off in a corner by himself, sitting on a folding chair, holding a can of Pepsi and a paperback book, worrying a fold of his sweatshirt.

He looked up, saw me, stared, returned to reading with the intensity of a finals-crammer. Nearby, two other men, one in a baggy tan suit and plaid tie, the other wearing an untucked white shirt and khakis, sat at a tiny table playing silent chess and smoking.

As my eyes accommodated, I noticed other games going, on the edges of the room. Another chess match—a woman and a man— moving pieces quickly and fiercely, a minute-glass filled with rapidly sifting white sand next to the woman's left hand. A few feet away, yet more table warfare. Scrabble. Cards. Backgammon. Go. Something that resembled chess but was played on a cubelike plastic frame by two bespectacled, mustached men wearing black who could have been twins—three-dimensional chess. On the near side of the kitchen partition, two other men did something intense with polished stones and dice and a mahogany chute. How did anyone concentrate with the noise?

Then again, these were *smart* people.

We made it to the drinks. The white paper was a butcher's roll cut unevenly. Soda, beer, bottled water, off-brands of scotch, vodka, bourbon, corn chips and pretzels, salsa and guacamole and shrimp dip still in plastic containers.

Zena used a chip to excavate the avocado paste, came up with a healthy green blob, ate, scooped again, and aimed the construction at my mouth.

"Good?" she mouthed.

"Excellent."

Grinning and fluffing her bangs, she blew me a kiss, reached out and took hold of my belt buckle and tilted her head at the glass doors. Her eyes were the brightest thing in the room.

She led me out to the balcony and closed the doors. "A dull roar. So the neighbors don't shit themselves."

It was quieter out here, but we weren't alone. About a dozen people shared the balcony, but no turning heads or vigilant eyes.

Lots of conversation; I tried to make out words, heard "economy," "texture," "bifurcation," "mode of deconstruction."

Zena maneuvered me into the left-hand corner and I felt the railing press into my back. Not much of a railing, thin iron, top and bottom pieces connected by widely spaced diagonal pickets. A large man would have had trouble slipping through, but anyone else would have found it easy.

Zena pushed up against me and the metal bit deeper. The air was warm, the view stunning.

Maybe that made it the party's romance zone, because right next to us, another couple made out feverishly. The man was beefy, balding, middle-aged, wore a tweed jacket too small around the shoulders; it rode up over corduroy slacks. His playmate was a few years younger, fair-haired, bespectacled, with a thin face but thick arms that jiggled in a sleeveless white dress as she masturbated her boyfriend's lapel. He said something, her hands flew around his neck, and they kissed again.

Next to them three men argued heatedly . . . about modems, software, morons on the Internet, how the meaning of cyber had been distorted from Norbert Wiener's original conception . . .

Zena turned my head and jammed her mouth against mine.

No one noticed.

The apathy was comforting. But also disappointing, because what did it say about my conspiracy ruminations?

A murder club? What I was seeing were some folk who craved sex and chitchat, checkmate, triple-word scores, whatever you aimed for in three-dimensional chess.

Sixty, seventy people.

How many killers?

If any.

The lovebirds next to us continued to go at it, even as the debating trio raised the volume, one man nearly shouting.

Zena's tongue continued to explore my palate.

My hands were on her shoulders; when had I placed them there?

Her tongue withdrew, regrouping for another attack, and I pulled away and massaged the back of her neck, such a small, delicate neck, then her shoulder. I could feel the bumps on her collarbone.

Smiling to camouflage the retreat, I said, "Nice party. Thanks for inviting me."

"Thank you for coming, sir."

"What, exactly, is the occasion?"

"Who needs an occasion?"

"Okay," I said. "What's the organizing criterion?"

She laughed merrily, guided my hand downward, across crepe, wedging it between her legs.

I felt heat, the butter of upper thigh, then a crinkly patch that puckered the silk.

No panties—no, there was something there, a waistband. But very sheer, very low. Bikini pants—why the hell was I conjecturing?

She tightened her muscles, capturing my fingers.

Her eyes were closed. Her mouth had parted and I smelled gin. One pink-nailed hand had gathered the fabric of my sportcoat as the other began moving down. . . .

Not again. . . . I played a frantic mental slide show: dead faces, bloody shoes, filthy alleys, grieving parents . . . I stayed soft.

She looked up at me. On her smooth, white face was that same flash of narcissistic rage.

I removed her hand, took hold of *her* face, kissed *her*.

When we stopped for breath, her confusion was gratifying.

"All these people," I said, shaking my head. "I'm not into displays."

I glanced at the passionate couple, now edging toward the glass doors.

Her lower lip twitched. She nodded. "I understand, A."

I turned, placed my hands on the railing and pretended to study the view. Lots of black between the house and the twinkles. Anything could be out there.

She moved next to me, put her head against my arm and I slipped my arm around her and touched her cheek. The necking couple had left but the three-man debate was still raging. Two women came out, holding plastic cups, laughing, and moved to the opposite end of the balcony.

"I repeat my original question, Z.: What's the occasion? Not simply a collection of friends."

I felt her tense up. "Why do you say that?"

"Because these people don't act like your friends." I rubbed her neck harder, slower, and she shivered. "No one's paying you any attention, and you're rather hard to ignore. So they must have their own agendas."

Her fingers reached under my jacket and kneaded my tailbone. "Oh, I don't know about that. Being hard to ignore."

"Oh, I do, Z. Any bunch that shines you on is either pathologically self-centered or dead."

Lifting her hair, I nuzzled the place where the fine strands met smooth neck flesh.

"They're acquaintances," she said. "Think of them as kindred spirits."

"Ah," I said. "The intellectual elite?"

"As a matter of fact, yes."

"Based upon what criterion?"

"Valid and reliable measurement, Andrew. Designed by *psychologists*."

"Oh, my. Why am I not convulsing with awe?"

She laughed. "I think we could be even more selective but it's a start."

"A smart club," I said. "And you provide the house."

She stared at me. "Tonight, I am. And that's my sole obligation, leaving me free for my own entertainment."

She grabbed my chin again. Nasty habit. Tickled my lower lip with a fingernail.

"Well," I said, "I feel privileged to be in such exalted company. Without even passing the test."

"You've passed mine."

"Thank you, ma'am. I shall apply for a federal grant based upon that."

"Such cynicism." She smiled but there was something tentative—wounded?—in her voice.

Still caressing her, I turned away and fixed my attention on the houses across the canyon. The air was a strange mixture of pollution and pines.

"Fun, fun, fun," I said.

"You're not an ascetic, are you, Andrew? One of those New Age killjoys?"

"What does ascetism have to do with cynicism?"

"According to Milton, quite a bit. He wrote a poem about that—'And fetch their precepts from the Cynic tub, Praising the lean and sallow abstinence.' "

"Lean and sallow," I said. "Haven't checked my complexion in the mirror, recently. But believe me, I know very well that abstinence does not make the heart grow fonder."

She laughed. "I couldn't agree more—what I'm getting at is you seem so . . . oppositional. I feel a certain resistance." She pressed closer.

I kept gazing straight ahead, then turned, looked down at her, and took hold of her shoulders. "The truth is, Z., I've been socially deformed. Too many years of listening to neurotics whine."

"I can understand that," she said.

"Can you? Then understand that parties bring out the worst in me. I came tonight because I wanted to see *you*. That makes anyone else two-legged refuse."

Her breathing quickened.

"How say we arrange some quiet time?" I said. "Are you free tomorrow?"

I tightened my grip on her shoulders. She felt breakable, so easy to hurt. Then I thought about Malcolm Ponsico and had to restrain myself from squeezing tighter.

"I—what about finding some quiet time right here, Andrew?"

I cocked my head toward the packed room on the other side of the glass. "You've got to be kidding."

"I'm not," she said. "Downstairs. My bedroom." She closed her eyes. "Come on, let me show you my stuffed animals."

BRILLIANT, DELAWARE. NOW WHAT?

She dragged me across the balcony and back through the room. A few heads turned, but still, no real interest.

Up front, the bathroom door was now ajar, lights left on, and she shut it as we passed, taking me down the stairs. Rickety; the steps quivered under our weight.

At the bottom was another closet-bath combo and a single bed-room door.

She reached for the knob. Twisted, frowned. "Fuck."

"Looks like someone beat us to it."

"Fuck, fuck, *fuck!*" A tiny fist beat the air. "They're not sup-posed to *do* that. I should pound til they—oh *fuck* it!"

Cursing, then shaking her head, she ran up the stairs and I followed.

I said, "I suppose the elite makes its own rules—"

"Stop *ridiculing,* already! I'm sopping wet and all you want to do is make fun, you misanthropic bastard!"

"I'd rather *have* fun than *make* fun but it's obvious this is not our night. So consider my original invitation: tomorrow. Or even to-night. After your soiree winds down. Come over to my place and I'll assure you privacy."

I touched her hair.

"God," she said, punching my chest very softly and looking at my zipper. "God, that sounds good . . . but I can't, dammit."

"Who's playing hard to get, now?"

"It's not that. I've got . . . to clean up, set my houseguests up. By the time they get settled—it's just complicated, A."

"Poor baby," I said, drawing her to me. "All those responsibili-ties to—what's the name of this club, anyway?"

"What's the difference?" she said, more weary than cagey.

"All those responsibilities to the What's the Difference Club."

She smiled.

"All right, then, Z. Tomorrow it is. If you put me off further, I'll know our karma-fate-cosmic-algorithm-whatever is accursed."

She put her arms around my waist. Even with the heels, she fit under my chin, breasts poking my stomach.

"So what's the answer?"

"Yes," she said. "Fuck *yes!*"

I TOLD HER I'D BE USING THE BATHROOM AND THEN leaving.

"So early?" she said.

"If I stay, I turn venomous. What time tomorrow?"

"At night, ten," she said.

I began reciting the Genesee address.

"No, you come back here," she said. "My guests depart tomorrow. I want you *here*. On *my* bed."

"You and me and the stuffed animals?"

"I'll show you stuffed, all right. I'll show you things you never imagined."

"Fine," I said. "The stage doesn't matter, only the performers."

"You bet," she said. "I'm a star."

One long, deep kiss and she was off, a blue flame burning through the crowd.

I went into the bathroom. Cramped and papered in brown foil printed with silver flowers, cracked white tile atop the vanity. No window; the stench of too many recent visits poorly dispelled by a noisy overhead fan.

Closing the commode, I sat on the lid and collected my thoughts.

I'd been here just over an hour and gotten nothing, not even Meta's name. Because what she was interested in was bedding me, not recruiting.

I could still taste her tongue, and the scent of her perfume stayed with me—I sensed it mentally rather than actually smelled it.

I rinsed my mouth out with tap water and spit.

If I went home tonight, Robin would ask how things had gone.

I'd say boring, the girl was crazy.

This was probably how female Vice cops felt standing on corners, waiting for hungry, frightened men to drive up and barter. . . .

But it was wrong to think of her as pathetic rather than dangerous.

Had Malcolm Ponsico made that mistake?

Kill the pity. Stop thinking like a therapist.

Time to get back, call Milo, decide how much further this should be taken.

I rose, washed my hands, and opened the door. Saw movement to my left. Two people coming up the stairs.

Zena's bedroom door open. But no lovers emerging from a tryst.

First came the wheat-bearded crew-cut guy in the gray sweatshirt, still grim.

He shot me another stare. I pretended not to notice.

Had we met . . . ? There *was* something familiar—

Then I saw the man behind him and turned my back, heart racing. Trying not to show the fear I felt, heading at a normal, but steady, pace toward the front door.

A split second had been long enough to register the details.

Older man in a white silk sportcoat. Short brown hair, silver temples. Tan face, gold eyeglasses, athletic gait, solid build.

Drinks at the marina. Calamari and a fine cigar.

Sergeant Wesley Baker, Nolan Dahl's training officer.

And now I knew where I'd seen the bearded man.

51

I WAS OUT THE DOOR NOW, BREATH STUCK SOME-
where down in my chest, walking down the black street as fast as I
could on ice-cold legs. Forcing myself to take slow, deep lungfuls
of the sweet, dirty air.

I drove the hell out of there.

At Sunset and Vine, I called Milo's cell phone with the one Daniel had given me.

"Where are you?"

"Fifty feet behind you," he said. "You didn't stay long."

I told him why.

"Baker," he said, and I knew he was remembering.

Baker's love of games. The porn-stuffed locker.

"Sure he didn't see you, Alex?"

"I can't be sure but I don't think so. It makes some other things
fall into place—let's talk somewhere private."

"Go home, I'll meet you."

"Which home?"

"Which do you want?"

"Andrew's place," I said. "This could take time and there are
things Robin doesn't need to hear."

AT GENESEE, I PUT THE KARMANN GHIA IN THE GA-
rage and was inside the apartment just before midnight. Past
Robin's bedtime but I called her anyway, certain the conversation
would be monitored by who-knew-how-many people at the Israeli
Consulate.

"Hullo."

"Hi, hon. Were you asleep?"

"No, waiting," she said, stifling a yawn. " 'Scuse me. Where are you, Alex?"

"The apartment. I may be here for a while. If things stretch too late I may just stay here. By the way, this is a high-tech party line."

"Oh," she said. "So when will you know? If you're coming home?"

"Why don't you just assume I won't be. I'll call you as soon as I can. Just wanted to say I love you."

"Love you, too. If you can make it home, please do, Alex."

"I will."

"The main thing is you're safe."

"Absolutely," I said.

I MADE INSTANT COFFEE IN THE KITCHEN AND SAT ON the dusty couch.

Baker. The bearded man. Houseguests. How many others?

Had Farley Sanger been at the party?

Vehicle in the garage.

Chevy van?

Because I remembered Wilson Tenney's driver's-license photo.

Mid-thirties, mid-sized, clean-shaven, long, light brown hair.

Cut the hair, grow a beard. Someone besides me had been aiming for disguise.

Baker and Tenney and Zena.

Maybe others.

A killing club.

Zena's place a refuge. Their safe house.

I thought of the atmosphere at the party.

Eat, drink, make merry; no paranoia, no suspicion. Most of the Meta people had no idea what the splinter group was doing for fun.

Games . . . Tenney had removed himself from the action, sitting in a corner alone. Reading. As he'd done at the park where Raymond was abducted.

Your basic loner . . . going downstairs with Wes Baker.

Impromptu conference of the club within a club.

A tight little murderous cell.

Baker and Tenney in Zena's bedroom, behind a locked door. Zena had been angry but she hadn't protested.

Knowing she was outranked.

Baker, the leader. Because of his charisma and his police experience.

A teacher, a trainer in police technique.

Who better to *subvert* the police?

Teacher and students . . .

Baker and Nolan?

Code 7 for hookers? Something worse?

Two cops in a park.

A young girl strangled and left stretched out on the ground.

Sweeping up.

Easy job for two strong men.

Could it be?

I thought of Nolan's suicide, so public, so self-debasing, executing himself in front of the enemy.

Like every suicide, a message.

This one said soul-rotting, strangulating guilt. The ultimate atonement for unredeemable sin.

A law-and-order guy. A smidgen of conscience had remained and the magnitude of his violation came to haunt him.

He'd passed sentence on himself.

But something didn't fit: If Nolan was aiming for expiation, why hadn't he gone public, exposed the others, prevented more bloodshed?

Because Baker and the others had some kind of hold on him . . . the photos? On-duty liaisons with teenage hookers.

Polaroids left in a family album.

Placed there deliberately for Helena to find. Not by Nolan. By people who didn't want her to probe further.

Break-ins at Nolan's place and Helena's house, days apart. Now, it seemed ridiculously coincidental. Why hadn't it bothered me then?

Because burglaries in L.A. were as commonplace as bad air. Because Helena was my patient and I couldn't talk about what went on in therapy unless lives were at stake. So I'd denied.

It had worked so well—shutting *my* mouth, driving Helena out of therapy. Out of town.

But, no, it still didn't make sense. If Nolan had been consumed by guilt over murder, dirty pictures wouldn't have stopped him from incriminating the others.

I was still struggling with it when Milo rang the bell.

HE WAS CARRYING HIS VINYL ATTACHÉ AND SAT right down next to me.

"There's something I need to tell you," I said.

"I know. Dahl. When you told me about Baker, my mind went on overdrive."

He unzipped the case, removed a sheet of paper, and gave it to me. "Here's why it took me an hour to get here."

Photocopy of some kind of chart. Horizontal grid on the upper three-quarters, several columns below a ten-digit numerical code and the heading DAILY FIELD ACTIVITIES REPORT. At the bottom, a series of boxes filled with numbers.

The top columns were labeled SPEC. SURVEY, OBS., ASGD ACT., TIME OF DAY, SURVEY SOURCE AND CODE, LOCATION OF ALL ACTIVITIES, TYPE OF ACTIVITY, SUPERVISOR AT SCENE, BOOKING #, CITATION #. Baker's name in every SUPERVISOR slot.

"Baker and Nolan's work log," I said.

"Daily report—the D-FAR," said Milo. "They're handed in at the end of each shift, stored in the station for a year, then moved downtown. These are Baker and Dahl's for the day Irit was murdered."

Everything in perfect block letters, the time notated militarily: 0800 W L.A. ROLL CALL TO 1555 SIGN-OFF.

"Neat writing," I said.

"Baker always printed like a draftsman."

"Compulsive. The type to sweep up."

He growled.

I read the report. "First call's a 211 suppression—armed robbery?"

He nodded.

"Wilshire near Bundy," I went on. "It lasted nearly an hour, then a 415 call—disturbing the peace, right?"

"It could mean anything. This one was near the Country Mart, but see here where it says 'no 415 found' under TYPE OF ACTIVITY? And no booking data in column 7? It didn't pan out."

He stabbed the paper with his index finger. "After that, they did traffic stops, ten of 'em in a row—Baker was always one for giving lots of tickets—then another no-arrest 415 in the Palisades, then lunch."

"At 1500," I said. "Three P.M. Late lunch."

"They list no Code 7s all day. If it's true, they were due for a break."

My eyes dropped to the final notation before checkout.

"Another no-action 415 at 1530," I said. "Sunset near Barrington. Are false calls that common?"

"Common enough. And it's not only false calls. Lots of times 415s end up just being an argument between two citizens, the officers calm 'em down and move on, no arrests."

I scanned the sheet again. "There are no details on any of the calls beyond the street location. Is that kosher?"

"On a no-arrest it is. Even if it wasn't kosher, with Baker being a supervisor, there'd be no one looking over his shoulder unless something iffy happened—brutality complaint, that kind of thing. Basically, D-FARS are stashed and forgotten, Alex."

"Wouldn't the calls come in through the dispatcher?"

"For the most part, but cruisers also get flagged down by citizens or the blues see things on their own and report to the dispatcher."

"So there'd be no way to verify most of this."

"Nope—anything else about it catch your eye?"

I studied the form one more time. "It's not balanced. All the activity's in the morning. You say Baker liked giving tickets but he issued ten before lunch and not a single one afterward . . . no real documentation for their activities for a solid hour prior to sign-off. More than an hour, if you include the Country Mart call. Even more if Baker bogused the entire afternoon log."

I looked at him. "During the time Irit was being stalked, abducted, and strangled, Baker and Nolan had the perfect alibi: doing police work. No way to disprove it—no reason to *doubt* it. Two with uniforms, a team. Watching the kids get off the bus, selecting Irit, grabbing her—both of them were strong and with two working together, it would have been a snap. Baker probably chose gentle strangulation because he wanted to pretend he wasn't just another psychopath. Wanting to set it up as a sex crime, yet *discriminate* it from sex crimes."

"God," he said in a voice that burst out of him like a wound.

Looking closer to tears than I'd ever seen him. "The fucking bastards. And they—I'm sure it was Baker's idea, that calculating
fuck—did more than set up a one-day alibi. They prepared for
weeks."

"What do you mean?"

He got up, made a move to the fridge, stopped, sat down. "I
looked through a whole bunch of their D-FARS. The pattern—busy
mornings, quiet afternoons—began two weeks before Irit's murder. Prior to that they had an even workload: calls throughout
their shift, Code 7s at normal times, normal lunch breaks. Two
weeks before Irit was murdered, they altered it, and they continued altering for three weeks after. That's how calculating they
were. Jesus!"

"Three weeks after," I said. "At which point, Baker headed over
to Parker Center and Nolan transferred to Hollywood. Distancing
themselves. Now we know why Nolan was willing to give up a
plum assignment."

"Covering his ass, the fuck."

"Maybe something else, too, Milo. He could have been distancing himself from the murder because the guilt started seeping in.
I'm sure that's why he killed himself. I'm also sure Baker and the
others took steps so Helena wouldn't look into it too deeply."

I told him about the break-ins, the snapshots in the Dahl family
album.

"Hookers," he said. "Dark-skinned street girls like Latvinia."

"Maybe Baker introduced him to Latvinia. Maybe Baker, by
himself or with a friend, came back and finished Latvinia off. But
what I still don't get is what kept Nolan from going public."

"Helena," he said. "Baker threatened to kill her if Dahl
squawked."

"Yes," I said. "Makes perfect sense. It would have intensified
Nolan's conflict, led him closer to total escape."

"So who are the others?"

"Zena, maybe Malcolm Ponsico, til he changed his mind and
received a lethal injection. Maybe Farley Sanger, though I didn't
see him at the party. *Definitely* Wilson Tenney. Because he *was*
there." I described the park worker's altered appearance.

"You're sure it was him."

"Do you have his DMV shot?"

He produced it from the attaché.

"Yes," I said, handing it back. "No doubt about it."

"Unreal—a goddamn psycho *club*."

"Club within a club," I said. "Meta offshoot. A bunch of eugenics freaks sitting around over their three-dimensional chess boards, telling themselves how smart they are, griping about the decay of society and one of them—probably Baker—says why don't we do something about it, the police are idiots—believe me, I know from experience. Just use different techniques, clean up the physical evidence, and distribute the murders one per district. Detectives from different districts never talk to one another. Let's have some fun with it. Or maybe it started off theoretically—one of those murder-mystery games—committing the perfect crime. And at some point, they took it further."

"Fun," he said.

"At the core, these are thrill crimes, Milo. They can't seriously think they're creating any societal impact. This is Leopold and Loeb taken a step further: pleasure-kill under a veneer of ideology. Pleasure at showing how brilliant they are, so just to be extra-cute, they leave a message. DVLL. Some coded in-joke the police are sure never to notice. Maybe an insult to the police, like Raymond's bloody shoes left at the Newton station. And even if the letters are discovered, they know the message will be impossible to figure out."

"Baker," he said. "That's exactly his style. Esoteric. Leader of the pack, sucking everyone into his goddamn games."

A vein, thick and knotted, was throbbing at his temple, and his eyes burned. "Killers in blue. Oh shit, Alex, you know the department and I don't have a perfect marriage, but *this*! Just what LAPD needs after Mr. Scumbag Rodney King and the riots and Mr. Scumbag O.J. Just what this *city* needs!"

"Which leads me to another question," I said. "Is Dr. Lehmann doing some butt-covering? He told me Nolan had problems Helena really didn't want to know about. I got a clear message to back off. If he knew Nolan had committed murder, he'd be under no obligation to report it unless another potential victim was in clear danger. I can see him wanting to keep the fact that his patient was homicidal quiet, for his sake and the department's—he gets lots of business from the department. But then why say anything at all?"

Why bother to meet with me in the first place? And now that I think about it, when I was there he tried to turn the tables. Asking *me* about *Helena*. Trying to figure out how much *she* knew."

He stared at me. "Checking you out? He was in on it, too? Instead of helping Dahl, he somehow drove the asshole to eat chrome?"

"Who better than Dahl's therapist, Milo? And as police consultant, working downtown, he's someone Wes Baker may have known. Someone to whom Baker could have referred Nolan."

"Oh, my," he said. "Oh my, oh my. . . . How far does it go?"

He looked at his Timex. "Where the hell is Sharavi? Haven't heard from him since he and Petra tagged Sanger to the Beverly Hills Hotel. She got Sanger's room number, went home, and Sharavi did a solo tail."

Pulling out his cell phone, he punched.

"The mobile customer is out. . . . Okay, let's lay out this blood-club scenario again: A bunch of Meta assholes get together, decide to play a different kind of game. How many members do you see in the club?"

"There couldn't be too many," I said. "Too dangerous sharing a secret like that with a crowd."

Without opening his mouth, he produced a frightening zoo-cage sound. "Okay, so Baker takes charge—he assigns Tenney to do Raymond Ortiz?"

"Maybe not specifically Raymond, just some kid at the park. A kid Tenney judged defective. Or maybe Tenney volunteered to go first and suggested Raymond because he'd seen Raymond, knew he was retarded. We know Tenney was bucking authority on the job, had been reprimanded. What better way to thumb *his* nose at the job than to *use* the job to commit murder?"

"Man with a uniform," he said, staring at Tenney's photo.

"Average-looking man in a uniform," I said. "Race discrimination goes both ways and this time it played in Tenney's favor: To the homeboys at the park, Tenney was just another faceless Anglo."

He rubbed his face. "No body, because Tenney wanted to be careful not to leave physical evidence. Then after he and Baker and the others saw no progress had been made, they left the bloody shoes on the steps of the police station."

"Blood they brushed in *after* they wrote DVLL," I said. "So they'd planned it. Maybe Tenney's idea, probably Baker's. Not as clean a murder as Irit's because unlike Baker and Nolan, Tenney never fancied himself a centurion with ideals. Just an angry, hate-filled guy with a supposedly high IQ who couldn't get a better job than sweeping up dog dirt and hated the world because of it. Also, because Raymond was a boy, Tenney might not have seen the killing as a sex crime, felt no need to desexualize it. He snatched Raymond in the bathroom, got him to the van and incapacitated him or murdered him right there, drove somewhere, disposed of the body. Then he quit his job, disappeared."

"Living at Zena's."

"Not all this time," I said. "Maybe he lived out of the van, maybe he crashed with other members of the club. And he won't be at Zena's for long. She said no more guests by tomorrow night. I got the sense some kind of movement's afoot."

"Another killing?"

"Could be. What districts haven't been hit?"

"Half the city," he said, "and the whole goddamn Valley. I could talk to Carmeli again about releasing that gag order—on the other hand, all we've got is supposition, not a shred of evidence, and if we alert Baker, anything he might have held on to will be destroyed, not a chance of ever getting to the truth—goddamn it, Alex, it's like having a map but no car—okay, onward. Irit. Baker and Dahl—they just happen to stake out the park, because they know kids go there?"

"Handicapped kids," I said. "After Tenney got away with Raymond, I can see the group going for another retarded kid in a park. But there's a big difference between Raymond's and Irit's murders. Tenney worked in that park, was familiar with the layout. Raymond was a local kid, his class was using the park daily while the school was being painted, so Tenney had plenty of time to study him. Maybe he'd even had a run-in with Raymond. Or one of Raymond's gang-banger brothers."

I motioned him to the door, led him out of the apartment, to the front steps.

"What?" he said.

"Just in case you don't want Carmeli to hear this," I said. "The conservancy wasn't part of Baker and Dahl's patrol area. And Irit's school only visited once a year. So why *was* Irit selected as victim? Baker's into control. Manipulative, a planner. He took the time to manipulate the daily log for *weeks,* so I can't believe he'd choose a victim randomly. What made Irit right for him? Could it have been something to do with work after all?"

"Carmeli?"

"We've both felt he's been hostile to the police from the beginning, Milo. Made remarks about police incompetence the first time we met him. I assumed he meant the lack of progress on Irit's murder but maybe it was something else. An unpleasant experience he had with LAPD *before* Irit's murder."

"A run-in with Baker?" he said. "Something bad enough to cause Baker to murder the guy's daughter?"

"Ideologically and psychologically, Baker was already there," I said. "He wouldn't need a big push, just a nudge. If Carmeli got on his bad side—something a mere mortal might have shrugged off—that could have been it. Both of us suspect Carmeli's Mossad or something like it. More than just the deputy consul for community liaison, but that's the face he presents to the public. Events organizer—the big Israeli Independence Day parade he ran last spring. LAPD would have had to be involved, for crowd management. Wouldn't it be interesting if Baker was part of the police contingent?"

We went back inside. The phone was ringing. I picked it up.

"It's Daniel. I'm down the block. May I join you?"

"Definitely," I said.

"I've got a key. I'll let myself in."

52

HE WORE HIS ELECTRICIAN'S UNIFORM UNDER A windbreaker and carried a small black backpack. His expression was one I hadn't seen before. Guarded. Tense. "How was the party?"

Before I could answer, Milo motioned him to a chair. "What's with Sanger?"

"He never went to the party. I followed him from the hotel, downtown, to a building on Seventh Street near Flower, where he met with a psychologist."

"Roone Lehmann," I said. The guarded look dropped off. I told him about Nolan and Baker, my meeting with Lehmann. My suspicion about Lehmann.

He sat there, eyes half-closed, both hands on his knees.

"Lehmann is confirmed," he finally said. "I got into his building, used a parabolic mike to listen to his conversation with Sanger. My station was a service closet. The mike's a small one, reception wasn't great. If I'd had a surveillance post in a neighboring building, I'd have chosen something more powerful. But I did manage to get most of it."

"On tape?" said Milo.

Daniel took a microcassette out of the backpack. Milo held out his hand and Daniel gave it to him.

"As I said, the quality's poor, sometimes words are hard to understand, but the general meaning's clear. Want me to summarize?"

"Yeah."

"Sanger and Lehmann are related—cousins. First they talked

about aunts and uncles, children, a family party last Christmas in Connecticut. Lehmann's a bachelor and Sanger asked if he was getting laid. Lehmann said wouldn't you like to know and laughed. Then Sanger laughed, too."

"There's a family resemblance," I said. "Both are big, thick, have flat features and baggy eyes. Both are probably related to the Loomis family—you said cousins ran the company now."

"The names we got weren't Lehmann or Sanger but you may be right. . . . Yes, there is a resemblance, now that you point it out."

"Something else," I said. "The Loomises pride themselves on links to colonial England. When I was in Lehmann's office he made a big deal about a piece of silver on his desk that had sat in British Parliament."

"Noble blood," said Milo. "These two jokers do anything besides reminisce?"

Daniel said, "There was nothing about Meta or the murders or DVLL, I'm afraid, though there was plenty of racism. Lehmann said, 'How's the hotel?' Sanger said, 'Not bad, considering it's owned by a towel-head.' 'Does that mean no hundred-thousand-dollar bar mitzvahs?' That kind of thing. Then they left the office and went down to a private club on the floor below. I couldn't figure out a way to get in there. Even if I had, all the cross-conversation would have made the mike useless. So instead, I entered Lehmann's office, because Sanger had brought a briefcase but didn't take it with him. I found it on a chair in Lehmann's inner office. We were guessing Sanger was a bagman for Meta, so I expected to find it full of money, but just the opposite: completely empty. In Lehmann's desk, however, I did come across a bag of cash. Two hundred thousand dollars."

"Right process, wrong route," said Milo. "The funds flow from west to east. Lehmann's the bagman."

"Looks that way," said Daniel. "They stayed in the club for an hour, came back smoking cigars and looking happy. They talked some more in the office, still no mention of Meta by name but Lehmann did say he was disappointed in 'the group.' It had deteriorated into a social club, he hoped New developed into something."

" 'New'?" said Milo. "Not 'something new'?"

"No, New, one word. The name of something." Daniel pointed to the cassette. "Would you like to hear it?"

"Later—New—so there's your subgroup."

"Maybe it's spelled N-U," I said. "As in New Utopia. In his article, Sanger called for that."

They looked at each other.

"What else did they talk about?" Milo asked Daniel.

"Lehmann said, 'Here's a little something from the family, it should tide you over for a while,' and they laughed some more. I heard a latch being closed—the briefcase—and a few minutes later, Sanger came out with it and left the building. I don't know what Lehmann did because I figured staying with Sanger made more sense. He drove straight back to the hotel and retired for the evening. I tried to call his room and the switchboard said he'd left instructions not to be disturbed. Just to be careful, I stuck around for another hour and figured he really had gone to sleep. Then I called again, impersonating his rental-car agent, and verified he'd be checking out tomorrow. I'll be watching him to make sure and then we'll have our New York people pick up his trail. We'll stay on him tighter, now. Helga Cranepool, too."

"One big happy family," said Milo. "So how'd Baker get connected?"

"Probably through LAPD," I said. "Lehmann consults to the department. That also could explain Zena's involvement. She was a police scout in Lancaster. Maybe she applied to LAPD, too, somehow ran into Baker and he gave her a private training course. Maybe Nolan Dahl wasn't the only one into young girls."

Milo shot up and circled the room and lit up a cigarillo.

"What bothered me," said Daniel, "was that Lehmann's name never came up in our investigations. We were concentrating on New York and the South, because of the Loomises' origins in Louisiana and Professor Eustace's sudden death in Mississippi. But I couldn't stop thinking that I'd heard the name before. As it turns out, I had."

He turned to me. "Do you have your copy of *Twisted Science* here?"

I nodded, retrieved the book from under the bed.

Turning pages, he said, "Right in Professor Eustace's article. One of the papers he cites as Loomis-funded nonsense was written by Lehmann ten years ago in a journal called *Biogenics and Culture*."

"Never heard of it."

"Neither has the Library of Congress. Here's Eustace's summary."

I read. "Intelligence, crime, and weather?"

"To me it's crazy stuff, Alex. Lehmann's main point is people from hot climates are inherently stupider and more 'dissolute' than those from Nordic regions because they have less need to build shelters from harsh weather, don't develop a sophisticated culture. In cold-weather regions, only smart and creative people are able to cope and propagate."

"Survival of the fittest," I said.

"Lehmann also claims that hot weather creates ill temper that leads to violence. Thus the expression *hot blood*."

He flexed the fingers of his good hand.

"Eustace uncovers this," said Milo, "and a few months later his car goes off the road."

"Something else about Lehmann," I said. "His degree's from a place called New Dominion University. That's one of the Loomis diploma mills, isn't it?"

"Yes," said Daniel.

"And his clinical training was at the Pathfinder Foundation. The same name as the Meta newsletter that carried Sanger's article. Lehmann told me he'd had a career in business before switching to psychology. Most of the books in his office were on management, not clinical psych. He even recited a business motto—'It's not enough that I succeed. You have to fail.' The guy's a Loomis put-up and he's wangled himself a position as a police consultant."

Milo stopped pacing but kept smoking.

"Not a banner day for gendarmes," he said. "Speaking of which, Daniel, what does Carmeli have against the department?"

"What do you mean?"

Milo came closer and stood over him. "This is not the time to be coy, friend. Your boss made it clear there's no love lost between him and LAPD. Did he have a run-in with someone? The parade? Something else?"

Daniel rubbed his eyes, removed his windbreaker. The black plastic gun sat in the mesh holster. "It was related to the parade. A security briefing at the consulate, run by Zev for LAPD and our people. Setting up perimeters, crowd control, security, both groups had agreed to share any information about terrorist threats, maintain full communication. Zev had been working overtime, hadn't seen his family much, so he decided to have Liora and the children over to the consulate. That day they were waiting out in the hallway for him to take the family to lunch. Zev ran overtime and as they waited, one of the LAPD officers came over to Liora and Irit— Oded was down the hall playing with a toy car—and sat down next to them. At first he was friendly, trying to talk to Irit, then he realized she was deaf and he concentrated on Liora. Asking her about Israel, Tel Aviv, telling her he'd traveled all over the world."

"Got to be Baker," said Milo.

"I'm sure you're right," said Daniel, very grim. "Liora told Zev the man made her feel uncomfortable. Too friendly, just sitting there when he should have been in the briefing. But she said nothing. That's Liora's style. Then, somehow, the officer turned it into something inappropriate. Sexually."

"He came *on* to her?"

"Not explicitly, Milo. But Liora said the connotation was clear. At that point, she got up and walked away. Later, she told Zev and he went—how do you say—ballistic. Complained to the mayor and was told the officer would be removed from parade detail and disciplined."

"Moved downtown. But he wasn't demoted," I said. "Still, maybe that's why for all his alleged brainpower he's still a sergeant."

"Baker," said Milo, punching his fist. "That son of a whore—so he knew Irit by sight. Knew she was deaf."

Daniel looked pained. "But to kill someone—a child—over *that—*"

"Think of it as a tracer bullet," said Milo. "After the Ortiz boy's murder went off perfectly, Baker and the other New Utopia assholes decided someone else was gonna die, it didn't really matter who, as long as it was someone they judged to be a life not worth living. Alex told me before that despite all the eugenics bullshit, this boils down to killing for fun. What greater fun for Baker than revenge? Mrs. C. rejects him, Mr. C. gets him disciplined, and their daughter just happens to be handicapped. It must have seemed like karma to the bastard. When I knew him, he was into Eastern religions, talked a lot about karma."

Daniel slumped, stared past us, into the kitchen.

"What?" said Milo.

"It's . . . disgusting. All of it's disgusting."

"Each murder has a connection to someone in the group," I said. "Ponsico and Zena, Raymond and Tenney, Irit and Baker. Nolan Dahl helped with Irit—Baker training him in all sorts of things. And I'll bet Latvinia was one of Dahl's playmates. Maybe Baker's, too. To them, a dark-skinned girl with handicaps was something to be used and thrown away. Baker could have killed her for fun, or because she knew about him and Nolan. Or both. *Probably* both."

"And Melvin Myers?" said Daniel.

"He got on the wrong side of someone in the group," I said. "Someone downtown. Baker or Lehmann?"

Looking into the backpack, Daniel removed a handful of papers and took out a color brochure. I examined it with him.

"The Central City Skills Center: For Fifteen Years, a Citadel of Hope." The photos showed blind people walking with guide dogs and operating computers, smiling amputees trying on prosthetic limbs.

The course list: sewing, crafts, mechanical assembly. A small-print list of funding sources was followed by a smaller-print professional advisory board. Doctors, lawyers, politicians . . .

Alphabetized.

Near the middle: Roone Lehmann, Ph.D., psychological consultant.

"Working with the handicapped," I said. "Must have given him a laugh. But maybe he got a bigger laugh playing financial games with the school. Taking candy from blind babies."

Milo hurried over and read the roster. "Myers discovers Lehmann ripping off the school and threatens to write an exposé. Maybe he tells Lehmann, even blackmails him, because one thing Myers doesn't lack is gall. Lehmann agrees to pay him off, calls a meet in that alley and someone—probably Baker—finishes Myers off."

He took the brochure from Daniel.

"The murders," said the Israeli, "are their way of mixing business with pleasure."

"The only problem is," Milo told him, "all we've got is theory. Because the only thing close to evidence—the Polaroids of Nolan Dahl's play-dates—were destroyed. Even if we find Tenney's van in Zena's garage, I have nothing that justifies a warrant."

"What would it take," I said, "to move on any of them?"

"A full confession would be peachy, but I'll settle for an incriminating remark. Anything that lets us focus on one of them—a weak link."

"That might be Zena. She spouts the eugenics line but it seems like role-playing. I'm not saying she's harmless. But so far, she's been less interested in politics than in partying. I have a date with her tonight at ten. Maybe I can get her to open up more about NU. Maybe eventually she can be made to see it's in her best interests to give up the others."

Milo frowned. "Don't know about the date, Alex. Tenney did make eye contact with you a couple of times and even though you don't *think* Baker recognized you, you're not sure."

"Tenney doesn't know me," I said, "so he's got no reason to suspect me of anything. He's probably just an antisocial guy. What would he tell Baker? Zena's got a new boyfriend? And if I break the date wouldn't that make Zena wonder?"

"Old Andy's a heartbreaker. He changed his mind."

"Then what?" I said. "Where do you go from there?"

No answer.

"Milo, the one good thing about these people being so arrogant is they have no idea they're under suspicion. On the contrary, they're probably gloating that everything's gone off smashingly. Five murders, all unsolved. They're getting cocky. That's why the pace has picked up. Think of what you said: half the city and all of the Valley. Thousands of handicapped people who can't be protected."

"And your date tonight is gonna change all that?" he barked.

"At least it's a connection to NU. Maybe Zena will tell me something important. At the very least, you can pull her in and lean on her a little. I repeat: What else is there?"

Longer silence.

"All right," he said. "One more time, but that's it. After tonight, you're out of it and we shift gears, go for full surveillance on Baker and Lehmann, keep Daniel's New York people stuck to Sanger and Cranepool, get a look at Zena's garage. If Tenney's van is in there and he splits like you think he's planning to, I'll use Baker's technique. Stop the bastard for a traffic violation and take it from there."

"Where does Baker live?" said Daniel.

"A boat in the marina called *Satori*." I described the location of the slip.

"Satori," he said. "Heavenly tranquility."

"The bastard's a pro," Milo told him. "Did Vice work and rob-bery undercover, meaning he understands surveillance."

"So I need to be careful," said Daniel.

"Start with being careful *tonight*, friend. I want both of us cover-ing Alex nonstop from the time he sets out to romance Little Ms. Murder til he gets home. A post on her street and another on the hillside behind the house."

"I can do the hillside," said Daniel.

"You're sure?"

"I've done climbing in Israel. Caves in the Judean Desert."

"Recently?"

Daniel smiled and flopped the dead hand. "Recently. One ac-commodates. Contrary to what our NU friends believe, life goes on for all kinds of people."

"Fine. Where you sleeping tonight, Alex?"

"Might as well go home," I said.

"I'll follow you." He faced Daniel. "After that, you and I meet back here."

53

8:00, awoke, put on fresh jeans, loafers, a black T-shirt, and his best
sportcoat, a black serge Hugo Boss jacket given to him by his
mother-in-law last Chanukah. After buying a morning paper, he
drove to Marina del Rey, where he walked through the Marina
Shores Hotel and out to the harbor.

Shielding his face behind the paper, he looked for Baker's boat.
Easy enough. Alex's description had been precise.

Satori was long, sleek, white. On a police sergeant's salary?
Or had Dr. Lehmann played share-the-wealth in all kinds of
ways?

He could smell the ocean, hear the gulls. Impossible to tell from
here if Baker was on the boat. One way or another, he'd find
out.

He strolled up and down the breezeway, pretending to sightsee.
Twenty minutes later, Wesley Baker came out on deck with a cup
of coffee, stretching and looking up at the sky.

Solid-looking in a white T-shirt and white shorts. Tan, muscular,
gold-rimmed glasses. A real California guy, absolutely nothing out
of the ordinary. Hannah Arendt would have been pleased. . . .

He gave another stretch, unfolded a deck chair, and brought it
close to the boat's pointed bow. There he sat, mug in hand, feet on
a lower ledge.

Face full of sun.

Just another golden day for the elite.

Daniel forced himself to watch.

. . .

HE GOT BACK TO THE HOUSE ON LIVONIA BEFORE noon and had something of a Sabbath, studying the weekly Torah portion, reciting kiddush, eating a light meal. Grape juice today, no wine.

Not allowing the murders to reenter his mind for an hour, but after that, they were all he thought of.

Milo arrived at 2:00 P.M. and the two of them discussed equipment. The German plastic gun interested the American the most—lightweight, convertible to automatic with the press of a button, two dozen rounds in a cartridge, easy to speed-load.

Daniel had three, offered him one. The big man thought about it, finally accepted, muttering about "the next time I want to sneak something onto a plane." They talked about long guns and agreed Daniel would take a rifle with a night-scope because he'd be on the hillside.

Milo had spent the morning reviewing Baker's police personnel files as unobtrusively as possible. Nothing in the records indicated Baker's transfer had been disciplinary. No record of any punishment or demotion due to Zev Carmeli's complaint. No documentation, at all, of the incident with Liora Carmeli.

"Figures," said Milo. "The brass investigates complaints enthusiastically. Like Michelangelo would investigate sculpting David out of dog shit."

The man had a way with words.

"Pencil pushers are the same everywhere," said Daniel.

Milo made that grumbling noise, then he left at 3:30.

The plan was for Alex to call Zena Lambert at 5:00 to confirm tonight's date. Anything unusual would mean calling the whole thing off—Milo was protective of his friend. That caused Daniel to think about things better left ignored and he stopped himself and concentrated on getting onto that hillside.

At 5:15, his phone rang and Milo said, "It's on."

DANIEL SET OUT AT 8:30. DARK ENOUGH FOR CON-cealment but enough time to be stationed behind the house well before Alex arrived at 10:00.

He wore ultralightweight black pants with paratrooper pockets, black shirt, black stocking cap. Concealing the rifle meant the long black coat with the Velcro-fastened pouch sewn in the lining. Other pockets for the plastic gun and ammunition. His backpack held the parabolic mike, a couple of tiny concussion grenades, mini tear-gas canisters, a combat knife that dated back to his Army days—he'd yet to find something better than the old blade.

He felt adrenalized and just a bit ludicrous. Big tough commando. Like one of those ninja movies his sons loved to watch. He'd assured Milo he could handle it. Because they weren't talking about freeing multiple hostages, here. Just getting onto that hillside, listening, recording, returning home.

As he headed for the door, the phone rang.

Milo, again? Change in plans?

"Yes?"

"*Shavuah tov.*" Zev Carmeli offered the traditional post-Sabbath greeting—have a good week.

"Same to you, Zev."

"I need to see you, Daniel."

"When?"

"Now."

"I'm afraid that's—"

"Now," Carmeli repeated.

"I'm in the middle of—"

"I know what you're in the middle of. Where you're *going* is *here*—the consulate. I've sent a driver for you, he's parked right behind the Toyota. Which has two flat tires."

"Zev—"

"And don't think about sneaking out the back door, Sharavi. Someone's watching."

"You're making a huge—"

The connection broke. As he put down the phone, two men came in, both young, one blond, one dark-haired. Dark suits, open-necked white shirts. He knew them by face and name. Guards from the consulate, Dov and Yizhar. He hadn't heard them enter. Carmeli had known the phone call would distract him.

Mr. Ninja, indeed.

"*Erev tov,*" said Dov.

And a good evening to you, too, schmuck. "Do you have any idea what you're doing?"

The man shrugged.

Yizhar smiled and said, "Following orders. Who says the only good Germans are Germans."

54

when Captain Huber called him in.

Huber was doing paperwork at a chaotic desk and didn't look up or speak. His bald spot was pink, slightly flaky.

"Sir."

"Your lucky day, Sturgis. Meeting downtown with Deputy Chief Wicks. What'd you do, solve a crime or something?"

"When?"

"Now. *Ahora*. They even sent a car and a driver—big Afro-Amer two-striper waiting just outside my office, you're really rating today."

Huber stopped writing, but kept his head down. "Maybe it's an affirmative-action thing, diversity and all that good stuff. Don't look so glum."

Never making eye contact, so he had no idea about Milo's expression.

"I—"

Now Huber looked up sharply, thick face mottled with anger. Wicks's call had caught him by surprise. Out of the loop.

Milo suddenly understood why and his bowels began to churn.

"What's that, Sturgis?"

"I'm on my way."

"Looks like you are, indeed. Making any progress on your cases?"

"Which ones?" said Milo.

"All of them."

"We're doing okay."

"Good. Don't keep them waiting. Close the door on your way out."

55

BODY-SEARCHED, POCKETS EMPTIED, DANIEL SAT SAND-
wiched between the two men in the consulate car, breathing in their
tobacco smell, knowing there was no chance to break free. He
feigned relaxation.

They drove him to the consulate, placed him in Zev Carmeli's
office, and remained outside the door.

He sat wondering if Zev would show.

Feeling like an idiot for neglecting the obvious. How could he
have not seen it? How could it have been any other way?

Denial, pathological denial.

Had Milo been intercepted, too? How far did this go?

Hopefully, it wouldn't matter, Alex walking into the date un-
protected. Just a date with a crazy girl and back to the Genesee
apartment.

More denial.

Alex was expecting full coverage, would behave accordingly.

He remembered the tranquil look on Baker's face, all those
murders and the guy was taking in the sun, unbothered by life.

Guy like that, *nothing* would bother him.

He looked around Zev's office. Saw something that could help,
pocketed it, and knocked on the door.

Dov opened it. "What?"

"Bathroom."

"You're sure?"

"Up to you, soldier. I can piss on his desk."

Dov smiled, took his arm firmly, and propelled him to a nearby
unmarked door.

No need for another search, the first had been so thorough.

"Have fun," Dov told him.

Once inside, Daniel urinated, flushed, turned on the faucet, took the cell phone he'd lifted from Zev's desk out of his pocket, and dialed a familiar number. Time for only one call—he hoped the phone was a normal line, not one of Zev's preassigned coded things.

Ringing. Good.

Pick up, friend, pick up, pick up . . .

"Hello?"

"Gene? It's me. I can't talk long. I need your help."

Knocking on the door. Dov's voice, "Hey, you drown or what? How long does it take to pee?"

"Wait til you reach my age," Daniel called out.

"Ain't that the truth," said Gene.

56

ZENA WAS AT THE STORE WHEN I MADE THE CONFIR-mation call.

"How gallant of you to verify, A."

"Just wanted to make sure you weren't too worn out from the party."

"Me? Never. On the contrary, bursting with energy. I shall prepare comestibles—pasta with clams, Caesar salad, fruit of the vine."

"The woman cooks, too."

"Oh, *do* I." She laughed. "I simmer and sometimes I boil over. I'll leave a key in the empty flowerpot near the door. I'll be ready."

AT 9:30 I PUT ON AN ANDREW UNIFORM: GRAY SHIRT, baggy gray pants, the same tweed sportcoat. The same cologne.

Starless night, a washed-slate sky, the air reeking of wet paper, damp around the edges.

I took La Brea to Sunset. The boulevard was rife with spandex and leather, delusions passing as hope. East of Western it changed: darkened buildings hemmed by shadow-strewn corners, everything murky, grubby, too quiet.

I drove automatically, slowly, as if riding a track, reached Lyric just after ten o'clock, and climbed the winding road, now stripped of cars.

Rondo Vista was mortuary silent. Zena's garage was closed and one car was parked in front of her house. Fifty-eight T-bird. Pink with a white top, faded and scarred.

Had to be hers.

The same faint light from her window. Setting the mood?

I parked and headed for the door. The covered pathway was dark, the dead spider plants shuddered in the night breeze. Feeling an inexplicable pang of first-date anxiety, I groped til I found the key in the pot, resting atop a mound of bone-dry planter's mix.

Music from inside.

Electric guitars played slowly.

Beautiful, dreamy music.

"Sleepwalk," by Santo and Johnny.

Zena setting the mood. I remembered the song from my childhood. She hadn't been born when it hit the charts.

I unlocked the door, expecting to find her downstairs in the bedroom, maybe some kind of cute note directing me to the stuffed animals.

She was right there in the living room.

Lit by a single pole lamp with a weak blue bulb.

Theatrical.

Nude, on the sofa.

She reclined, one arm extended along the top of the couch, like Goya's "Naked Maja." Wide-eyed with eagerness, her tiny white body perfectly formed, pearly in the steely light. Nipples pink and erect, oversized for the small, white breasts, black hair sprayed static. Her legs were spread just enough to offer a view of bleached-blond pubic patch. Her other arm rested on her flat, smooth belly.

I smelled clam sauce but the lights were out in the kitchen.

No preliminaries. How to get out of this—

"Hi," I said.

She didn't speak. Or move.

I came closer, was inches away before I saw the ligature around her neck. Copper wire, biting into the slender stem, so tight it had been invisible.

Wide, wide blue eyes. Not seductiveness. Surprise, the final surprise.

I turned to run, was caught by the elbows from behind.

A knee in the small of my back sent a jolt of pain up my spine and made my legs give way.

Then hands around *my* neck, more pain, different—an entire new definition of pain, as the back of my head exploded.

57

MILO'S DRIVER WAS NAMED ERNEST BEAUDRY AND HE was coal-black, maybe thirty, handsome, impassive, a devout Baptist, with a bristly mustache that looked laser-trimmed and an eighteen-inch neck turned to asphalt by shaving bumps.

The car was a blue unmarked Ford, same model as Milo's but newer and much cleaner, parked in the West L.A. station lot. Beaudry stayed close to Milo as they approached it, held the door open for him.

"Some service, Officer."

Beaudry didn't answer, just shut the door and got into the driver's seat.

He managed the car skillfully. Driving was one of his favorite things. As a kid he'd fantasized about becoming a professional race driver til someone told him there were no black ones.

The police radio was on, reciting that night's epic poem of coded violence, but Beaudry wasn't listening. Turning out of the lot, he headed for the 405.

"Downtown?" said Milo.

"Yup."

As they got on the ramp, Milo said, "So what's this about?"

No answer, because Beaudry had none, and even if he had, he was smart enough to keep it zipped. The 405 was clogged with nighttime airport traffic and they barely moved for a while.

Milo repeated the question.

"No idea, sir."

A few car lengths later: "You work for Chief Wicks?"

"Yup."

"Assigned to the motor pool?"

"Yup."

"Well," said Milo, "all these years on the force and I never got driven before. So this is my lucky day, huh?"

"Looks like it." Beaudry let his left hand sink to the driver's-door handrest as he one-fingered the wheel.

Traffic started moving.

"Okay, I'll just sit back and enjoy this," said Milo.

"There you go."

Sturgis stretched his legs and closed his eyes. They cruised slowly but steadily.

Nice and easy—then Beaudry heard, "Shit—Jesus."

Rustling motion on the passenger side. Beaudry glanced to the right and saw that Sturgis was sitting up.

"Oh—Jeesus, I can't—" The last word was guillotined by a gasp and Beaudry saw Sturgis slump, one hand on his barrel chest, the other fighting to loosen his tie.

"What's the problem?"

"Stomach—chest—probably just gas . . . the shit I had for dinner—oh, man, here's another—*Jesus*, it hurts like a mother—oh, shit, this is not—"

Sturgis sat up again, suddenly, as if pierced by something. Gasping, rasping, yanking the tie loose but holding on to the limp fabric. Clutching the left side of his chest. Beaudry heard a button pop and plink against the dashboard.

"You all right—"

"Yeah, yeah—get the hell over to Parker, maybe they've got a—no . . . I dunno—oh *shit!*"

The long legs stiffened, knees knocking against vinyl. Sturgis's eyes were shut now, and his color looked bad—grayish, his face screwed up tight.

"Ever have this before?" said Beaudry, fighting to sound calm.

Milo's response was a deep, bearish moan.

"Sir, have you ever experie—"

"Ohh! Jeez—get me—oh—*ah!*" Sturgis arched his back, bit his lip, and Beaudry heard fast, rough breathing.

Beaudry said, "I'm getting you to a hospital—"

"No, just get me—"

"No choice, sir—where's the closest one—Cedars, okay, Robertson exit's just a ways up, hold on—"

"No, no, I'm oka—*ahh!*"

Left hand back on the wheel, Beaudry switched to the fast lane and floored the unmarked, using his right hand to snatch the handset and call in an emergency.

No one answered at Deputy Chief Wicks's office. Of course; they'd asked him to bring Sturgis straight to that conference room on the fifth floor, some kind of high-level detective stuff—what was the extension there? No idea. Should he go through the Parker switchboard? No, they'd made it clear this was confidential. Meaning they were trusting him with more than just chauffeuring, probably preparing him for something bigger and better—

Meanwhile, his charge was moaning and gasping like a fish out of water, sounding like he was gonna die right here in the car—look how heavy he was, probably didn't exercise, ate all kinds of garbage—just his luck, Ernest Beaudry's golden luck. All that clean living and raising his kids right, doing his job without a hitch, getting assigned to the motor pool and making Delores happy because he wouldn't get shot by some crackhead. Pushing for motor pool because his uncle had started that way and made sergeant even with all the departmental racism. Because his uncle and other relatives had told him a smart young guy like him, with presence, could do even better. Driving, the connections you made, maybe he'd get to drive for the chief.

Heck, driving could *make* you a chief. Daryl Gates had started off driving for Saint William Parker. Then again, look where Daryl Gates had ended up, so maybe it was just the opposite and driving was really *bad* luck, a curse, a hex. This sure wasn't a good sign, he wished Sturgis would just stop having his heart attack, decide it *had* been gas, start breathing normally again—

Silence. Oh, no— "You all right?"

No answer. But Sturgis was still breathing, Beaudry could see the big belly heaving.

"It's all right," he said soothingly. "We'll take good care of you, almost there."

Sturgis's face screwed up tighter as he seized again and landed almost prone on the seat, sliding down. Thank God he had his seat belt on. Bucking and heaving . . . that wheezing—

Robertson, 1 mile. Beaudry checked the rearview and slid across all four lanes, raced down the exit ramp, which was thank-God clear, ran an amber-to-red at National, and jetted north. Cedars just a couple miles away.

Don't die here, man, at least wait til we get there—Pico, Olympic, another iffy amberoo, some cross-traffic that honked at him.

Forget *you*, I am *allowed*, I am the *po*-lice—Wilshire, Burton, here we go, here we go, here we go—Cedars, *yes*! Swing in on Alden, into the covered parking lot, up to the emergency entrance—no one there, Sturgis quieter—but looking worse—was he still breathing, oh, Lord, please give him just a few more breaths—CPR? No, no, no, of course not, not with all these doctors around . . .

"We're here, just hold on, man," he said, slamming the car into park. "Help's right on the way."

He left the engine running and track-starred into the E.R. reception area, yelled at the sleepy-looking clerk that an officer needed help.

The place was full of sick old people and accident victims, various species of lowlife. Before the clerk could answer, Beaudry ran past them and grabbed the first person in uniform that he saw—a nurse, Filipina—then a female intern in scrubs, the three of them hustling to the unmarked.

"Where?" said the intern, red-haired, looking maybe sixteen, but her badge said S. Goldin, M.D.

"Right here." Beaudry threw open the unmarked's passenger door.

No one inside.

His first thought was that Sturgis had been gripped by another attack, had somehow opened the door, fallen out, crawled somewhere to die. . . . He ran around the car to check, then looked under the vehicle.

"Where?" said the intern, now looking skeptical.

She and the nurse stared at Beaudry. Taking in *his* badge, the uniform, the two stripes, the Sam Browne loaded with gear, the nine-millimeter.

Figuring, he was for real but what the hell was his *story*?

Beaudry raced around the parking lot, looking over, under, between every damn vehicle, greasing up his uniform, soaking his tapered-to-the-muscle shirt with stress sweat.

When he came back, Intern S. Goldin repeated, "Where? What's going on, Officer?"

Now Beaudry was breathing hard and his own chest hurt.

Stand tall, show no stress.

"Good question," he said.

So much for family advice. Driving was *definitely* a hex.

58

NEWLY RETIRED POLICE CAPTAIN EUGENE BROOKER, thirty pounds overweight, slightly hypertensive, and a non-insulin-dependent diabetic, walked uphill.

Old man and the mountain; some image. When his daughters inquired about his health, he always said, "Feel like a kid."

So, live the lie tonight.

Danny's surprise call—talking twice as fast as usual, from that consulate bathroom—had ended with, "It'll probably be nothing. Do what you can, Gene, but don't put yourself in danger."

Sneaking a phone into the john? Why were Danny's own people doing this to him?

He trudged up Lyric, staying in the shadows when he could. He'd parked his car a long way down on Apollo, brought the only two weapons handy: the old service revolver, which he'd continued to clean and oil out of habit, and the nine-millimeter that he kept in his bedside nightstand. No long guns because all three of his were already packed away in the U-Haul and they were for quail, not people. Another reason: Rifles were too conspicuous. An overtly armed black man walking the hills at night was beyond a joke.

Up, up, and away. . . . He forced himself to breathe slowly. How long had it been since he'd done real-life, break-a-sweat police work? He didn't even want to think about it.

Pathetically out of shape, but with the diabetes you had to be careful about your exercise—who was he kidding, since college football and walking a beat on Central, he hadn't done a damn thing, athletic-wise. . . .

Climb every mountain, ford every stream, huff huff, the old Nikes nice and quiet.

He'd memorized the address on Rondo Vista.

Slow and steady, it wouldn't do to have a heart attack up here and end up roadkill or worse.

No reason to hurry, probably a quiet night, as Danny had said. Just a precaution for the shrink's sake.

Danny hadn't had time to give many details. The main thing was that a cop named Baker, whom Gene didn't know, might be part of it, so watch out for him, he drove a Saab convertible.

A cop behind all that blood? It could make the Rodney King case look like musical comedy. Beyond that, all Gene knew was that a crazy girl was also part of it and the shrink was on an undercover date with her.

Why a shrink for bait?

How had Danny and Sturgis put it all together?

He'd find out tomorrow. Tonight his job was to keep an eye on the house. If something looked treacherous for the shrink, pull some kind of distraction.

More, if necessary.

He made it to Rondo Vista nearly out of breath, wanting to clear his throat but the street was too silent for that kind of noise so he lived with the phlegm.

He'd made sure to eat an orange before leaving, keep the old blood sugar steady, he should probably test more often, but sticking himself was such a hassle.

As he stood there, searching for the house, he became aware of pounding in his ears. Like a fast tide, the high blood pressure. Luanne had died of a stroke—no, stupid to think about that. . . . Lord, it was quiet up here.

Manson Family terrain; you could dismember someone in the middle of the road, no one would notice til sunrise. . . . There was the house, small place, white with dark trim, gray or blue.

He studied the layout, examined nearby cars.

One in front, the Karmann Ghia Danny had given the shrink, and an old pink T-bird in the driveway that had to be the girl's.

Nothing else except the few vehicles he'd passed on the way up. Couple of compacts and one honey, a white Porsche 928, no doubt some hill-house guy's toy. Porsches and hill-houses went together, the old L.A. lifestyle he'd never much tasted . . .

Danny had said look out for three things: a Chevy van, it could be in the garage, Baker's Saab, and a Mercedes sedan owned by some other shrink named Lehmann.

What the hell was this all about?

He looked carefully. None of those were around. Maybe in the garage.

If he'd been official, he'd have run a make on every vehicle within a half-mile radius, the compacts, the white Porsche, but now . . .

Retirement.

He realized he was breathing fine, felt good, great, no more pounding, no clammy skin or other warning signs of impending hypoglycemia.

Revolver in his shoulder holster, nine-millimeter tucked in his waistband at the small of his back.

This was good. A send-off before he died a slow death in Arizona.

TEN MORE MINUTES OF SILENT WATCHING FROM BE-hind a tree, and he decided to get a closer look at the house.

A narrow space ran between the crazy girl's place and its southern neighbor and Gene could see lights—more hill-houses way across a canyon.

From what he could tell, the ground sloped down sharply, probably not much backyard.

Danny'd said that if Sturgis was there, that's where he'd probably be stationed, but he had a feeling Sturgis wouldn't make it.

Cold, quiet anger in the Israeli's voice. Unusual . . .

Sturgis. Gene didn't know the guy, had only seen him from a distance and he didn't look in any better shape than Gene. Usually you thought of those gay guys being obsessed with their bodies. Luanne had once remarked that they seemed to be the best-looking guys, probably because they didn't have families, plenty of time for the gym—

The conversation in his head came to an abrupt halt; had he heard something?

A rustling?

No, just silence. And nothing around the house had changed.

He examined the place some more. Not much in the way of

front windows, and the way the structure was stuck into the hillside, the entire bottom floor was below street level. Probably lots of windows in back, to catch the view. How to get back there—was there some foothold? Had to be for someone like Sturgis to obtain a position.

Enough idle curiosity. The idea was to stay here, on the chance—the less-than-unlikely, minuscule off-chance—that his old bones would see some action.

If Luanne were alive she'd say something like, *You're doing what? Can't you work your midlife crisis out some other way, sugar?*

That night, finding her on the kitchen floor . . . stop. Don't even think her name, don't visualize her face.

God, he missed her—

He decided to go past the house, check out the northern edge of the girl's property.

As he took a step, something pressed against his left mastoid and a voice whispered, "Don't move, don't even blink. Hands up, very slowly—behind the head, grab the head."

A hand took hold of his shoulder and turned him around.

Suppressing *Oh, shit!* thoughts, Gene mentally prepared a plan: Size up the enemy, figure out a way to catch him off-guard, land a sucker punch, maybe trip him, distract—

It was Sturgis and he looked furious. His eyes were green—God, they were bright, even in the darkness. The guy stank of exertion and stress.

They stared at each other. Sturgis's shirt had a button missing. Something black and plastic, probably one of those German Glocks, was a foot from Gene's nose.

"Hey," whispered Gene. "I'm a civilian now, but shouldn't rank count for something, Detective?"

Sturgis kept staring.

"Can I drop the damn hands, Detective Sturgis?"

The Glock lowered. "What're you doing here, Captain?"

Gene told him about the bathroom call. The guy didn't look surprised, just angrier.

The disheveled appearance. They'd tried to keep *him* away, too, but he'd managed to get away.

Gene said, "You, too?"

Half a nod.

"The Israelis actually grabbed you?"

Sturgis's lips pulled back, showing teeth—something out of a horror movie, and Gene was glad the guy was a cop.

Then the realization hit him.

"The department?" said Gene.

Sturgis didn't answer.

"Damn . . . and you escaped."

"Yeah, I'm a fucking Houdini."

"And now you're in deep manure."

Sturgis shrugged and lowered the black gun to his side. "Keeps life interesting." He guided Gene back behind the tree.

"How long you been up here?" said Gene.

"Got here right before you."

"How far down did you park?"

Sturgis hooked a thumb. "The Porsche."

Hill-house guy; so much for his powers of detection, thought Gene. It was good they were putting him out to pasture.

"You and Daniel had a two-man plan," he said. "He was going behind the house. You figuring to do it now?"

Sturgis didn't answer.

Wasn't *this* a picture. Alone in this dark, quiet place with a gay guy and it didn't bother him a whit. Years ago . . .

"He was supposed to go back there with a microphone and a tape recorder," said Milo. "I'll go back there but if the drapes are drawn, I won't be able to see anything. I don't like it, but Dr. Delaware's in there already."

"See what you mean," said Gene. "Daniel also said it would probably turn out to be nothing."

"Hopefully. Dr. Delaware's putting himself on the line."

"Dedicated, huh?"

"You have no idea."

"You know," he said, "I worked a case with Sharavi. Serial killer before they were calling them that. The guy's righteous as they come. Never met a better detective."

Sturgis kept looking around, those wild eyes on full alert. As if he heard something that Gene wasn't hearing.

Gene said, "Now that I'm here, at least you have backup. Let's get some signals."

"We were supposed to use cell phones but that's fucked, too. I had all the stuff at my house before they grabbed me at the station."

"Except the gun."

"Except that. Had it in a pants holster, the driver never searched me, they were trying to make it look like something positive, getting called downtown."

"A driver," said Gene. "You've got to worry when they escort you."

Sturgis gave a weird half-laugh, half-grunt. Big lunk, you'd never know he was gay.

"Okay, signals," he said.

Gene waited a long time for him to come up with something. Deferring, because Sturgis was still active-duty, knew more details than he did.

Finally, the guy said, "How about this: You stay here, keep a special lookout for cars—"

"Saab ragtop, Chevy van, Mercedes."

"Good. Two could be in the garage, though I've been up here several times today, never saw them enter or exit. I go in back of the house, step out every half-hour, over there, in that space between the houses, and hold up my hand to let you know everything's okay. You'll be able to see me because of the lights shining from those houses in the distance. I'll only hold it up for a second, so we need to get our times straight. If I don't come out, wait another five minutes, then come checking. If you don't see me right away, pull some distraction—"

"Knock on the door?" said Gene. "Pizza man? Chinese-food delivery?"

Instead of answering, Sturgis looked around some more, though Gene still couldn't see any reason why.

"Yeah, fine, whatever works," said Sturgis. "Okay, let's play bad spy movie and synchronize our goddamn watches."

Both of them peeled back their cuffs. Gene was squinting at the dial of his Seiko Diver when sudden activity threw him off-balance. He had time to see a black-gloved hand chop down on Sturgis's gun arm, sending the Glock falling to the ground with a dull clunk.

As he watched Sturgis fall back into darkness, he was grabbed from behind, arms pinioned, yanked behind his back, and cuffed—Sturgis, too. Glove leather over both their mouths.

Black-garbed figures coming out of the shadows.

Out of nowhere—where the hell had they been—

At least three of them, armed for bear and more—Jesus, look at those machine pistols, Gene had seen them in gang roundups, never fired one because, unlike lots of other cops, he'd never been much of a gun freak.

Sturgis was dragged out of his vision and Gene felt himself pulled in the opposite direction.

Damned Keystone situation and now he was probably gonna die from something else, not the damned diabetes.

Fool, fool, fool—never underestimate the enemy—a cop like Baker would be a serious enemy—but, still, both he and Sturgis were pros, how could they have—

Hands guided him down the hill.

"Shhh," a voice said into his ear, and he blotted out images of Luanne's reproving face.

Oh, honey.

Yeah, I screwed up, baby. Joining you soon.

59

MY EYELIDS SLAMMED AS TIGHT AS METAL SHUTTERS. My mouth *tasted* metallic. Breathing was difficult, each inhalation a rip in my lungs, and the pain in my head was a scarlet-orange-black thing.

Drowsy, but I hadn't lost consciousness. I tried to open my eyes. Too heavy. I could hear, smell—so much metal—feel, think—feel myself being lifted, pressure at wrists and ankles. Meaning at least two of them . . . bumpy ride.

Steps—the stairs down to the bedroom.

Lowered onto something soft. Perfumed.

Zena's perfume—Zena's bed.

New pressure bore down. Wrists, ankles, belly. Weight—dry, warm, crushing weight, like a big dog sitting on me.

The snap of clamps; now I couldn't move.

The back of my head was hot and caustic, as if something larval and fanged had hatched inside my skull and was chewing its way out . . . lesser pain in the crook of my right arm.

Cold sting—an injection.

I tried again to open my eyes. A sliver of light before they collapsed.

Everything okay, because Milo and Daniel knew. Daniel was listening.

Then I wondered: Not a sound had been made since I'd entered the house and said hi to Zena.

Were they assuming Zena'd made good on her promises, the lovemaking beginning spontaneously, silently?

Or were they unable to hear—an equipment malfunction? Those things happened. Space shuttles went down.

Waiting for some kind of signal from me?

My lips wouldn't function.

Rest up, stay calm, regain your strength.

The plan had been for me to open the living-room curtains. Did the fact that I hadn't alarm them?

Where *were* they?

I needed to *say* something for the parabolic mike.

Breathing was so hard, my throat a pinpoint—now I did black out.

UP AGAIN, NO IDEA HOW LONG IT HAD BEEN. EYES wide open, pupils aching as they expanded to take in the bright light of the bedroom.

The bedroom ceiling, I could see little else.

White ceiling, sparkle-sprayed.

The light from a cheap plastic fixture. White, circular, brass finial in the center, like the nipple of a big, white breast, Zena's breasts so small—

I pressed my head to my chest to see what was holding me down. Leather restraints. Thick, brown hospital restraints; as an intern on the psych wards, I'd wondered what they felt like. . . .

Flashes of color off to the left. I struggled to get a better look, my neck tremoloed with pain that traveled down my spine, as if someone had run a filleting knife down my center.

Say *something* for the damned mike.

My tongue was a soft, useless pillow, taking up space in the garbage can claiming to be my mouth.

I strained some more, studying the color to my left.

Eyes. White eyes with flat black irises.

Dead eyes—plastic.

Stuffed animals, what seemed to be a mountain of them stacked against the left-hand wall. Behind them, another curtain. Behind it, no doubt, another glass slider.

Teddy bears, a gigantic panda with a lolling head. Disney characters, a killer whale that was probably a souvenir from Sea World, more kapok and felt that I couldn't make out clearly.

Zena's collection . . . that surprised look. I'd taken it for wide-eyed arousal—

The wire around her neck, gritted with blood, just a twist away from decapitation.

I moved and the restraints compressed my chest and my forearms and my shins.

But I was breathing better.

"Good," I said.

It came out "Guh."

Loud enough for the mike to pick up?

I tried to relax. Pace myself. Save the energy for *talking*.

As I worked myself up for another syllable, a face blocked out the light.

Fingers pinched my left eyelid, lifted it, let it snap as something tickled my nose—bristly, the face so close I couldn't focus.

Then it drew back.

Dirty-blond beard-hairs raking my chin on the way up.

Smelly beard—fermented-food stink—over red skin, dandruff flakes.

A hair-framed mouth breathed on me, hot and sour. A pus pimple nested in the fold between nostril and cheek.

More distance and I saw Wilson Tenney, dressed again in a sweatshirt, this one green and reading ILLINOIS ARTS FESTIVAL.

"He's up."

"Nice recovery," said another voice.

"Must be in good shape. The rewards of a virtuous life," said Tenney. Then his face shifted to the right and vanished, as if moving offstage, and another one, freshly shaved, ruddy, sunburnished, took its place.

Wes Baker folded his arms across his chest and studied me with mild interest. His eyeglass lenses glinted. He wore a pink button-down shirt, beautifully laundered, sleeves folded up crisply on thick bronze forearms. I couldn't see past the third button.

His right arm held a small hypodermic syringe filled with something clear.

"Potassium chloride?" I said, for the mike, but it didn't come out right.

"Speech will return in a few minutes," said Baker. "Give yourself a little more time for your central nervous system to bounce back."

I heard Tenney's hoarse laugh from behind me.

"Potassium chloride," I tried again. Clearer, I thought.

Baker said, "You just won't relax, will you? Obviously a striver. From what I've been able to gather, pretty bright, too. It's a shame we never got a chance to discuss issues of substance."

How about right now? I thought.

I tried to say it. The result was a series of mouse squeaks. Where were Daniel and Milo?

Taping, wanting evidence? But . . . they'd never let me down . . .

Baker said, "See how peaceful he looks, Willy? We've created another masterpiece."

Tenney joined him. He looked angry but Baker was smiling.

I said, "Zena was . . . artistic." Almost perfectly clear. "Goya . . ."

"Someone who appreciates," said Baker.

"Posed . . ." Like Irit and Latvinia and—

Tenney said, "Her life was one big pose."

"No gentle . . . strangulation?"

Tenney frowned and glanced at Baker.

"Why kill her?" I said. Good, the words were out; my tongue had shrunk to normal size.

Baker rubbed his chin and bent closer. "Why not kill her?"

"She was . . . a believer—"

He held up a silencing finger. Professorial. I remembered what Milo had said about how he loved to lecture. Keep him talking, get it all on tape.

"She was," he said, "a *receptacle*. A condom with limbs."

Tenney laughed and I saw him pick something out of the corner of his eye and flick it away.

"Zena," he said, "exited this mortal coil with a bang." One hand touched his fly.

Baker's expression was that of a weary but tolerant parent. "That was terrible, Willy." He smiled at me. "This may batter your self-esteem, but she was as sexually discriminating as a fruit fly. Our little barnyard gimcrack."

He turned to Tenney. "Tell him Zena's motto."

"Cock-a-doodle-do," said the bearded man. "Any cock will do."

"She was a lure," I said. "For Ponsico, me—others?"

"A lure," said Baker. "Have you ever gone fly-fishing?"

"No."

"It's a marvelous pastime. Fresh air, clear water, tying the lures. Unfortunately even the best ones unravel after too many bites."

"Malcolm Ponsico," I said. "He lost enthu—"

"He lacked commitment," said Tenney. "A weak trout, if you will. It soon became clear something smelled fishy."

"Willy," said Baker, reprovingly, "as Dr. Alex here can tell you, inveterate and inappropriate punning is a symptom of mood disorder. Isn't that so?"

"Yes." The word sounded perfect. At least to my ears. My head was clearer—back to normal.

"Feeling better?" said Baker, somehow sensing it.

He flourished the hypodermic, then I heard a metallic clank as he put it down somewhere. The leather restraints were killing the blood flow to my limbs and my body seemed to be disappearing. Or maybe it was the remnants of the drug, pooling in low places.

"What axis?" Tenney asked me. "Depression or mania?"

"Mania," I said. "And hypomania."

"Hmm." He stroked his beard. "I don't like to think of myself as hypo-anything." Sudden smile. "Maybe hypo-dermic. Because I do have the capacity to get under people's skin."

He laughed. Baker smiled.

"Perhaps *that's* why I've been feeling crabby. Or perhaps my moods just shift for the halibut."

"What a wit," I said. He reddened and I visualized Raymond Ortiz, snatched in the park bathroom, bloody shoes.

"I wouldn't irritate him," Baker said, almost maternally. "He doesn't take well to irritation."

"What did Raymond Ortiz do to irritate him?"

Tenney bared yellow teeth. Baker turned his back on me. "Want to tell him, Willy?"

"Why bother?" said Tenney. "I have no need to clear my sole— petrale, Dover, take your pick. To assuage my admittedly shrimpy conscience by confessing what I did to the stupid little squid. The scales of justice are in equilibrium. No pearls of wisdom. I prefer to clam up."

Suddenly, his beard loomed above me and his hand was around my neck.

"All right," he said, spraying spittle. "Since you insist. What the obese little degenerate *did* was destroy the quality of my life. How? By filthying the bathroom. Inevitably. Inexorably. Every single time he used it, he filthied it. Do you understand?"

He bore down, increasing the pressure on my neck, and I gagged, heard Baker say, "Willy."

My field of vision grew black around the edges and now I knew something was wrong, Milo would never let it get this far—the fingers loosened. Tenney's eyes were moist, bloodshot.

"The stupid gobbet of scrambled DNA couldn't figure out how to use *toilet* paper," he said. "He and all those other limpy, loopy defectoids, day after day."

He turned to Baker. "It's a perfect metaphor for what's wrong with society, isn't it, Sarge? They *shit* on us, we clean up."

"So you killed him in the bathroom," I said.

"Where else?"

"And the bloody shoes—"

"Think!" said Tenney. "Think what he did to *my* shoes!"

I gave the closest thing to a shrug the bonds would allow. *On my own—what to do—*

"I got tired of *stepping* in it!" Tenney was shouting now, raining saliva. "They didn't *pay* me for that!"

His fingers touched my neck again, then he reversed himself suddenly and walked away and I heard footsteps, a door opening and closing.

Alone with Baker.

"My neck hurts," I said, throwing out another cue, but my faith was dying. "Can these restraints be loosened?"

Baker shook his head. The needle was back in his hand.

"Potassium chloride," I repeated. "Same as Ponsico."

Baker didn't answer.

"Raymond's shoes," I said. "Nothing random, everything had a reason. Irit Carmeli's murder simulated a sex crime. Her mother read you as a sexual aggressor, so the payback had to have sexual overtones. But you needed to differentiate yourself from just another pervert. You and Nolan. He got off on dominating little girls."

Baker showed me his back again.

"Was Irit mostly Nolan, or both of you? Because I think you shared Nolan's tastes. Young girls—dark girls. Girls like Latvinia.

Did you do her yourself or with Tenney's help? Or someone else I haven't had the pleasure of meeting?"

He didn't budge.

"Like Ponsico," I said, "Nolan lacked the will eventually. More important, he had some sort of conscience, what he did eventually got to him. You sent him to Lehmann but it didn't help. How'd you prevent him from bringing you down?"

No answer.

"The sister," I said. "You told him what you'd do to her if he destroyed anyone but himself. And if his will had failed again and he didn't eat his gun, you'd have taken care of him?"

His left shoulder twitched. "Think of it as euthanasia. He was suffering from a terminal disease."

"Which one?"

"Malignant regrets." I heard him laugh. "Now we'll have to get the sister, anyway. Because you might have educated her."

"I didn't."

"Who else knows besides Sturgis?"

"No one."

"Well," he said. "We'll see about that. . . . I've always liked North Carolina, the horse country. Spent some time years ago, raising Thoroughbreds."

"Why doesn't that surprise me?"

He turned around and smiled. "Horses are immensely strong. Horses kick hard."

"More killing, more fun."

"You're right about that."

"So ideology—eugenics—had nothing to do with it."

He shook his head. "Strip away what passes for motives and motivation, Alex, and the sad truth remains: For the most part, we simply do things because we *can*."

"You killed people to prove you were able to get—"

"No, not to prove it. Simply *because* I could. Same reason you pick your nose when you think no one's watching."

The silencing finger touched my lips. "How many ants have you stepped on during your lifetime? Millions? Tens of millions? How much time have you spent regretting the fact that you committed ant genocide?"

"Ants and people—"

"It's all tissue, organic material—jumbles of carbon. So simple, until we elevated apes come along and complicate things with superstition. Remove *God* from the equation and you're left with a reduction as rich and delicious as the finest sauce: It's all tissue, it's all temporary."

He righted his glasses. "Which is not to say I don't create my own excuses. Everyone does, everyone has a cutoff point. For you, it's ants, perhaps you'd spare a snake. Someone else might not. Others draw the line at vertebrates, mammals with fur, whichever arbitrary criterion defines lovable or cute or sacred."

He straightened, looked wistful. "You can't really understand unless you travel and expose yourself to different ways of thinking. In Bangkok—a beautiful, putrid, very scary city—I met a man, a master chef, artist with a Chinese cleaver. He was working in a luxury hotel, preparing banquets for tourists and politicians, but before that he ran his own restaurant in a harbor district where tourists never go. His forte was cutting—slicing, cubing, julienning at unbelievable speed. We smoked opium together several times and eventually I gained his trust. He told me he'd trained as a child, working his way up to sharper and sharper knives. Over thirty years he'd cut everything—sea slugs, grasshoppers, shrimp, frogs, snakes, beef, lamb, monkeys, baboons, chimpanzees."

Smile. "You know the punch line. Under the knife, it all splits apart."

"Then why even bother picking targets?" I said. "If it's a game, why not just strike randomly?"

"Deconditioning takes time."

"The troops need a rationale."

"The troops," he said, amused.

"So you gave them one: inferior tissue. Your ants."

"I didn't give anyone anything," he said. "Deafness is inferior to hearing, retardation is inferior to an adequate intellect, not being able to wipe your own anus is inferior to studying philosophy. There is intrinsic value in cleaning house."

"New Utopia," I said, fighting to speak clearly, calmly. Was anyone *listening*? "Survival of the fittest."

He shook his head again, Mr. Scoutmaster showing a dull scout how to tie a complex knot for the fiftieth time. "Spare me the sloppy compassion. Without the fittest there *will* be no survival. Retardates don't discover cures for diseases. Spastics don't steer jumbo jets. Too many of the unfit, and we'll all be enduring, not living. The way Willy was forced to endure that bathroom."

He removed his glasses, cleaned them with a tissue. The house was silent.

"A nice mix," I said. "Pop philosophy and sadistic fun."

"Fun is good," he said. "What else do we have to show for our time on this planet?"

He raised the syringe again. No help coming, but play for time, time was all I had.

"Melvin Myers," I said. "A blind man trying to live a normal life. What was his sin? Learning something about Lehmann while fooling with the computers? Embezzlement? Shunting grant money to New Utopia?"

Big smile. "Ah, the irony," he said. "Money allocated for the inferior finally used productively. Myers, that place—pathetic."

"Myers was intelligent."

"It's all the same."

"Damaged tissue."

"Spoiled meat can be gussied up and sautéed, but it remains unfit for consumption. The blind don't lead the blind. The blind get led around like barnyard animals."

He aimed the needle at the ceiling, squirting liquid. A toilet flushed. Footsteps, again.

I heard Tenney's voice. "Whew, no more Mexican for me."

Baker tapped the syringe.

No rescue.

Daniel, Milo—how could you abandon me?

My body started to shake. "You can't hope to—"

"Hope has nothing to do with it," said Baker. "What you know amounts to supposition but no evidence. The same goes for Sturgis. The game needs to end. Here's a true test of your belief system: Is there an afterlife? Now you'll find out. Or"—he smiled—"you won't."

"DVLL. You're the new devils?"

The needle caught ceiling light, sparking white.

His mouth tightened. Irritated. "How many foreign languages do you speak?"

"Some Spanish. I learned a little Latin in school."

"I speak eleven," he said.

"All that travel."

"Travel enriches."

"What language is DVLL?"

"German," he said. "Nothing like the Goths when it comes to matters of principle. The crispness, none of that useless Gallic lassitude."

Zena's comments about French. Parroting her guru.

The needle lowered.

"So what does it mean?" I said.

No answer. He'd turned grave, almost sad.

Daniel, Milo . . . the limits of friendship . . . just another delusion . . .

"Potassium chloride?" I tried for the third time. "Freelance executioner. At least the state offers sedation."

Tenney said, "The state offers a last meal and prayers and a blindfold because the state's game is insincerity—pretending to be humane."

He laughed very loudly. "The state actually takes the time to sterilize the *injection* site with alcohol. Protecting against *what*? The state is an *ass*."

"Don't worry," said Baker. "Your heart will explode, it won't take long."

"Dust to dust, carbon to carbon."

"Clever. Too bad we never got a chance to spend more quality time together."

"Executed," I said, barely able to restrain the scream that kept growing within me. "What's my crime?"

"Oh, Alex," he said. "I'm so disappointed in you. You still don't understand."

"Understand what?"

A sad shake of his head. "There are no crimes, only errors."

"Then why'd you become a cop?"

The needle lowered a bit. "Because police work offers so much opportunity."

"For power."

"No, power's for politicians. What law enforcement offers is choice. Possibilities. Order and disorder, crime and punishment. Playing the rules like a card hustler."

"When to fold, when to draw," I said. Stall, stretch every second, don't look at the needle. Robin— "Who to arrest, who to let go."

"Exactly," he said. "Fun."

"Who gets to live," I said, "who doesn't. How many others have you killed?"

"I stopped counting long ago. Because it doesn't matter. That's the point, Alex: Everything is *matter* and nothing *matters*."

"Then why bother to kill me?"

"Because I want to."

"Because you can."

He came closer. "Not a *single* one of them was missed . . . no impact, nothing changed. It made me realize what I should have known years before: Sensation is all. One passes the time in the least onerous way possible. I like to clean house."

"A sweeper," I said, and when he didn't answer: "The elite takes out the trash."

"There are no elites. Just those with fewer impediments. Willy and I will end up worm-food like everyone else."

"Smarter worms, though," said Tenney. He grinned at me. "See you for chess in hell. You supply the board."

"Sensation is all," I said to Baker.

Baker put down the needle again, unbuttoned his shirt, and spread the placket.

His chest was tan, hairless, a grotesque plane of ravaged flesh. Scores of scars, some threadlike, others raised and welted.

He displayed himself proudly, rebuttoned. "I thought of myself as a blank canvas, decided to draw. Please don't talk to me about mercy."

"At least tell me about DVLL."

"Oh, that," he said, dismissively. "Just a quotation from Herr Shickelgruber. Pure mediocrity, that one, those sickening watercolors, but he did have a way with a phrase."

"*Mein Kampf?*" I said.

He got very close. Sweet breath, soap-and-water skin. How did he tolerate Tenney?

" '*Die vernichtung lebensunwerten Leben,*' " he said. " 'Lives not worth living.' Which applies, I'm afraid, to yours."

Tenney moved in and held my right hand down, elbow to the mattress. Oh, Milo, the bastard is right, nothing matters in the end, nothing's fair—fingertips drummed the crook of my arm, raising a vein.

Baker lifted the syringe.

"Happy heart attack," he said.

Robin—Mom—go out with style, don't scream, don't scream—I prepared for the jab, nervous system crashing, alarm bells jingling—

Nothing.

Baker straightened. Perturbed.

Still the jingling.

The doorbell.

"Shit," said Tenney.

"Go see who it is, Willy, and be careful."

Clang. The needle disappeared and in its place Baker held a machine pistol—black, banana-shaped handle, rectangular body, nasty little barrel.

He looked around the room.

The bell rang again. Stopped. Three knocks. More bell.

I heard Tenney's rapid climb up the stairs.

Voices.

Tenney's, the other high-pitched.

A woman?

Her voice, Tenney's, hers.

"No," I heard Tenney say, "you've got the wrong—"

Baker moved toward the door, pistol held high.

The woman's voice again, irate.

"I'm telling you," said Tenney, "that this—"

Then, a low, muffled stutter that could only be one thing. More footsteps, racing, as Baker pointed the machine pistol at the door, ready.

Thunder behind him—breaking glass, a glass roar—from behind the curtains, then a flute arpeggio of tinkling shards as the curtains parted and men burst in shooting.

More stutter, much louder.

Baker never had a chance to see them. His pink shirtback sucked up crimson and the rear of his head dissolved in a red-brown mist.

The front of his head followed, facial features blanketed in red oil and white jelly, the substructure disintegrating, features losing integrity, turning to port wine. Melting. A wax figure melting.

His chest exploded and soft things flew out, plunking wetly against the wall.

One of the shooters ran to me. Young, sharp-featured, black hair. One of the guards I'd seen at the consulate. Behind him, a big, heavy, white-haired black man in navy blue sweats. Older, at least sixty. He glanced at Baker's body, then at me.

The young, hawk-faced man began undoing my restraints, only to be yanked away.

By Milo, disheveled, wet-eyed, sweating, breathing hard.

"Sir," said the young man, Milo's big hand still on his arm.

"Get lost! Do your job and I'll do mine."

The young man hesitated for a second, then left. Milo freed me. "Oh, Alex, such a fuckup, such a goddamn idiotic *fuckup,* I'm so— oh, man, we almost lost you—it really went bad—never again, never fucking again!"

"You always were one for drama," I said.

"Shut up," he said. "Just shut up and rest—man, I am so sorry, I will never let you talk me—"

"Shut up yourself."

He lifted me.

HE CARRIED ME PAST BAKER, LYING IN A BROTH OF gore, crossed the white room, now candy-striped, bits of brain and bone a free-form collage. Out to the stairs. Tenney's corpse was sprawled on top.

"Up we go." His breathing was too hard, too fast. I felt strong enough to walk and told him so.

"No way."

"I'm okay, put me down."

"All right, but we've got to get the hell out of here. Be careful not to trip over that piece of shit."

A woman came into view at the top of the stairs. Very short, heavyset. Rosy cheeks, bulbous nose.

Irina Budzhyshyn, proprietress of the Hermes Language School. Small pistol in her hand, nothing fancy.

In her Russian accent, she said, "No one else in the house. Get him out of here and then we bring in the cleanup crew."

A man appeared behind her, in black. Late twenties but already bald on top with a brown mustache and goatee.

He was breathing hard, too. Everyone was.

"I've got transport," he said in a thick voice. Not acknowledging me, though we'd met.

The landlord at Irina's building—what name had he used? Laurel. Phil Laurel. *As in Hardy.*

Everyone's a comedian.

60

WE GOT INTO RICK'S PORSCHE.

Milo said, "You all right?"

"I'm fine." I was coated with icy sweat and fought not to shake.

He made a too-fast U-turn and raced down the hill.

"Oh, man," he said. "What a—"

"Forget it."

"Sure, forget it. Biggest fuckup of my life—forget it is exactly what I won't do—how the hell could I have been so goddamn stupid—!"

"What happened?"

"I got ambushed is what happened. Sudden meeting with a deputy chief. Sharavi was pulled off, too, by his own people. Til I found out, I thought *he* set it up—did you see an older black guy in there?"

"Captain Brooker?" I said. "The one who got hold of Raymond's file and shoes?"

"Sharavi managed to call him from the john in the consulate. . . . The guy ended up being righteous."

"Think Sharavi's bosses will punish him?"

He reached Apollo, turned sharply, sped. "Bosses don't like being bucked. . . . I'm taking you to my place, Brooker's gonna meet us there and we'll all get cleaned up."

"How'd you get free?"

"Faked a heart attack, scared the hell out of the department lackey they sent to drive me. He zoomed to Cedars, ran for help, I split, got to the E.R. the back way, found Rick, borrowed the Porsche."

He was still breathing hard and his color was bad.

"Laurence Olivier," I said.

"Yeah, maybe I'll switch jobs, become a waiter."

"Meantime, calm down. We don't want a real heart—"

"Don't worry, I won't drop dead on you, too pissed off to die—Jesus, Alex, this was the worst thing that's ever—the department pulled me off but *I* screwed up by not anticipating it. Big-time. Should have known Carmeli would be listening in to every word. Knew from the start the guy was no social director—what'd he call himself—an arranger. He arranges all right."

He cursed.

"You predicted it," I said. "The Israelis would take care of business themselves."

"So I'm a goddamn prophet. But a stupid one. I kept seeing Sharavi as the hit man, got thrown off. Truth is, he was just like me, fucking bait. . . . The whole thing went to shit—I *am* leaving the fucking *job*. Switch to something quiet—I'll use my goddamn master's, teach English somewhere—elementary school, not in L.A., where ten-year-olds shoot you, some backwater, kids who still say aw, shucks and—"

"What exactly happened?" I said.

"What happened? *Shit* happened is what happened. Brooker and I were up there playing *I Spy* when they grabbed us. Two guys and that little Russian girl and they managed to get us cuffed before we knew what hit us. Finally, we convinced them we weren't the enemy and they freed us, demanded we leave, it was their operation. Brooker and I refused because we didn't trust them to protect you, said we'd spoil whatever plans they had if they didn't share the wealth. Bluffing, because I knew that if the debate stretched out I'd have to split. Because I wanted to make sure *someone* was watching you—didn't want you in there without surveillance."

He blinked hard—wet eyes? Rubbing them hard, he coughed.

"They agreed to let us in on it but *they* had to call the shots. *She* did—Irina, Svetlana, whatever. She agreed to let us be part of the rear attack if we didn't 'cause problems.' The arrangement was Brooker and me and one of them—the black-haired guy—in back of the house and her and the other guy—the fucking landlord—at the front door. The guy with us had a mike, parabolic, like Sharavi's, but it wasn't working well and by the time he got it going, Baker was ready to . . . I'm sorry, Alex, when I heard you say potassium chloride I nearly—I told the guy we're going in right now, bucko, he tells me he needs a signal from her, I say fuck you, and he uses his beeper to signal *her* and she says she's already at the front door, just hold on one second, but I'm already up, running for the glass door anyway and the black-haired one is holding *on* to me, I'm fighting with him, come this close to shooting *him*. Finally Svetlana and Landlord pull the front-door thing, do Tenney, we can hear them shooting him and we do the rear attack on Baker—I'm sure all of us perforated him—what a *mess*, Alex."

He gripped the wheel and turned to me.

"Not that *they're* unhappy. What went down is exactly what they planned. There were never gonna be any arrests."

61

OTHER THAN A FALSE STORY ABOUT WILSON TENNEY, none of it ever hit the news.

Wes Baker's heart-attack obit was printed only in the police protective association newsletter.

Baker had been right about one thing: So few things had impact.

I never saw Daniel again.

"Carmeli's gone, too," Milo told me. His fifth visit to my house in one week. He was drinking more. I kept trying to look my best, assure him I was fine.

"The whole family, him, the wife and son. Ditto, Baker's boat. I went down to the marina, harbormaster said Baker had sold the boat to 'some guy with an accent' who'd decided to dock at Newport."

All of Andrew Desmond's identity papers had disappeared from my pockets. I'd given the clothes to Goodwill.

"How're you and the department getting along?" I said.

"They still claim they love me."

He sat at my kitchen table and ate a corned beef sandwich, noisily. Wonderfully, reliably gluttonous.

Some things *do* matter.

"What do you think happened to Daniel?" I said.

"I'd like to think they didn't hold it against him, but . . . tried to contact Brooker, he's split for parts unknown. . . . Daniel was a good soldier, Alex. Up until the last moment, he did exactly what they wanted."

"Defining the target."

"He was their hound, just like me. Spotting—pointing. They

used us both to pinpoint the prey, then brought in the attack dogs for the kill."

"Revenge," I said. "Carmeli heard everything. Including why Baker had chosen Irit. Now he knows it wasn't just random madness. Wonder how it affected him."

"Who knows . . . bet you he never told the wife."

I smiled.

"What's funny?"

"Your big performance: Mr. Chest Pain, rogue cop on the lam."

He slapped his sternum and rolled his eyes.

"Debonair," I said. "So tell me about this promotion. And why."

"Kicked back up to D-III but removed from West L.A. They're giving me an office at one of those little mini community outposts they're putting up all over town. Cop-lite, the guys call 'em, but I get my own space, separate entrance. The title is major case investigator—troubleshooter on nasty stuff, anywhere in the city. The promise is I don't have to deal with red tape, get total departmental support and backup."

"Sounds good."

He rubbed his face. "I'm not kidding myself, Alex. They want me out of the station—any station. And I know damn well this can go either way: the best thing that ever happened to me or they marginalize me, ease me out. If it's the second, fuck 'em, I'll deal with it. Meanwhile, they've upped my pay and promised lieutenant within a year."

"Still sounds good," I said. "Now, tell me why."

"The official reason is that they were intending to do it all along—the meeting with the deputy chief was about that. Because of my solve rate, people in high places had put in a good word for me."

"Carmeli. Wanting you out of the way."

"Carmeli *and* the department," he said. "The *real* reason is they need to shut me up. Because Carmeli told them about Baker and NU and what he was going to do about it, and they didn't try to stop him."

"Common interest," I said. "The last thing LAPD needed was a psycho-killer cop."

"Clean slate, Alex. Can't say I'd rather see Baker in court."

"And the story about Tenney being picked up for Raymond

Ortiz and Latvinia and dying in a shoot-out with police gives their families some peace of mind. Too bad Raymond's body will never be found."

"They told his parents Tenney had burned it completely—confessed it before he went for his gun."

"Convenient," I said.

Frowning, he took something out of his pocket and placed it on the table.

Two neatly cut squares of newsprint.

This morning's paper.

Two papers, same date. *Los Angeles Times, The New York Times.*

The local story was slightly bigger, a front section, page 12, the lower right-hand corner:

PSYCHOLOGIST PERISHES IN HOUSEFIRE

SANTA MONICA—Fire investigators said an early-morning blaze that killed a psychologist yesterday was the result of faulty electrical wiring.

Roone M. Lehmann, 56, died in his bed of smoke inhalation during the fire that erupted in a secluded area of Santa Monica Canyon and consumed his house along with nearly half an acre of surrounding vegetation. Neighbors' houses were spared. The structure had been outfitted with smoke alarms but apparently they failed to go off.

Lehmann, a bachelor, had served as a consultant to the Los Angeles Police Department as well as to several other foundations and institutions, including the Central City Skills Center. Funeral arrangements await notification of next of kin.

The smaller scrap said:

BOATING ACCIDENT CLAIMS TWO

A couple boating on Long Island Sound drowned yesterday evening in what police are terming a freak accident.

Farley Sanger, 40, and Helga Cranepool, 49, had apparently embarked on a nighttime sail when their craft sank after a previously undiscovered hole in the bottom widened and filled the twenty-foot sailboat with water.

''Mr. Sanger boated all the time,'' said a Manhattan neighbor, preferring to remain anonymous, ''but never at night.''

Sanger, an attorney, was a partner in the firm of . . .

I gave him back the clippings.

"Same day, probably the exact same time," I said, sliding the papers toward him. "Perish the careless."

"Hey," he said, "they made the rules."

62

I ENDED UP TELLING ROBIN A VERSION THAT LEFT her shocked, but relieved, eventually able to sleep again.

My sleep was another matter but after two weeks, I was starting to settle down.

I'd never forget any of it, knew I had to get back on a routine.

Taking referrals, seeing kids, writing reports. Feed the fish, walk the dog.

Thinking about Helena, from time to time. The things she'd never know . . . sometimes ignorance *was* bliss.

Thinking about Daniel, too. What *had* happened to him?

I filled the hours. Doing the usual things because I *could*.

The small white envelope that arrived on a sunny Tuesday was punctuation of sorts.

No stamp, no postmark, stuck right in the middle of the day's delivery.

Post-office oversight, if you believed that.

Embossed Hallmark trademark on the back flap.

Inside was no card, just a photograph.

Daniel, along with a pretty, slender woman around his age. He wore a white shirt, dark slacks, sandals, and she had on a loose blue dress and sandals. Several inches shorter than he was, with curly blond hair. Her arm in his.

Flanking them, three children.

A gorgeous, dark-skinned but fair-haired girl of college age wearing an olive-drab Army uniform, and two little black-haired boys in T-shirts and shorts and yarmulkes. The older boy grinned mischievously but the younger one looked serious, a clone of Daniel. Daniel and the woman and the girl all smiled evenly. The girl had Daniel's features, her mother's hair.

Stone wall behind them. Big, rough, golden stones.

Nothing else.

On the back was a typed address:

PINSKER STREET, JERUSALEM, ISRAEL.

Below that:

NEXT YEAR IN JERUSALEM? YOU ARE ALWAYS WELCOME HERE.

My service phoned. "A Mr. Brooker, Dr. Delaware."

"I'll take it."

"Doctor? My name is Gene Brooker and I'm—"

"I know who you are, Captain. We . . . encountered each other briefly."

"Did we? Anyway, the reason I'm calling is to deliver a message, Doctor. From a mutual friend. He sent you something and wanted to know if you received it."

"I did. Just now, as a matter of fact. Perfect timing."

Silence. "Good. He said to tell you he's fine. Thought you might be wondering."

"I was. Thoughtful of him."

"Yes," he said. "He's always been thoughtful."

ABOUT THE AUTHOR

JONATHAN KELLERMAN, America's foremost author of psychological thrillers, turned from a distinguished career in child psychology to writing full-time. His works include eleven previous Alex Delaware books—*When the Bough Breaks, Blood Test, Over the Edge, Silent Partner, Time Bomb, Private Eyes, Devil's Waltz, Bad Love, Self-Defense, The Web,* and *The Clinic*—as well as the thriller *The Butcher's Theater*, two volumes of psychology, and two children's books. He and his wife, the novelist Faye Kellerman, have four children.